MW01127997

The
WORLD'S GREATEST DETECTIVE
and
HER JUST OKAY ASSISTANT

The
WORLD'S GREATEST DETECTIVE
and
HER JUST OKAY ASSISTANT

LIZA TULLY

BERKLEY
NEW YORK

BERKLEY
An imprint of Penguin Random House LLC
1745 Broadway, New York, NY 10019
penguinrandomhouse.com

Copyright © 2025 by Elisabeth Brink
Penguin Random House values and supports copyright. Copyright fuels creativity, encourages
diverse voices, promotes free speech, and creates a vibrant culture. Thank you for buying an
authorized edition of this book and for complying with copyright laws by not reproducing,
scanning, or distributing any part of it in any form without permission. You are supporting
writers and allowing Penguin Random House to continue to publish books for every reader.
Please note that no part of this book may be used or reproduced in any manner for
the purpose of training artificial intelligence technologies or systems.

BERKLEY and the BERKLEY & B colophon are registered trademarks of
Penguin Random House LLC.

Library of Congress Cataloging-in-Publication Data

Names: Tully, Liza, 1956- author.
Title: The world's greatest detective and her just okay assistant / Liza Tully.
Description: New York : Berkley, 2025.
Identifiers: LCCN 2024046067 (print) | LCCN 2024046068 (ebook) |
ISBN 9780593816776 (hardcover) | ISBN 9780593816783 (ebook)
Subjects: LCGFT: Detective and mystery fiction. | Novels.
Classification: LCC PS3602.R5318 W67 2025 (print) | LCC PS3602.R5318 (ebook) |
DDC 813/.6--dc23/eng/20241023
LC record available at https://lccn.loc.gov/2024046067
LC ebook record available at https://lccn.loc.gov/2024046068

Printed in the United States of America
1st Printing

The authorized representative in the EU for product safety and compliance is Penguin Random
House Ireland, Morrison Chambers, 32 Nassau Street, Dublin D02 YH68, Ireland,
https://eu-contact.penguin.ie.

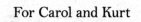

For Carol and Kurt

The
WORLD'S GREATEST DETECTIVE
and
HER JUST OKAY ASSISTANT

CHAPTER 1

The Interview

A ubrey Merritt opened the door. "You're late," she said.

She was tall, silver-haired, formidable. In her sixties and still going strong. Her eyes—a vivid dark blue—bored into me with such ferocious concentration that I had to suppress an urge to run.

Still panting, I checked my watch. "By one minute. One minute only."

"That counts as late."

"Technically, I suppose, but—" *Don't argue,* I told myself. *This is your dream-job interview. At least* try *to be agreeable.* I plastered a nice smile on my face and said, "Of course. I'm so sorry."

Her eyes narrowed. "I don't like apologies. They're usually insincere, which yours clearly was."

I caught myself before I apologized again. The interview was deteriorating faster than it had any right to. I needed to turn it around quickly. Perhaps if the nationally renowned private investigator knew the reason for my very slight tardiness . . . ?

"I'm not usually late, at least not as a general rule," I explained. "It's just that the plumber was supposed to come this morning at nine a.m., and then at noon he called to say he was running late. If it had been anyone else, I would have canceled—I mean, if it had been the mayor of New York, I would have canceled—so as not to risk being late for this interview. But our kitchen sink has been leaking like crazy for more than a month—even when the water wasn't running!—and the landlord was no help at all. I tried to fix it myself, and so did . . . um, the guy I live with." I never knew what to call Trevor. *Boyfriend* was passé, *partner* sounded too functional, and *fiancé* was too French. "Nothing worked, and we've been desperate to get it fixed. I was really worried that if I told the plumber guy, *Sorry, you missed the appointment; come back another day,* he'd get annoyed and refuse to return at all! I thought that as long as he showed up very soon, as he assured me he would, because he was already in the neighborhood, I could wait while he fixed the sink and still make it here by two p.m. Which I did! Minus one minute, of course."

"Stop, please." Aubrey Merritt was holding up her pale white hands, palms out, as if I were aiming a gun at her. "Excuses are even worse than apologies. They tend to go on far too long, as yours just did. And the longer they go on, the less convincing they become."

I could feel my face reddening. Not convincing? Really? Anyone who'd ever experienced the scourge of a leaking sink wouldn't *need* convincing. First there's the constant drip, drip, drip. Then the stench of water collecting in a saucepan under the sink and sitting there (and overflowing) while you're at work. Then the job of dumping the dirty water. Where are you supposed to put it? You can't pour it down the kitchen sink, because it will just leak out again in a big rush. You can't throw it out the window of your apartment either. Try doing that on East Fourteenth Street and see how far you get! No, you have to pour it slowly down the bathroom sink or shower drain, or flush it down the toilet a little at a time, because the toilet is the most ancient fixture of all and always seems to be on the verge of giving up. Your day is thereby ruined. Now multiply that by weeks.

But as I peered past Aubrey Merritt, into the apartment where she lived and worked, I saw a possible reason why my explanation had failed to garner sympathy. The place was gorgeous and looked to be enormous. Even the foyer was huge. Its decorations included a tall Chinese-looking vase on a marble plinth, and a wall-sized, museum-quality nineteenth-century oil painting of men in a small boat harpooning a shark. And the building itself was one of the finest New York had to offer—a nine-story Gilded Age confection of brick and terra-cotta that bordered private Gramercy Park (its keys given only to near neighbors). Chances were good that Aubrey Merritt had never lived in a fourth-floor East Village walk-up with antiquated plumbing and a landlord who didn't return calls, so how could she possibly understand the desperation I'd felt and the risky calculation I'd had to make?

"Come with me," she said briskly, apparently having decided not to shut the door in my face. As I followed her down a corridor, I spied a man with the silhouette of a linebacker disappearing into a back room. I wondered what relation he had to the detective. Was he her husband? Lover? Friend? Employee?

"That's Gilbert," Aubrey Merritt said over her shoulder. She gave no further explanation, and I didn't ask for one. I was too unnerved by the ridiculous thought that she must have eyes in the back of her head.

We entered a large sunny room that I took to be her office. Crammed bookcases lined three walls. A faded Persian rug covered a portion of scuffed mahogany floor. Two old leather chairs were set on either side of a deep-cushioned couch of dark green velvet, and a single window, high and wide and gracefully bowed, looked over a garden ringed by a tall brick wall. Soaking up the cool late-April sunshine falling through this lovely window was a round oak table showcasing a collection of odd, eye-catching items: city maps, brass statuettes, an ancient South American mask, and other things.

But what really drew my attention was a wooden easel angled so that it caught the window's light. A low table next to it was home to charcoal pencils and dirty rags, and the floor surrounding it was covered with rudimentary charcoal sketches, some of them mere lines and shadings, pieces that appeared to have been ripped from the easel in dissatisfaction.

I couldn't help being drawn to one of these sketches, of a quaint ivy-covered cottage with a lush front garden in which a shadow in the shape of a man worked. Was it an actual place, I wondered, or only a fantasy? I hadn't studied it for more than a few moments when I heard a sharp cough. I looked up to find the detective waiting for me. She was seated behind a Louis XV–style writing desk with intricate inlaid wood and gold filigreed edges. The desktop was clear but for an iPad and a fluted vase filled with black-spotted tiger lilies.

Honestly, the room and everything in it had almost overwhelmed me. I could have spent an hour there by myself contentedly, simply reading the spines of the books, running my fingers along the well-aged leather of the desktop, and turning all the fascinating artifacts over in my hands. I'd grown up in a small house on a busy street in Queens. At night I'd fallen asleep to the tuneless music of nonstop traffic and the rumble of jets flying into and out of LaGuardia. It was just my dad and me in the house. He was a handyman/carpenter (no job too small), and in the entire seventeen years I'd lived with him before I went off to Queens College the decor had never once changed. Our idea of a luxury vacation was a long weekend every August in a motel on the Jersey Shore.

As Aubrey Merritt tapped her fingers on her desk impatiently, I weaved a path through the cast-off drawings and lowered myself into the armchair in front of the desk.

She picked up the iPad and settled stylish black reading glasses halfway down her nose.

"Let's see. . . . You are . . . ah, is it Laura Portman?" Her voice was low and a little rough, her cadence unhurried.

"Blunt," I supplied. "Olivia Blunt."

Frowning, she swiped an index finger, slightly bent with age, across the screen, then another and another. I imagined the job applications of dozens of more qualified applicants flying past under her fingertips.

"Oh, I see what happened. I was on the wrong day. Let's see. . . . Yes, there you are. Olivia Blunt."

A long moment of silence followed. I wondered if I should fill it with something. Gushing admiration would just embarrass us both, but I needed to let her know that I deeply and sincerely respected her, that I had never wanted anything as much as I wanted this job.

"How did you hear of this opening?" she finally asked.

"*PI Today*," I replied promptly.

"Good. You follow industry news. How long have you been a subscriber?"

A subscriber? I swallowed awkwardly. I would have given anything to be able to say that I devoured *PI Today* every month, and that I'd worked brilliantly in the field of private investigation for at least two years and had impeccable references. That, additionally, on a basic-skills level, I could answer phones with chronic pleasantness, keep schedules up-to-date and nonconflicting, and balance books so that they always came out ahead. But it seemed unwise to lie to a seasoned detective. Some subtle tell would probably give me away. Plus, she had my résumé.

I wobbled a rueful smile and said, "I'm not a subscriber. I've actually never read the magazine at all." *For god's sake, Olivia, you didn't have to be* that *honest!*

Her eyebrows were silver like her hair. Delicate and sparse, they blended into her milky skin. Nevertheless, I saw them rise. "No? How's that?"

"I have you on a Google search. Several, actually." Hearing how creepy that sounded, I reddened once more. But the words were out and there was no way to reverse the path I was on, so I forged ahead. "I know how you found the Native American teenager in Idaho who was missing for over two years, and how you identified the killer of that famous Instagram influencer whose body washed up on a Florida beach. I know you were down in Mississippi for a couple of weeks in February, solving the very public and scandalous murder of a state prosecutor. But somehow you always manage to keep your processes dark, despite the swirl of media attention that increasingly surrounds you, so I haven't been able to figure out how you do any of it. Basically, Ms. Merritt, whatever can be known about you from available sources, I know it. I even looked you up in your high school yearbook and found out that you played Puck in *A Midsummer Night's Dream*. And shooting guard on the girls' basketball team." In genuine disappointment, I continued. "I was honestly surprised to learn that you didn't graduate at the top of your class."

Aubrey Merritt removed her reading glasses and set them carefully on her desk, then stared at me without expression. I squirmed internally. Had I really just scolded the famous detective? How epically stupid of me!

I finished weakly. "And you sang in the children's choir at St. Anne's Episcopal Church."

She waited, and when I said nothing more, she asked, "Is that all?"

"Well, no. But you get my point."

"I do indeed. Tell me, Ms. Blunt, how long have you been keeping such a close watch on me?"

"About four months. You see, I work as a fact-checker for an online news bureau—you probably know that from my résumé—and in about mid-December, I think it was, our publication ran a profile on you, and it was my job to check the basic facts. That was the first time I'd ever heard about you, and I was fascinated, of course, as anyone would be. I've always been fascinated by detectives, ever since I was a kid. I've read mysteries all my life." Hearing how naive that sounded, I hurried to qualify the statement. "Of course, I do realize that detective novels and real-life investigations have absolutely nothing in common, but still, it must be so interesting to solve mysteries—especially unsolvable ones, which you do all the time, apparently—without the heavy reliance on forensics that character-izes modern detective work. You use mostly logic, observation, and psychology—skills available to us all, as you've pointed out many times at the various conferences you've spoken at."

"How do you know that? Only licensed PIs are allowed to attend those conferences." She seemed suspicious, as if I must have done something illicit.

I explained patiently. "The best bits of the proceedings are often televised and put up on YouTube afterward. I've seen all your talks. Congratulations, by the way, on the lifetime achievement award from NALPI, the National Association of Licensed Private Investi-gators."

A light flickered in Aubrey Merritt's dark blue eyes, and a corner of her mouth twitched slightly. "Tell me, Ms. Blunt—do you own a double-breasted winter coat and a red beret?"

I nodded in dread and astonishment. It was actually a bucket hat, but I wasn't going to correct her.

"You were the young woman outside my window last December. December eighteenth, as I recall."

"Y-es," I stammered. "That was me. I didn't mean to bother you. I just—" I sighed. There was no excuse. But I kept going anyway, needing to smooth over the awkwardness. "You see, I'd just read that profile I told you about, and I knew you lived here, on the first floor—"

7

"How? My address isn't public."

"It wasn't hard to find. I mean, for a fact-checker." I wobbled a sheepish smile. "And when it turned out we're so close—I'm just a few blocks south of here, on Fourteenth—I thought I'd just stroll by and maybe catch a glimpse of you. I had no intention of loitering in front of your building the way I did, but it was night and your curtains were open, so I suppose I did peer a bit—"

"You were spying on me. Very badly, I might add. May I give you some advice?" She didn't wait for an answer. "Unless you *want* to be seen, and recognized by your mark months later, I don't recommend positioning yourself under a streetlamp directly in front of their window. At the very least, across the street would have been better. Or inside a parked car."

"I'm sorry. I didn't mean to—"

"What did I say about apologies? And don't attempt to disavow your actions either. Spying is *exactly* what you meant to do, and what in fact you have done. Both in person and online."

"You're right," I admitted. My voice sounded flat and mechanical. *I might as well leave now,* I thought. *This interview has failed.*

"Good. Now that we have that settled, why don't you tell me exactly what fact-checking entails? From your red eyes and slumped shoulders, I assume it involves staring at a computer screen in dim light for hours every day."

After I'd thrown back my shoulders and blinked several times to lubricate my eyeballs, I told her about my job. How I tracked down information from multiple traditional sources and from the furthest corners of the internet. How I mapped entire social networks and traced life stories back through years of social media postings. How I quickly assessed the reliability of sources, and cross-checked data looking for inconsistencies. How I had, as a result, saved my employers from making countless embarrassing, even dangerous, errors.

"Just a quarter turn of the dial would turn fact-checking into fact-finding," I said, pointing out how my skill could be helpful in detective work.

Aubrey Merritt tented her fingers before her mouth. Her gaze became sharper and more impersonal, while her thoughts seemed deep and far away. She stayed that way for some time. I felt briefly like an exotic flower at a botanical garden, blooming from so much rapt attention; then like a fat sow at a pig farm, shrinking from a butcher's cold assessment; then like a speck of dust. In defense, I conducted my own close inspection.

She was dressed casually but elegantly in loosely cut gray trousers and a dark purple tailored shirt of good quality—silk, I think it was. Her features were severe—high cheekbones, strong straight nose, sharp chin—but attractive in their perfect proportionality. She wore her hair short and smooth, layered in the back with a long swooping bang in front that at the moment was sitting obediently behind her ear. No makeup attempted to bring color to her ghost white skin or to disguise the webs of tiny wrinkles around her mouth and eyes, and her only adornments were a pair of silver stud earrings and a modest analog watch with a brown leather strap.

I felt awkward and uncouth sitting opposite her. She was clearly a woman who knew who she was and dressed to please herself, while I spent hours in the fitting rooms of cheap boutiques trying on dozens of shirts, skirts, and pants, then walked out without buying a thing. Most clothes felt wrong when I put them on my body. My present outfit was a good example of that: a tight black skirt, a confining maroon jacket, and leather pumps that squeezed my toes and chafed my heels. It had been wrong to dress up in interview clothes, I realized. I didn't feel like myself. But a person can't wear jeans and a sweatshirt to an interview. Or can she?

Her inspection over, the detective gently shook her head. "No. It doesn't suit you."

"Excuse me?" I thought she might be referring to my mismatched outfit.

"A computer in a cubicle. Dry facts. Social isolation. It doesn't suit you. You're no Bartleby."

"Excuse me?"

She swiped a few times and leaned forward to consult her screen. "Hmm. Did I get this wrong? No, I was right. It says here that you were an English major."

"Oh!" I suddenly grasped the reference. "You mean Bartleby the Scrivener. The Dickens character."

"Melville," she corrected sternly.

"Oh, right. Melville. Of course. Melville. I knew that." Honestly, I'd never read much Melville. Or Dickens, for that matter. In college I'd waitressed nights and weekends, with little time left for serious study. I'd managed to squeak by academically by doing the absolute minimum. I'd actually believed it was rather clever of me. Now, of course, I regretted it.

"May I ask"—I realized I might not want to hear her answer, but I was curious—"why you think I'm not like Bartleby?"

Aubrey Merritt changed the subject. "I saw that you took quite an interest in my office when you came in. Tell me, Ms. Blunt, what precisely did you find most intriguing?"

"Why, the drawing, of course. The one of the cottage. It was so"—I hardly dared use the word with such a serious and accomplished woman—"*sweet*. Is that a real place?"

"Anything else?" she asked, evading my question.

Feeling miffed at having two questions in a row ignored, I hurtled on to a different topic. "Okay, well, there was something else, on that round table there, that I thought was very interesting. It looked like a fossil of some kind." I was telling a white lie. What I'd found most interesting wasn't what I knew quite well to be a fossil but the note card tucked under one corner of it, almost hidden. It read *For Aubrey, love always, Harry.*

This answer pleased her more. "Yes, that's one of my favorite things. It's a fossil of a coelacanth found off the coast of Madagascar. Do you know what a coelacanth is?"

"Well, from the fins and gills, I'd say it's a type of fish. And because it's a fossil, it must be very old."

"Coelacanths have survived on this planet for four hundred and ten million years. That's quite an accomplishment for a species, wouldn't you say?"

"Oh, definitely."

Aubrey Merritt smiled slyly. "I have two more questions for you. They may seem unrelated or frivolous, but how you answer them is very important. The first: am I left-handed or right-handed?"

I scrambled for the answer. Which finger had swiped across the screen of the iPad? Had I seen her pick up a pen? I couldn't remember! But as I gazed at her in helpless horror, I realized the clue was directly before my eyes.

"Left-handed," I said.

"Why do you say that?"

"Your watch is on your right wrist."

"Second question: what is your favorite word? You have four seconds to answer."

My favorite word? What kind of game was she playing now? Whatever. I'd play along. *Detection* popped into my head, but that was too obvious and would sound like sucking up. The next word I thought of, *stress*, was certainly apropos but would paint me in a negative light. The word I ended up blurting was *serendipity.*

No comment came my way. Aubrey Merritt simply inclined her head. "Thank you for coming, Ms. Blunt. You'll hear from either me or Gilbert in a week or two."

I walked home in a miserable stupor. The interview couldn't have gone worse. With painful self-reproach, I counted my mistakes.

1. I'd been one minute late.
2. I'd blathered on stupidly about my kitchen sink.
3. I'd blithely admitted I'd never read the industry's only professional magazine.
4. I'd confessed to cyberstalking and spying on her—very badly, as she'd pointed out.
5. I'd had poor posture and bloodshot eyes.
6. I couldn't tell Dickens from Melville, despite my college degree.

And:

7. I was no Bartleby, which now seemed like a bad thing.

I'd gone into the interview with one simple and, I'd thought, achievable goal: to convince the great detective that, even though I had no training in her field, I could be useful in my way. And I'd completely failed.

I didn't hear anything for several days. Then a phone call came. It was from Aubrey Merritt herself, offering me the job. I nearly fell off my legs. But I rallied quickly, accepting the position immediately, before she could change her mind, before salary or start date or anything else practical had been discussed. I thought I felt her smiling through the phone, which gave me the courage to ask why she'd chosen me from her presumably long list of applicants.

"I like to keep my processes dark," she said.

Only later did I realize she'd been quoting my own words back to me.

She asked what my present salary was. I was not so starstruck that I didn't inflate it by ten percent. This she gamely raised another ten percent. I was thrilled at this too, until later, when I did the math and realized that twenty percent of a little isn't actually that much, which meant that Trevor and I would not be moving out of our stamp-sized apartment in the East Village. Nevertheless, my world felt fresh and clean and newly illuminated, as if a light had suddenly switched on. I knew for a fact that the constant noise, the non-opening windows, and the occasional dead rat on the stairway wouldn't bother me as much anymore. At the age of twenty-five, after much stumbling, I'd finally landed a job that truly excited me, one that I was sure would lead me into a magical future. I was going to be an assistant to the most famous PI in America!

I went into the newsroom the next morning and gave my two weeks' notice.

CHAPTER 2

Testing . . .

Two months later, I was despondent. The job wasn't what I'd hoped it would be. I'd imagined myself walking shoulder to shoulder with the great detective in the field, helping her to solve one fascinating mystery after another, but so far all I'd done was sit in a tiny windowless office (a former closet?) off the foyer, answering the phone, scheduling meetings, relaying messages, and doing endless research on the internet.

Sure, she sometimes used me as a sounding board, testing out her theories and puzzling through clues in whatever case she was working on, and once she'd let me tag along to a tony art gallery in Chelsea to investigate the theft of a painting worth millions. But that case had been solved over the course of one long rainy day (spoiler: the gallery owner stole it himself), with my entire role consisting of nothing more than holding the detective's umbrella as she got into and out of taxis.

One Monday afternoon in early August, I slipped quietly down the corridor past my boss's closed door to chat with Gilby in the kitchen. Gilbert Dixon had been Aubrey Merritt's housekeeper for over a decade, and he occasionally performed investigative duties such as surveillance and undercover work. He was a large man, and he lifted weights at a gym nearly every morning. If you met him in a dark alley, you would immediately hand over your money and beg for your life, never guessing how gentle he really was.

"Be patient, Olivia. She's watching you," he said when I complained that my new job was turning out to be just as dull as my old one.

"Watching me do what?" I said, bewildered. "Get floor plans of suspects' homes off real estate websites? Compile exhaustive dossiers on business tycoons? Look up criminal records in state and national databases? Minutely examine the backgrounds of thousands of Instagram posts for clues to geographic locations?"

"She's *testing* you," he amended. "She's observing how you do things, how you react to challenges and frustrations. She takes her work very seriously, and she won't allow just anyone to be part of it. She needs to know what they're made of first. The two assistants before you didn't last a month. The fact that you're still here is actually pretty impressive."

He got a leash off its hook. "Here. Why don't you take Sarge for a walk and get yourself some fresh air? If she asks, I'll say I sent you to the store for something."

Sarge was Gilby's dog, a solid 130 pounds of bullmastiff. The detective tolerated the large, slobbering animal because she knew Gilby would quit if he couldn't bring his dog to work with him. As far as I could see, Gilby was the only person on earth who could on occasion impose his will on Aubrey Merritt. As he was a noble and fair-minded individual, he used his power only rarely, and only for the common good, as he saw it. He had gently but firmly explained to the detective that bullmastiffs were known to be effective guard dogs, and as it was possible that she would someday be targeted by one of the violent criminals she had unmasked, or by a disgruntled former client whose case had been resolved in a way that did them more harm than good, she would benefit from a guard dog's protection.

I found that reasoning doubtful, given that Sarge had the heart of a kitten. He also had droopy eyes; baggy jowls; soft, floppy paws as big as catchers' mitts; and gray whiskers that showed his age (fourteen years). On hearing his name he had lifted his large head, and he had lumbered onto his four legs on hearing the word *walk*. He knew other words too, but those were his favorites. I clipped the leash onto his collar and led him down the long hallway to the front of the apartment. He trudged slowly, with a swerving waddle in his rear half, because he was still waking up and because his old joints were creaky. We passed the closed door of Aubrey Merritt's office. I strained my ears but didn't hear anything inside. She could have been asleep in there for all Gilby and I knew. Or dead.

Sarge and I were almost out the door of the apartment when ringing emanated from my office. It was from the agency's landline phone, whose number was on the agency's website, and it was my job to answer it and take messages. The people who called that number were usually cranks, journalists, or prospective clients.

I dropped the leash and darted to my desk, glad that I hadn't left the office yet. Jarred fully awake by my sudden shift in direction, Sarge careened clumsily after me in a spirit of adventure.

I picked up the receiver. "Good afternoon. Merritt Investigation Agency."

"I'd like to speak to Ms. Merritt, please."

"Ms. Merritt is in a meeting at the moment. May I ask who's calling?" This was what I'd been told to say.

"My name is Haley Summersworth. I'm from Vermont."

Was the state supposed to be a selling point? If so, Ms. Summersworth had missed the mark. Aubrey Merritt had solved cases in numerous states and a smattering of foreign countries. Vermont, though lovely, was unlikely to entice her.

"To what are you calling in regards?" Oof. My own tortured syntax made me wince.

"It's really very personal and . . . complicated." The sad hesitation in her voice melted me a bit.

"I understand. My name is Olivia Blunt. I'm Ms. Merritt's assistant, and I can assure you that the agency's communication with clients and potential clients is kept strictly confidential." This was my standard response to a reticent caller.

She capitulated easily. "Oh, all right. It's about my mother. She died last week."

"I'm sorry to hear that."

"Everyone thinks it was suicide. I don't agree. I think it was murder. I know it was, actually. Murder."

The word *murder* came out of her mouth in a muddled, self-conscious way, as if she were speaking a new language and trying hard to get the pronunciation right.

"Do you have any evidence?" I asked hopefully, getting ahead of myself.

"Well, not exactly . . ."

"Never mind. It's not a requirement."

"Is this the kind of case Ms. Merritt would be interested in?" she asked.

"Possibly. I can't say for sure. A number of factors will influence her decision. She'll need to talk to you herself, of course. Then there's her schedule to consider."

"Yes, I imagine someone as famous as she is must be very busy."

"Very." I was supposed to give the impression that my boss was always terribly busy. This made it easier for her to refuse a case if she didn't like the sound of it.

As it turned out, she had wrapped up a case that morning. The client, an elderly gentleman who claimed to have escaped three nearly fatal accidents in a row and suspected his business partner of trying to do away with him, had stopped by the office at ten to hear the detective's conclusion. I had enviously watched him disappear into her office. I would have given anything to be included in that meeting!

"I truly hope she can help me," Haley Summersworth was saying. "I don't know where else to turn. No one around here will believe me. My family, my friends—they all keep telling me I'm just in shock. They say I need to let go of my suspicions and try to move on with my life. But I can't do that. I know my mother wouldn't have taken her own life. I know it! I just can't prove it!"

"You definitely have my sympathy, Ms. Summersworth. Honestly, I can't think of anything more crazymaking than having the people closest to you casually dismiss your deepest concerns."

"Oh, thank god. You don't know how good it feels to talk to someone who understands."

"I do understand. Now, why don't I take down your phone number and email, and if Ms. Merritt wishes to pursue the matter, I'll get in touch with you to set up a meeting. Ms. Merritt usually prefers to talk to prospective clients in person, but she's willing to use Zoom when necessary." I scribbled down the contact info.

"Please tell her what I said," Ms. Summersworth said. "I am very, very sure a murder was committed, and I know she'll be able to find it if she looks. It would mean the world to me if she would try. Please convince her for me, would you? Please?"

"I'll definitely try, Ms. Summersworth. Good-bye."

I hung up the phone and woke up my computer. Before I passed a potential new client on to my boss, I was supposed to compile a portfolio of basic information about the client, the case, and the victim if there was one. Usually this information would consist of whatever I could glean from an hour or so of internet research—just enough background to help Aubrey Merritt decide whether a Zoom call was warranted.

For a while Sarge sat patiently beside my desk, staring at me with roused expectation, but when he heard how rapidly my fingers were clicking across the keyboard he heaved a great sigh of resignation and headed back to his dog bed in the kitchen.

An hour later, armed with facts, I knocked on my boss's door and was told to enter.

CHAPTER 3

A Suspicious Death

Aubrey Merritt was standing at her easel in front of the bay window that looked onto the garden. She had her back to the room. "Oh good. You've brought me a new case," she said expansively, without turning around.

"How did you know?" I was standing in the doorway.

"Let's see. The landline rings, the hairy creature lumbers back to his lair, and for fifty-five minutes no footsteps sneak past my door. Then there's a very businesslike—not a tentative!—knock, and you enter my office with a dozen or more index cards clutched in your hand."

"There's no way you can know I'm holding index cards," I said stoutly.

"For goodness' sake, it's a *guess*, Blunt. A very reliable guess, I venture to say, as you rarely make notes on anything else. Like any good craftsman, you're loyal to your tools. I expect there are a half dozen colored pens scattered across your desk at the moment, and ripped-up index cards in a tidy little pile off to one side."

She lightly brushed a line of her charcoal drawing with the side of her little finger. "Well, come in. I promise I won't bite."

I sat on the green velvet couch, which was so low and soft that it seemed to swallow me. As I arranged my note cards on my lap, I was dismayed to see that my fingers were trembling. I was always a little uneasy around my boss, and what Gilby had just told me made my uneasiness worse. Two assistants before me had been fired. Were my days numbered? Or had I survived the first elimination round, as Gilby had suggested? If so, what was I doing right?

I began to describe the case. "A woman appears to have committed suicide. Her daughter thinks it was murder."

"Egad. Standard fare," Aubrey Merritt groused.

I didn't say anything. At that point I'd been with her long enough to know that she wasn't as indifferent as she was pretending to be. New cases *always* intrigued her. Though she preferred complex, high-profile, high-paying gigs, I had yet to see her refuse a worthy person in need. She had even done a quick pro bono job for a local postal worker who had claimed (correctly) that he was being framed by a colleague for stealing Social Security checks.

"Her name was Victoria Summersworth," I continued. "She died from a fall from her balcony during the early-morning hours of July thirtieth after celebrating her sixty-fifth birthday at a party attended by seventy friends at the Wild Goose Resort on Lake Champlain."

The detective took a step back and considered her drawing thoughtfully for a moment, then laid her charcoal pencil on the ledge of the easel and wiped her hands on a rag. She untied her smock, lifted it over her head, and hung it on the corner of the easel's wooden frame. She was very deliberate in all her actions. I'd never seen her hurry, yet she always seemed to be miles ahead of me and everyone else.

"Go on." She sat down at her ornate desk and fixed me with her steady, skeptical gaze.

Conveniently for me, the dead woman's Facebook page had virtually exploded after her death. An impressive number of her 773 friends had posted passionately appreciative comments about her, while the wide array of agencies and institutions she'd supported had cataloged her numerous unselfish deeds. It was an impromptu online memorial service that, while obviously skewed to the positive, seemed honest and heartfelt.

"She had a truly astonishing number of friends and acquaintances who seemed to genuinely care about her," I said.

"Surely you don't believe what people post on Facebook."

"Of course not," I assured her. "But if only a fraction of the love and affection on her Facebook page is authentic, it's still quite a testament to her character."

My boss raised her eyebrows, clearly unimpressed with my reasoning. "If she was as saintly as you're suggesting, then we have to assume she was a fool."

My jaw dropped. "Why?"

"Truly good people—a *very* rare breed, by the way—tend to assume other people are just like them. They give their friends the benefit of the doubt, minimize conflicts, explain away any lapses they observe. They skip blithely down dark alleyways, allowing their happy whistling to drown out the echoes of the predatory footsteps following them. People like that don't sniff out their enemies the way the rest of us do. It's a dangerous state of affairs for them."

"That's such a . . . well, such a *dark* way of looking at things."

She lifted her sharp chin and squinted down her nose at me. "We're not here to weave daisy chains, Blunt. A woman is dead. Either she killed herself or someone did it for her. Where is the lightness in that? Now, tell me what else you've got scribbled on those cards in your lap."

Chastened, I supplied a brief biography of the deceased. "She was born Victoria Mary O'Shaughnessy in Vergennes, Vermont, a little town not far from Burlington and only a few miles down the road from the highbrow Wild Goose Resort, which she probably never visited in her youth but would eventually own. The daughter of a carpenter and a secretary—neither of whom attracted any public notice at all, as far as I could tell—she attended public schools, where she apparently did not distinguish herself in any way. She graduated from state college with a teaching certificate but veered off course by taking a job at Kingfisher Development Corporation in Burlington. There she steadily climbed the ladder. First she was communications assistant, then communications associate, then communications director. Her professional career ended when, at the age of thirty, she married her boss, Warren Summersworth, aged fifty-one, owner and CEO of the company."

I took a breath and noticed that Aubrey Merritt's eyes were closed, which meant she was listening intently. With slightly more confidence, I went on.

"She instantly became stepmother to Warren's two children—Neil, age nine, and Lauren, age seven—whose mother had died of cancer the previous year. Another two children—Scott and Haley—came along within the first five years of the marriage. Warren Summersworth died at age seventy-one, leaving her as the majority stockholder of both Kingfisher Development and its subsidiary, the Wild Goose Resort. She tapped the eldest son, Neil, to head the development company while she assumed the leadership position of the resort. She continually expanded and modernized the resort until, a couple of years ago, she stepped back from the day-to-day operations, passing the responsibility to the couple's third child, Scott, to whom she gave the title of general manager."

The detective's eyelids fluttered open. "Most murders are committed by people close to the victims. That's especially likely in this case, given that Victoria Summersworth appears to have had an utterly conventional life."

"But we don't know that she *was* murdered," I pointed out. "Shouldn't that be decided first?"

The detective waved her index finger in the air like a prim schoolteacher. *Tsk, tsk.* "The difference between murder and suicide is immaterial for our purposes. The fact is that *someone* killed Victoria Summersworth. Either it was the deceased woman herself or an as-yet-unidentified assailant. We need to adjust our thinking in this case only to the extent that we must begin by treating the victim as the primary suspect."

"Haley Summersworth was adamant that her mother didn't kill herself," I offered, adding hastily, "Not that I believed her."

"Very good, Blunt. Don't believe her. Don't believe anyone. It's facts we're interested in, only facts. Carry on."

"Victoria had a boyfriend named Monty Draper. He's all over her social media, where they appear to have been quite the lovebirds. Apparently, he's a bridge champion who plays in tournaments around the country in the winter. In the summer he teaches bridge at the Wild Goose Resort."

"He'll be a major suspect, of course, along with the four children."

I blanched. "You think one of her children might have killed her?" I didn't know what I'd been thinking, but it wasn't that.

"What's the matter? Does the specter of matricide make you quake?" There was a definite trace of mockery in her voice.

"It does, in fact," I answered honestly. "Think how sick you'd have to be to murder the woman who carried you in her body for nine months and took care of you when you were a child."

"What if the mother was abusive? And one day the adult child's rage boiled over? Or what if the adult child was a malignant narcissist? Or a psychopath?"

"Okay. I've heard of cases like that. But matricide is still very rare, isn't it? Even the Greek and Roman gods didn't go in for it as a regular thing, and they were always murdering family members."

"Well, well. I see you learned something in college after all. I assume you're referring to Orestes and Clytemnestra?"

I gulped. Was I? I thought it best to agree.

"Do you remember what motivated Orestes?"

"Not off the top of my head." *Not at all* was more like it.

"Orestes was the son of Clytemnestra and Agamemnon, the king of Mycenae. When Agamemnon was away, Clytemnestra had an affair with his cousin Aegisthus. Then, when Agamemnon returned home, Aegisthus killed him. Orestes avenged his father's death by murdering both his mother and her lover. Does that jog your memory?"

She was looking at me with actual hope.

"Yes, now that you mention it. Clytemnestra. That was his mother. Orestes killed her for sleeping with Aga—Aga—with another guy."

She rolled her eyes. "Don't ever play poker, Blunt. You're a terrible bluff. Your thoughts and feelings virtually write themselves on your face."

I solidified my face, hoping to make it blank. But if Aubrey Merritt was right (I didn't think she was, not completely), it was probably blaring my discomfort.

She went on. "Orestes's motive was revenge. Same as Hamlet's, only Hamlet didn't have the guts to do the bloody deed. The ancient playwrights, Shakespeare, and all the great writers of the past understood that families are breeding grounds for strong emotions. Torrents of rage can be boiling under the smoothest of surfaces. Never forget that."

I nodded solemnly and made a mental note: *don't forget familial rage.* I might have quibbled with her reading of Hamlet (perhaps he'd had the guts *not* to kill his uncle). But that was a topic for another day.

"There's one more thing worth mentioning," I said. "It's about the deceased woman's husband, Warren. He died in a boating accident on Lake Champlain. Victoria was with him at the time. A storm came up, the wind shifted, the boom came round suddenly, and Warren was knocked overboard. Victoria brought the boat around but couldn't find her husband. Warren's body wasn't recovered until the next day."

"Dear me. How terribly sad," she said, brightening up considerably.

Who's bluffing now? I might have asked.

"The accident happened fourteen years ago. I don't see how it could be relevant," I added.

"Fourteen years *is* a long time. But the tragic death of someone deeply loved . . . or deeply hated . . . A family never really emerges from its shadow. Questions can linger for decades. For example, how can anyone be sure what really happened on that boat? The boom came round suddenly—so the widow said. There was nothing she could do—so she said. Shall we take her at her word? I imagine the children have some ideas about that. . . ."

Her face had softened; her body had visibly relaxed. I marveled at the change that had come over her. She looked as contented as if she'd just been told a cozy bedtime story.

"Set up a Zoom meeting with Ms. Summersworth right away," she said dreamily, her eyes half-closed. "I've decided to accept this case. Just think, Blunt. By this time tomorrow we'll be on the shore of Lake Champlain, with more fascinating questions just like that one in front of us, and not a hint of an answer in sight."

The pleasure she was taking in a situation that would appall most people was certainly worth noting, but it was the pronoun that snagged my attention. "*We?* You mean I'm going to Vermont with you?"

Her eyes snapped open. "I can't very well get there on my own."

This answer perplexed me for a moment, until I remembered that she didn't drive, a fact that had struck me as odd when I first learned it. I suspected there was a story behind it (a terrible crash in her past, perhaps?), as she was a staunchly independent woman. Yet when it came to local travel she depended completely on Gilby, or on hired cars whose drivers she often complained about. On my first day of work she'd asked if I had a driver's license and a vehicle, and I'd replied yes to both. It was a tiny lie, as I didn't actually own a vehicle. I did, however, have access to my father's old car, which he kept in addition to the pickup truck he had for work, and he always let me use it when I needed to.

"If you're asking me to drive you, that's no problem. I'd be happy to." I smiled, but only briefly, as an image of me standing in the rain, holding aloft the detective's black umbrella on a Chelsea street corner, floated before my eyes, and the frustration that had been gnawing at me for weeks swelled inside my chest. Had I just agreed to be a chauffeur? Only a chauffeur? It was entirely possible. A voice in my head hissed, *Don't be a wuss. If you don't get more assertive fast, you'll be opening car doors and holding umbrellas for the rest of your life!*

"Whatever you're thinking, do spit it out," Aubrey Merritt said dryly.

I swallowed and plunged ahead. "Well, when you offered me this job, I was naturally completely thrilled at the prospect of working with you. But I think I just assumed that being your assistant would mean, like, working on cases with you. Yet so far, with the exception of that art heist, in which I played no meaningful role, all I've done is secretarial stuff and internet research—a *lot* of internet research. And now, maybe, driving. It's not that I don't want to do that stuff; it's just that I'd really like to help with other things too."

"By 'other things,' you mean . . . ?"

"Investigative work. Detection." I met her eye, even though my insides were turning to jelly.

She picked up the reading glasses on her desk and twirled them lazily by one temple. "You think you're ready for that?"

"Yes, I do." *I've always been ready,* I might have added.

"Hmm." Her eyes glimmered at me darkly. "What would you do if I said I simply needed a driver? Just a driver, nothing more."

A terrible sadness flooded my heart. In my mind's eye I saw my rain-battered dreams being swept into the gutter. At the same time, I sensed that she was testing me, that she wanted me to step up and be heard.

"You see, Ms. Merritt . . . I can't just sit in a cubicle or tiny office all my life. I need more . . . more challenge or something. I need to learn things. If I don't, I'm afraid I'll just—I don't know—wither away. I'm sorry if that sounds dramatic, but surely you can understand? You said yourself, I'm no Bartleby. You knew that only because you're no Bartleby either!"

Silence filled the room. I closed my eyes and waited for her response. After a few moments, when nothing had happened, I opened one eye and saw that she was leaning back in her chair, chewing thoughtfully on her glasses' temple. I sat still. Another span of time passed. Finally she sighed and said, "I'm sure Gilbert informed you that I attempted to professionally train two different assistants this year. Each one proved inadequate. One of them failed to catch a suspect's blindingly obvious lie, and the other lost her case notebook on a subway car—at least that's where she *thought* she'd left it." The detective grimaced in disgust. "It was a waste of my time, frankly, and my time is far too precious to squander on another talentless wannabe."

"I am not a talentless wannabe. I'm different."

I expected her to say something biting, dismissive, or skeptical, but she didn't. She tossed her glasses on the desk and shrugged. "All right, Blunt. It hasn't escaped my notice that you've fulfilled your duties thus far with a degree of stubborn tenacity and dogged attention to detail that does speak well of you. And one or two conversations we've had about cases have been marginally helpful. I suppose I owe you the opportunity to be of greater use, and it would be mildly interesting to find out if you have half the potential you seem to think you do. But beware: my patience is already thin."

"Thank you, Ms. Merritt. Aubrey."

The index finger went up and waved. "Did I say you could call me by my first name?"

"No. Ms. Merritt."

"You can drop the *Ms.*"

"Okay. Merritt. I promise you won't regret giving me this chance." I was too relieved to be thrilled. I'd asserted myself—and prevailed!—and now all I wanted was to get out of that office as quickly as possible and see if I was still in one piece.

"Mm. We'll see about that. Be here tomorrow at eight a.m. Park on the street and I'll come out. And for god's sake, don't be late. It's a long drive and we need to get there ASAP, before the trail gets any colder."

CHAPTER 4

Conflicts of Interest

I hurried home that evening—following my usual route, from East Twentieth to Irving Place to East Fourteenth—and ran up the four flights to the apartment I shared with Trevor. I was dying to tell him my good news.

I found him reading a dog-eared script in our tiny kitchen. He was wearing gray sweatpants, a T-shirt, and flip-flops, and he was snacking on Doritos, out of the bag, with a jar of extra-hot salsa.

"Really?" he said weakly when I finished explaining my planned trip to Vermont with Merritt the next morning. He had rich brown eyes and an ultraslim physique and he took things at face value. I could always count on him to keep the earth under my feet.

"Is something wrong?" I asked.

"No, no. Not at all. I'm happy for you. It's just that . . ."

"What?"

"When will you be back?"

"Whenever Merritt and I have solved the case."

"How long will that be?"

"There's no way to know at this point. It depends on the situation. A week? Maybe longer."

"Did you forget?"

"Forget what?"

His brow creased in pained disappointment. "You forgot."

"What are you talking about?" I scanned my memory: this week . . . this weekend . . . Saturday night . . . "Oh shit. Your opening."

He nodded sadly.

Trevor had graduated from NYU with a degree in performing arts. He'd had bit parts in small productions for several years and had done a few commercials. Four months ago, when he'd tried out for the part of Bernard in *Death of a Salesman,* he'd said it was a long shot. He told me afterward that when he got to the studio to audition, there were so many actors waiting in line in front of him that he almost turned around and went home. But he didn't; he stayed. Then, by some miracle (and because he is very talented) he got the part, and we were both ecstatic. The rehearsals had been grueling but he'd thrown himself into the work with all his heart, and now, in just five days, the curtain at the Tank, one of the best and most famous off-off-Broadway theaters, would go up, reactions would start flooding in, and his future career as an actor would be decided by hypercritical reviewers who didn't care one bit about what a nice guy he was and how hard he'd worked.

He wanted me in the audience, cheering him on, and I wanted to be there.

I sank into a chair, covering my face with my hands. "Oh no. I forgot about your opening! I was so excited about the case. . . ." I picked up my head and looked him in the eye. "I know: I'll tell Merritt I can't make it. I have preexisting plans that can't be changed.

She can't expect me to just drop what I'm doing and rush off to another state whenever she calls!" On an emotional level, I meant every word. On a practical level, I knew Trevor would never let me forfeit the trip.

"No. Don't do that," he said. "It's okay, I promise. It's just an opening night. There'll be plenty of other opportunities for you to see the production, if they don't close us down first." He gave a nervous chuckle that betrayed his paralyzing fear of failure.

"I bet we'll be back in time." I suspected that this was overly optimistic, but I went with it anyway because I wanted it to be true. "Merritt is extremely good at her job. She'll probably crack the case in a couple of days. And with me there to help it could go even faster."

"Don't stress about it, Olly. This is a big opportunity for you and you've got to make the best of it. Your career is on the line here too, not just mine."

We reached across the table and gave each other's hands a squeeze. We tried to smile, but both of us were a little shaken. We were getting married in the spring, and I suppose we were wondering if this was what our future would be like—the two of us straining to go in different directions, missing each other's big events. We'd talked about having kids too. How on earth would that work?

Neither of us felt like cooking after that, so we sent out for Thai food.

Later that night, Trevor's mother, Zuzanna, called him. I knew it was her from the tone of his murmuring voice. She brought out a complicated kind of tension in him—frustrated, patient, hopeless, diplomatic. I heard him say, "We don't care, Mom. We really, really don't care."

I knew he was referring to the wedding plans. Zuzanna was a Polish immigrant who'd married Trevor's dad, an Indian American neurologist, when she was only twenty years old. She'd never worked, choosing instead to pour herself into her two sons: Trevor, who was wonderful, and Clark, who was wonderful and severely autistic. Ever since she'd been a bride herself she'd dreamed of having a daughter and planning a big wedding for her, and now it looked as if I was as close to a daughter as she was going to get and Trevor's and my wedding was the only one likely to come her way. As she had plenty of money since Trevor's dad's death, she'd offered to pay for the entire event if she could be "involved" in planning it. Given that Trevor and I were scraping by in low-paying jobs, that my widower father wasn't exactly a tycoon, and that planning the wedding clearly meant so much to her, we'd agreed. We'd told her we wanted to keep it small and simple, but that idea hadn't lasted long—as, in hindsight, we should have expected.

Trevor got off the phone and came into the bedroom, where I was working on my laptop.

"She really wants your input on the flowers," he said.

"Can't you give her input?"

"No, Olly. It has to be you."

"Why?"

"Because you're a woman and she's a woman. Flowers are a woman thing."

"I don't know what to say to that, Trevor. I don't know where to start."

"I'm not saying that's what *I* think. That's what *she* thinks. Just say you'll call her, okay?"

"Okay, but not tonight. I have work to do."

"Thank you," he said sincerely, and went back to whatever he was watching on TV.

I went back to scouring the internet for more information about the Summersworth family. This afternoon's research had been a

cursory first sweep. I knew there was likely plenty left to uncover, and I wanted to be prepared for any question I might be
asked. I had no intention of becoming Aubrey Merritt's third failed
assistant. She wanted to know what I was made of? Well, I would
show her.

CHAPTER 5

The Wild Goose Resort

My dad's car was a thirteen-year-old Jeep with almost two hundred thousand miles on the odometer. I'd called it Horace once—as in *horror*—and the name had stuck. He was army-camo green, with ripped fabric seats and nonfunctioning shock absorbers. Riding in him felt like ass-bouncing on a broken trampoline. Part of his metal floor was rusted through in the back, the resulting gaping hole covered up by a moldy and disintegrating bathroom rug. Before heading over to Merritt's, I took this valiant, pathetic vehicle for a rare ride through a car wash, shook the grit out of the worn floor mats, and tidied up the interior as best I could.

At seven forty-five I double-parked outside Merritt's elegant building, turned off the engine, and waited for her to come out as I'd been instructed. It was cool and sunny, one of those fresh, uplifting summer mornings when it was hard to imagine cold-blooded murderers dwelling among us. But of course they were there—they were everywhere—slyly masquerading as normal people. Working at a PI agency was making this dark fact ever more apparent to me, and my outlook was gradually changing as a result. For one thing,

I was more suspicious of everyone I saw—dog walkers, delivery people, folks I'd seen before in the neighborhood, and anyone I hadn't.

At exactly eight o'clock Merritt emerged from the building. She was always punctual and abhorred people who weren't. Her disapproval extended to early birds as well as latecomers, which was why I hadn't gone to her door when I'd arrived fifteen minutes ahead of schedule. I watched as she paused on the arched portico, and I clearly registered the exact moment when, looking up the street, she caught sight of me sitting behind the wheel of my ancient rusted vehicle. Her standard resting face, never free from a pinch of suspicion, was overcome by a surge of horror, which curled into snobbish disgust, which subsided into resignation.

I gave an awkward little wave.

Gilby emerged from the building carrying two large suitcases. I scrambled out of the car, went around to the rear, and yanked open the stiff door to Horace's cargo area. Gilby ferried Merritt's bags up the sidewalk and hoisted them inside. They looked smart and expensive and took up almost the entire space. Crammed into the remaining sliver of cargo area, my nylon duffel and two canvas totes looked like a pile of woebegone junk.

"She's not going to like this," Gilby said under his breath, referring, of course, to Horace.

I shrugged. What else could I do?

To her credit, Merritt didn't say a word about my car, even when we were on I-87 and the highway wind was whistling through the gaps in the thin doors and the constant high-pitched engine whine was making it impossible to talk. I was glad for the noise, actually, as Merritt lacked ordinary conversational skills. I'd tried a bit of small talk with her on a few occasions, hoping that she might catch the conversational ball and toss it back, but all she'd done was glare at me as if I were a blazing moron.

The trip should have taken about five and a half hours, but Horace's top speed was fifty-eight miles per hour, so for us it was closer to six. We rolled between the stone pillars at the entrance to the Wild Goose Resort just after two p.m.

The resort was more beautiful than I'd expected—all towering pines and feathery fir trees and massive ancient oaks. Smooth, perfect lawns stretched in all directions, gardens of colorful wildflowers were scattered artfully about, and there were enough blooming rhododendron bushes to suggest an infestation. We passed a gently rolling golf course, the fertilized grass so green that it hurt my city eyes; a checkerboard of precisely painted tennis courts; and a low concrete building that presumably housed the mechanical underbelly of it all.

Signs along the access road directed visitors to the Lodge—so named, I supposed, to suggest that there could not possibly be another. We chugged along a semicircular driveway and stopped in front of a huge Victorian mansion with two modern wings stretching out on either side, exactly like wings.

The instant we pulled up to the entrance, a fresh-faced bellhop who'd been waiting on a porch studded with mostly unoccupied rocking chairs jogged out to greet us and carry our bags inside. Wearing the staff uniform of navy canvas pants and a white polo shirt, he would have been indistinguishable from many of the resort's paying customers were it not for the green-and-gold Wild Goose logo on his shirt.

Merritt pried open Horace's rusted passenger door until it stuck; then she proceeded to kick it, with surprising force, until the opening was wide enough for her to attempt an exit. She grabbed the overhead strap for leverage, but it soon became clear that she was having trouble hoisting herself out of the Jeep. The bellhop extended a helping hand, but she waved him away with a curt "For god's sake, I can do it myself."

After she and our luggage had disappeared inside the building, I drove the car across the road to a woody parking lot—an apparently exclusive club of sleek, statusy vehicles to which my proletarian auto could not hope to belong—and returned on foot to the Lodge. Its lobby was rustically elegant and much larger than I would have expected from the building's facade. I would soon learn that the entire structure, including the original house and its two wings, housed twenty guest rooms and suites, a function hall for private parties, a five-star restaurant, a piano lounge, a conference room, a cozy library, a billiards room, a children's game room, a tiny gift shop, and a warren of administrative offices.

I arrived just in time to meet Merritt as she was being escorted to the elevator by the helpful bellhop, who was also maneuvering a brass trolley containing her suitcases. Her hair was disheveled, her gait slightly wobbly, and the extra pinkness in her cheeks suggested that her blood pressure was up. She looked as if she'd aged on our journey.

"Meet me back here in forty-five minutes," she said with startling ferocity.

"No problem." My luggage was in a heap at the reservation desk. I hurried over to check in.

The desk was manned by two clean-cut workers in green vests with gold buttons, and I gave my name to one of them.

He clicked his keyboard and consulted his computer screen. "I'm sorry," he said. "I don't have anything for a Ms. Blunt." He offered me a look halfway between bemusement and pity, as if I were a harmless little critter that had waddled in from the woods and was now lost. A plastic tag on his vest identified him as Jason, reservation specialist.

"Could you look again, please, Jason? I'm here with Ms. Aubrey Merritt. Perhaps you've heard of her? She's a nationally renowned private investigator. I'm her assistant."

Jason ran a finger down his screen. Pressing his lips together, he allowed several seconds of apparent concentration to pass. Then he said, "I do see a reservation for an Aubrey Merritt. She's booked into our luxury Blue Heron Suite. But there's nothing here for an Olivia Blunt." He glanced up with gently quizzical eyes, as if kindly allowing for the possibility that I'd mistaken my own name.

I realized what must have happened. During our Zoom call yesterday afternoon Haley Summersworth had offered us free lodging at the resort for the duration of the investigation. It appeared now that she'd booked only one room. Not knowing Merritt (or me), she'd mistakenly imagined that a luxury suite would be big enough for both of us.

"The Blue Heron Suite can accommodate up to four people," Jason pointed out with an optimistic bounce in his voice.

"That's a firm *no*, Jason," I replied. Riding in the car with my boss had been stressful enough. Living with her—sharing a bathroom, possibly hearing her snore—was out of the question, and there was no doubt in my mind that she would feel exactly the same way about me, only more so.

"I absolutely must have a separate room, preferably one next door to or on the same floor as the Blue Heron Suite," I said.

He wagged his head in a semblance of regret. "I'm sorry; we're completely booked."

"Say again?"

"It's the height of the season. We're completely booked."

My thoughts began to race. What if I couldn't get a room? Would I have to put myself up at a nearby motel, provided there was one? Or sleep in my car and sneak into the resort's ladies' room to wash?

"Jason. Please. Look again. There's got to be something." I made no attempt to camouflage the desperation in my voice. I even dialed it up a notch, hoping to come across as a patron capable of hysteria.

Jutting out his lower lip for some reason, he once again consulted the magic screen, this time jerking the mouse around erratically, as if to demonstrate the added determination he was bringing to the search. Finally he said, "Well, it looks like a room in the staff dormitory is available. Will that work?"

"The staff dormitory? Are you sure there's nothing else?"

He did some more mouse jerking, adding a frown suggesting extra effort, then looked up at me with a sad-eyed smile. "I'm sorry. That's all I can offer you at this time."

"All right. If there's no other choice."

He asked how long I'd be staying.

"Indefinitely. The same as Ms. Merritt. And you can put it on her tab."

He appeared dubious. "I'll have to check with management on that."

"So you will."

He reached under his desk, brought out an 8½ x 11 piece of paper, and swept it briskly under my nose. "Let me show you where you'll be staying," he said.

It was a printed map of the Wild Goose Resort that appeared to have been drawn by an untalented child. Numerous dotted lines that indicated walking and biking paths, and a few unbroken lines that represented paved roads, crisscrossed the seven hundred acres of the resort. Little squares and rectangles indicated various structures, such as a clubhouse, game room, snack bar, greenhouse, and gym. Everything had a sugary name, like Wisteria Lane and Children's Castle and Froggy Pond. Tucked among tiny sticklike trees were dozens of tiny cabins. More cabins dotted the shore of Lake Champlain, a portion of which was represented by a light blue blob in the map's northwest corner. The harbor had very small boats in it. The golf course was kelly green, and there were four bright turquoise swimming pools—one a normal size, one Olympic, one kidney shaped, and one a little blue speck. The whole map looked like the kind of board game I'd never wanted to play.

"We're *here*." He marked the Lodge with a slashing X of his ballpoint pen. "The staff dormitory is *here*." He circled a rectangle on the far side of the golf course.

"That couldn't be any farther away," I observed.

"It's about a twenty-minute walk if you go this way." He swept his pen along a dotted line. "Twenty-five minutes if you take the shore path." Another dash of the pen.

"How about if I drive?"

"Sorry. There's no parking over there. If you need to get there faster, I suggest you rent a bicycle."

"Where do I do that?"

"Here. At Uncle Bob's Bike Shed." He circled something far away.

"Any other options?"

"I can get someone to take you and your luggage in a golf cart."

I checked my phone for the time. "Okay. But I need to leave right away."

He nodded toward the map on the counter. "You'll want to take that with you." As there was a distinct warning tone in his voice, I folded it hastily and stuffed it into my pocket.

He made a call, and a minute later a golf cart pulled up in front of the Lodge. A tanned, good-looking guy about my age hoisted my motley array of bags into the back. He had an easy, relaxed manner and a very white smile, which he used to good effect. I settled myself on the flat vinyl seat up front and checked my phone again. If I hurried, I would have just enough time to drop off my bags in my room and make it back to the Lodge in time to meet Merritt.

"Drive fast," I told the good-looking guy.

He smiled his very white smile and said, "There's a speed limit. I get fined if I go over it."

"Don't you ever break the rules?"

He winked. "For you I suppose I could."

"Oh, please," I said and looked away.

CHAPTER 6

Clemmons and Grout

"You're late," Merritt said, emerging from the shadow of the Lodge's front porch as I raced up the steps.

"I'm sorry," I said, forgetting that she didn't accept apologies. She didn't care for excuses either, so I didn't bother offering mine. The truth was, I would have been on time if Jason's map had been a little clearer. As it was, I'd taken a wrong turn at the junction of several loosely dashed lines, which had brought me through some thick woods and out to a lovely sandy beach, inexplicably deserted, where I'd lingered for a minute or two, rendered helpless and forgetful by the beauty of the scene. It had been a long time since I'd taken a real vacation, and it felt quite special to stumble upon the grassy hills, the red cliffs, and the placid sapphire lake that stretched as far as I could see. I might have said it looked like a postcard, but that would have made no sense, as postcards were just pictures on stiff paper and this was real.

"Look alive, Blunt. We have an appointment at the police station in Burlington in twenty minutes," Merritt said.

"I'll bring the car around right away."

We were a few minutes late, which did nothing to improve Merritt's mood. The temperature between us was a good ten degrees cooler than Detective Jim Clemmons's air-conditioned office.

The man himself was big and burly and round like the trunk of a sequoia. He had foggy gray eyes and a saggy pale face, and his handshake was warm and soft.

"This is my assistant, Officer Grout," he said, referring to the uniformed female officer standing next to him. Not much older than me, she was short and squarish, with a needlessly hostile stare. Her handshake felt like a death grip.

We all took seats around Clemmons's metal desk—Merritt and me across from him, Grout off to the side. A thick manila folder occupied the space between us. I could see the edges of some photographs peeping out.

"Welcome to Burlington, Mrs. Merritt. I'm aware of your work in the field of private investigation, and I want you to know that we here at the Burlington Police Department are honored to have you. I understand that Haley Summersworth hired you to look into her mother's death. She's asked me to share the results of our investigation, and I have no problem doing that. Suicide's rough on a family, and Haley's taking it pretty hard. She's a sweet girl, and I'd like to do what I can to help settle her mind. But frankly, Mrs. Merritt, speaking as one professional to another, I'm afraid she's wasting her money and your time."

"Possibly," Merritt said. "Tell me, Detective, before you start, how well did you know the deceased?"

"I wasn't a personal friend, but I knew her well enough to say hello when I ran into her, and to call her by her first name. She was a public figure in this city—all around the state, actually. Her husband, of course, was Warren Summersworth of Kingfisher Development, and they owned the Wild Goose Resort as well, which you probably know."

"So you would say she had a wide circle?"

"Oh, definitely. She was in the local paper a lot for various things: five-K fund-raising walks, charity events, arts organizations. Every year she made big donations to the library, the YMCA, and our two homeless shelters, and this past spring she organized a gala to raise money for the expansion of the children's wing of the hospital. She was also on the diversity outreach committee, I think. Everyone knew Vicki Summersworth. Everyone who was anyone, as they say."

"What was her reputation in town?"

"People loved her," Clemmons said without hesitation. "There was something about her.... I can't put my finger on it.... She had a way of drawing you in and making you feel good. She was always smiling, and she made everyone around her smile too. Whenever I ran into her she would ask me how Klondike was." He smiled at the memory, proving his point.

"Klondike?"

"My Saint Bernard."

"Ah, I see. Did she remember your name as well?" Merritt asked archly.

"Mine? Oh, sure. She called me Jim. She was on a first-name basis with everyone. She even remembered Sarah's name." He nodded toward his second.

She had kept her belligerent eyes on me since we sat down, as if I were a lawbreaker she wished she could throw in jail. I tried a small smile, hoping to disarm her, but it had no effect.

"Any conflicts you know of? Turf battles? Grudges? Unhappy customers?" Merritt asked.

"Not that I ever heard of."

"All right, thank you. Now, what have you got for me?"

Clemmons opened the folder in front of him and recited his findings. "No forced entry. No sign of a struggle. No robbery, as far as we know. No known enemies. Basically, no evidence to suggest foul play. In addition, there was a suicide note."

"May I see it?"

He slid a clear plastic bag across the desk. Craning my neck, I could see a cream-colored note card inside, with *From the desk of Victoria Summersworth* embossed in a swirling gold font at the top. Merritt shook open her black reading glasses, settled them on the bridge of her nose, and raised the plastic bag to within an inch of her face. I'd seen her do this a few times before—stare at something so closely—and she had occasionally asked me to read fine print out loud or describe the backgrounds of grainy photographs. I'd started to suspect that there was something wrong with her near vision that even her bottle-thick glasses couldn't entirely fix, but I hadn't asked her about it directly. I knew she wouldn't appreciate having any limitations pointed out.

She studied the note for a long time—long enough that the air in the room seemed to grow heavier, as if thickened by her concentration. Clemmons glanced at me quizzically, and I had to smile with an assurance I didn't feel. I had no idea what Merritt was doing with that transparent bag held so close to her face. Certainly its contents couldn't be *that* intriguing.

"It's a suicide note," Clemmons said, perhaps hoping to hurry her along.

"Either it's a suicide note or someone wants us to think it is."

Clemmons smiled tolerantly, as if he'd expected some theatrics from the famous investigator. "It's been authenticated, Mrs. Merritt. Haley identified the handwriting as her mother's right off the bat. Later she had second thoughts and asked to have the note analyzed by an expert. I decided to humor her, given her fragile emotional state. The verdict of the graphologist was that the handwriting definitely matches Mrs. Summersworth's. Unfortunately, that wasn't what Haley wanted to hear."

Merritt passed the note to me. A bit of excitement fluttered in my chest. This was the first time I'd touched real evidence from a real possible crime scene. I read the note several times, until the words were stamped on my memory:

> Thank you from my deepest heart to the beautiful, loving friends who made my days so precious. It breaks my heart to say good-bye, knowing that no apology can ever heal the hurt you'll feel. There's still so much joy and pleasure in this world for you. Don't be sad, my darlings.
>
> Vicki

I won't deny that I teared up. It was humbling to hold such a sacred message in my hand. How could a woman with so much love in her heart possibly have taken her own life?

I felt Merritt's steely gaze on me. "Blunt, are you going to document that?"

"Oh, right." I quickly got out my phone and took pictures. Front and back, even though there was nothing written on the back, unless in invisible ink.

This would be my job going forward: to document every aspect of the investigation in the form of notes, photos, and audio recordings, all of which I would label and catalog at the end of each day. The idea was that if specific information was ever needed, it could be quickly and easily retrieved. As I would soon discover, though, my exhaustive files would be rarely consulted, for the simple reason that Merritt had a truly remarkable memory. Whether it was photographic or not, I couldn't say. Her ability to retain facts surprised me at first, as she often seemed to be paying no attention at all. Yet she could effortlessly recall not only what a witness said but their specific words and phrases, and when I would check the audio later,

I'd find that she'd been exactly right. She also had impressive observational skills. No detail escaped her, from a book abandoned on a park bench to the return address on a piece of mail. My painstaking records were like an external flash drive—good to have but seldom used.

"Where was this found?" Merritt asked Clemmons, referring to the suicide note I held in my hand.

"In the bedroom, on her dresser. Right in the middle. Obviously meant to be conspicuous."

I stole a last glance at the note before returning it to Clemmons. The penmanship was loose and loopy, with a smudge on the last line. I imagined Victoria Summersworth scribbling it with a limp hand, knowing she was about to die. It occurred to me that the words might not represent her true feelings, or at least not all of them. They might have been offered simply to assure her survivors that she bore no grudges, that her death was not their fault.

Clemmons produced photos. Merritt examined each glossy eight-by-ten with extremely close attention, then handed it to me for documentation. The images, taken from different angles, made my blood run cold. They showed Mrs. Summersworth's body mere hours after the life had gone out of it. She was lying on her back on a boulder, black lake water inches from her right arm, which was flung out from her body in a theatrical gesture. Her left arm was folded under her, and her legs were the same: one thrust out, the other bent at the knee. She looked like a wooden puppet severed from its strings.

I tried not to let my horror show, but my hands were visibly trembling as I trained my camera lens on each photo and snapped a picture, then stacked all the photos neatly and pushed the pile back to Clemmons, glad to be rid of it.

One corner of Officer Grout's lip curled into a tiny smile of superiority. Apparently she had noticed my unprofessional reaction to the crime-scene photos and found it amusing. I flashed a prickly "back off" glance in her direction. This earned me an outright smirk.

"The coroner's report," Clemmons announced, taking an official form out of the folder and placing it before us. "You can see here"— he pointed to a line at the top—"that the cause of death was blunt force trauma to the head. The distance between the deck and the rocks is about forty-eight feet, or roughly four stories. That's enough to kill a person, except in rare instances. Bruising on the body was consistent with a fall. There were no defensive wounds. Time of death: between two and four a.m."

Merritt nodded. "Toxicology?"

"Alcohol, slightly above the legal limit. No surprise, as she'd come from her birthday party. No drugs."

"Financial records? Phone records?"

"Usually we only ask for that information when there's reason to suspect it might be useful. That wasn't the case here, but Haley insisted on it. She also gave us her mother's phone and computer and asked us to examine them. There was nothing out of the ordinary."

"Where are the phone and computer now?"

"They were returned to Haley."

"Who found the body?"

"The housekeeper, a young woman named Pia Valente. Mid-twenties, nice girl, trusted. This is her fourth summer working at the resort. Mrs. Summersworth sent her a text at eleven thirty-six Saturday night asking her to come to the house the next morning to clean."

"You didn't find that strange?"

"At first. But Mrs. Summersworth was apparently in the habit of hosting impromptu get-togethers at her house—the family calls it the Bungalow—and Pia was used to being summoned on short notice. She arrived at the house at approximately eight a.m. Unfortunately, she cleaned the entire first floor before she discovered the body, thus thoroughly contaminating the scene. As she never went up to the second floor, you'll find that area untouched."

"The get-together you're referring to was a luncheon Victoria was planning for her children the day after her party," Merritt said. "That plan casts some doubt on the suicide theory, wouldn't you say?"

On yesterday's Zoom call Haley had explained that Victoria had texted her children at eleven thirty-five the night of the party, inviting them and their partners to lunch at her house the next day. She had something important to tell them, she said. This text was one of the reasons Haley was so certain that her mother hadn't taken her own life.

Clemmons puffed out his cheeks and let out a noisy sigh. I got the impression that he would have preferred it if this topic hadn't come up. "I know Haley was upset about that text, and I don't blame her. It was definitely an odd twist. But, as I explained to her, her mother was likely in a distraught state. She might easily have reached out to her children at one point that night, hoping to get them all together, and then, hours later, been overcome by despair. There's not necessarily a contradiction there."

Merritt's mouth turned down at the corners. She didn't like Clemmons's theory, but there was no denying that it made some sense.

"I assume you're done at the house," she said.

"Yes. You can go in whenever you want, provided the family agrees." He'd been fiddling with a paper clip, standing it up on one end and letting it fall on its side. "One thing, Mrs. Merritt, before you go . . . If you happen to find something we overlooked . . . I trust you'll let me know."

"Of course. I'll gladly pass along any significant new information I collect, on one condition: that I get your complete and timely assistance if and when I need it. Records, forensics, manpower if it's called for. We share the same goal, Detective—to find a killer, assuming one exists, and get him or her off the streets—so there's every reason for us to cooperate. Don't forget that if it turns out there was a murder and I'm able to identify the killer, you'll need to be ready to make an arrest."

Clemmons looked a bit disconcerted, as if he was just now grappling with what it would mean for him to be bested by a famous outsider.

As if she'd read his mind, Merritt added, "I'm a private investigator—emphasis on *private*. I don't need or want public credit for my work."

I raised my eyebrows at that. Aubrey Merritt certainly didn't lack for public credit. But it was true that she didn't seek it, at least in any overt or egotistical way. The only people she seemed to want to please were her clients, but even there her loyalty went only so far. If they tried to control her or interfere with her work, she had no problem walking away, with her usually hefty retainer fee firmly pocketed.

Merritt went on. "As far as I'm concerned, if there are kudos to be given at the end of this, they can all go to you and the Burlington Police Department—provided we've worked together as partners."

Clemmons visibly relaxed. "No problem there, Mrs. Merritt. Just let me know how I can help."

We said cordial good-byes, all but Officer Grout, who stood next to towering Jim Clemmons like a trained attack dog leashed at its master's side. The odd little woman was definitely getting on my nerves. As Merritt and I left the office, I offered her a brisk "Nice to meet you, Officer Grout." She looked right through me, as if she hadn't heard.

Merritt and I piled into Horace for our trip back to the Wild Goose Resort.

"Where to now?" I asked excitedly. "The crime scene?"

"Easy does it, Blunt. It's not a crime scene yet. First we have to prove there was a crime."

CHAPTER 7

A Rumpled Bed

S oon the majestic Green Mountains were streaming past the window and clear Vermont sunshine was beaming through the bug-spattered windshield. Merritt put on her big Gucci sunglasses, and I followed suit with my knockoff Ray-Bans. I felt my blood getting warmer, quickening its pace, felt my brain shifting into a higher level of attention. With Clemmons and Grout behind us, our work could begin in earnest.

As I mulled over what we knew so far, one question kept coming back to me. "What kind of mother would invite her kids to lunch and then kill herself?"

"I take it you don't buy Clemmons's theory that Victoria simply changed her mind?"

"No way. Not at all. Do you?"

"It's plausible." Merritt paused. "What did you think of the suicide note?"

"I thought it was sad and generous. It made me like her."

"Is that all?" The sly tone of her voice suggested that the question was a test. She was probing to see what I was made of.

I went over the words of the note carefully in my mind. They seemed pretty straightforward. *Thank you. Don't be sad.* That about covered it. "Yeah, that's all."

Merritt sighed, clearly disappointed.

"What? Did I miss something?"

"She never said she was sorry."

"Was she supposed to?"

"As a general rule, that's what suicides do. They know they're leaving their loved ones with a lot of guilt and confusion, in addition to the usual grief, so they say they're sorry. That, and *I love you.* To make them feel better. But she didn't say that either."

"She said, 'Don't be sad.' Isn't that the same idea?"

"Not really. Oh, and she forgot to mention that she was going to kill herself."

"I think that'd be obvious from her dead body."

"Sure. But the note made no reference to the act. And why did she need to thank everyone under the sun? All her *beautiful friends* and that rubbish? Did she really think the whole gang would be lining up to read her last words? Did she *want* them to? And, frankly, if her days had been so precious, why was she killing herself at all?"

"You think the note's a fake?"

"I've no idea. But it's a question, isn't it?"

There it was again, the same hum of contentment that I'd heard in her voice yesterday. We'd apparently stumbled onto one of those fascinating questions whose answers, to her strange delight, were nowhere in sight.

We passed between the resort's stone pillars and drove along the smoothly tarred road abutting the golf course. I noticed a group of male golfers standing around a putting green, one leaning listlessly on his club, the others watching intently as a heavy fellow in bright yellow shorts prepared to putt. It looked like a Norman Rockwell painting—all the colors so vivid, and the one man so bored while the others were so avid. And the putter himself was an oddly endearing figure—such a big man hunched knock-kneed over a little white speck of ball. The resort seemed designed to produce such perfect set pieces of Americana, from the sedate Schwinn bicycles, with their wicker baskets, that we also passed, to the old-fashioned ice-cream stand with the red-and-white-striped awning up ahead.

Horace let out a noisy belch as we rumbled past the Lodge, causing an older couple who were crossing the road to look up in alarm. I beeped and waved to assure them that there was nothing to fear, but I'm afraid that only startled them more.

We turned left at an unmarked road and headed up a shallow slope into a pine forest. The road soon changed from macadam to dirt. The coils in the seats sounded like an orchestra tuning up as Horace bucked and swayed in the hardened ruts, and Merritt and I bounced and dipped more than usual.

We passed a half dozen narrow driveways. I peeked down each one, hoping to catch sight of the cabins I figured must be at the ends of them. But all the cabins were hidden, either around bends or among the trees. I'd learned from my research the night before that there were about seventy of these houses, rentable by the month or the season, scattered all over the resort. Seasonal rental of a large waterfront cottage could top fifty thousand dollars. At the rate I was going, I wouldn't see the inside of any of them in this lifetime, except as a guest.

Victoria Summersworth's home was tucked away by itself at the end of the road, where a tight cul-de-sac encouraged stray visitors to turn around and go back the way they came. It was far from being the small, cozy affair that the word *bungalow* implied. Instead, it was rustic yet sprawling, with enough steeply pitched gables to make Nathaniel Hawthorne proud. The unpainted cedar shingles were nicely weathered; the trim was painted dark green. Thick shrubbery sculpted into smoothly rounded shapes looked like a necklace of oversized beads adorning its foundation. Off to one side there were a garden of zinnias and black-eyed Susans, a large sundial of polished granite (rather tomblike, I thought), and, on a pole, a wooden bird feeder carved and painted into a perfect mini replica of the White House. We parked, then walked up a path of gray stones embedded in moss. A wide covered porch was home to several clay pots of red geraniums—flowers so ubiquitous at the resort that they looked less cheerful than they should have—and a row of rocking chairs with mismatched plaid and floral cushions.

Haley had told us where to find the key, and Merritt fished under one of the flowerpots and produced it.

I snorted unprofessionally. In the city, a key under a flowerpot was practically an invitation. "Any idiot could break into this place."

"Maybe an idiot did," she said.

We entered a spacious hallway with polished hardwood floors, a brass coatrack, and an antique colonial hutch that held, among other things, a leather tray for car keys and a glass vase full of murky water and drooping black-eyed Susans. A muddy heaviness hung about the place. The air hadn't circulated in days.

A fancy satin clutch lay beside the vase. I pictured Victoria Summersworth tipsily tossing it there when she returned home from her birthday party the night she died. It struck me as poignant that her little purse should still be here when she wasn't.

Merritt saw me looking. "Well . . . ?"

"You want me to—?"

"That's what we're here for."

I opened the clutch gingerly and removed its contents: a compact, a lipstick, and two business cards—one for Butternut Farm, provider of fresh produce and maple products; the second belonging to a Mr. Stephen Hobbs, CPA, with an address in Burlington. I snapped a picture of each card and returned them to the clutch. I wondered where her phone was, until I remembered that Haley had turned it over to the police.

The hallway led to a living area that stretched all the way to the back of the house, where tall glass doors admitted a stunning view of the lake and a flawless blue sky. The decor was bland and comforting in a matronly way: a thick wheat-colored Berber rug, cranberry tasseled couches, an overabundance of floral chintz pillows, unremarkable watercolors of birds and plants, and a formidable array of family photos in sterling silver frames.

The place appeared to have been tidied up. There were no shoes abandoned on the rug, or sweaters tossed across the backs of chairs. On the coffee table, a couple of art books—Rembrandt, Salvador Dalí—were stacked next to a big handcrafted ceramic bowl and a bulky old-style photo album with slightly yellowed pictures kept in place by clear cellophane sheets. I peered curiously at the open page and snapped pictures of the three photos on display: (1) a young man, about seventeen or eighteen years old, tall and good-looking, in a graduation robe with an embroidered patch on the chest and wearing a mortarboard with the tassel hanging down; (2) three rows of soccer players in team jerseys posing on a green field, the same young man standing in the back; (3) the same guy again, this time grinning in a stiff tuxedo next to a demurely gowned and corsaged girl with her hair in a French twist.

From there I followed Merritt out to the deck. The furniture consisted of several spa-like chaise lounges, a long wrought iron dining table with eight cushioned chairs, and the biggest propane grill I'd ever seen. It all looked rich and ordinary. There was nothing to suggest that a woman had spent her last moments here. Yet I was acutely aware of what had occurred, and the metal railing, just above waist height, drew me like a magnet. With ghoulish fascination I peered over it to the rocky shore below, imagining Victoria Summersworth's fall through the soft night air and the terrible smashing force of the sudden impact. I wondered whether she had died immediately or had spent some minutes or hours lying there helplessly, in agony, conscious of the fact that her life was ebbing away. In those terrible moments, if they occurred, did she find herself regretting her act? Did she wish she could rewind the tape, somehow spirit herself back up through the night air to tumble in reverse over the railing and be deposited back on the deck of her beautiful house, with the chance to take a different path?

I didn't know how long I was mesmerized there before Merritt appeared at my elbow. "How do you suppose she got herself over the railing? It's fairly high. And look: the supports are vertical. There's nowhere to put your feet to climb onto the top of it."

I stepped back to get a better look. Merritt was right. The bottom was made of vertical slats. Additionally, the top of the railing was too narrow to stand on. Mrs. Summersworth had been a petite woman, shorter than almost everyone else in the group photos on her Facebook page. I was probably three or four inches taller than her, not to mention younger, and I would have a hard time getting myself over it.

We went upstairs and entered the dead woman's bedroom. Unlike the tidy downstairs, this room revealed a life in progress. Books were stacked on both night tables. I saw a couple of Louise Penny's mystery novels and a whole stack of self-help books by Brené Brown. Jewelry and perfumes (Joy by Jean Patou and Un Jardin sur le Toit by Hermès) were scattered across the dresser where the suicide note had been conspicuously placed, according to Clemmons. The king-sized bed with its high linen headboard was a rumpled tangle of ivory sheets and rose velvet coverlet.

I wanted nothing more than to exhibit the sangfroid of the seasoned investigator, especially in front of my boss. But I couldn't manage to repress the normal human emotions that bubbled up from my heart. I felt guilt for still being alive while the recent inhabitant of this room was irrevocably gone; shame for snooping in her private space; and sadness at her senseless loss, especially as she had been by all accounts a very decent human being.

"What do you see here, Blunt?" A sweep of Merritt's arm took in the entire room.

The question sounded casual, but I knew it wasn't. It was the second test of the day, and I didn't want to fail a second time. I studied the bedroom carefully, trying to see what a person with investigative talent might see—i.e., a clue. But when nothing had jumped out at me after a minute or two, I turned to Merritt and shrugged. "Ah . . . a messy dresser and an unmade bed?"

She raised a silver eyebrow at me as she turned away.

I told myself I'd do better next time.

We went into the bathroom. It was very large and very white, with gleaming double sinks, a glass-enclosed shower big enough to park a Harley-Davidson in, and a deep soaking tub set next to a lake-view window. I immediately coveted the tub. I wondered if I'd ever be so lucky as to have a bathtub like that myself. It was outfitted just as it should have been: with jars of bath beads, little pink soaps shaped like seashells, and about a dozen votive candles. A plush white bathrobe lay in a crumpled heap on the floor beside it. The only thing missing was a shallow bowl of rose petals.

Tearing myself away from the tub, I joined Merritt, who was perusing the sink area with singular focus. The white marble was nearly covered with a panoply of hair-care and skin-care products and other cosmetics. I recognized several different collagen firming lotions, and a facial moisturizer that sold for a small fortune. When Merritt flipped a switch, Hollywood lightbulbs around a huge mirror erupted into brilliant life. Glass bottles gleamed like jewels in the megawatt glare, and our own somber faces stared back at us in needless and unwelcome detail.

Merritt opened the medicine cabinet and started taking things out. "What does this say?" she asked, holding out a brown medication vial.

I took it from her and read the label. "Lisinopril, fifty milligrams."

"And this one?"

"Rosuvastatin, twenty milligrams."

"High blood pressure and high cholesterol. Perfectly ordinary." She seemed disappointed. I handed the vials back and she returned them to the shelf.

We returned to the first floor and entered the kitchen—a perfect chef's dream of marble countertops and modern stainless steel appliances. It boasted pendant lights, a center island big enough to accommodate three cooks at once, and colorful Persian runners scattered nonchalantly about. The only things that ruined the *Architectural Digest* effect were olfactory: the moldy smell of dead flowers and the sour odor of discarded food rotting in the trash.

Merritt suddenly barked, "Rémy Martin!" My gaze followed her pointing finger to an amber bottle on the counter beside the sink.

"There are two brandy snifters in the dish drainer," I said.

"I saw them. They've been washed. Check the dishwasher."

I opened it. "It's empty." I pulled out the top rack. "Wait—no, it's not. There are two glasses and a plate here."

"Are the glasses large or small?"

"Just regular kitchen glasses. Water glasses, I guess." I paused to think. "Wait a minute. Brandy is a late-night drink. So Mrs. Summersworth must have had a late-night visitor. Maybe someone who came over after the party. But that person wouldn't also have used a water glass, would they? So there could have been a second person here earlier in the evening, maybe before the party." I stood up a little taller, proud of my deductions.

"Nice try, Blunt. But you're going too far, too fast. Those glasses can be explained a lot of different ways. However, I do believe someone was with Victoria Summersworth the night she died. The open brandy bottle and the snifters suggest that, but the bed is even more telling."

"How so?"

"Small woman, big bed. A California king, I think it's called. She would have disturbed only one side if she'd been alone. But the bedding was disturbed on both sides—a fact you failed to notice."

"She could have been a messy sleeper." I tried not to sound defensive.

"Both pillows had indentations, and the covers had been flung back on both sides. Two people got out of that bed the night Victoria Summersworth died."

I was determined not to be a mere yes-woman, spinelessly agreeing with everything my employer said, so I pressed my lips together and concentrated on finding a way to disprove her supposition. Was there any way that Victoria *alone* could have messed up both sides of her king-sized bed? The best answer I could come up with was a mental video of her flinging back the covers on one side, then getting out of bed, carefully crawling back in, scooching to the other side, flinging back the covers on that side, and emerging from the bed again. Technically possible, but unlikely without a specific intent to deceive.

I leaned into the counter. "So, who do you think she was in bed with? Must have been her boyfriend, Monty Draper."

"Not necessarily. There could have been someone else."

I certainly wouldn't have gone there. I was having a hard enough time picturing a sixty-five-year-old woman cavorting with her lover in a California king. That she could have had a second guy in the wings was beyond what my knee-jerk ageism would let me imagine.

My eye fell on two child-sized Red Sox hats resting on the gleaming marble. A name—Colby—was handwritten in black marker on the brim of one of them. The other bore the name Caleb. Grandchildren?

It surprised and irked me that my research had missed them. What else might have escaped my notice?

Merritt was rummaging around in a wicker basket stuffed with flyers, store receipts, sticky notes, and scribbled lists. The basket was on a little built-in desk that was also home to a mug crammed full of pens and pencils. She passed a weekly planner over her shoulder. "Here. Get photos of the last three months."

I opened the planner so it lay flat on the island. It had come from the Metropolitan Museum of Art in New York and its facing pages bore pictures of Impressionist paintings. As I trained my camera on the most recent page, I noted that someone had written *Party!*—with an exclamation point—on the last Saturday in July. That same day, at two p.m., was the word *hospital*. I paused and stared in perplexity at the next day, Sunday, until I realized what I was (not) seeing.

"This shows the party on Saturday night, but Sunday's blank— nothing about a family lunch," I said.

But Merritt was gone. I found her in the living room, one hand cradling her chin as she gazed thoughtfully at a grouping of photos in sterling silver frames. They were the usual family photos: graduations, weddings, a lakeside barbecue, and a darling chubby baby laughing at the camera as he grabbed his toes.

"Where's the husband?" she asked. "Where's Warren?"

I tried to come up with a reason for his absence. "Maybe . . . since he's dead . . . it pains her to remember him?"

"Or she doesn't *want* to remember him. Maybe she didn't like him very much. Maybe for good reason. In which case it might have been a great relief to her when he drowned. You said she was on the boat with him when the accident occurred—is that right?"

"Yes."

"Hmm."

I knew exactly where her mind had gone. But it wasn't Warren's untimely death we had come to investigate. And it seemed rather churlish to invade the dead woman's house and rifle through her things only to insinuate that she herself might have been a murderer.

Merritt turned toward the sliding glass doors. "I need to see that deck one more time. Something out there is bothering me, and I'm not sure what it is."

I obliged by opening one of the doors for her. It was surprisingly heavy and hard to slide along its tracks. Before we stepped into the fresh air, she flicked a nearby wall switch. Nothing happened. She did it again and nothing happened.

"I wonder what this switch is for," she said.

I went out and craned my neck, looking for a fixture. Close under the eaves was a large floodlight.

"Try it again," I said.

She flicked it several times. Still nothing happened.

"The light's not working," I said.

"Can you get up there and see if it's the bulb?"

I pulled over one of the chairs from the dining table and climbed on top of it. When I twisted the bulb clockwise, the light flickered on. "Just a loose bulb," I called down.

A crafty smile passed across her face.

I clambered off the chair. Once again, I could guess what she was thinking. "Bulbs come loose all the time," I said, embracing my role of spoiler. "Especially if they aren't screwed in tightly to begin with."

"Do they? I don't recall ever having a bulb that unscrewed itself."

"Well, they do, I think." I honestly wasn't sure.

"You're probably right. It's probably just an innocent malfunction. Or . . ." Her eyes took on a deep violet hue as they glimmered at me in the dusk.

I finished her thought. "Or the floodlight was intentionally disabled to prevent eyewitnesses."

"Mm." She sounded like a purring cat. "Something to think about."

We stood together at the railing, quietly contemplating the waters of Lake Champlain. There weren't any boats on this relatively secluded area of the lake at present, and it was very unlikely that any boats would have been bobbing about between the hours of two and four a.m. Which gave me pause. Because it was safe to say that even if the deck had been ablaze with electric light, there would have been no one out there on the water to witness Victoria Summersworth plummeting to her death. So why would a hypothetical murderer have bothered to unscrew the bulb?

CHAPTER 8

Queen Victoria

Look. Someone's there," I said. We were pulling out of the cul-de-sac in front of the Bungalow, and my eye caught a flash of bright yellow through the trees. A mailbox up ahead marked the entrance to a driveway.

"Turn in. Let's see who it is," Merritt said.

The driveway took us to a house much smaller than the Summersworths' but similar in design. An older woman stood smoking on the porch. She wore a yellow T-shirt and she was glaring at us. Though thin and frail looking, she managed to give off an impressively aggressive vibe. I felt a little wary as I brought Horace to a stop. She looked like the kind of starchy old crone who kept a shotgun in her closet.

"I saw you over there. You've no right to be going into that house," she called angrily after I'd switched the engine off.

Merritt got out of the car. "My name is Aubrey Merritt. I'm a private investigator hired by the Summersworth family to look into Mrs. Summersworth's death. Could I speak to you for a moment?"

The woman gave Merritt the once-over. Then her eyes flitted to where I was sitting, behind the wheel of the Jeep.

"That's my assistant, Olivia Blunt. We're talking to anyone who might be able to shed some light on what happened that night."

"She killed herself. Jumped off the balcony."

"Most likely, ma'am. But the family wants to be sure."

The old lady squinted. "You mean they're *not* sure? They think it was something else?"

"Not necessarily, Mrs.—"

"Tucci. Pat Tucci."

"The family just wants to get all the facts, Mrs. Tucci. Do you think we could speak to you for a few minutes?"

"Sure. Speak away."

"Could we come in?"

"All right." The woman dropped the cigarette at her feet and ground it out with the toe of her shoe. She bent over stiffly to pick up the extinguished butt, then wrapped it in a tissue she took from the pocket of her baggy gray sweatpants.

"Can't let my daughter know I was smoking." She jerked her head toward the door. "Come on in."

Once we got inside it became obvious why her daughter would object to her smoking. In the living room an oxygen apparatus consisting of a storage tank, a plastic mask, and thin plastic tubes was set up next to a clunky recliner upholstered in greenish brown tweed.

She caught me looking at it. "Everyone keeps telling me I have to stop smoking, but I say you go when you go, so you might as well enjoy yourself while you can. Robin doesn't see it that way, of course. If I light up around her, she acts like I'm putting a gun to my head."

"Robin is your daughter?" Merritt said.

"That's right. She was the Queen's assistant. She worked for that woman for thirty years, maybe more. It's been so long, I can't re-member."

"I see. And do you and Robin live here together?"

"We do. We've stayed in this house every summer since the Queen took the one next door. She liked to keep Robin close. I don't know what we're going to do now that the old lady's gone. If the family has any decency, they'll let us stay until Labor Day, like we usually do. I hope the Queen left my daughter some money in her will, and a lot of it. She certainly deserves it. Nobody did more for that family than Robin did."

"I take it you didn't like Mrs. Summersworth."

"I didn't have anything against her personally. I just didn't like the way she treated my daughter. She expected her to come when-ever she called, and do whatever she asked. Any time of the day or night, any day of the week. Robin was like a servant to her, or a lady-in-waiting. That's why I called her the Queen, like Queen Vic-toria. She would never have had such an easy life if Robin hadn't been there to take care of things. You know what they say: behind every great man . . . Well, Robin was the power behind the Queen's throne. That woman couldn't have screwed in a lightbulb by herself."

My mind darted to the loosened lightbulb on the deck. Was it just a coincidence that the subject of lightbulbs had come up twice in so short a time? Scenarios began to form in my mind:

1. After decades of thankless servitude, Robin Tucci defiantly refuses to screw in a lightbulb when she's asked. Her refusal pre-cipitates an argument that ends in the older woman's fatal fall from the balcony.

2. Robin Tucci, stuffed full of a servant's repressed resentment, deliberately tampers with the bulb so she can throw her boss over the railing in total darkness, leaving no possibility of being seen.

Whoa. My imagination was certainly galloping ahead. Guiltily,

I glanced at Merritt, who less than an hour ago had scolded me for overanalyzing the water/brandy glasses. What would she say if she knew what was in my head now?

Not having become overexcited by the lightbulb reference herself, Merritt was carrying on a normal conversation with Pat. The tone was friendlier now. The two tough-minded seniors had taken each other's measure and found each other acceptable.

"How do you see it, Pat? You think she killed herself?" Merritt asked.

"How would I know? I wasn't there, was I? Sure, I was surprised when I heard she'd jumped, but not *that* surprised. In my opinion, everyone's a whole lot sicker than they look."

"What about your daughter? What does she think?"

"Robin hasn't said much of anything. It worries me. It's not like her to be so quiet. Of course, she's devastated, poor thing. She dedicated her life to that woman. I'll never understand why. But she did, and now she's hurting—that's for sure."

"I'd like to talk to her if she's around."

"Sorry. She's off somewhere, on one of her hikes. She does that whenever she's upset. Just disappears up some blasted mountain trail and comes back covered with mosquito bites. I have no idea where she is right now, probably couldn't even get her on the phone. The reception's spotty, as you can imagine. But I'll try if you want me to."

As she reached for a mobile phone on the small table beside the recliner, Pat started to hack—deep, rolling coughs that sounded alarmingly unhealthy. She went to pick up the oxygen mask but stopped herself midway, letting her empty hand fall to her side, and just stood there, coughing miserably. I got the impression that she didn't want us to see her with the plastic mask over her nose.

"Can I get you a glass of water?" I asked.

"It's nothing," she wheezed, waving me away. The fit subsided a few moments later.

Merritt handed Pat a business card as if nothing had happened, as if the woman hadn't just been coughing up her guts on the way to her grave. "There's no need to interrupt your daughter's hike. Just let her know I'd like to speak to her when she gets in."

"Is this her?" I pointed to a framed photo on a table.

"Yeah, that's Robin."

The photo showed a woman with bone-straight black hair, a thin-lipped smile, and heavily penciled eyes standing by the side of Victoria Summersworth in front of the Lodge. Robin was wearing a gauzy red thing like a shawl, only longer and flowier. Though her face was quite pale, almost ghostlike, she looked happy. Victoria was giving the camera a big, delighted grin. She wore enormous sunglasses, a short Lilly Pulitzer skirt, and a matching lime green polo shirt. Victoria looked to be in her forties, Robin somewhat younger, so the photo must have been about twenty years old.

I peeked out a back window as Merritt and Pat continued talking. The Tuccis' house had an attached wooden deck that was much smaller than the Summersworths', and it didn't abut the cliff in the dramatic way their neighbors' did. Instead, it opened onto a nice green lawn that swept a fair distance down to a portion of cliff adjacent to the Summersworths' house. Someone had put a weathered wooden bench at the point where the lawn ended. Beyond that, a dirt path traversed the property, running close along the rocky cliff edge—perilously close, in my opinion. A thick forest separated the two properties, creating a sense of privacy.

I heard Merritt say, "One thing I don't understand, Pat—how did you know we were at the Summersworths' house just now? I checked when we came in, and you can't see their house from the porch."

"Oh, that's my little secret," Pat said, as gaily as a child showing off her cleverness. "Come into the kitchen and I'll show you."

Merritt and I traipsed after her, and the three of us stood in a semicircle around the sink. Pat pointed out the window.

The forest was thinner there, and the front door and driveway of the Bungalow were visible through the trees.

"I was doing dishes when you drove in," Pat explained.

"Did you see anyone the night Mrs. Summersworth died?" Merritt asked.

"I certainly did. There was a big American car in the driveway at about one in the morning. A black sedan. I know whose it was too."

"Really? Whose?"

Pat lowered her voice. "It belonged to that sleezy guy she was hanging around with, that Draper fellow. Robin says he's a gold digger. Apparently he dazzled the old gal with a lot of attention and flattery, and she fell for him right away. Not very smart of her."

My jaw dropped. This was clearly a mega clue. Pat was putting Victoria's boyfriend at the house one hour before the estimated time of death. If she was right, this investigation was progressing very quickly indeed. Maybe I would be back in New York in time for Trevor's opening.

"You're sure it was his car?" Merritt asked.

"As sure as I need to be. He drives the only big American sedan I've seen around here all summer. Most people at this place drive foreign cars or SUVs."

"You didn't happen to notice the license plate, did you?"

"I didn't think to look."

"Did you see anyone in the car? Or anyone going into or coming out of the house that night?"

"No. Wish I did."

A frustrating pause ensued. We were all probably thinking the same thing: if only she'd laid eyes on him.

"Did Mrs. Summersworth have a lot of visitors?" I asked. I was clearly butting in, and I half expected Merritt to silence me, but she didn't.

"Her boyfriend, of course. He was over there a lot in the evenings, which, thankfully, gave Robin a break. The Queen didn't like to be alone, ever. Of course, it didn't matter that *I* was left alone, did it?" Pat said with a huff. "Her children came by fairly often as well. Three of them, anyway. Neil visited about once a week. He brought his two kids—nice-looking boys about six and ten."

"Colby and Caleb?" I said.

"Yeah, that's them. Their grandmother spoiled them for about an hour, and then they left. Lots of hugs for the boys, no hugs between mother and son. A duty call, if you ask me."

"What about Scott? Did he come by?" He would have been closest in proximity, as he worked at the resort.

"Oh yeah. He was there several times a week. He used to bring dinner from the Lodge on those tin room-service platters with the big curved tops. He and his mom seemed very close, but not always in a good way. They argued a lot. When their windows were open I could hear them going at it. Not the words, just the raised voices."

"So you don't know what they argued about?" asked Merritt.

"Robin said it had to do with the resort. Vicki didn't like the way he was handling things."

"Nothing more specific?"

"Robin wouldn't share specifics. She was very closemouthed where the Queen was concerned. She knew how I felt about her, and I suppose she didn't want to give me any more ammunition than I already had. She probably didn't want me to gossip either, but who was I going to tell? I don't have any friends here. I don't fit the type, if you know what I mean."

Pat hesitated. "There was one thing, actually. Happened a couple of days before the party—Thursday, I think—around dinnertime. I was here, at the sink, with the window open, and I saw Scott come storming out of the house. He yelled back over his shoulder, 'Stop accusing me!' Then he got in his car and drove away fast. The Queen was at the front door. She looked all sad and slumped, just staring after him."

"And you heard those words clearly?" Merritt said.

"Very clearly. 'Stop accusing me!' Clear as a bell."

"Hmm. Interesting."

"Isn't it just?" Pat said with the sly smile of someone who knows she's just passed on a juicy bit of gossip.

"And the third child who visited . . . who was that?" Merritt said.

"Oh, Haley, of course. The two of them adored each other. Lots of smiles and hugs when those two got together. Robin says Haley's a peach."

"So, by process of elimination, the one who didn't visit was Lauren."

"Correct. That one's a nasty piece of work, Robin says. I wouldn't know, myself. I met her a few times when she was a teenager, but I haven't laid eyes on her for years. She lives over by Stowe. She and her husband have a farm, and she makes skin-care products in her barn. She's pretty successful, apparently. She and the Queen never got along."

Pat opened the refrigerator. "Can I get you two something to drink? Soda or iced tea?"

I asked for iced tea. Merritt declined, but Pat put three glasses on the table anyway, along with a pitcher, and invited us to sit down.

"It would be helpful if you could walk us through what you remember of that night," Merritt said when we were settled.

"I didn't go to the party. I was here by myself, watching TV," Pat said.

"What time did your daughter leave for the party?"

"That would have been around four or four thirty. The party

didn't start until six, but she needed to be there early to make sure all the preparations had been made. She's very organized and detail oriented. If an event goes off well, the family takes the credit. If it doesn't, Robin takes the blame. As usual."

"And after she left, you watched TV?"

"That's right. About nine thirty I went out on the porch for a smoke. It was a nice, warm night. Very still and dark. Moonless. There's something sinister about a moonless night, don't you think? The dark is so black, you can't walk ten feet without tripping. So, I was standing there, on the porch, when I noticed a light coming down the road. I figured it was Robin coming home early from the party, and I didn't want her to see me smoking, so I stubbed out the cigarette and came inside."

"A light. What kind of light?"

"A flashlight. Everyone around here uses flashlights at night. You always see little beams wavering around in the dark from people going from the Lodge to the game barn or the snack shack or back to their cottages. The resort discourages driving, you see. They want to keep the place as rustic as possible, so they ask people to leave their cars in the parking lot across from the Lodge. Most people do. They pay an awful lot for the privilege of walking instead of driving. Go figure."

"Robin carries a flashlight with her?"

"Always. At night, that is."

"So, you went inside to watch television. And she came in shortly after? Around nine thirty, you say?"

"No. That's just the thing. She didn't come in then. The light I saw must have belonged to someone else, someone going to the Summersworths' house. That's the only one past ours."

"I see. You're sure of the time?"

"Yes. I was surprised that Robin was coming back so early, so I checked the clock in the kitchen when I came in. I wondered if maybe it was later than I thought. But no, it was just about nine thirty. A few minutes past that, actually."

"Very good. And what time did Robin get home?"

"Don't know. I fell asleep in my chair, the way I always do. I woke up again around one a.m. and Robin's bedroom door was closed, so I figured she'd come home while I was asleep. I decided to have a little smoke before bed. It was a bit chilly outside by then, and I don't like all the animal noises that late at night. The raccoons are out then, and they're mean little things. So I went into the kitchen and opened the window over the sink. You know, this one that I just showed you. That's when I saw there was a car—his car—in the Queen's driveway."

"And how sure are you of *that* time?" Merritt asked.

"I can't say I'm absolutely sure. But I do believe it was about one a.m. I must have checked my phone absentmindedly when I woke up."

"After that what did you do?"

"I went to bed, slept through until maybe seven. When I came into the kitchen to get my morning coffee I checked again—just curious, you know—and the car was gone."

"Thank you, Mrs. Tucci. You've been a big help."

Pat's hand darted out. Her fingers curled around Merritt's forearm, preventing her from getting up. "Look, I need you to be honest with me, Mrs. Merritt. I think you'll agree that I've given you a lot of information, so it's only fair that you give some to me. Victoria Summersworth was murdered, wasn't she? Isn't that really why you're here?"

Merritt kept her voice steady. "As I said, Pat, there's no evidence of foul play. The police concluded that Mrs. Summersworth's death was a suicide, and I don't have any information that contradicts their finding."

Pat emitted a trembling sigh. "I don't like thinking there might be a murderer roaming around. We're kind of isolated up here, Robin and me. And now, with the house next door empty, it's even worse. Honestly, I wouldn't mind as much if he did it—Monty Draper—because then I'd know it was just a personal thing. But if it was a random killing . . . if there's some kind of psycho lurking out there . . ."

"At this time I don't see any reason to worry," Merritt assured her.

Looking unconvinced, Pat muttered, "That's just what Robin said."

CHAPTER 9

Trade Secrets

Looks like Monty Draper has some explaining to do," I said as we made the short drive from Pat Tucci's house to the Lodge.

"Pat saw a car at the house, not a person," Merritt reminded me.

"Well, someone had to be driving it."

"True. But we don't know if that person was Draper."

"He's the most likely candidate, isn't he? By far."

Merritt didn't comment. She was staring out the window at I don't know what. The towering pines, so distinct and majestic an hour earlier, had blurred together in the fading light.

"It fits perfectly," I said, eager to connect the dots. "They're drinking heavily at the party. Then they go to her place, they drink brandy, they have sex—hence the brandy glasses in the drainer and the bed rumpled on two sides. Then, for reasons we don't know, things get tense. They end up fighting, it gets physical, and he pushes her too hard. She falls off the balcony and dies. He's completely stunned, didn't mean to do it. He writes a fake suicide note in her messy handwriting, figuring it's the only way out of a murder charge. Then he gets the hell out of there. I bet he started breathing a lot easier once the cops concluded it was suicide. He doesn't know that Pat Tucci saw his car. Or that you were hired to investigate."

Still Merritt was quiet.

"You've got to admit, it's a pretty good theory." I was proud of having come up with it so fast.

"Tell me, Blunt, have you ever stopped to wonder why I have a career?"

"Because being a private investigator is what you always wanted to do?"

"You're talking about yourself now, of course, as so many people tirelessly do. I'm asking a different question. I'm asking you to consider what it is about our criminal justice system that creates a demand for someone like me and allows that individual to achieve a degree of fame and fortune that far exceeds what any publicly funded detective can hope to achieve."

Now I was quiet.

"It's because police departments have constraints," she continued. "Constraints of time, money, manpower, politics, and public pressure. Even their vaunted forensic labs aren't the magical places we think they are; they're frequently slow and overburdened. And wrong. All too often, police detectives don't have the resources they need to do their jobs the right way, with the necessary care and patience. How do you suppose they handle that?"

"No idea."

"Well, what would *you* do if you were given too few resources to do your job?"

The words *cut corners* and *cheat* came to mind, but I bit my lip.

"I'll tell you," she said. "The minute they get a likely suspect in their sights, they start building a case, searching for evidence that will prove them right. Once they get enough evidence, they haul the suspect in and start questioning him to get even more evidence to take to the DA. And while they're busy doing that, they're blind to all the evidence that points a different way. The real culprit skips town and the trail goes cold. That's not how it always happens, of course. But when the police call me in, or the relatives call me in, it's very often what I see. The cops started chasing the wrong guy right off the bat, thinking they could score an easy win, and their botched case gets dumped in my lap."

"You think that's what I'm doing."

"Is it?"

We both knew the answer.

I said, "So, your advantage is that you don't have those same constraints."

"Exactly. There's no pressure on me of any kind. I can take all the time in the world if I want. I get paid by the day, and if I fail to solve the case, I don't lose a dime. No one loses face, because the only people who are likely to know about it are the client and me. Clients typically have no desire to publicize the fact that they just spent a lot of money on something that didn't work. See? No financial pressure, no public pressure, no time pressure. I can afford to fail, and that's a big reason I succeed. It's not glamorous, but that's my secret—one of them, anyway."

She softened her tone. "You said you wanted instruction, right? So here's your first lesson: slow down. Way down. Stick with the simple acts of listening and looking at first, and do those things exceptionally well. Notice the flat notes, the cracks in the plaster, and file them away in your memory just as they are, without interpretation. And if you find that, in your innocent enthusiasm, you really can't resist positing a loosely plausible theory based on scant evidence, then for god's sake, don't fall in love with it."

I ought to have been committing this valuable advice to memory. But I'd gone a bit foggy after she said *I can take all the time in the world if I want.* I was holding on to the hope that I'd be back in NYC in time to attend Trevor's opening night. Now that hope was being undermined. How long was it going to take to find this alleged killer anyway? Days? Weeks? Months? The resort would close for the season in mid-October. By then the leaves would have changed from green to gold to red to brown, and some of them would have been whisked off the branches by a cold north wind. I pictured myself trekking miserably around the resort in Merritt's chilly wake, the thrill of the chase long since dissipated, while Trevor knocked about our empty apartment, languishing in solitude, wondering why he'd gotten himself involved with the assistant to a globe-trotting PI who might spend weeks away from home.

I swept that worry out of my mind as best I could. Trevor and I had a strong, solid relationship. If I didn't want to drive myself batty, I needed to believe that together we could handle whatever challenges life threw at us. Because we definitely could. I hoped.

The Lodge was coming up on the left; the parking lot was on the right. It was full of Japanese and German cars. I pulled into a spot next to a BMW and turned Horace's sputtering engine off.

"Pat was right about one thing, at least: you don't see a lot of American cars around here," I said.

"Come on, now. You didn't fall for that nonsense about the American car, did you?"

"What nonsense? Pat said the car in the driveway was an American make. A black sedan. That's how she knew it was Monty Draper's."

"You saw how far the driveway was from the kitchen window. And don't forget it was the middle of the night—a moonless night. Pat even commented on how dark it was. How could she have known the make for sure? Chevy, Ford, Honda, Toyota—they all make large sedans that would look very similar from that distance in the dark."

"She seemed pretty sure it was his."

"Don't forget that she called Monty Draper sleazy and a gold digger. She doesn't like him, not at all. When she saw a dark sedan in the driveway, she might have unconsciously linked it to him." She hesitated. "It's also possible that she was deliberately trying to frame him by putting his car at the scene."

"What? Are you serious? She didn't strike me as the kind of person who would do something like that!"

Merritt shook her head at me. Once again, I'd disappointed her. "Honestly, Blunt, do you really think you know what kind of person would do something like that?"

She didn't wait for an answer. "There's a third option too. Pat Tucci is not a stupid woman. The minute she saw us, she understood what our being there meant—that potentially the suicide verdict was erroneous and an unsolved murder was on the table. It scared her. Did you hear what she said at the end of our conversation? She said that if it turned out that Monty Draper had killed Victoria she wouldn't mind, because that would make the murder personal instead of a random thing. She'd be less worried that way."

I had to ponder that for a moment before I understood what she was suggesting. "Okay. Let me see if I've got this right. Now you're saying that Pat Tucci identified the car as Monty's as an unconscious wish fulfillment, that on some deep psychological level she needed the car to be his to lessen her fear that it might actually belong to a serial killer who might show up one night to murder her and her daughter." I shook my head. "I don't know, boss." That was all I was going to say. It wasn't my place to explain to the great detective that her idea was bonkers.

"You think that's far-fetched."

I figured I might as well admit it. "Yes. I do."

"Maybe it is." As she pushed open Horace's creaky door, she said slyly over her shoulder, "That doesn't mean it's wrong."

CHAPTER 10

A Winning Personality

Ms. Merritt! I'm so glad to meet you in person. I'm really honored that you agreed to take this case. I know how in demand you are."

Haley Summersworth was a plump brunette with a round, pleasant face. Her dark hair was piled on the crown of her head, held there by a scrunchie that was a little too loose, so that her thick topknot was on the verge of sliding down the side of her head. She was dressed in light-wash jeans and a baggy sweatshirt bearing the slogan: *Keep calm and let HALEY handle it.*

We were meeting her in the Fainting Goat Lounge on the first floor of the Lodge. The poster outside the door advertised upcoming karaoke nights, and performances by a local blues singer and a Celtic band. The inside of the lounge smelled like stale beer and air freshener and was furnished the way you'd expect: a polished mahogany bar with dozens of gleaming bottles arrayed along a mirrored wall; open tables in the middle of the room; semicircular banquettes lit by low-hanging lights along the walls. A shiny black piano dominated an entire corner, a raised wooden platform next to it. The place felt cramped even though, objectively, it wasn't.

Merritt and I were seated in one of the booths. It was six p.m. on a Tuesday, and the only other patrons were a tired-looking, sunburned couple at the bar. Haley Summersworth's bustling two-minute-late entrance felt like a fresh breeze.

Merritt introduced me. Haley turned smiling eyes to me and I found myself briefly and unexpectedly mesmerized. Her eyes were large and liquid, warm and welcoming. They were light brown, the color of chestnuts, and they seemed to exude sympathy and understanding. When she said she was pleased to meet me, I almost blurted, *Will you be my friend?*

"I brought you this," she said to Merritt, sliding a laptop out of her canvas tote and placing it on the table. "Mom always used the same password—it's the name of her dachshund who died last year, poor thing. Seventeen years old, kidney disease. Mom was devastated. His name was Bunyan. As in Paul Bunyan, not the gross things people get on their feet. B-u-n-y-a-n. All lowercase."

I had to think for a moment. "Wasn't Paul Bunyan that giant lumberjack? The folk hero they make gigantic sculptures of in states from Maine to Oregon?" This was one of the many random things I knew from my fact-checking days.

"That's the one. He had an ox: Babe the Blue Ox. The two of them went around together chopping down trees and hauling lumber." Haley gave a little laugh. "It's kind of an odd name for a dog, especially a dachshund. But this whole resort started out as a lumber camp in the nineteenth century, so I guess it fits. Anyway, everyone called him Bunny. The dog, I mean."

"You already searched your mother's computer—is that right?" Merritt broke in, never a fan of chitchat.

"Yes, but I didn't find anything. I gave it to Detective Clemmons's digital forensic team as well, and they didn't find anything either."

"Were you looking for anything in particular?"

"Threatening messages, I guess. Anything that might shed some light on her death."

"Blunt here will take another look. She has some experience with this kind of thing."

I sat up straighter and Haley gave me a smile. She seemed as pleased as I was that I'd been recognized as having a helpful skill—though I honestly had no idea what Merritt was talking about. I'd never searched a computer in my life.

A waitress came over and we ordered drinks and fried gherkins. Merritt went for sparkling water and, good assistant that I was, I followed suit. Haley asked for a beer.

"I know this is a hard thing to talk about," Merritt said, "but I need to get this question answered. Had your mother ever been treated for depression or complained about her moods? Did you ever notice anything like that?"

"Oh, no. She was always in a good mood. She was a very happy person."

"There was a tragedy in the family, though—your father's death fourteen years ago. That must have been difficult for her."

Haley nodded solemnly. "Absolutely. My father was the kind of person . . . well, you just couldn't imagine him dying *ever*. And then it was so sudden, so random. We were all devastated, especially Mom and Scott, because they were with him when it happened."

"Scott too?" I broke in, surprised. "The newspaper said only your mother was in the boat."

"Oh, that was Mom's idea. She worked in PR at Kingfisher before she married my dad, and she was friends with the editor of the *Burlington Free Press*. She convinced him to keep Scott's name out of the paper. He was seventeen at the time, and he'd been struggling with . . . some things . . . and she thought it would make everything worse for him to be publicly connected to Dad's death. Some people were questioning why more hadn't been done to save him. It was all nonsense, of course. He was seventy-one years old and he was hit in the head. He went under right away."

"So, your mom . . . she recovered from the loss okay?"

"Sure. I guess. My parents weren't exactly close. So, you know . . . um, but it was very hard on her anyway." Haley's voice trailed off.

Merritt smiled gently. "I see."

I wondered if she was going to dig a little more, try to ferret out what the source of the marital difficulty was, but she seemed to decide that she'd pushed Haley far enough on that topic, and she smoothly moved on to the next.

"Tell me about Monty."

"Oh, Monty," Haley replied with weary good humor, as if he were a harmless subject too often discussed. "He's caused quite a stir in the family. Neil and Lauren absolutely hate him. Think he was after Mom's money. And he's a bit rough around the edges; you'll see what I mean when you meet him. I wasn't too keen on him myself at first. He seemed to show up out of the blue. A bridge champion? I didn't even know there was such a thing. And that awful moussed-up hair! *Messed up* is more like it. But he grew on me after a while, mostly because I could see how happy he made my mother. She lit up when he was around. They laughed a lot together—secret jokes—and they were always touching and giving each other little smooches. It was lovely to see Mom so happy. I figured, if she liked him, so what if he was a fortune hunter? That's what prenups are for, right? Mom would have absolutely hated the idea of a prenup, but I knew Neil would twist her arm until she agreed, and in the end she'd do it to keep peace in the family."

"Were they talking about marriage?"

"Yes, he proposed a few weeks ago. Mom confided in me. It's kind of a secret, though I suppose it doesn't matter now. Anyway, she hadn't accepted his proposal yet. Said she had some things to straighten out first." Haley leaned forward. "See, Ms. Merritt? More proof that she didn't kill herself. Do you believe me now?"

"I never disbelieved you, Ms. Summersworth."

"You can call me Haley," she said confidently, offering her charming smile.

"Actually, I would prefer to keep our relationship on a more formal footing. You see, Ms. Summersworth, you're my employer in this case, and there's more than a small chance that you'll find my work unsatisfactory. I might fail to solve the mystery. Or, if I do solve it, my conclusion might disappoint or shock you. It isn't inconceivable that at some point in the future you'll find yourself wishing you hadn't hired me. If that happens, it will be easier for both of us if we're not on a first-name basis."

"I can't imagine that ever being the case," Haley said resolutely. At the same time, she was blushing. She hadn't expected that response and didn't know how to take it. Like her mother, she was the kind of person who went through life spreading warmth and sunshine wherever she went. This attitude probably worked for her most of the time, and now it was being rebuffed, leaving her at a loss about how to behave. To make matters worse, Merritt was raising a troubling prospect about the case itself that Haley apparently hadn't foreseen: namely, that if Victoria was murdered, someone had to have done it, and that person wasn't necessarily the stranger Haley imagined. It could be someone known to her, someone close.

The waitress returned, setting down our drinks and putting the plate of fried gherkins in the middle of the table. Haley and I immediately dug in. Merritt abstained. It occurred to me that I'd never seen her eat. When I suggested stopping for lunch on the drive up, she'd refused, and I'd never shared a meal with her back at the office, or seen anything beyond a glass of ice water or a cup of coffee on her desk.

"You said your mother had some issues to straighten out before she could decide whether to marry. Do you have any idea what they were?" Merritt asked.

Haley wiped her mouth with a napkin. "I wish I could tell you, but she didn't explain herself, and I didn't ask."

"You must have an idea."

"I figured it was business. She usually had Kingfisher or Wild Goose on her mind. I didn't go into those topics with her. I left the family business to open my own café, and I take pains to keep my distance." She seemed uncomfortable suddenly, pressed her lips together firmly.

Merritt squinted at her. "What is it, Ms. Summersworth?"

Haley stayed silent for a moment, then said, "I didn't come here to air my family's dirty laundry."

"I didn't come here to hear it. But I would very much like to know what was on your mother's mind in the days and weeks before she died."

Haley sighed, letting her resistance go. "The resort's been having money problems, apparently. I don't know all the details. All I know is that my brother Neil was accusing Scott of mismanagement, and Mom was in the middle. Neil wanted her to fire Scott, and Scott insisted that Neil was lying out of . . . spite, I guess, because they never got along and because of that whole thing about Dad's death." She rolled her eyes. "Welcome to the family."

Merritt and I exchanged glances, remembering what Pat had overheard Scott saying to his mother: *Stop accusing me!*

"Tell me about the will," Merritt said.

"Mom's lawyer has it. There'll be a formal reading on Saturday."

"Do you know what will happen to the business?"

"Not the specifics. The four of us have equal shares in the company, and I don't expect that to change. But Neil will have a lot more power without Mom around. As CEO of Kingfisher, he'll basically be running the whole operation. I imagine we'll all just do whatever he says. That's what we've always done."

"You trust him, then?"

"Yes, absolutely. He's a very ethical person. We all are, frankly. We got it from our father, who was always going on about honesty, hard work, and civic responsibility. And from Mom too, of course, who never met a worthy cause she didn't support."

She sipped her beer. "But that doesn't mean Neil will turn a blind eye to management problems. In fact, I wouldn't be surprised if he fired Scott now that Mom isn't around to protect him." Her face fell. "Gosh, I hope he doesn't do that. That's the last thing Scott needs right now."

"Sounds like your mother was in the habit of looking out for Scott."

"God yes. She always watched out for him, shielded him. He's had his issues, shall we say, and she was always there to bail him out. Some people would say she should have tried tough love instead."

"What kind of issues?" Merritt asked.

Haley shook her head. "That's not relevant, is it? Besides, he's doing well these days. He's put a lot of stuff behind him, and that's where it should stay."

"Fair enough." Merritt gave a brief nod of acquiescence. Of course, I knew that she fully intended to find out what "stuff" Brother Scott had allegedly put behind him.

"Moving on," she said, "there are a couple of things I need your help with."

Haley brightened. "Really? I'll do anything you want me to. Truly. I'd love to help. Anything is better than sitting around missing my mother."

"I need the guest list for the party, and the photos from that night as well—there are photos, I trust."

"Absolutely. We had a professional photographer come. The proofs might not be in yet, though. I'll ask Robin Tucci. She takes care of things like that."

"Good. And one more thing: did your mother always keep her house key under the geranium pot?"

Haley groaned. "I'm afraid so. I suppose dozens of people know about it. It's been there since I was a kid. Honestly, most of the time we didn't lock up at all. Mom used to say the Wild Goose Resort is one of the safest places on earth. We always want to give that vibe for marketing purposes, naturally, but it also happens to be true. The worst crimes committed here are occasional petty thefts. Guests are supposed to use the in-room safes, but you'd be surprised how many don't. They leave their valuables lying around in plain sight, and once in a while something gets nicked. We usually suspect the housekeeping staff, but it's awfully hard to prove, especially if you don't have the missing item. Oh, and once someone stole a boat, a Sunfish. Sailed it all the way up the lake and left it on the northern shore, half-hidden by leaves and branches. Since it was recovered a few days later, nobody was too upset."

"Do you have a security force?"

"We do. It's pretty small. There are probably eight or ten guys on the roster, but usually only two are on duty at a time. You'll probably see them riding around in golf carts. They wear black polo shirts that say SECURITY on them. Mostly, they help lost children find their parents, and break up late-night fights at Big Red's Big Red Game Barn."

"There was no special security detail at your mother's party?"

"We never do that for a party. Not even a wedding."

"CCTV in the lobby, perhaps?"

Haley shook her head. "We've never needed anything like that."

"I'd like to see the venue, if you don't mind."

"No problem at all. I can take you there now."

Haley called the waitress over and had a brief word with her about the bill. Apparently, all the charges that Merritt and I incurred were to be on the house. We had only to sign our names and note our room numbers. It all seemed rather magical to me (presto, no financial stress!), but having been a server myself in college, I naturally worried about the waitstaff. Resorts usually added an eighteen percent gratuity to a bill automatically, but there was no way of knowing how much of it trickled down to the individual server, so I took a twenty out of my wallet and put it on the table for a tip she could pocket immediately.

Merritt didn't notice. She seemed to float above such grubby matters. She didn't touch cash or credit cards and had barely spoken to me about expenses, other than to pass the responsibility for them over to me. On my first day of work I'd been handed an agency credit card, which I'd yet to use, and I had access to the agency bank account, to make deposits and pay invoices. (This was how I knew Merritt charged quite a lot for her services.) Merritt's trust in me had amazed me until Gilby informed me that she also employed an outside accountant, who dipped into the books periodically to keep an eye on things. Still, I had a good deal of autonomy in money matters, and given that my boss seemed perfectly indifferent to the issue, I fully intended to scatter large tips around the resort in solidarity with the working class.

Haley led us out of the Fainting Goat Lounge, down a wide corridor, through a set of double doors, and into a function hall that could probably handle a wedding with two hundred guests if they squeezed a bit. At the moment there were ten or twelve round tables set up, each with a capacity of eight to ten guests. Similar tables, whose legs had been collapsed, leaned vertically against the inner wall, and in the corner nearest us there were a half dozen serving stations and a maze of rolling room dividers. Haley flicked some switches and a row of big crystal chandeliers bloomed into incandescence across the high ceiling, allowing us to see clearly that the walls were painted pale green, with brass sconces set at intervals, and the floor was dark, polished parquet. At the far end there was a dais where a speaker's podium, a conference table for panelists, or a small band could be set up. At the other end were a movable bar and swinging doors into the kitchen.

It would all have been very bland, very chain-hotel-ish, were it not for the French doors lining one side of the hall. They opened onto a flagstone terrace and a green lawn that sloped down to a small harbor. The fine white sand of its beach had likely been imported from a sunnier clime and spread like a soft carpet over New England's own grainy dirt and pebbles.

Merritt took a look around. She seemed disappointed, which was how I felt. There wasn't a fascinating detail in sight, much less a fascinating question. "All right, Ms. Summersworth. That's all for now," she said.

But Haley wasn't ready to be dismissed. "You'll check in with me regularly, right? Let me know when you've uncovered a clue? I'm so curious about how you do things. More importantly, though, I desperately want the truth about my mother's death to be revealed. It's not fair that she should be called a suicide when I know she wasn't one. She would be here today if she could—to marry Monty, and be with her children, and watch her grandkids grow up. I know that in my very soul. Now you have to prove it. You'll do that for me, won't you, Ms. Merritt?"

"I'll do my best to discover what happened the night your mother died."

"And you'll call me every day, keep me apprised of your progress?"

Merritt stiffened. I could see she was irritated. "No, Ms. Summersworth. I won't do that. I don't give progress reports or daily updates to my clients. In fact, you'll likely hear very little from me until my investigation is complete. When it is, I'll present my conclusion at a time and place of my choosing, to a group of my choosing, either with or without a police presence, as I so choose. In the meantime, it's you who must answer my questions, not the other way around."

Haley's face reddened at this sharp rebuff. So did her eyes. For a moment I feared she might burst into tears, but she got ahold of herself. This was the second time Merritt had shot her down. Maybe she was finally getting the picture that although she had hired the famous detective, she hadn't bought her—that this process she'd initiated could spin wildly out of her control.

CHAPTER 11

Questions

Merritt and I parted in the lobby. She hadn't asked me to dine with her, for which I was glad, as I didn't want to sprain my brain trying to make conversation with a dinner companion who seemed utterly determined to give nothing of herself away.

Of course, her personal life wasn't a complete mystery to me. I'd done my research and had managed to uncover some of her story, though not as much as I would have liked. She'd married at twenty-two, just one month after graduating from Sarah Lawrence—a fact that had intrigued me right away. It spoke of either unbridled passion or starry-eyed romance, both of which seemed at odds with a woman whose most prominent attribute was hard-nosed logic. The groom, Theodore (Ted) Ferro, graduated from Juilliard the same year. The marriage lasted six years, after which point Ted moved to Los Angeles. He dropped out of public sight about a decade later, after an undistinguished music career.

What had caused the divorce? Alcohol? Money troubles? Affairs? There was no use in speculating, given the limited information I had. It was more interesting to speculate about my boss's postdivorce romantic life, starting with the mysterious Harry, who had given her the strange memento of a coelacanth fossil and had professed his undying love on an accompanying note card. When did that happen? Was the love requited? Had there been other relationships? Love affairs long or short? The occasional romantic dalliance? If so, they'd magically stayed out of sight of the internet. In any case, Merritt seemed comfortably single now. Set in her ways, sufficient unto herself.

With Victoria Summersworth's laptop tucked under my arm, and with the help of Jason's resort map, I found my way from the Lodge to a snack bar down by the docks, where I had a cheeseburger and a Diet Coke. There was a long line to place my order and a long wait to get my food, but I didn't mind, as the wait gave me time to decompress and people-watch.

The place was crowded with parents and children, many under the age of six. It seemed to me that about a third of these children were crying and another third were screaming, while the last third were rubbing ketchup into their shirts. I tried to picture myself as a mother and Trevor as a father, but my mind refused to cooperate. I literally couldn't imagine it. Was this a sign that I wasn't cut out to be a parent? That I might never be?

I called Trevor. He didn't pick up. He was probably at a rehearsal, his phone turned off. I left a quick voice message saying that Merritt and I had arrived safely and had started investigating right away, and that we'd lucked into a pretty amazing clue right off the bat. If the clue panned out, I said, I could be back in New York in a matter of days. I didn't know why I said that. It was wildly optimistic, as Merritt had all but convinced me that the black sedan in the Summersworths' driveway could have belonged to virtually anyone, and even that it might not have existed at all.

I slipped my phone into my pocket and gazed across the lake to a breathtaking orange and rose sunset happening on the western horizon. In the city I was usually hemmed in by buildings and traffic. Everything moved; everyone was going somewhere. Even the ants on the sidewalk appeared to be on a mission. Here the world was big and empty. The lake stretched as far as your eye could see, inviting you to fill it with your own thoughts and feelings if you wanted, in whatever way you wanted, and in your own time.

I felt a little opening, a little breath of freedom. On its heels, a pinch of anxiety. What was I doing here, anyway? Lake Champlain seemed a random place to find myself. I was actually a homebody. I liked my tiny apartment and the bed I shared with Trevor. I liked laying my head on his chest and listening to his heart. I even liked cleaning out cabinets and vacuuming up dust bunnies and growing herbs in pots on the windowsill. I wasn't a stern, friendless loner like Aubrey Merritt. I didn't want her solitary life.

And yet . . . working with her on this case was the most exciting thing I'd ever done. It captured me like nothing ever had. Even as I sat here truly and painfully missing Trevor, I sensed that nothing, not even Merritt's prickly personality, could tear me from her side. I would stay on the trail with her even if I did miss Trevor's opening night, even if the investigation dragged on for months.

The staff dormitory was a three-story rectangular structure bereft of architectural interest. My room was on the lower level—the basement, actually—but the building was situated on a hill so that the back side had a surprise outdoor area, a little flagstone patio that was separated from my neighbor's patio by a decaying six-foot fence laden with scraggly vines. The room was nicer than I'd expected a dormitory room to be. It was clean and freshly painted, though the furniture was old and creaky and the bedspread was pilled polyester.

The minute I got there I opened my laptop and connected to Wi-Fi with the password I'd been given when I checked in. The photos on my phone immediately uploaded to my computer. To my surprise there were more than fifty. I organized them into albums— one labeled Police Evidence, one labeled Crime Scene. When I saw what I'd done, I changed the label to The Bungalow. At this point there was no proof that a murder had been committed, and I was determined to take Merritt's advice not to get ahead of the facts.

I closed the laptop feeling unsatisfied. I'd accomplished all that was required of me for the day, and I believed I'd done a competent job, but surely more was needed. Though the investigation had barely begun, tantalizing questions were piling up, just as Merritt had said they would. Eventually each one would have to be answered or accounted for in some way if the truth was going to emerge.

Maybe my brilliant boss could immediately home in on the most significant facts and keep them neatly filed in her mind in perpetuity, but I wasn't in her league. My brain collected details haphazardly, then jumbled them all together in a useless mental goo. If I wanted to be truly helpful in this investigation, I needed to focus my thinking. Bring discipline to bear.

I'd brought along a small suede-bound journal that I'd purchased in a bookstore shortly after college graduation, thinking that I might, someday, given just the right circumstances, become a writer. A mystery writer, naturally. Nothing had come from that ambition, which I'd allowed to remain soft and foggy and laden with obstacles, the biggest of which was this: writing fiction wouldn't pay for food, clothing, and shelter, not to mention my student loans. And then there was this: I'd never written anything remotely creative before, so I didn't know if I could.

The journal had sat untouched in my dresser's bottom drawer for several years. Then, this morning, out of the blue, as I was about to leave my apartment to pick up Merritt, I suddenly remembered it, and on an impulse I dug it out from under old T-shirts and tights and stuffed it into my duffel bag. I had no idea what I was going to do with it; I knew only that I wanted to bring it along.

Now I took it out and looked at it. The suede was very soft, sort of a creamy brown; it fit loosely, like a big cozy sweater, around the hard cover. On the front there was a cutout where I guessed I was supposed to put a picture or maybe a title.

Feeling a bit tentative, I opened the journal and wrote down a few questions pertaining to the case.

1. *Suicide note. Written by V?*
2. *Text message to children. Ruse or real? If real, what important news did V intend to reveal?*
3. *Car in driveway. Monty Draper's? Someone else's? Pat Tucci's diabolical attempt to frame MD? If so, why?*
4. *Light seen, 9:30 p.m. Flashlight? Whose? Going where?*
5. *Loose lightbulb on deck. Significant?*

That was it. Five questions I could not afford to forget, five threads that needed to be pulled and ultimately tied up. Finally satisfied with my day's work, I glanced at my phone. It was ten thirty. Time for bed. As I was brushing my teeth, another question popped into my head. I dashed out of the bathroom and wrote down the following:

6. *Was V being treated for depression secretly, without her children's (Haley's) knowledge?*

Yes, I thought proudly, staring down at my raggedy penmanship. *A lot of people who are depressed don't want it to be known, because of the stigma or because they think it would upset their kids. And if she was depressed, it's much more likely that she* . . . Before I could follow that thought to its obvious conclusion, more questions rained down on me, one after another. I scribbled as fast as I could.

7. Did V murder husband fourteen years ago by pushing him off boat? Did then-teenager Scott do it? (OMG: Did they <u>both</u> do it?!?!) Note possible motive for revenge killing.

8. What were money/management issues at resort, according to Neil?

9. Complicated relationship between V and Scott. Relevant?

10. Why did V have poor relationship with stepdaughter Lauren?

11. Brandy glasses, water glasses, indentation on pillow. All Monty Draper's?

12. Photo album. Why? Young man (soccer player). Who?

The flow of questions stopped abruptly, as if a spigot had been shut off. I held my pen motionless above the paper, just in case any stragglers decided to come out of hiding and be counted. When nothing stirred, I gently laid down the pen and read over my list. It was longer than I'd expected; even so, I had an uneasy feeling that I'd missed some things. Possibly a lot of things.

Out of some nascent investigatory instinct, or maybe just morbid curiosity, I returned to my laptop and clicked on Clemmons's crime-scene photos, then held my breath as a picture of Victoria Summersworth's corpse appeared on my screen.

There she was, splayed out on the rock, arm and leg akimbo. Her body must have rolled during the fall, because her flimsy nightgown was screwed around her waist in a way that left her lower half naked. I couldn't help being unnerved by the sight of an older woman so exposed. Given the public-facing person she had been—always well-dressed and aware of appearances—she would probably be horrified that this undignified image existed, and that it was the last photo that would ever be taken of her.

But what most riveted me was her face, bleached to stark whiteness by the photographer's bulb, framed against the dark gray surface of famously hard New England granite. Her open eyes were clear glass marbles. Her lips were bloodless alabaster, no different in color than the surrounding skin. She couldn't have looked less like the vibrant individual she'd allegedly been.

Like most people, I'd heard plenty of stories about spiritually advanced folks wearing beatific smiles as they passed away peacefully in their beds, and I had no reason to doubt those accounts of end-of-life serenity, but I was far from spiritually advanced. I couldn't picture death as anything but terrifying—cold as a robot, venomous as a rattlesnake, predatory as a wild beast. It was the ultimate serial killer, an entitled bastard who cackled in your face because he knew he would always prevail in the end. In fact, he *was* the end.

As I gazed unblinkingly at Victoria Summersworth's ugly—yes, *ugly*—remains, I felt the brutal tragedy of her death clamping my gut. This image wasn't just a piece of evidence. It was a photo of a real dead woman, and it was awful to see. I cried quietly, glad to be alone and unseen. After a few minutes I dried my eyes and wondered if I'd made a terrible mistake. I just might be too softhearted to be a PI. Had the young Aubrey Merritt ever cried over a photo of a corpse? Somehow I doubted it.

The day had been long. My eyelids felt heavy. I started yawning like a sea lion does, loudly and with a wide-open mouth. I was just about to flop into bed when the opening drumbeat of Billie Eilish's "Therefore I Am" reverberated through the room. I picked up my phone.

"I need you here right away," Merritt said. "Robin Tucci just showed up."

CHAPTER 12

Chronic Unhappiness

The night was very dark. A sliver of crescent moon illuminated a corner of the sky without doing much for the earth. I was used to streetlights and neon signs making the night as accessible as the day. Here there was nothing to guide me but the flashlight beams of other guests, the bright floodlights of Big Red's Big Red Game Barn, and the porch lights of the cabins I passed on my way. Small groups of revelers shouldered past me on the gravel path, punctuating the air with peals of laughter that quickly faded.

It was almost eleven thirty when I arrived at the Lodge. The lobby was empty except for a knot of middle-aged partyers in front of the Fainting Goat Lounge, their voices loud and their eyes bright with alcohol. A syrupy piano-bar rendition of Elton John's "Your Song" floated through its open doors.

I rode the elevator to the third floor and padded down a quiet, shadowy corridor until I reached the heavy oak door of the Blue Heron Suite. I knocked and heard Merritt's voice telling me to come in.

Robin Tucci was perched on a long couch in the middle of the

THE WORLD'S GREATEST DETECTIVE AND HER JUST OKAY ASSISTANT

room. I recognized her from the decades-old photo of her and Victoria I'd seen earlier that day. Her eyes were the same—dark and feral—but she'd put on weight, and her formerly long, raven black hair was now short and streaked with gray. She was dressed in a shapeless, sleeveless tunic of swirling earth tones, her legs bare, her feet encased in flat brown leather sandals with complicated crisscrossing laces. They looked like the Roman gladiator shoes I'd seen in *Ben-Hur*, an old movie about ancient Rome I'd been forced to watch in high school in what passed for a history lesson. Robin came across as restless and wary. I got the feeling that she startled easily, that at any moment she might jump up and dart away.

Merritt introduced me, and I took the chair next to hers while Robin swigged from a plastic bottle of spring water that Merritt must have given her.

"If you don't mind, Ms. Blunt will record our talk," Merritt said to our guest.

"Wait. Really? I thought this was supposed to be a conversation," Robin said, shooting a hostile glance in my direction.

"The recording is solely for my personal use. I like to keep track of what people tell me so I don't have to call them back in because I've forgotten a detail."

As if forgetting a detail is even a possibility for Merritt, I thought.

Robin shrugged a grudging acquiescence, unable on short notice to marshal the gumption needed to object to the visiting investigator's professional methods, especially when that person was employed by the family that signed her own paycheck.

I placed my phone on the coffee table in a careful, obvious way, as if to prove our transparency, and pressed the record button. Robin glanced at it with distaste and turned back toward the detective.

"I suppose Haley hired you," she said sourly.

"Yes, that's right. How did you know?"

"She's the only one who would. What did she tell you? How did she phrase it? Did she say, *Please prove that my mother was murdered so I won't have to deal with her suicide?*"

"Not at all. She simply wants to rule out foul play."

"Right," Robin scoffed. "She might have said she wants to rule it *out*, but what she really wants is to rule it *in*."

"How so?"

"Obviously, this death isn't easy on any of the children, but it's especially hard on Haley. She adored her mother. Imagine having to cope with the fact that someone you loved so much, someone you really looked up to and depended on, didn't care enough about you to stick around. It's devastating. Haley's got a big heart that bruises easily, just like her mother, and she's very stubborn and determined when she wants to be—that's just like her mother too. She's not going to let Vicki disappoint her. She's going to put up a fight. And you're her weapon, Mrs. Merritt. You're going to prove it was murder so her illusions about her mother's love for her won't be crushed."

"You think Mrs. Summersworth didn't care about her family?"

"Oh, Vicki cared all right. I'm not saying she didn't care, only that Haley sees her mother's suicide that way—as a cruel abandonment. She would want it to be anything else, even murder, because murder wouldn't have been her mother's choice."

"So you believe that Mrs. Summersworth did kill herself. What makes you so sure?"

"Vicki was unhappy, and she'd been unhappy for a long time. You can call it depression if you want. Others didn't see it. They fell for the sparkly facade, which was what she wanted them to do. But there was a lot of sadness under that party-girl exterior."

Merritt leaned back, eyes narrowed, fingers tented before her mouth. Something was bugging her, but I didn't know what. As far as I could see, Robin was turning out to be every bit as useful as one would hope such a close and constant observer of the family would be. She'd offered a reasonable (and rather poignant) insight into Haley's behavior, as well as a valuable assessment of Victoria's state of mind. I was delighted by how much Robin had given us in so short a time, and I would have followed up immediately with questions about the dead woman's alleged chronic sadness.

But Merritt went a different way. "How did you two meet?"

Robin emitted an annoyed huff, as if she'd been dumped at the start of a long, tedious path that she was now pointlessly required to traverse. "A long time ago, when Vicki was communications director at Kingfisher, she hired me as her assistant. We worked together very successfully for a couple of years. You could say we made a good team. Warren Summersworth was the boss, obviously. His wife, the first Mrs. Summersworth, died shortly after I was hired—some form of cancer—leaving Warren with their two kids, Neil and Lauren. They were only eight and six when their mother died, and Warren worked all the time. He was never home. You could see that the kids were suffering. Six months or so after his first wife died, Warren started courting Vicki. I couldn't tell whether he actually cared for her—they were such different people—or he just needed another wife to create a reasonably normal home for him and his kids. Anyway, they dated, got engaged, and married. All done fairly quickly but perfectly correctly, with thoughtful gifts and surprise roses and weekends away. Vicki was thrilled. Warren was twenty years older than her, but he was fit and very good-looking. Even when he died, at seventy-one, he was still a handsome man. She was just a middle-class girl from Vergennes who'd never expected much, and everything about him dazzled her, not least his money. I wouldn't call her materialistic or greedy—she was too kind and humble for that—but she knew she'd lucked into something good. She told me once, in all seriousness, that she felt like she was living in a fairy tale."

"How lovely," Merritt said, with zero conviction.

"Not really," Robin replied. "After they married she quit her job to be a full-time wife and mother. It wasn't long before she realized that was a harder job than writing press releases at Kingfisher. At first I just went over on weekend nights, to babysit. Then I started doing errands and some grocery shopping. Then I was there all day Saturday, ferrying Neil and Lauren to their practices and other activities. It was all working out well. I enjoyed the kids and the various domestic tasks, and Vicki and I were still a good team. Eventually she and Warren offered me a full-time job with a generous salary, paid vacation days—the whole thing. They even paid for my health insurance. I became nanny, housekeeper, cook, and personal assistant. Basically, I did whatever I was asked."

"You must have liked the job, given how long you stayed."

"Honestly, I did. It was better than shuffling papers in an office. I like managing projects. That's how I saw it, as a kind of project-management job, the project being the household. Their home in Burlington is beautiful, by the way; I didn't mind being there at all. And we were here, at the resort, every summer. I had my own little cottage next to the Bungalow, and Vicki let me bring my mother so she wouldn't have to be alone. I never would've predicted I'd be with the family this long, but I never had a reason to leave."

"You said Mrs. Summersworth was unhappy. Why was that?"

"Once Scott came along the marriage went downhill. Warren lost interest in her. At some point he started an affair with a woman in Burlington, one of those new age types, who sold aromatherapy candles and homeopathic remedies in a shop with a beaded entranceway; you probably know the type. Vicki didn't know what to do. She was devoted to the marriage and the family. Haley came along a year after Scott, and Vicki just couldn't see a life for herself as a divorced mom. I think if it had been a matter of just her own children, she might have left Warren. But she felt responsible for

Neil and Lauren too. She worried about what would happen to them if they lost another mother, this one through divorce. Those two kids were not easy on her. Typical stepchildren, they never forgave her for not being their real mother. But she was there for them anyway, no matter how badly they treated her. I honestly think it was mostly for their sakes that she stayed, though of course she never got credit for that."

"So she ignored the affair?"

"That's right. She just looked the other way for years, and eventually it ended. But the damage was done. She and Warren were living separate lives. They were together when they had to be, at business functions or the children's events, but the only time you'd see them touching was in photographs."

"You think that was the source of her unhappiness?"

"Absolutely. It hurt her terribly. The light went out of her eyes, but instead of crumbling or starting to drink, she got this larger-than-life personality. Always positive, always caring, always doing something fun for the children or throwing a party for one of her friends. And all the charities and benefits—I lost count after a while. Women's shelters, halfway houses, food banks, hospital fund drives . . . you name it. Vicki was busy making the world a better place. It was all just a facade—a good one, a worthy one—that covered up a broken heart."

"So you weren't surprised when you learned that she'd taken her own life."

"Surprised? No, not really. Shocked, yes—the way you are when your worst secret fear suddenly comes true."

"Why now, do you think? Did anything happen recently that would have destabilized her, triggered her choice?"

"No, I don't think so. Nothing in particular. She had a lot going on as always—the resort, the family, various commitments—but no more than usual." Robin's gaze drifted toward the night-blackened window. "But I did sense . . . I don't know . . . a shift in her."

Merritt waited through a few silent moments before prodding her. "A *shift*. What kind of shift?"

With a barely visible shiver, Robin returned her attention to Merritt. "I can't describe it. It was just a feeling I had. Honestly, it might just be something I'm feeling now, looking back on what happened. But I don't think so. There were signs. . . ."

"What signs?" Merritt was quicker with this question, hoping to pin her down.

Robin shrugged off the question. Again she looked toward the window, as if the truth lay out there, in the dark. "Oh, I don't know. Feelings, signs. How stupid of me. I can't be sure what I'm talking about. It's just that . . . somehow . . . I think I actually knew." She glanced back at us with a startled expression on her face. "Does that make me a bad person, that I actually knew and did nothing to stop it?"

"Did you really know, Ms. Tucci? Even now you're not sure of it."

"I guess not. It's only hindsight, I suppose. I *should* have known, though. I was closer to her than anyone else. I was the one who could have stopped it. If I *did* have suspicions, if I saw signs—and now I'm not sure I did—I obviously didn't pay them enough attention."

"It's natural to feel confused, to feel guilty even. But you must know that if it was suicide, there was nothing you could have done."

"You're right, of course. Vicki had a strong will. If she'd decided—really and truly decided—then no one could have stopped her."

Merritt pursed her lips. "I need to ask. . . . Did Mrs. Summersworth have any enemies that you know of? Anyone who might have wished to harm her?"

"Not a soul wished Vicki harm. Honestly, no one."

"You seem quite sure of that."

"I am." Robin stared coldly at her questioner, as if the mere suggestion of someone wanting to harm her boss was offensive to her. Then she shifted her position on the couch, yanking the hem of her tunic dress and tucking it under her thighs. "Look, Mrs. Merritt. I obviously don't know exactly what happened the night Vicki died, but the police investigated, and as far as they could tell, the answer is obvious. I don't see what's to be gained by raking over dead coals. This family has been through enough. As far as I'm concerned, your investigation is just protracting the agony for everyone. But more than that, I'm worried you're going to do something terrible, like unfairly cast suspicion on one of the children. That would be a truly horrible thing to do. It would rip the family even further apart, not to mention ruining one of their lives. I care about those kids. I know they're adults now, but I remember them as children and I still feel very protective of them. If you're going to accuse one of them, I'm telling you right now that you'd better be very sure you're right, and you'd better be able to prove it."

Merritt nodded. "I hear you loud and clear, Ms. Tucci, and I respect your concern. This is obviously a difficult time for the family, and the last thing I want is to make unnecessary trouble for them or you, but a murder, if one occurred, needs to be exposed and punished. Don't you agree? We owe that much to Mrs. Summersworth and her family. We owe it to society too, to get a killer off the streets, assuming one exists here. There's no proof at this point that foul play was involved, but I need to do my job. If you want this investigation to conclude quickly, the best thing you can do is cooperate. Now, if you don't mind, I'd like you to walk me through that evening, as clearly as you remember it."

"All right, if you insist." Robin's eyes darted a bit as she shepherded her memories. "I got to the Lodge early, at about four thirty, to make sure everything was in order. The kitchen gets very busy when we're hosting a private event in the function hall, especially on a Saturday night, when the restaurant is busy. There's a lot of energy and anxiety flying around. I talked to the chef to make sure he had everything he needed. Then I saw that the bar was properly stocked and the hall was set up correctly—table settings, floral centerpieces, and so on. I also called the band to make sure they were coming; I've had some close calls on that front before. The worst thing was, the cake I'd ordered from a specialty baker in Burlington was delivered very late, and when it finally arrived it was absolutely not what I'd ordered. It looked like a wedding cake and was twice the price we'd agreed on. But at that point, what could I do?"

"And did the evening go as planned?"

"Other than the cake, everything went off without a hitch. The party was a big success." She smiled briefly, a shred of pride poking through.

"Did you notice anything unusual? Out of the ordinary? Surprising? Even something small could be important."

Robin's brow furrowed as she considered the question; then she slowly wagged her head. "I can't think of anything, but I was busy. I didn't sit down all night. Even when things are going well there are always little fires to put out."

"What time did you leave the Lodge?"

"Midnight, I'd say."

"Did anyone see you leave?"

Robin frowned. "Does it matter?"

"If you'd just answer the question . . ."

"I have no idea if anyone saw me walk out the door. What I can tell you is that I talked to Scott shortly before I left, that I walked home alone, that my mother was asleep in front of the TV when I arrived, and that I didn't wake her up. I went into my room and went to bed. I was exhausted. You get tired when you put on an event for seventy people and everything has to go perfectly. When I woke up the next morning, I found out Vicki was dead."

"How did you find out?"

"I saw the police lights and the ambulance in the driveway."

"What time was that?"

"Must have been about nine thirty, ten a.m."

"What will you do now that Mrs. Summersworth has passed?"

Robin leaned back against the couch cushion, letting a little of the fight ease out of her. "I don't know. I'm not sure how much longer my mother and I can, or ought to, stay here at the resort. I really don't belong here anymore. I'm not part of the family, I'm not a paying guest, and I'm not staff either, at least not resort staff. When Vicki was alive, I was mostly invisible, and I was okay with that. Now that she's gone, I feel like I don't exist."

I feel like I don't exist. I glanced at Robin sharply, but she seemed unaware of just how brutal that statement was. I wondered if it wasn't *she* who was depressed. Or maybe I just didn't appreciate the toll that being a longtime servant—a mostly invisible being, in Robin's own words—took on a person's self-esteem. I recalled that Pat had intimated that Robin's life was a failure. It couldn't be easy when your own mother blithely circulated such a devastating opinion. Maybe the mother's attitude had seeped into the daughter's soul.

Robin sniffled and wiped under her eyes with a curled index finger, smearing the mascara she was trying to keep intact. Her grief was now tinged with self-pity. I didn't blame her. She was in a tough spot. Finally she looked up at us.

"Is that all? Am I done here?" she demanded, but her voice was weaker than it had been.

"That's all for now, Ms. Tucci. Thank you for coming. I appreciate your help."

Robin stood up and smoothed the wrinkles in her tunic with stiff palms. She gave Merritt a proud but brittle glare. "I knew she would do it. There was a shift, like I said. I sensed it. I'm sure of that now. I'm afraid you're wasting your time, Mrs. Merritt."

———

"A *shift?*" I said when Robin was gone. "Do you believe that?"

"It's possible. She was close enough to Mrs. Summersworth that she could have felt a subtle change. Then she doubted herself and ignored it, like most people do when they have a premonition."

"Or she was putting it out there to give credence to the suicide theory, knowing it can't be proved."

"Correct. Which is why it's not useful information. On the other hand, if she's right that Mrs. Summersworth was chronically unhappy, it's important. We didn't find antidepressants in her medicine cabinet, but that doesn't mean she wasn't being treated. I know Haley thinks her mother was just fine, but that doesn't mean she was. We need to check Victoria's medical records for mood disorders."

I nodded, pleased that I'd identified this issue myself in my journal earlier this evening. "If she had an online health account and kept her passwords on her laptop, I can probably view her file."

"Do that. And while you're at it, see if she'd recently been diagnosed with the kind of incurable illness that makes suicide an attractive option." She raked stiff fingers through her limp hair and briefly closed her eyes. She looked quite ragged after our long day. "I'd give anything for a cup of tea," she said.

I took the hint. Coffee, tea, and other things were arranged on a table in a corner of the suite. I cracked open a sealed bottle of local spring water, filled a mug, dropped in a bag of chamomile tea (figuring it was better to avoid caffeine this late at night), and set the mug in the microwave. When the tea was ready, I served it and sat across from her.

She sipped and immediately grimaced. "What on earth is this?"

"Chamomile."

"Chamomile?" She squinted at the tag on the tea bag to double-check. "It tastes like . . . nothing. Like colored water."

"It might need to steep a little longer."

She sighed with annoyance. "For the future, Blunt: when I say *tea*, I am referring to a drink made with tea leaves, not flowers."

"I'm sorry. I thought . . . since it's so late . . ."

She stared at me baldly, daring me to continue my unwanted caretaking behavior.

"I can make another cup," I said quickly.

"Never mind. I just wanted something hot." She wrapped her fingers around the mug. "By the way, what did you think of Robin Tucci?"

"She seemed a little . . . I don't know . . . weird."

"She's a very unhappy woman," Merritt said wearily. "And there's a lot she's not telling us."

CHAPTER 13

Dirty Shoes

The dew was still sparkling on the grass as I hurried over to the Lodge the next morning. Several meetings had been scheduled for the day. The first was at eight a.m. with Pia Valente, the housekeeper who'd discovered the body.

I arrived three minutes early, feeling inordinately proud of my punctuality, especially since last night's meeting with Robin Tucci had gone past midnight, and afterward my mind had been so full of thoughts that I'd had a hard time getting to sleep. I'd set my alarm at the loudest volume possible, worried that after I finally did nod off I'd power sleep right through the morning hours. I'd done that a few times in my previous job. My old boss had merely scolded. Aubrey Merritt would probably fire me on the spot.

I shouldn't have been surprised to discover that she'd beaten me to Scott Summersworth's office. So had he. He was leaning against his large mahogany desk, his arms folded across his chest—not in a defensive way, more as if he just needed a place to put them. Merritt, seated comfortably in one of two club chairs, was drinking coffee out of a paper cup. They were chatting together amiably.

The office was determinedly Vermont-ish. Thickly carpeted in forest green, it was home to several carved wooden ducks and a large framed map of the state. A hunting rifle was mounted on the wall behind the desk, which was covered with messy stacks of paperwork and a brass nameplate: SCOTT SUMMERSWORTH, GENERAL MANAGER. THE BUCK STOPS HERE. Under this tired saying was a machine-tooled image of an antlered deer. (So stupid.)

Merritt introduced me. Scott smiled a bit absently as we shook hands. His grip was warm, bordering on hot, and a bit sweaty. He had a ruddy complexion and watery blue eyes. Greasy blond hair fell rakishly over his forehead, setting him apart from the clean-cut members of his staff, as did his clothing, which teetered on the edge of unkempt. The crisp navy blazer (I imagined it kept on a hanger on the back of his door for special meetings) couldn't offset the combined effect of wrinkled khakis, worn-out Sperry boat shoes, and the food stain—or was it a wine dribble?—on the front of the light blue open-necked polo shirt that complemented his eyes.

"Happy to meet you, Ms. Blunt." His smile fell short of believable, but I gave him credit for the attempt. "My sister instructed me to make your stay as comfortable as possible. I hope everything is okay so far?"

"It's very nice," I said, taking the chair next to Merritt. This seemed like the wrong time to complain about my room in the distant, drab staff dormitory. In fact, it seemed like the wrong time to discuss lodging at all.

"My condolences for the death of your mother," I said.

"Thank you. It was a terrible blow to all of us. Frankly, it still feels unreal." Honest emotion trembled in his voice.

He looked toward the door and a smile broke out on his face. This one seemed genuine, if sad. "Oh, here she is. Come in, Pia. Have a seat. Don't worry. This is just a formality."

A woman about my age entered the room nervously, no doubt

feeling the eyes of three people on her, and perched on a love seat under the room's only window. She was wearing crisp blue Bermuda shorts, clean white trainers, and a light gray sweatshirt with the words HELPING HANDS printed in big blue letters across the front. Her dark hair was brushed back smoothly into a low ponytail, and her makeup consisted of nothing more than a brushing of mascara and a sheen of coral lip gloss. Her brown eyes darted apprehensively around the room—from Scott to Merritt, to me, and back to Scott, where her gaze lingered for several seconds.

"Thank you for coming, Ms. Valente," Merritt said. "My name is Aubrey Merritt. I'm a private investigator, and this is my assistant, Olivia Blunt. We're looking into the death of Victoria Summersworth. I have a few questions for you about the morning you found her body."

Pia nodded, tight-lipped.

"I'd be grateful if you'd describe exactly what happened that morning."

Pia looked to Scott again, as if asking for his permission to proceed.

"You may leave the room now, Mr. Summersworth," Merritt said firmly. There was no way she was going to tolerate having one witness coach another surreptitiously.

A sour expression indicated that he didn't like being dismissed. But he gave a slow, unwilling nod and shuffled out of the room, casting a single backward glance at the housekeeper.

"Proceed, Ms. Valente. That morning. What time did you arrive at the house?"

"About eight o'clock. That's when Mrs. Summersworth told me to come. She wanted me there early so I would be done with the cleaning at ten or ten thirty and she would have time to get things ready for lunch."

"You'd worked for Mrs. Summersworth before—is that correct?"

"Yes, many times. But not for her directly. See, the company I work for, Helping Hands, has a contract with the resort. We do all the hotel rooms, cottages—all the guest areas. Mrs. Summersworth called us whenever she needed cleaning services. She always asked for me, because I'd been to her house so many times, I knew how she liked things. Like, she really wanted the lampshades dusted every week. And she could tell the difference too. I don't know how she did it, but she did."

"How did you enter the house?"

Pia looked confused. "With a key . . . ?"

"You had a key in your possession?"

"No. There's a hidden key. That's what I used if Mrs. Summersworth wasn't home, but sometimes she just left the door open for me."

"I see. And on that particular morning, the morning of your employer's demise, the front door was locked, so you used the hidden key to gain entrance to the house. Have I got that right?"

"Yes," Pia said, but she looked a bit doubtful.

"Are you sure, Ms. Valente? Or are you having second thoughts?"

Pia's brow creased. "I mean, I *think* the door was locked. I do remember getting the key out from under the pot, so it must have been locked. But I wasn't really paying attention, so I could be wrong, I guess, about the door. But I'm pretty sure."

Pia's hands were twisting in her lap, and her posture was stiffly erect. She was trying to hold up under the detective's rapid-fire questioning, but anxiety was getting the better of her.

My heart went out to her. I knew just how she felt. I too had squirmed under Merritt's pitiless gaze, at times becoming so flustered that I feared I might forget my own name. I had no idea what Merritt was trying to accomplish by interrogating the housekeeper so sternly. Did she *want* to make Pia Valente feel like a murder suspect? What would be the benefit in that?

"Where exactly was the key hidden?" Merritt continued in a

tone that implied that she already doubted the veracity of whatever answer Pia might give.

"Under the geranium pot."

"There are several on the porch. Which one are you referring to?"

Oh my god, I thought. *Leave the poor woman alone.*

"The one closest to the door." Pia seemed sure of this.

"So, you unlocked the front door and went inside. What happened next?"

"The house was quiet," Pia said. "It was the morning after her big party, so I figured Mrs. Summersworth was still asleep. I went into the living room and started picking things up. Quietly. I didn't want to wake her."

"What things?"

"Two glasses and a brandy bottle."

"Where exactly were they?"

"One glass was on the coffee table; the other was on the table next to the big chair. The bottle was on the coffee table too. I brought them into the kitchen and washed the glasses by hand."

"What then?" Merritt asked.

"I washed the counters with marble cleaner and a soft rag, the sink with Bar Keepers Friend and a scouring pad, the floors with a Swiffer, then a thin coat of floor wax . . ."

I waited for Merritt to stop her, as we certainly didn't need an entire litany of cleaning products. But Merritt let her go on and on, detailing her methods precisely, as if she were testifying at a housekeeping tribunal.

"When I was done with the downstairs bathroom, I knew I couldn't hold off on the vacuuming any longer or I wouldn't finish in time. There hadn't been any noise from upstairs for almost an hour, and I thought maybe Mrs. Summersworth wasn't asleep after all. She might have gone out to meet her friends for an early breakfast—she did that a lot with her 'hat ladies'; that's what she called them—so

I went upstairs and peeked into her room. The bed was empty, so I went back downstairs and turned on the vacuum. The living room rug was very bad. Someone had not taken off their dirty shoes when they came in." Pia sat up primly, looking as critical of this miscreant as Mrs. Summersworth (or Merritt, for that matter) might have been.

"You vacuumed up the dirt, I presume," Merritt said.

"Of course," Pia said stoutly.

"Did you notice anything about it?"

"Excuse me?" She faltered a bit, obviously finding the question odd, as I did.

"Was it mud, mulch, gravel, grass . . . ?"

Pia pressed her lips together as she tried to picture the exact nature of the offending particles. "Umm . . . just dirt, I think. Brown dirt. Clumps of it. I'm sorry, but that's all I can remember. There was a trail across the whole room, all the way from the front to the back."

"Thank you. When exactly did you discover your employer's body?"

"When I noticed that the door to the deck was open a crack. I went to close it. That's when I saw the chair." She paused, seemed to lose her train of thought.

"The chair," Merritt prompted.

"The chair, yes. Lying on its side by the railing. It wasn't supposed to be there, and it definitely wasn't supposed to be lying on its side. I got a little annoyed, actually. I figured whoever knocked it over had been too lazy to pick it up. When I went out on the deck to put it back where it belonged, a bad feeling came over me. Why was the chair where it didn't belong? Who'd knocked it over? I knew then—I felt it in my bones—that something bad had happened."

"So you looked over the railing."

"Yes." Sitting very still and upright, Pia stared into the middle distance without blinking.

Merritt didn't ask Pia what she saw, and the room was quiet for a few seconds.

"You called nine-one-one, I assume," Merritt said, offering no acknowledgment of the trauma the housekeeper must have experienced in that moment.

"Um, no."

"You called your employer, Helping Hands, to ask for help," Merritt suggested.

"Not exactly. I called Scott . . . I mean, Mr. Summersworth."

"Hmm. Interesting choice. May I ask why?"

"Mr. Summersworth is in charge of everything around here. Plus, it was his mother. I figured he'd want to be told first, and then he could come over and take care of things the way he wanted to."

"I see. Have you ever met Monty Draper?" Merritt said, switching tracks abruptly.

"You mean Mrs. Summersworth's boyfriend?"

"That's the one."

"I did meet him a few times when I was at the house." Her upper lip curled slightly at the edge. It was a snarl—a very small one, but there was no mistaking it.

"Do you like him?"

She shrugged. "He's all right."

"You can be truthful with me, Ms. Valente."

Her eyes flashed. "If you really want to know, I don't like him at all."

"Why not?"

"He always acted super sweet to Mrs. Summersworth—kissing and hugging her all the time. Then, the minute her back was turned, he'd be cold and mean. To me, anyway, because I'm just staff and don't count for anything. A lot of people around here are like that. They act all nice to their friends and the opposite way to us." She paused to tuck a loose strand of hair behind her ear. "Another reason

I don't like him is that he drinks a lot. I could always tell when he'd been at the house, because there'd be empty bottles in the trash. Mrs. Summersworth didn't drink at all when she was alone."

"Thank you, Ms. Valente. That's all for now."

"I can go?"

"Yes. If I need anything more from you, Ms. Blunt will be in touch."

"Wait. I have a question," I said. My voice sounded overly loud in the room.

Both Merritt and Pia turned to me with surprise. I didn't blame them, as I hadn't said anything but *hello* to Pia before then.

"Pia," I said, "do you remember a big photo album being open on the coffee table?"

"Yes, I remember it."

"Was it always there, in that specific place?"

"I'd never seen it there before. There are a lot of old photo albums just like it on the bookshelf in the den, and I assumed it was one of those. I thought about putting it back but I figured Mrs. Summersworth left it out for a reason, so I didn't put it away."

"Do you remember the page it was open to?"

"I didn't look."

"Here—let me show you." I pulled up one of the pictures I'd taken—the one of the young man in his black graduation gown—and passed my phone to the housekeeper. "Do you recognize him?"

She glanced at the screen. "Never saw him before."

"Thank you, Pia. I know it isn't easy to have so many questions thrown at you about such a difficult subject. Ms. Merritt and I really appreciate your help."

There was a shade of gratitude in Pia's eyes when they met mine. Wordlessly, we acknowledged to each other that the famous investigator had treated her badly, just as many other people at the resort apparently had.

Pia stood, smoothed her sweatshirt, and swung her straw bag over her shoulder.

Her hand was reaching for the doorknob when Merritt called after her, "One more thing, Ms. Valente, before you go. When you contacted Mr. Summersworth to tell him that his mother's body was lying at the bottom of the cliff, did you call the main office here at the Lodge and ask to speak to him?"

The question seemed to cause the housekeeper some difficulty. She shuffled clumsily, cast a sidelong glance at the door through which she'd almost escaped.

"Ms. Valente?" Merritt prodded.

Pia turned troubled eyes to her inquisitor. "I called his cell phone."

"You have Mr. Summersworth's personal cell phone number in your contacts?"

"Yes, I do." Her voice was stiff with something—pride, or rebellion, or both.

"I see. You and Mr. Summersworth are personal friends?"

"There's nothing wrong with that, is there?"

"Not at all. Are you more than friends?"

Pia took a step back, clearly affronted by the frankness of the question, and immediately denied that they were. Then she seemed to reconsider. Straightening her spine, she said, "Maybe. I don't know. Why don't you ask him?"

"Thank you, Ms. Valente. I will."

Pia left. A moment later Merritt and I heard her and Scott murmuring in the corridor outside the office, their tone intimate and urgent.

"What do you suppose they're whispering about?" Merritt asked me.

"No idea." I took a moment to marshal my courage. "Did you have to be so hard on her?"

"Was I hard on her?"

"You know you were."

Merritt sniffed. "The young woman made it clear through her body language and general demeanor when she entered the room that she was quite anxious. Overly so, in my opinion. We need to ask ourselves why that should be the case."

"Isn't it enough that she discovered the body?" I answered hotly. "Or that there's already been one investigation and now there's another, and she's being called in again to answer questions, only this time by an overly harsh interrogator? Added to the fact that people around here don't think much of her and they get away with treating her badly? Or are you seriously suggesting that Pia Valente could have murdered Victoria Summersworth?"

Merritt's lips came together in a thin line. She was clearly not impressed by my reasoning. "In this business, Blunt, a suspect is guilty until proved innocent. Every suspect. Even the ones you sympathize with and want to protect. We're detectives, not social workers. Please try to remember that. Now, tell me what in the way of facts and evidence you gleaned from this interview."

Another test. I took a deep breath, buying myself a few seconds to cool off and gather my thoughts. "Hmm, let's see. It's impossible to say whether the relationship between Scott and Pia has any relevance to Victoria's death. I'm inclined to think it doesn't. But at least the mystery of how Victoria got herself over the balcony railing is solved. By standing on the chair first, she could have stepped up onto it, and kicked the chair inadvertently as she launched herself into the air. Beyond those things, what did we learn that we didn't already know?" I considered the facts carefully. "Just that someone, at some point—which could have been anytime since the rug was last vacuumed—walked across the carpet in dirty shoes. It doesn't seem like much."

"Are you sure about that? How long do you think Victoria Summersworth would have tolerated a long trail of dirt across her beige Berber carpeting?"

I saw her point. "Probably not long."

"Precisely. I strongly suspect that the dirt was left there on the night of the victim's death. And not by her. That dirt is critically important, Blunt. It will need to be accounted for."

CHAPTER 14

The Second-Best Son

The office door opened and Scott came in. He looked distracted and worn-out. "I hope we can keep this meeting short," he said, lowering himself into the chair behind his desk. "There's a lot going on at the resort today. I'm sure you understand."

He seemed to be aiming for a tone of authority that he couldn't quite achieve. Instead, I got the sense that he was out of his depth, that his feet hadn't yet grown into the professional shoes he was wearing. I could easily commiserate. Impostor syndrome is a real thing. But shouldn't he have passed through that stage by now?

Merritt buttressed him. "I certainly do understand, Mr. Summersworth. The Wild Goose Resort is a very busy and, I might add, *very* impressive operation. I imagine there's a lot to keep track of. Hundreds of guests, a large seasonal staff, four restaurants . . ."

"Five," Scott said.

"Five restaurants," Merritt amended. "Not to mention the hotel and all those cabins. Also a greenhouse and vegetable farm, a day care and children's camp. The roads, the landscaping. And the harbor! How could I forget the harbor? Rental sailboats, waterskiing, sunset cruises, swimming lessons. You clearly have an enormous job, yet everything seems to run very smoothly. The online reviews are outstanding. How on earth do you do it?"

I glanced at my boss with a mix of horror and respect. She'd managed to switch roles from harsh inquisitor to sniveling syco-phant in the space of a few minutes, displaying a degree of thespian talent I hadn't known she possessed. Her goggle-eyed flattery seemed too obviously fake to me, but it was having the desired effect on the resort manager, who was apparently too needy to sniff out the in-sincerity. He relaxed, his face softened, and his chest puffed out.

"Love. That's how, Mrs. Merritt. I love this place, all seven hun-dred acres of it. I know it like the back of my hand, and I can do every job there is. Except maybe the chef's job—I can't cook for shit." He chuckled at himself. "You see, my dad insisted that we kids learn the business from the bottom up. He made us work in every area at one time or another. I scooped ice cream, waited tables, washed dishes, even made beds and cleaned bathrooms. I did a lot of the fun stuff too, like driving the waterskiing boat and leading nature hikes. When I was in college, I helped with marketing and publicity, scheduling, reservations, hiring, firing. I learned to source practically every item this club uses: food, alcohol, mattresses, beach chairs, tennis rackets, and god knows how many other things. You name it, I know where to get the best quality at the cheapest price. You're absolutely correct that running the day-to-day operations is a lot of work. My sisters and brother opted out of the general man-ager role early on. But I love it. It's all I ever wanted to do."

"Day-to-day operations—would those include financial aspects, like payroll, accounting, investing?"

"Payroll is handled by a firm in Burlington. Everything else happens at our parent company, Kingfisher Development. They take care of accounts receivable, accounts payable, and all sorts of other financial matters, including taxes. They do our marketing as well—with significant input from me, of course. And they make the big financial decisions, investing and the like."

"Your brother runs Kingfisher—isn't that right? I can only imagine what it must be like to work for a sibling. Is that a problem for you, your brother holding the reins?"

Scott shrank a bit, as if a puff of air had been squeezed out of him. "I wouldn't say Neil *holds the reins*, exactly. But . . . well . . . I guess he does to some extent. He was always going to run Kingfisher someday. He had the aptitude and the interest, and my father groomed him for it since he was in high school. I always wanted to work here, at Wild Goose. I guess you could say I'm more of a people person, less of a numbers guy, so things worked out the right way."

"Not a math whiz, huh? Me neither."

I nearly choked. *Merritt is pushing this suck-up act way too far*, I thought.

"How do you get along, you and Neil? Outside the office, I mean," she asked innocently.

Scott's face reddened. He tried to cover his discomfort with a stiff smile. "Uh, well . . . I guess I have to plead the Fifth on that one."

"Siblings can be tough," Merritt said, her voice dripping with sympathy. "How about your mom? Did you get along with her?"

A few beads of sweat popped out at his hairline. "My mother? Of course. I loved her. She was my mother."

"I'm sure you did." The word *saccharine* wasn't sweet enough to describe her tone. "We always love our mothers, don't we?"

Not Orestes, I thought.

Merritt went on. "Was there any trouble, any conflict, between you and her? Concerning the resort?"

As I was starting to learn, a good liar lies smoothly and fairly quickly—because the lie, long rehearsed, has been waiting on the tip of his tongue, and when its moment to shine finally arrives, it falls from his lips like a plump, perfect raindrop, by all appearances the purest, most natural thing in the world.

Scott Summersworth was a terrible liar—slow and clumsy. Even I, rookie that I was, could see him wrestling with himself, wanting to lie but not being able to. Finally his shoulders slumped as he surrendered his effort to be a worse person than he was.

"Well, there usually is, isn't there? Especially in a family business."

"Yes, that's very true. Family businesses can be the worst. Did you argue about money?" Merritt prompted ever so gently.

"Good guess, Mrs. Merritt," he said wryly. "My mother thought I was mismanaging the resort's finances. It wasn't true, but no matter what I said, I couldn't convince her. I felt like she was hounding me, badgering me, over a nonexistent problem. So yeah, we argued. It wasn't nice."

"How long had the conflict between you and your mother been going on?"

His eyes narrowed. "Why are you asking about this? I thought you were here to investigate my mother's death."

"I'm just looking for context," she said.

"I hope you're not suggesting that this conflict I had with my mother could be a motive for murder. Is that where you're going with this?"

"I'm just getting the lay of the land, Mr. Summersworth. I'm not going anywhere at the moment."

"Well, for your information, the real conflict wasn't between me and my mother at all. It was between me and my brother. Neil had been whispering things to Mom about me, accusing me of screwing up the resort financially. She finally confessed that. He should've talked to me directly if he had concerns about what I was doing—or what he thought I was doing—but I don't believe he actually wanted to know the truth. He just wanted to spread rumors. He has a low opinion of me, sorry to say. I used to feel hurt by that, used to try to change his mind, but I gave that up long ago."

"Was there a falling-out over something specific?"

His face grew rigid. "Nothing worth talking about." With a fresh glare in his eye, he said, "So, this is what you came here to talk about, is it? Family dynamics. Sibling rivalry. Money problems. You're investigating *us*, aren't you? Me and my siblings, as if one of us could possibly have killed our own mother. It's outrageous that you would even think such a thing."

"I'm just doing my job, Mr. Summersworth. Ticking all the boxes. With your cooperation, I'll be able to wrap up my inquiries quickly and get out of your hair. Now, if you don't mind, I need your timeline for that evening, and whatever you can tell me about your mother's movements, in as much detail as you can remember."

"I went through all this with Jim Clemmons. It must be written in a report somewhere."

"I'm sure it is, but I never rely on reports. I like to hear things with my own ears. Since you're such an old hand, I probably don't need to give you the usual caveats about details—you know, to be sure to mention anything unusual, even if it was small."

Scott drew in a ragged breath and sighed it out. "As far as my mother goes, I can't tell you where she was or what she was doing every minute, obviously. I do know that she arrived at the Lodge at around six forty-five. The party had started at six, so she was more than fashionably late. It pissed me off, if you want to know. I mean, I can understand someone being fifteen or twenty minutes late, but the guests were there to see her, specifically, and forty-five minutes was too much. People had started asking if she was going to show up."

"Did she usually arrive late to events?"

"Depended on what it was. No one wants to be the first to show up to a party, and that's fine. But there are events where it's important to be on time. My mother knew the difference. She was very good at timing her entrance. She could read a room, as they say."

"She came alone?"

"No, she was with Monty Draper, her boyfriend."

"Then what happened?"

"The usual: a lot of cheek kissing, hellos, *happy birthdays*, and hugging and gushing about how nice everyone looked. We had an open bar, and the guests had been hitting it hard. They usually do in the hour before dinner at a big function. They like to get their buzz on fast, because once they sit down and the wine is served it's déclassé to be seen drinking the hard stuff. The band was playing cocktail music, light jazz, just background stuff. Dinner was from seven to around eight thirty. Three courses: salad or appetizer, entrée—beef, chicken, or vegetarian—and dessert. There was a cake, of course, a big, elaborate thing. Mom blew out the candles and everyone cheered. Then the band came back on for real, started playing swing music. My mother loved swing. The whole 1920s vibe really turned her on. She would have made a great flapper."

He drifted a little, wearing a wistful expression. I supposed he was imagining his mother doing the Charleston in a headdress, a long beaded necklace, and a skinny sequined dress.

"After that?" Merritt prompted.

He shrugged. "It was a typical party. People danced, they sat in the lounge and talked to their friends, they played pool in the billiards room, visited the kids in the playroom, or they just planted themselves at the bar and pounded 'em down. Usually at this kind of function—weddings especially—someone ends up getting pushed into the swimming pool, and then there are always a few who jump in after them. As long as they keep at least some of their clothes on, we pretend not to notice. As far as I know, that didn't happen the night of my mother's party. It was an older crowd."

"Do you recall where your mother was during the dinner, the dancing, and so on?"

"Well, she had dinner at the head table, obviously, with Monty and me; Neil and his wife, Allison; my half sister, Lauren, and her husband, Eric; and my sister, Haley, and her wife, Sumiko. Neil and Lauren both have kids. They were in the Kids' Klub, on the lower level, along with eight or nine other kids. At some point during dinner the child minders—that's what we call them—took the kids outside. It was still light out, and you could see them playing croquet in their party clothes on the lawn. It was a pretty sight. Mom ran out and hit some balls with them. She loved her grandkids—she loved all kids. It disappointed her that Lauren didn't visit very often, so she didn't get a chance to develop good relationships with her three granddaughters."

"After that?"

"After dinner, Mom made a round of the tables, chatting with everyone. When the band started, she and Monty danced a bit. Then he went off to play billiards and she chatted some more, and then she left." He paused. "I guess that was one unusual thing. Yes, it was definitely unusual."

"How so?"

"She asked Monty to take her home early, about nine thirty. The party was still going strong. She loved parties, almost always stayed to the end. So that was unusual."

"Were you concerned?"

"A little. But I figured she was tired. She is . . . was . . . getting older, you know. Not that I'd ever really noticed it before. She was always so determined not to act old; you'd never hear her complaining about a stiff joint or a moment of forgetfulness. But it had been a big night, lots of people and commotion, and I figured maybe she'd just had enough. She'd done her bit: kissed cheeks, and oohed and aahed, and heard everyone's news, and danced to her favorite song, 'La Vie en rose,' and she was ready to call it a night."

"So, the last you saw of her and Monty Draper that evening was at about nine thirty."

"No, I saw Monty again later. Maybe an hour later. I caught up with him at the bar and we had a few drinks."

"How did he seem to you?"

"Perfectly fine."

"What did you talk about?"

He sighed loudly to let us know how irrelevant he thought the question was. "Well, let's see if I can remember. The PGA tour was on the TV. We record it and play it on a loop for the guests. So we talked about that. Monty follows sports like I do. Loves games of all kinds. He first came to the resort last summer, as a bridge coach—we have a lot of avid bridge players here—and he liked it so much, he never left."

"What time did he leave the Lodge that night?"

"About eleven thirty, I'd say. That's when the night manager comes on and the bar closes. We said good night, and that was that."

"Did he say where he was headed?"

"He didn't say anything about going back to my mother's, if that's what you're asking. I assumed he was going home."

"I want to ask you this one more time, Mr. Summersworth, if you don't mind; think about it hard, please. Did you notice anything else that was unusual that evening? Any interaction or behavior that might be worth mentioning?"

"I really don't remember anything else out of the ordinary. Except . . . well, I did see my mother go outside at one point. Must have been about nine o'clock. She was by herself. I thought that was a little strange, so when she returned I asked where she'd been."

"What did she say, exactly?"

"That she'd needed to get something out of Monty's car. I didn't think anything of it."

"She returned alone?"

"Yes."

"Was she carrying anything?"

"Um . . . let me think. No, not that I recall." A moment later he realized what he'd said, and he gave an awkward grimace. "So maybe she *didn't* get something out of the car?"

"Think back. Perhaps there was something in her hand, something small, or she was wearing an article of clothing—a shawl, for example—that she didn't have on when she went out."

Scott frowned. "No to both those things."

"Do you know how much time elapsed between her leaving the Lodge and returning?"

"Fifteen, twenty minutes? I was talking with some buddies of mine in the lobby, and as I was facing the main entrance, I could see who was coming in and going out, but I wasn't keeping track of the time."

As Merritt and I both knew, the parking lot was right across the street. It shouldn't have taken more than five minutes to retrieve an item from a car.

"Good. That's helpful. Now, where did *you* go, Mr. Summersworth, at the end of the night?"

"Me? I went to bed."

"You live nearby?"

"I live right here. I've got a nice suite all to myself on the other side of the Lodge. Bedroom, little living room, kitchenette. I take my meals right here at the resort. What more could a bachelor ask for?"

"Can anyone vouch for your whereabouts in the hours between two and four a.m.?"

"Oh, so now you want my alibi. Ticking the boxes—is that it? Okay, I'll give it to you, Mrs. Merritt. I was sleeping in my bed between two and four a.m. Alone."

"Uh-huh. And what kind of car do you drive?"

"A BMW 330e."

"Color?"

"Black."

"Very good. Thank you, Mr. Summersworth. You've been very helpful."

"That's it?"

She paused. "Well, no. I do have one more question. What's your opinion of Monty Draper? Do you like him?"

"I do, actually. Though I might be the only one."

"Really? How so?"

"My two half siblings, Neil and Lauren . . . they think he's kind of sleazy, that he was going after Mom for her money. Haley had her reservations too, at first. But I think she's come around some now. I've gotten to know him better than the others, and I think he's actually a very decent guy."

"Would you say you're close, you and Monty?"

"I suppose I would. We became friends, and I hope we'll continue being friends."

"Were you aware that he'd asked your mother to marry him?"

"Had he?" Scott let out a delighted chortle. "The old codger! Works fast, doesn't he? I'll have to give him a hard time for that!" Then his face fell, and he lowered his head. He seemed to have remembered that his mother was gone. There would be no happy wedding to usher in her sunset years.

"Have you spoken to Mr. Draper since your mother's death?"

He shrugged sadly. "A couple of times, right afterward. It's all a blur; I can't remember what was said. I suppose I ought to call him, see how he's doing. He probably thinks Mom's death was his fault, just like I think it was mine. But it was no one's fault. I know that rationally. And I'm trying like hell to convince my heart of that."

"You have my sympathy, Mr. Summersworth." Merritt smiled like an angel, then went in for the kill. "By the way, how long have you and Ms. Valente been lovers?"

He glanced up in sharp surprise. "What did you say?"

"I'm sorry. Was the question unclear?"

"No, no. I just . . . I didn't say anything about that. Did Pia tell you?"

"She didn't need to. It couldn't be more obvious. Are you trying to keep it secret?"

"No, not at all," he sputtered.

Merritt's eyebrows went up, and stayed aloft until the resort manager continued.

"Well, maybe a little. Pia's not a resort employee—just to get that straight. She works for an outside agency. So there's no sexual misconduct going on."

"Good to know," Merritt said mildly.

"But . . ." He looked at the floor, kneaded his brow with stiff fingers. "As I said, my mother thought I was screwing up the resort, and my brother is convinced of it. If they ever found out I was dating a housekeeper, especially the one who cleaned Mom's house . . . well, that would just give them more ammunition to use against me, so we were keeping it on the Q.T., at least for now. There are other reasons too. Pia's unsuitable, if you know what I mean, in their book. She's . . ." Scott stumbled, unable to find the right word.

"Hispanic?" Merritt supplied.

"Yeah. She's Hispanic. From an immigrant family. And she doesn't have a college degree. Not yet, anyway. But she's planning on getting one very soon. She just needs a little help." He sighed. "Pia understands all this—my job, my family, everything. That's why she refused to come to Mom's party with me even though I invited her. She said she'd rather go out with her friends. I tried to convince her to come with me, said I was ready to face the wolves, so to speak. But she insisted Mom's party wasn't the right time for that. She wants me, and us, to be in a better place before we go fully public, because she knows that as soon as we do, people will talk." He raised his head, looked Merritt in the eye, and said with unexpected force, "What Pia and I have together is very real, very special. We love each other, and we're going to make our relationship work, whatever anyone says."

I wanted to jump up and cheer. I'm a total sucker for declarations of love. But Merritt was unimpressed.

"So, you stand by your statement that you were alone on the night of your mother's death?"

"Yes," he said firmly. "I was alone that night."

"You're aware that you're leaving yourself without an alibi."

"I didn't know I needed one," he said icily.

CHAPTER 15

An Intriguing Woman with a Lot to Offer

Just then the door flew open and a woman barged in. "Scott! I need to speak to you!"

I recognized Lauren Perry from the photos on her company website, but just barely. On her website she appeared lithe and lovely, innocent and dewy faced (a fitting advertisement for her skin-care products). A short video showed her wearing an endearingly simple cotton dress and twirling with gentle abandon in a field of wildflowers against the majestic backdrop of the Green Mountains. She looked like Julie Andrews singing "The Hills Are Alive" in *The Sound of Music.*

In person she was very different. Her body was more scrawny than slender—an awkward assemblage of thin bones and pointy angles—and the face that had been so well made-up and attractive on the website was in real life pallid and pinched.

Her eyes flashed scornfully when she saw Merritt and me sitting there. She snapped at her half brother, "Who are they?"

"This is Aubrey Merritt, the private investigator Haley hired, and her assistant, Olivia Blunt."

Lauren reared back, horrified. "Haley did *what*? She hired a *what*?"

"Ms. Merritt is here to investigate Mom's death. She and Ms. Blunt drove up from New York City yesterday."

"Oh great. Another investigation. Just what this family needs right now. And Haley never thought to mention this to me?"

"Why would she? You two barely speak."

"I think I have a right to know when strangers have been brought in to dig around in my family's business," Lauren said hotly.

"They're not digging in anyone's business, just investigating Mom's death."

"*Your* mother's death."

Scott sighed wearily, as if he'd heard this distinction a hundred times.

Lauren continued. "This is going too far, even for Haley. Why are you indulging her?"

"Because it means a lot to her, Lauren, and I really don't see the harm."

Lauren cast a withering glance toward Merritt and me before turning back to Scott. "How much access do you intend to give these people?"

"They're asking about the party, Lauren. And the night Mom— my mother—died. That's all."

"You'd better hope that's all. I'm sure you wouldn't want them nosing around too much. I mean, in case anything came up . . ."

"What's that supposed to mean?" He looked more hurt than angry.

Lauren tilted up her chin and offered a smirk.

All this time I'd been expecting Merritt to jump in and say something, to defend our investigation, or Haley's right to hire us, or even Scott's right to indulge his younger sister's whims. But she seemed content just to sit back and listen.

Scott changed the subject. "Are the girls with you?"

"They're right here." Lauren stepped aside, and I saw for the first time that there was a little girl standing behind her; and behind her another, smaller one; and behind her a third, even smaller one. I judged their ages to be about eight, six, and four. They were blond like their mother, and also thin and bony; they were dressed in matching one-piece pink bathing suits and had matching French braids woven tightly at the sides of their heads. The only things that distinguished them from one another, besides their sizes, were their flip-flops, which were different colors, and the fact that the smallest child clutched a stuffed purple pony with a flowing white mane. They gave the strange impression that they'd been put in a straight line years ago and had simply decided to stay that way.

Scott waved them in, and they filed into the room obediently, staring at Merritt and me with unblinking eyes. "Mrs. Merritt, Ms. Blunt—I'd like you to meet my nieces: Constance, Viveca, and Paulette."

Merritt and I said hello, and before I could ask to meet the pony, Lauren said sharply, "Girls, wait outside."

They left the same way they'd entered, with neither a smile nor a skip.

"Your daughters are very well-behaved," Merritt said with apparent approval.

Well-behaved? I would have gone with *robotic*.

"My daughters are none of your business."

Scott sighed again. "Lauren, what can I do for you?"

"I need to draw your attention to a few issues around this place that need immediate action, but I think I'll wait until these two"— she jerked her head in our direction—"have left."

Merritt got to her feet, and I followed suit. "We were just going, as a matter of fact. Thank you for your time, Mr. Summersworth. It was nice to meet you, Ms. Perry."

Lauren turned her back, and Merritt and I walked past her, out the door.

———

"Wow. Pat Tucci wasn't kidding. Lauren really is a nasty piece of work," I said as soon as we were out of earshot.

"She's an intriguing woman, isn't she?" Merritt was unruffled, even oddly pleased by the rude behavior we'd just been subjected to. "She clearly has a lot to offer our investigation. We ought to sit down with her as soon as possible."

"Didn't you hear her? I doubt she'll talk to us."

"Oh, she will. But not until she knows for sure that we're not going away."

CHAPTER 16

The Purple Hat Ladies

Merritt told me to meet her in the lobby at noon for the drive to Monty Draper's apartment in Burlington; until then she had some matters to attend to. Finding myself with about two and a half hours to spend however I wanted to, I hurried back to my room to put on my bathing suit, and then I set out carrying my towel, sun hat, sunscreen, water bottle, and a book about the Boston Strangler that I'd borrowed from Merritt's library. (*Thank you, Olly, but I'd rather not know,* Trevor had said when I offered to describe exactly how Albert DeSalvo carried out his thirteen grisly murders.)

It was a beautiful morning, warm and sunny, and I was looking forward to a swim. Unfortunately the sandy beach near the dock was crowded with families, and the roped-off swimming area was rather small, though that didn't prevent it from being hawkishly surveilled by several lifeguards with mirrored sunglasses and triangles of white sunscreen on their noses.

Disappointed with the beach, I decided to try one of the four pools at the resort. I thought it might be fun to check them all out and see which one I liked best. Guided by my now-wrinkled map, I visited the Olympic-sized pool, where sinewy swimmers wearing goggles stroked down watery lanes at high speeds; the kidney-shaped pool, with its own Polynesian-style thatched-roof bar, where well-oiled sunbathers were already (it was only ten a.m.!) sipping exotic drinks and making slinky eyes at one another; and the family pool, with a curvy slide for children and a very wet sandbox for toddlers. At this point I couldn't help feeling a bit deflated. My specific needs (beauty, quiet, privacy) were not being met by any of the pool types on offer, which reminded me that I didn't quite fit into the resort as a whole. First, because I was too poor—I could never afford to vacation here on my own. Second, because if I *did* have more money, I wouldn't spend it here. I would go someplace much more exciting, maybe the Azores or the Amalfi Coast.

I was making my way back to the lakeshore when, at an intersection of gravel paths, three older women in bathing suits, cover-ups, and hats crossed in front of me. I looked after them with curiosity. Each of their hats was some shade of purple; one was a lavender floral bucket hat, one a plum plaid baseball cap, and one a deep royal purple hat with a wide, floppy brim. I proceeded on my way, but I hadn't gone very far when I remembered something Pia Valente had told Merritt and me that morning—that Victoria had a group of friends she called her "hat ladies." I had no idea whether that had anything to do with the trio of seniors who had just crossed my path. Nevertheless, I turned around. It couldn't hurt to find out, and I had nothing else to do anyway.

I hurried back to the intersection and turned left to follow them. I soon caught sight of their purple heads bobbing up ahead, and I quickened my pace until I was close enough that I could hear snippets of their conversation but not so close as to alarm them. It was rather exciting, this bit of independent sleuthing. I didn't expect anything to come of it until I heard one of them say:

"But *why*? That's what I want to know. She seemed so happy."

"That's what she wanted us to believe," another responded.

The next chunk of dialogue was lost as the path skirted a playground filled with shouting children. But as we moved into a quiet grove, I picked up the following:

"Honestly, I think she would have told us if she was depressed."

"They don't, you know. They're too ashamed."

"Ashamed? Why? She knew we loved her."

"There's a stigma. Still."

I couldn't hear anything but murmuring after that, and the next thing I knew, we were passing through a beautiful flower garden. The air was full of a loud buzzing. Fat yellow bees, what seemed like hundreds of them, were suspended before the open petals of roses and other flowers, whose names I didn't know. When the ladies stopped to watch and exclaim, I hung back, pretending to admire the flowers as well.

They soon proceeded to the end of the garden and let themselves through a gate in a brown picket fence. Tall, skinny, pinelike shrubs hid whatever was on the other side. I waited a decent interval before I followed them through the gate, hoping I wasn't entering the grounds of a private residence.

A great welcoming cheer went up, and I stopped in my tracks, startled and self-conscious, but the cheering had nothing to do with me. The ladies I'd followed were being greeted by three friends who'd been relaxing in chaise lounges along one side of a lovely little pool. There were hugs in every direction; then the six women started fussing around one another, making a lot of friendly noise. One was wearing a grape-colored visor; the others had purple hats on their lounge chairs.

A corpulent woman in a flowery skirted bathing suit noticed me and called out in a resonating contralto, "Come in, young lady! Any traveler who discovers this grotto is welcome to sit by its cool water and be healed!"

I smiled stiffly to hide my distaste. I couldn't stand amateur theatrics. Exaggerated vibrato and exalted diction had the same effect
on me as fingernails scraping a chalkboard. The woman was right
about one thing, though: the pool did resemble a grotto. Its uneven
bottom was painted blue-gray, making the water look as transparent as it really was, and the pool was surrounded by mossy cobble-
stones instead of the usual concrete. A small wooden utility shed at
the far end was thickly covered with dark green ivy. In front of it
was a rock garden that would have been completely lovely were it
not for an obviously fake outcropping through which a stream of
water trickled, making a soft musical sound.

The friends settled themselves in a cozy grouping on the chaise
lounges and a couple of plastic chairs someone had pulled over from
a nearby table.

I couldn't believe my good luck. These women were very likely
Victoria's "hat lady" friends, and the talk I'd overheard was very likely
about Victoria herself. But what should I do now? I must have been
standing there gaping like an idiot, because one member of the gang,
looking quite fit in her white one-piece, looked over and said, "Don't
let us bother you, dear. We're just a bunch of harmless old dames."

I smiled again, this time with more sincerity, and set my towel
and other things in a spot across the pool from them. I figured I
ought to act like a normal resort guest, so I took off the old denim
shirt of Trevor's that I'd worn over my bathing suit and I lowered
myself gingerly but happily down one step after another into cool,
clean water that didn't smell of chlorine. I started to swim a breast-
stroke the short distance to the far end, keeping my head up while
my body adjusted to the temperature; then I ducked and swam un-
derwater in slow, languid strokes, with my hair streaming behind
me. There was probably a smile on my face.

After a few lazy laps I eased out of the pool, lathered up with
sunscreen, and, with my Mets baseball cap resting gently on my

face, stretched out on a lounge chair. The hot sun was beating down, warming my skin, and I was deliciously drowsy from my swim, but that didn't keep me from tuning in to the conversation happening not far away. The women were all bridge players, apparently, and they were discussing the previous afternoon's bridge game and the potluck dinner they'd had afterward. One of the ladies said:

"Vicki would have loved it."

This remark was met by a few moments of silence. Then a cascade of voices:

"She was a terrible bridge player herself."

"So true. She only ever won when she partnered with Monty."

"She was definitely the teacher's pet."

"It was sweet how in love they were."

"Love? Is that what you call it?"

Once more the conversation paused at a door no one wanted to walk through. Finally someone said:

"Do you think something was going on with her we didn't know about? Some kind of awful problem?"

"Her son, you mean," another replied.

I recognized this voice. It was the contralto belonging to the lady stretched out on the chaise, with her hands clasped over her belly.

"Carla, what are you talking about? What about her son? Which one?"

"Scott, of course. You know he's a drug addict, don't you?"

"No! I didn't know that! Are you sure?"

A couple other voices admitted that they'd also been ignorant of that fact.

"Really? You didn't know? Well, I suppose she didn't tell everyone. It was a very private matter, and very painful for her."

Carla sounded pleased to be the only friend in the group with whom the dead woman had shared her secret.

"Tell us, Carla. Details, please."

A murmur of voices concurred that it was time for Carla to spill the beans.

Needing no further persuasion, Carla launched into a fulsome account of Scott Summersworth's alleged addiction and his mother's response to it. Now her thundering, theatrical voice was music to my ears as it carried well across the space between us. I pretended to doze.

A condensed version of the story, which was much longer in Carla's dramatic retelling, would go like this: all was well for a year or two after Scott assumed the role of general manager. Then, on a fateful day known only to Scott himself, cocaine entered the picture, and then by slow degrees Scott's life and the lives of everyone around him began to resemble a not-so-fun carnival ride. He would be proudly clean for weeks at a time; he'd be smiling and handsome, and the resort would look and feel like a happy place. Then he'd start using again. Back would come the runny nose and the puffy eyes, the tremor in the hands and the raunchy whiff of unwashed clothes. The fits of anger would resume. There would be missed meetings, unreturned calls, and mysterious absences. Servers would cry; landscapers would grouse; guests would complain that the bath towels were not soft and the golf carts needed repair. As the staff learned to avoid their boss, one problem after another went unsolved. The resort lost some of its mojo.

On the really bad days, Scott hit his mother up for money. She always gave it to him, always believing his ardent vow to get clean and stay that way forever. A few days later he'd be back for more money, and she'd be crushed, and sometimes she would have the courage to refuse. That was when Scott's evil twin would appear—that shameless being that looked just like Scott but said and did things Scott himself would never say or do. He broke things and he insulted and berated her, and when she still didn't capitulate he stole from her. It was ugly and heartbreaking and terrifying and hopeless. Vicki suffered from it, Carla said, more than anyone knew.

"Anyway, he's supposedly in recovery now," Carla said lightly, pleased to be wrapping up her story with a happy ending, though the word *supposedly* left the door open for a sequel.

The little group was stiffly quiet. No doubt they'd heard similar stories before, but this one was more troubling. This one was about Vicki and Scott—a dear friend and her usually affable son, who one woman said she remembered as a skinny blond kid riding a bike and climbing trees.

I remembered Scott too, from an hour earlier, when I'd noticed his sweaty handshake and unkempt appearance, and the way his eyes reddened easily at the mention of his mother. He'd seemed shaky to me—like a man still reeling from an emotional body blow. Now I wondered if there was more to it. Was he using, as Carla had hinted he might be? If so, what, if anything, did that mean for the investigation into his mother's death?

After a while a stilted voice announced:

"I'm not surprised. I had a feeling something like that was going on."

And another replied, "Why go and kill yourself, though? Just because of that. I mean, I know how hard addiction can be on everyone involved. Believe me, I do know. But how would suicide help that? It would just make everything worse. And you said he was in recovery."

"Carla said *supposedly*. Supposedly in recovery."

"I agree with Lisa. An addicted son is not a good enough reason to kill yourself."

"I'm sorry, girls. . . . This is a terrible non sequitur, but it really bothers me and I can't stop thinking about it. I just can't picture

Vicki throwing herself off a balcony. Can you? It's so violent, so messy. She just wasn't that kind of person. Pills would have been more her style."

"None of it was her style. Not the decision, not the doing. Nothing."

"In any case, it was cruel of her not to say good-bye."

"The party was her good-bye."

"Oh god. You're right, now that I think of it. That wasn't just her birthday party; it was her farewell, her *bon voyage*! Now, *that* was Vicki, one hundred percent. Going out on a high note while the people she loved were just down the road, dancing up a storm."

The women fell silent again, sunk in their grief and awe.

A breeze whispered past, carrying the smells of warm earth and flowers. I had half a mind to sit up and identify myself as the assistant to the famous private investigator Aubrey Merritt, who'd been called in to make short work of the very questions that were haunting them. I even toyed with the idea of interviewing them myself— on my boss's behalf, of course. I would've relished the opportunity to flap my fledgling detective wings, but even if I'd had the moxie to do that, risking Merritt's ire in the process, it likely wouldn't have been a productive path. The women's discussion showed that they had no more clues about the cause of Victoria Summersworth's death than I did. Tellingly, the possibility of murder hadn't been mentioned at all, much less any hint of a likely motive or suspect. And I had to consider that any information I shared with these talkative girls would no doubt spread around the resort like a blazing wildfire, providing advance warning to the as-yet-hidden killer, if he or she existed.

I was lost in these thoughts when a fresh voice made itself known. It was soft and hesitant. I might not have heard it at all if the other women hadn't been quiet.

"What if she was killed?"

"Killed? By whom?"

"A serial killer."

"Oh, Sandra, don't be ridiculous. Has Vermont ever had a serial killer? Even one?"

"Wait. Sandra's right. What if she *was* murdered? Maybe not by a serial killer, but by a violent psychopath wandering around the resort."

"Or a burglar. What if a burglar knew about Vicki's party—honestly, who *didn't* know about Vicki's party?—and broke in while the party was going on, figuring the house would be empty? Then Vicki went home early, for whatever reason, and caught him in the act?"

"You're saying a burglar threw her off the balcony?"

"Why not? That makes just as much sense as her killing herself, doesn't it?"

The ladies seemed about to embark upon another round of speculation when the small voice intervened, with a bit more energy than before.

"Do any of you remember that young man who was loitering at the pool when we were doing water aerobics? It was a couple of weeks ago. The children were having swimming lessons at one end and we were at the other with our kickboards—four or five of us, anyway, including Vicki. Remember I said I thought he was a pedophile stalking the children?"

A few snorts of derision followed this question. Apparently Sandra was not a favorite. Nevertheless, she went on.

"Oh, come on. You must remember. He was dressed very inappropriately for the pool, in jeans and a hoodie and sunglasses, with a canvas hat pulled down over his face. And on such a warm day! I expected him to follow after the children when they left—I was ready to say something to their parents if he did. But he stayed right where he was. That's when I realized it actually wasn't the children he was after. He was stalking *us*—a bunch of old ladies! Which is quite disturbing too, when you think about it. You better believe I kept a sharp eye on him after that, but I soon realized that no, I was wrong again. It wasn't *us* he was interested in. It was Vicki. Specifically. He was watching her every move. His eyes were positively glued to her."

"How would you know that if he was wearing sunglasses?"

"I just knew. I can't say how, but I knew."

"Did you tell Vicki?"

"Of course. I wouldn't dream of not telling someone if I thought they were in danger. She admitted that she'd noticed him too but didn't think anything of it. Told me I was letting my imagination run away with me. I didn't argue with her, but I didn't forget about that young man either. I kept my eyes peeled for him, and I'm pretty sure I saw him hanging around the resort a few times after that. Always alone and always with the sunglasses and hat."

"Sandra, *everyone* around here wears sunglasses and a hat!"

"That's not all. He was at Vicki's birthday party too."

This gave the women pause. Finally one of them spoke up.

"Are you sure about that?"

"Well, not one hundred percent. But there was definitely a young man standing out in the lobby, near the door. A tall young man, quite slim and lanky, just like the one at the pool. I'm quite sure he wasn't there as a guest. He wasn't dressed right, and I hadn't seen him during dinner. He was just *there*, if you know what I mean. Not doing anything, not talking to anyone. Just watching. It gave me an eerie feeling, and I've always thought that as women we need to pay attention to those feelings, because we never know where danger might be lurking, do we?"

"That sounds kind of vague, Sandra, but if you really think that guy was up to no good, you should have told the police."

"I did! They said they'd look into it, but it was obvious they didn't take me seriously. Like you all don't."

No one rushed to assure Sandra that she was believed. Instead a hush descended over the pool. I supposed we were all wondering the same thing. Did Vicki have a stalker? If so, who? And why?

Despite that alarming possibility, I was quietly excited. I couldn't wait to share what I'd learned with my boss. I checked my phone and saw that the time I'd spent eavesdropping had really flown by. I would have to hurry if I wanted to get to the Lodge in time to meet Merritt. I didn't dare keep her waiting again.

CHAPTER 17

The Bridge Champion

On the drive into Burlington to meet Monty Draper, I told Merritt what I'd overheard about Scott Summersworth's alleged cocaine addiction and a possible stalker.

"If Carla was right," I said, "and Scott routinely flew into rages when his mother refused to give him money for drugs, we can assume he was capable of murdering her. So a possible scenario is this: Scott is still using. He needs money, and, hoping to steal cash or valuables of some kind, he drives to the Bungalow in the wee hours after the party. He knows Monty won't be there, because Monty told him he wouldn't be, and he assumes his mother will be asleep. Only she wakes up, they have a huge fight, and off she goes over the balcony. He writes the suicide note in a forgery of her handwriting that was good enough to fool the graphologist."

"So you believed this woman, Carla, the storyteller. You accept that Scott is an addict, either using or in recovery."

"Using is my guess, unless he's gotten cleaned up since killing his mother ten days ago. But I don't think so. He didn't look so good this morning, remember? He had red eyes and his hands were trembling. Dirty clothes, unshaved, hair not combed. Honestly, his staff looks more professional than he does."

"And you equate lack of polish with active addiction."

The flatness of her tone made me pause. Out of the corner of my eye, I saw her knead her forehead as if a headache was coming on.

"Blunt, we discussed this . . ." she said.

"All right, all right. I'll slow down," I said.

"Way down."

"Way down."

"Good. Now, there are a couple of things I want you to do when you're back in your room this evening. First, see if you can get a feel for the kind of money problems the resort is having. I don't know how you're going to do that, but you're a fact-checker; I'm sure you'll figure something out. Next—you got a picture of that business card that was in Mrs. Summersworth's evening purse, right? The one belonging to the CPA? Get me some background on that guy and his company. Was he someone she ran into for the first time that night, or was there a special reason she needed his contact info all of a sudden? I trust you're continuing to make your way through Mrs. Summersworth's laptop and you'll have a report for me soon. When you're done with all that, go back to the Bungalow and search her office."

"The Bungalow? Me? Alone?"

"What's the problem? Do you need an escort?"

"Of course not," I said quickly. But I wasn't thrilled at the prospect of entering a dead woman's house and spending a few hours rifling through her stuff. Alone. At night.

"There will likely be a file cabinet with important documents: insurance policies, bills, receipts, personal papers. . . . A lot of people her age still rely on paper. Get in there and see what you can find."

"No problem," I said, suppressing a groan.

"You know where the key is," she added.

"Sure do." *Along with everyone else at the Wild Goose Resort, includ-ing a possible murderer,* I thought.

Monty Draper's apartment complex on the outskirts of Burlington was called Meadow Gate, because, I supposed, it was on a rise over-looking a meadow. I saw no sign of a gate. The place might have lived up to the first half of its bucolic name if the meadow hadn't ended abruptly at the shoulder of Route 89, the interstate highway that snakes north to Canada and south through the Green Moun-tains before crossing over into New Hampshire. From the parking lot of the apartment complex I could trace its silver asphalt path for at least a mile in both directions.

The apartment building, an eight-story concrete monolith, was as bland as its setting. Back in the seventies it had probably aspired to be chic and sophisticated. Now it just looked like something that had never belonged there in the first place.

I buzzed the correct buzzer and received a protracted buzz in response. Merritt and I went through the double glass doors and piled into an elevator whose thin carpet exuded a whiff of dog pee and whose buttons had been worn away by the pressing of many thumbs. The elevator made slow, clanking progress, and I experi-enced my usual grip of anxiety at being trapped inside a tiny en-closed space. Finally the mechanical box unclenched its metal jaw and, trailing Merritt, I stumbled with relief into a windowless cor-ridor.

Monty Draper opened the door to his apartment before we got there. He was on the short side, with a soft girth, a weather-beaten face, and a rather startling shock of stiff gray-blond hair. His wist-ful smile revealed a mouthful of large, brilliantly white teeth.

"Come in," he said soberly, though he had the rough red com-plexion of someone who often wasn't sober. His floor plan matched

Victoria's—dining room to the left, kitchen to the right, living room straight ahead, sliding glass door, balcony—only his apartment was smaller and uglier than Victoria's house. A *lot* smaller and uglier.

Merritt and I sat side by side on a cheap too-low couch set against a long wall of unbroken beige.

Draper remained standing, looking uncomfortable. He had agreed to meet, but now he seemed unsure of what to do with us. He was wearing saggy blue jeans held up with a braided leather belt. His shirt had two chest pockets with buttoned flaps and a smaller pocket on one sleeve. It looked like a safari shirt, only it was white and made of soft jersey material. Like the apartment building, it seemed to have started its life with a vague ambition that had fizzled out.

"Can I get you anything?" he asked.

Merritt declined in a frosty voice. I knew right away that there would be no flattery or cajoling in this interview.

Feeling a need to warm up the atmosphere, I piped up with the old standby "I'm sorry for your loss."

"I still can't believe it," he said, sinking into a chair across from us. "I was dancing with her that night, and she seemed so full of life. I thought . . . I thought . . ." He seemed helpless in his grief. "It's my fault. I should have known how unhappy she was. If I'd known, I would never have left her alone that night. But I had no idea. The party had been wonderful; she was glowing. There was no sign of what she was about to do. I'm still in shock. I simply can't believe it."

"You drove Mrs. Summersworth to the party that night—correct?" Merritt asked.

"I did."

"I assume you left your car in the parking lot across the road from the Lodge."

He nodded.

"Did you lock it?"

"Lock it? Why do you ask?"

"Just answer, please."

"Well, yes, I must have. I lock my car with my key fob whenever I leave it."

"So if Mrs. Summersworth had wanted to get something out of your car, some item she'd left there, she would have had to ask you for the key fob."

"That's right."

"Did she ask you for the key fob at any time that night?"

"No."

"Are you aware that she left the Lodge between approximately nine and nine twenty?"

"No, I wasn't aware of that. Did she?"

"She did, Mr. Draper. She said she was going out to your car, but your car was locked and you hadn't given her the key. Nevertheless, she was seen leaving the Lodge at roughly nine o'clock, returning at roughly nine twenty. Do you have any idea where she might have gone?"

Draper looked genuinely puzzled. "I can't imagine where she would have gone."

"Think carefully, please."

He slowly shook his head. "I have no idea. It wouldn't have been far, though."

"Why do you say that?"

"She was wearing sky-high heels—a good five inches of lift, I'd say. I joked that she could break an ankle in those things. But she loved her shoes, had about fifty pairs in her closet. These in particular were . . . well, sort of a shiny gold color. They matched her dress. She was okay in them on a floor, but she couldn't have gone very far outside."

"Where were you between nine and nine twenty, Mr. Draper?"

"Probably in the billiard room. We'd already had dinner and

danced. I'm not much of a dancer, and Vicki gave me permission to go after I'd swung her around on the floor a bit. I went off and played pool with some buddies of mine until she came to get me. That must have been about nine thirty or quarter to ten, somewhere in there. It surprised me when she said she wanted to go home. If she'd been any other woman, I would've assumed I hadn't been paying her enough attention. But Vicki wasn't the kind who needs you by her side every minute. That girl could have partied all night without help from me."

The hairs on the back of my neck rose like the scruff of a hostile dog. I didn't appreciate the way Monty Draper was talking about women, as if we were just a bunch of stiletto-heeled dames who regally gave men "permission" to escape and do the guy things they'd much prefer to be doing after they'd fawned over us sufficiently. As if, like toddlers, we deserved praise when we were capable of socializing without them.

"Did she say why she wanted to leave the party early?" Merritt's tone had gone from frosty to below zero.

His shoulders slumped. Again, he gave off an air of overwhelmed helplessness. "She didn't. It was all very mysterious. When I dropped her off, she didn't even want me to come in. That was a first, and I was a little miffed. I asked if she was angry with me about something. Typical guy, right? Thinking it must have been about me. She said she wasn't angry at all but she wanted me to go back to the party and have a good time, and she would call me in the morning and we could talk then. That got my blood pumping. You know what it means when a woman says she wants to *talk*, don't you? It means she's either going to break up with you or tell you she wants to take it to the next level."

Merritt's eyebrows rose, and stayed aloft for several seconds—a mix of surprise and scorn.

Draper seemed not to notice. "If you really want to know, I'd asked her to marry me, and she'd said she needed to think about it. I didn't take that personally at first. I knew she had a lot to figure out, but it was getting to be time to decide, wasn't it? Her old man had been dead for . . . what? Twelve, fifteen years? And her kids were well past grown. She was turning sixty-five. It was time for the next stage of life, the part where you don't have to give a damn about anything. Your second childhood, only without the parents around. She knew she could enjoy life with me. We'd travel the world together and love every minute of it. She was always up for an adventure. Not a complainer, ever. You know that old advice about spending three nights in a tent in the rain before deciding to marry someone? Well, I didn't have to do that. I knew the kind of lady she was. Three days in a damp tent with her and we'd be laughing the whole time, having pillow fights and telling each other stories. She was a one-in-a-million gal. I loved her something fierce, god help me. Like a house on fire."

"Uh-huh," Merritt said without enthusiasm. "So, when she said she wanted to talk . . ."

"I was excited and terrified. I figured either I was going to be joining the family or I was going to be out on my ass. A hope and a fear. I didn't know which it would be."

"How did she seem to you when you dropped her off? Happy? Sad? Tired? Tipsy? Aching feet?"

"It was strange. I definitely got the feeling something was going on with her. Her eyes were bright and sparkly, and she seemed excited. I asked if she was okay, if there was anything I could do. She just said she didn't need me right then. I thought that was a weird way to put it. What was she going to do that she didn't need me for? But there was no point in bugging her about it. She was up to something, and she didn't want me around."

"So you didn't go inside with her? Just left her at the door?"

"I watched to make sure she got in safe, of course."

"Are you very sure you didn't enter the house that evening, Mr. Draper?"

I stiffened, wondering how he would answer Merritt's rather aggressive question, given that we suspected they'd been in bed together. His hand snaked out for a glass of ice water (it was too early for vodka, wasn't it?) beside him, but he didn't pick it up.

"Vicki wanted me to go back to the party, and that's what I did," he said glumly. "You can ask Scott Summersworth if you want. I had a couple of drinks with him at the bar."

"Did you return to her house later that night, after you left the Lodge?"

"For god's sake, if you're asking whether I killed her, the answer is no."

"I was asking if you went back to her house after you left the Lodge."

"No. I did not. I went home."

"What time was that?"

"Eleven? Eleven thirty? I really don't recall."

"Can anyone vouch for your whereabouts between two and four a.m.?"

He made a sweeping gesture that took in the span of his anemic apartment. "As you can see, I live alone."

"What kind of car do you drive?"

"A Buick Regal. Why do you ask?"

"Color?" she said.

"Color? What difference does it make?"

"Just answer, please."

"Look, I don't have to answer your questions at all. You're just a hired PI."

"Quite true. You're under no obligation to assist with this private investigation, but when someone is unwilling to work with me it makes me wonder why."

"Okay, okay. My Buick Regal is dark blue. A nice color, a very nice color. I like my dark blue Buick Regal very much."

"Thank you, Mr. Draper."

I expected her to confront him with the fact that a car similar to his was seen in the Summersworth driveway at approximately one o'clock on the morning of Mrs. Summersworth's death. But she didn't. She moved on smoothly.

"On your way back to the Lodge after dropping off Mrs. Summersworth, did you pass any cars or notice anyone on the road or in the woods?"

"Didn't see any cars that I recall. Don't remember any people either. I wouldn't have expected to see anyone. Hardly anyone goes up that way. Sure, there are about a half dozen houses up there besides Vicki's, but they're occupied by seasoners who tend to keep a low profile. Most of the guest cabins are south of the Lodge; that's where the beach and the docks are, and the pools."

Merritt said, "She sent a text message to her children shortly before she died, something about wanting to get together with them for lunch the next day. Do you know anything about that?"

"Yeah, I heard about that from Scott, but I have no idea what was in her mind." He paused. "If you really want to know, I kinda hoped she was going to tell her kids she'd decided to marry me. To get their blessing. Or just test them out. Now that I hear myself say it, it sounds kind of stupid. Not Vicki's style at all to go asking for permission. But that was the thought that crossed my mind."

My eyes were roaming around the apartment. I was trying to get a fix on the guy, the kind you can get only by studying the environment a person has created for themselves, but there wasn't much to latch on to. The place was devoid of personal style or artifacts. The furnishings might have come from a generic furniture store or one of those staging companies that people use to make their homes look attractive to potential buyers. The only thing missing was the factory smell.

"Where are you from, Mr. Draper?" I asked.

"The Southwest," he said.

Couldn't get much vaguer than that. "New Mexico? Arizona?"

After some prodding on my part—Merritt looking on, I sensed, with approval—it came out that Monty Draper was from Phoenix, where he'd worked in sales for a large electronics firm. A brief early marriage had produced one child, a son. He'd been single since the marriage ended. At fifty he'd retired with a pension and taken up his passion: bridge. Nationally ranked, he played in tournaments all over the country, some of which offered generous cash prizes.

He'd arrived as a bridge coach at the Wild Goose Resort the previous summer. There were a lot of players among the guests, and the resort had given him a small stipend and the use of a big room in the Corner Clubhouse to offer individual and group instruction and, eventually, to start the Tufted Duck Bridge Club, which hosted a weekly roster of games at various levels, from beginner to advanced. Over the course of that first summer, Monty Draper had fallen in love with the Wild Goose Resort, Lake Champlain, and the state of Vermont. He'd also fallen head over heels for his least talented student, Victoria Summersworth.

"Is that your son?" I asked, pointing to a framed photo—the only photo in the room—of a handsome young man in an army uniform, an American flag in the background.

"Yes, that's Jeremy. That was taken . . . oh, must be ten years ago now, when he first enlisted. He did four years in the army, got some IT skills under his belt, and went to Arizona State. He's in Sacramento now, working for a tech company. Don't ask me what the hell they do. Some kind of AI stuff. I don't understand a word of it."

Merritt stood up. "Thank you for your time, Mr. Draper. I'll be in touch if I have any more questions."

He saw us to the door. "I'm sorry if I got a bit touchy there, Mrs. Merritt. I know you're just trying to help."

"No worries," Merritt said in an airy voice. "By the way, I forgot to ask, what do *you* think, Mr. Draper? Did Victoria commit suicide?"

His face fell and his voice got quiet. "It sure looks that way."

CHAPTER 18

The World in Black and White

"You didn't like him," I said.

"Neither did you." Merritt blotted her neck with a napkin. Her silver hair lay flat and limp against her head, the bangs slicked to one side and tucked behind her ear. She spent most of her time in her air-conditioned apartment or in artificially cooled city buildings, and now the heat was getting the better of her, even though the temperature was only in the mid-eighties.

We had claimed a picnic table in the shade of a big oak tree behind a roadside café. We'd ordered sandwiches at a window and were waiting for our order to be called. Squirrels had skittered up the tree trunk when we sat down, and they were chattering in the low branches. Birds twittered in the higher branches, their songs sweet and gay. I had no idea what variety of birds they were. For the first time in my life, my blithe ignorance of birds and practically every other aspect of the natural world felt like a limitation I wanted to rectify.

"He's a sexist," I said. "All that stuff about Vicki being such a superlative example of womanhood because she didn't cling. Were all the men of your generation like that?"

"Not all. Just most." She tried waving a napkin in front of her face, which was half-hidden behind her big sunglasses, but the napkin was too floppy to create much of a breeze.

"That must have been horrible, especially in the workplace," I said. She'd never once mentioned her past career to me. Of course, I'd done my digging into this aspect of her life, so I knew that back in the eighties she'd been an assistant curator at the Metropolitan Museum of Art, before some kind of dustup there got her fired and, in a surprising career switch, she'd turned around and opened her own PI agency. There must have been loads of misogyny and gender discrimination in the workplace all those years ago, and I supposed I was hoping she would open up and vent her feminist rage about men like Monty Draper and the bad old days when attitudes like his were commonplace and competent women like herself were driven into boring support roles or washed out of the game entirely when they refused to put out. What she said next came as a surprise.

"The problem with your generation is that you expect things to be easy."

My brow furrowed. I had to pause and search for the right response. "Easy? No, not easy. Fair. We expect equal pay and equal opportunities for promotions and things like that. And equal respect in the workplace."

Now she was blotting her pale décolletage with strange drama, as if we'd just emerged from the Amazon. "The second problem with your generation is that you expect things to be fair."

"What's wrong with that?" I said, feeling heat rise in my cheeks. "And by the way, you've got us wrong. We don't expect things to be fair; we demand it."

She gave a brief, derisive snort. "Good luck with that."

I fumed silently for a few seconds. "What about the Me Too

movement?" I said finally. "It made a real difference in society. I bet if you'd had it your work life would have been a lot easier than I assume it was. So what if it makes a few assholes nervous? As long as they behave themselves, they have nothing to worry about."

"Okay, Blunt. I'll give you that. Me Too is a good thing for the most part. But don't fool yourself into thinking sexual harassment is going to go away. The fact remains that any individual who is smaller and weaker, or a member of any marginalized group, runs the risk of being exploited. Why? Precisely because they're smaller, weaker, or at the wrong end of a power imbalance. Humans are just another species of animal. Individuals in a group who have the power to exploit often do exploit. It's as simple as that, and the sooner you accept that fact, the better."

"That's just . . ." I struggled to find the right words and couldn't. I had to settle for blubbering out my reaction. "It's awful that you think that. If I believed that, I'd be depressed all the time. It's like you're saying nothing can ever get better; society can never improve. But things *do* get better. There are plenty of examples of that. Look at the civil rights movement, and women's suffrage, and a lot of other things that have made society more just."

Merritt removed her dark glasses, laid them on the chipped paint of the picnic table. Her sweaty, lined face looked extra pale and defenseless without them. "I'll tell you one thing that will never change. Human nature. Specifically, a human being's propensity for violence, for murder. It's been happening since Cain and Abel, and it will be going strong long after we die. There are murderers in every country and every era—the few who get caught and the many, many more who don't—and not one of them gives a damn about Me Too or human rights or any of that stuff. If you stay in this line of work, murderers will be your life. You'll be chasing them during the day and dreaming of them at night. Your starry-eyed idealism will be a liability. So will your empathy. You need to ask yourself if you can handle that." She waved the flaccid napkin pointlessly. "Personally, I have doubts."

I felt a swirl of confusion. I knew she was sharing something important with me, something about the stark black-and-white nature of the work she did, and how it had changed her and might change me. I knew I ought to take what she was saying to heart, and to find some quiet moments later in the day to reflect honestly on my temperament and suitability for the work. That was what my head told me. My gut had a different reaction. My gut suddenly knew with total clarity that Aubrey Merritt's bleak outlook didn't come from her job alone. There was something else, something dark *in her.*

I wondered what it was.

"I was calling you. Didn't you hear me?" the girl from the café said. She was carrying a tray heaped with our sandwiches and drinks.

"Oh, sorry. Thanks for bringing the food over." I made a lame attempt to brush off the picnic table, as if that would help her somehow.

Merritt and I unwrapped our sandwiches. She had a turkey club and I had a chicken wrap with French fries. We both had iced teas. We ate in silence for a while. I was still trying to absorb our recent conversation, which had gone off the rails. I decided to ignore her stated doubt in me. I would rely on time to prove her wrong. Eventually I returned to our original topic.

"What did you think of Monty Draper? Besides not liking him."

"His grief seemed genuine. But something about him didn't add up."

"Like what?"

"His apartment bothered me. Looked like no one actually lived there."

"Agreed. Maybe it's a single-guy thing. He needs a wife to decorate his living space. And dress him. That shirt, for example." I shook my head sadly.

"And his hair," Merritt added. She took a bite of her sandwich.

She hadn't touched the fried gherkins at the Fainting Goat Lounge, and we hadn't dined together last night or breakfasted together this morning. This was our first meal together. Surely there was no reason for it to feel so awkward, but it did.

"What about that picture of his son, Jeremy?" I asked, dipping a French fry in ketchup.

"That bothered me too. Looked like a stock photo he got off the internet. When you're doing your research tonight, check them both out—Monty and Jeremy Draper. Dig up everything you can."

I winced. My to-do list was getting long. "You think Draper could have murdered her?"

"If Victoria told him no, refused to marry him, I can see him taking it hard. And he drives a dark blue Buick Regal, which fits the description Pat gave. Then again, so does Scott Summersworth's black BMW."

The rowdy squirrels were throwing nuts down from the branches above our heads. One landed on the picnic table and rolled toward me. I picked it up and twirled it in my fingers, marveling at its little woody crown.

"You know what I think is odd?" I said. "If Draper had wanted to, he could have strengthened the suicide hypothesis. Or the random-killer hypothesis, for that matter."

"What do you mean?"

"Well, he could have done what Robin Tucci did and told us Vicki was struggling with depression. It would be evidence in support of the suicide hypothesis that couldn't be refuted. But he didn't do that."

Merritt didn't say anything. She was listening, and when she listened, she listened *hard*. It made me nervous—like when the teacher called on you in school and you had to give an answer in front of the class. Even when you knew you were right, you stumbled a bit.

I continued carefully. "Also, you offered him an opportunity to claim that he'd noticed someone on the road or in the woods when he was driving back to the Lodge from her house—a mysterious character, a stalker or burglar maybe, someone up to no good. If Draper was the murderer, and he was worried that the suicide hypothesis wasn't going to fly, you'd think he'd want to muddy the water by giving us that additional angle to pursue. But he didn't do that. He didn't take either of those opportunities to deflect suspicion from himself."

"Because he has nothing to cover up, you're suggesting."

"Exactly."

"So, where does that leave us?"

"Both Robin Tucci and Monty Draper knew the dead woman intimately, yet they said opposite things about her state of mind. Robin said she was chronically unhappy, that lately there had been subtle changes in her mood that signaled what she intended to do. Monty said Vicki was feeling great when he dropped her off, that she was actually excited about something. They both knew her very well, probably better than her kids, so both their opinions have merit. But they're completely contradictory." I spread out my hands, palms up, as if revealing a secret. "Ergo, one of them is lying."

"You're pegging Robin as the liar, I assume."

"That makes the most sense, as she was the one steering us toward the suicide hypothesis, which she would obviously want to do if she was guilty."

Merritt looked at me as she never had before. With respect. "Not bad, Blunt."

I was wildly pleased and tried not to let it show.

"Let's leave all that aside for the time being," she continued briskly. "At the moment what I'm interested in is whether Monty

Draper went back to the house after he left the Lodge. We know someone was there, and I'd very much like to talk to whoever it was. Monty is the most obvious possibility, but he says it wasn't him. And we can't forget that Pat Tucci saw a light on the road at about nine thirty p.m., a flashlight, headed to the Bungalow. I'd like to know who was behind that light. So, that's where we are now."

She sipped her iced tea, then continued. "There was a CCTV camera in the lobby of the Meadow Gate apartment building. I trust you noticed it."

I nodded, even though I hadn't. Next time I'd be sure to look.

"I want the footage for that night. Handle that with Clemmons, would you? ASAP."

Another item added to the list. There was no way I'd remember them all. I got out my phone and started jotting notes.

CHAPTER 19

Spandex Adonis

What on earth is taking so long?" Merritt groused, loudly enough for the receptionist to hear.

The receptionist, a woman in a tired middle age whose cheeks drooped like melted wax, pretended she hadn't.

Feeling obliged to bridge the gap, I went over to her desk. "Excuse me. We've been waiting twenty minutes. Are you sure Mr. Summersworth knows we're here?"

"He ought to be back any minute," she said, repeating earlier statements.

"Can you call him?"

"Sorry, no. He's on his bike. He usually does fifteen miles up the shore road and back at lunchtime. Something must have delayed him. But I do expect him soon."

I returned to my seat and opened the puzzle app on my phone. I'd never once finished the *New York Times* crossword puzzle, but that didn't stop me from trying.

Next to me, an idle Merritt sat scowling into empty air, no phone in her hand, no magazine on her lap, nothing to gainfully occupy her mind. She was being forced to wait, she didn't like it, and she didn't care who knew.

After a while she looked over my shoulder. "You do keep after that thing, don't you?" She'd seen me hunched over the puzzle a few times before, in the office. "Have you ever wondered if you're just not up to it?"

"Never. Someday I'm going to do the whole thing in under an hour." I wasn't nearly as confident as I sounded, but that wasn't her concern.

A soft chuckle reached my ears. "You really are quite admirable on occasion, Blunt."

My heart soared. Another compliment! In an instant all the grim things she'd said earlier that afternoon about human depravity and the never-ending flow of killers in this world was completely forgotten, replaced by the conviction that becoming her assistant was the best decision I'd ever made.

Eventually a very tall man burst through the door. He was wearing skintight bicycle shorts that showed off thighs of iron, buttocks of steel, and a bulky crotch area I tried not to stare at. A skintight nylon shirt in brilliant yellow and blue was stretched over chiseled pectorals and rock-hard abs. There wasn't one jiggle of fat on his long, lean body. He was splendidly, stupendously fit. I could almost hear his metabolism humming under his skin like the quiet engine of a Maserati.

Snapping off thin black gloves, he strode toward us in a wind of purposeful energy.

"Sorry to keep you waiting, Mrs. Merritt. I hate to be late. It's a long-standing peeve of mine. Shows disrespect for others. Hate to make excuses too, but I think you deserve to know the reason for my tardiness. I got a flat tire on the way here. Must have run over a piece of glass or something. The tires on these Danish racing bikes are much too thin. A design flaw, obviously, but it keeps the bike light, which is an advantage on race day." He turned to me. "And you are . . . ?"

"Olivia Blunt, assistant to Ms. Merritt."

"Excellent. If you two will give me a minute to get cleaned up, I'll meet you in my office and we'll get down to business."

The receptionist ushered us into his office while Neil Summersworth hurried in the opposite direction. She offered us water, a soft drink, or coffee, all of which Merritt declined with such frosty impatience that the poor woman practically ran back to the safety of her desk. First he'd kept us waiting. Now we were expected to wait again while he carried out his après-exercise toilette. It galled her.

The office was of an uncluttered Scandinavian style, not a dust speck in sight. Long windows let in crystal clear sunshine. Merritt took a seat across from a stunning desk of polished tiger maple.

"What kind of getup was that? Looked like a clown suit to me," she said.

"He's a bicyclist," I supplied, knowing it wouldn't help.

"I got that. Danish racing bike, et cetera. But why the gloves?"

She didn't really want an answer, but I gave one anyway. "So his hands don't slip off the handlebars."

She grunted.

I was drawn to a glass display case along one wall. It turned out to contain a pictorial representation of the nearly 150-year history of the company that had come to be called Kingfisher Development. The early photos, curled and yellowed with age, showed various construction sites—each one involving huge piles of logs, big stacks of cut lumber, and a small army of sturdy-looking men. Much of the company's early work had apparently been done on barren snow-fields ringed by ghostly, leafless trees under leaden gray skies. I got chilly just looking at it. The corporate history got a bit cheerier as color photography supplanted black-and-white. Even so, all those gruff men standing lifelessly around huge holes in the ground bored me nearly to tears. I skipped over about a hundred years until I got to the most recent photos, which showed big yellow dump trucks, and workers in hard hats and bright orange vests. A few were actually smiling. *There. That's better*, I thought.

Neil Summersworth strode into the room, now attired in stiff khakis, leather loafers, and a crisp button-down shirt with the top button undone. Damp hair was evidence of a recent shower, and a scent of spicy aftershave wafted in his wake. Like his half brother, Scott, he had a plain face that seemed to occupy the exact middle point on the attractiveness scale, equidistant from Ryan Reynolds and whoever the ugliest man on the planet was. Unlike his half brother, though, he appeared supremely confident, comfortably ensconced in the sacred temple of his superlative body.

We said a second round of hellos, and I placed my phone on his desk to show that I was recording.

"Oh no," he said immediately. "My lawyer wouldn't like that."

"It's standard procedure." I figured that as a businessman he would respect procedure.

"Absolutely not." His chin tilted up, and he stared down his nose at me, smug in his foreknowledge that I would be the one to fold.

I glanced at Merritt. Her eyebrows arranged themselves into a sentence that read, *This isn't a hill worth dying on.* I made a show of putting the phone away, but I was feeling peppery and didn't turn the recorder off.

Neil turned to Merritt. "I'll be honest. When I heard that my sister had hired a private investigator to look into my stepmother's death, I was annoyed. I saw no reason to doubt the police's verdict of suicide, and I would have preferred to close the book and move on. Since then, though, it's occurred to me that Haley might be right in one respect: the Wild Goose Resort needs to be seen as taking the possibility that a violent crime occurred on its grounds very, very seriously. Given the facts as I know them and the conclusion of the police, I believe that possibility is remote. But rumors have a way of cropping up. It could be helpful to be able to point to the fact that we commissioned a private inquiry to supplement the police investigation. As you may be aware, the best way to handle potential negative publicity is to be on top of the issue right from the start, controlling the narrative."

"Controlling the narrative?" Merritt asked innocently, as if she'd never heard the phrase before.

By now I knew her methods well enough that I could appreciate her strategy in this case. It was rather elegant. She was offering an alpha male the time-honored masculine role of explainer in chief.

He assumed it with pleasure. "Getting ahead of the story to disarm the rumor mill," he said with a condescending smile. "You see, Mrs. Merritt, we could lose a lot of business if word started to spread that there'd been a murder at the resort. I know that sounds crass, to be thinking of PR at a time like this, but it's one of the things you've got to do when you're running a hospitality business. In hospitality, ratings and reviews are everything. A mouse under a bed or one broken showerhead or burned-out lightbulb will cost you bookings. Imagine the damage a whiff of murder would do. The loss would be incalculable. We'd be under a dark cloud for seasons to come. I don't doubt that we'd even lose some of our regulars, families who've been summering with us for years, for generations, whose trust and loyalty we've earned by consistently maintaining the highest standards. Too many people seem to think that the Wild Goose Resort has been around so long that it can't go under, but they're wrong. We're as vulnerable as any other business to fluctuations in the marketplace, to fads and changing consumer preferences. Our bottom line is affected by the weather, for god's sake. We simply couldn't survive a rumor of that kind."

"You seem very confident in the police's verdict."

"You're not really suggesting there *was* a murder, are you?" He chuckled gently, as if we were all in on the same joke—as if Merritt and I had stopped by just for the laughs.

Merritt ignored the question. "What can you tell me about your stepmother? What kind of a relationship did you have?"

He sighed from somewhere deep inside himself. "Well, she was a stepmother, wasn't she? My own mother died when I was eight, and Dad married Vicki a year later. A lot of people thought it was too fast; I know I did. I resented her. Kids do. I missed my real mother, and I didn't want a replacement that wasn't nearly as good as the original. My mom was soft-spoken, kind, nurturing. She didn't make a big deal out of herself, stayed in the background, which I think suited Dad well, as he was always so public and dominant. Vicki was . . . well, she was Vicki—always onstage, it seemed. Even when the show was over and the lights were dimmed, she still seemed to be wanting to prove herself. Most folks thought she was wonderful; I always thought she was trying too hard. It's exhausting to be around people who are that insecure."

A shadow of sadness passed across his face, and he went on at a slower pace. "I think in the end I recognized that she was basically a good person who was doing her best, and I was able to respect her for that. I'll always be grateful for the way she assumed the burden of caring for two children who weren't her own. My sister Lauren would disagree, but Vicki was a warm and generous stepmother to us. I admit that as an adult I kept my distance to some degree. She drove me crazy with her opinions on every subject you can imagine, from eating insects to space travel."

"Space travel?"

"The next frontier in the hospitality biz. She wanted to beat Marriott to Mars." He rolled his eyes. "About an hour in her company was all I could take."

"Did you get together often?"

"With my kids, yes. We visited about once a week, usually after church on Sunday. I wanted them to have a connection with her. She adored them, spoiled them like crazy. They loved going to Nana's house."

Duty call was the term Pat Tucci had used.

"What's going to happen to the family business now that she's gone?"

"It's going to be a thorny mess for a while; transitions always are. But in the end things will be settled according to my late father's wishes. All four of us kids have equal shares in the company, and that won't change. I'll continue running Kingfisher, as I have for the last ten years, and I'll take a more active role in the management of Wild Goose. Whether my brother will stay on there is yet to be determined."

"Who makes that decision?"

"I do." He made the fact sound like an immovable concrete block.

"When I spoke to him this morning I was struck by how much he loves his job. Why wouldn't you want him to stay on?"

Neil fiddled with a pen, buying himself time. "We've got there already, have we? All right. I'll give it to you straight, Mrs. Merritt. The Wild Goose Resort is on the road to bankruptcy—not from lack of business, mind you, but from simple mismanagement. When my father died, he left Kingfisher in my stepmother's hands, and she very wisely put me in charge. But she insisted on managing Wild Goose herself. The club had always been her love, and she had a lot of ideas about how to improve it. Unfortunately, she was a terrible businesswoman. She eventually brought Scott on to help her, but that just made things worse. Let's just say my brother has his problems."

"Drugs, you mean."

"Yes, drugs. Cocaine. A long-standing habit. It's a miracle he's still alive."

"I've heard he's clean now." I was surprised to hear Merritt say that. She'd given such short shrift to the pool gossip I'd relayed.

Neil snorted. "Is he? Really? This isn't the first time I've heard that story. He always had a knack for cleaning himself up when he needed his mother to pay off his debts. Then he went right back to using. If he's truly clean now, good for him, but I'm not holding my breath. If history is precedent, it won't last."

"Did you and your stepmother discuss the resort's finances?"

"God yes, many times. I begged her to fire Scott and find someone with actual managerial skills. There are some very qualified people out there who could have turned the place around in a year or two and put it on sound financial footing."

"How would they do that?"

"Stop all the extravagances, for one thing. The fresh towels in every cabana, heaping bowls of fruit at every breakfast bar . . . Wild Goose throws out twice as much fresh fruit and vegetables as it consumes. And that's just the tip of the iceberg when it comes to waste. But there was no talking to her. She'd just say, *But we've always put fresh towels in the cabanas! We've always held a sunset ice-cream social on the lawn! We've always offered flower-arranging seminars for free!* Well, I would say to her, what would be the harm in charging for them? If they don't pay for themselves, get rid of them. She'd react like I was spouting heresy. My stepmother lived in la-la land, Mrs. Merritt. I blame it on my father, frankly. He indulged her pipe dreams, because as long as he was around, she couldn't do any actual harm. Then he died, and she gave herself carte blanche to do all the things she'd talked to him about. And she indulged Scott, who is just as impractical as she was, only worse, because he's an addict, who has probably had his hand in the till all along, in addition to being incompetent. Together they made a poisonous feedback loop, and Wild Goose was paying for it with its life."

"How did she react to the idea of firing Scott?"

"At first she flatly refused, but lately she'd been coming around. The last time we talked, she shared that she was seriously considering letting him go. She sent a text the night she died. . . . Maybe you heard about it."

"Yes. She invited you kids to lunch, said she had something important to tell you."

"That's right. When I saw that text—this was before I knew she was gone—my first reaction was hell yes, she finally did it."

"You thought she was bringing the family together to announce a change in management at the resort."

"Exactly. But now I'll never know."

Merritt and I exchanged glances. Either wittingly or not, Neil had just given his hated stepbrother a motive for murder.

"I'm asking everyone to walk us through the night of the birthday party," Merritt said, "from the time they arrived to the time they left the Lodge. Anything they saw, heard, or otherwise noticed, especially regarding your stepmother. Would you mind?"

"Sure, no problem. I've got an online meeting in a few minutes, though, so I'm going to have to wrap this up pretty quickly after that." He laid the pen on his blotter. "I arrived with my wife and our two boys at around six. The boys had brought Nana presents. Colby, who's ten, gave her a wooden boat he'd built from a kit, and Caleb, who's six, gave her a pine cone he'd painted and decorated with glitter. We encourage crafts at our house—anything to get the kids doing things, instead of being passive in front of a screen. So, the boys left their presents with Robin, my stepmother's assistant, and ran directly to the Kids' Klub to see their friends. Allison and I went in to the party." He threw up his hands, a gesture halfway between irritation and helplessness. "I don't know how much detail you want me to go into. The night was typical. Cocktails, dinner, a little dancing. We were ready to leave by nine o'clock. The kids were antsy by then, and we always try to get them into bed at a reasonable hour. We live outside Burlington, and we were home at about nine thirty, I'd say."

"Did you go out again that evening?"

"No. Why would I? I'm an early-to-bed kind of guy, and frankly, I find parties tiring." Narrowing his eyes, he said, "If you want corroboration, you can ask my wife."

Merritt offered him a mordant smile. "Is she a heavy sleeper, Mr. Summersworth?"

"Oh, for god's sake."

"Think back. Did you notice anything unusual at the party? Anything at all, even something small."

"Unusual? Let me think. No, nothing unusual. One of the servers dropped a platter, which made a mini crisis in the kitchen. Had to be cleaned up, the meals replated. There was a kid hanging around, a teenager. I was passing through the foyer on my way back from the bathroom and saw him standing there by himself, looking awkward. He was wearing jeans and a hoodie, so I knew he wasn't there for the party. I figured he was a son of one of the guest families and had wandered in by mistake. I told him this was a private party and asked him to leave, and he did."

"Did he say anything?"

"Not a word. Just left like I asked him to. Seemed like a nice kid."

I rolled my eyes. It's interesting the way adults approve of kids who keep their mouths shut and do what they're told.

"Had you seen him before?"

"No. But I'm barely at the club these days."

"How would you describe him?"

"Tall, thin. Lanky. Yeah, that's the right word: *lanky*. Dressed exactly like every other teenage boy I see around town. Only things missing were the earbuds."

"What about his face?"

Neil shrugged. "A normal face, I guess. Honestly, I didn't look that hard."

"Does that happen often? People wandering in to private functions?"

"Happens all the time. Guests are used to the Lodge being open, and it is, of course, twenty-four seven. But when there's a private party in the function hall, that section of the Lodge is closed. We put up signs, but people ignore signs—that's a fact of human behavior you're well aware of when you work in hospitality—so people wander in accidentally. Teenagers are the worst. They come in on purpose, I think, to see if they can filch a few beers." He glanced at his smartwatch. "If you don't mind, I've got to wrap this up now."

Merritt didn't move. "One more question, Mr. Summersworth. Do you know a Stephen Hobbs? Your stepmother had his business card in her purse the night she died. I assume she was given it at the party."

"Stephen Hobbs? Never heard of the guy. I wouldn't put too much stock in it, though. Vicki was forever collecting business cards."

"He's a local CPA. Any idea why she would be interested in someone like that?"

"None whatsoever." He hesitated, and his eyes slid down to the right. He was remembering something. "Well, maybe . . . At one point I did suggest that she hire her own accountant. I was half joking, but maybe she took me up on the idea."

"Why did you think she needed her own accountant?"

"She kept insisting that she didn't trust the numbers I was giving her about the resort—which was exactly the kind of thing she *would* say. Deny, distract, stonewall, shift the blame—Vicki would do anything before she'd face the truth. I got to the point where I was willing to say anything to get her to understand and accept the dire financial straits the resort was in, so in a heated moment I told her that if she didn't believe Art's numbers, she ought to get a second opinion. Said she could ask Art to turn over the resort's financial records and she could damn well have her own accountant check the math."

"Art? Who's Art?"

"Arthur Doyle, our CFO. He's been with Kingfisher since the beginning. He was originally a friend of my mother's, and he became a close friend of my father's after my parents got married. He was a constant presence in our family. He's Lauren's godfather, in fact. He's older now, of course—early eighties. He's had a couple of medical issues to deal with lately and is planning to retire at the end of the year, but he's as sharp as ever, and has a good staff under him. There's no way he made a mistake."

His smartwatch was vibrating softly. He tapped the screen to stop it. "Time's up, ladies. My meeting's about to start."

Merritt and I thanked him and filed out of his office. When we were alone in the elevator, I muttered, "Too bad Victoria died before she had a chance to check those numbers."

"Schedule an appointment with Stephen Hobbs right away," Merritt said.

CHAPTER 20

Robbery!

I was right. There *was* a robbery!" Haley's excited voice came through the speakerphone. "A thief was in her bedroom stealing her jewelry the night she died!"

"Slow down, and start at the beginning," Merritt said. "You're on speakerphone, by the way. Olivia is here with me. We just met with your brother Neil, and we're on our way back to the resort."

"Oh my god, where do I start? I'm absolutely frantic right now. The funeral was delayed by the police investigation, and Mom's cousin wanting to fly in from Seattle, and now, suddenly, it's tomorrow and no one has done anything to prepare for it. The four of us should have sat down days ago and talked it out, come up with something really nice—music and eulogies and whatnot—but naturally that didn't happen, so the pastor called me with some questions. He'd called Neil first, apparently, and Neil palmed him off onto Lauren, and Lauren said I was in charge of the funeral and pushed him over to me—thank you, Neil and Lauren, and fuck you both—so now I'm stuck with it. I tried to get Robin Tucci to help me, but she's up a mountain somewhere, and her mom started yelling at me for no reason, said Robin damn well better be in the Queen's will, and from now on the Summersworth family can damn well take care of itself." Haley took a breath. "Honestly, I have no idea why she needed to be so bitter. I mean, I barely know the woman."

Merritt and I exchanged worried looks. Haley's emotional state was alarming, but who could blame her? Planning a funeral was enough to stress anyone out. Only, what did funeral arrangements and Pat Tucci have to do with missing jewelry?

"Tell me about the robbery," Merritt said.

In many more words than were needed, the story came out: Haley had gone to the Bungalow to get the lovely oil portrait of her mother that was hanging on the wall in the den. It had been painted when Victoria was in her early fifties—she looked like a mature woman, obviously, but she wasn't so old that you couldn't see how beautiful she'd once been. Haley intended to prop the framed painting on an easel near the altar, where everyone could see it during the funeral service and be reminded of the very special person whose body was inside the casket. She was certain that her mother would absolutely adore this idea. (I imagined a delighted Victoria in heaven, clapping little white hands.)

Once in the house, though, Haley had become distracted and ended up poking around in her mother's jewelry box, only to notice that her mother's favorite piece of jewelry was missing. It was a jade necklace that Victoria had received from Warren as a wedding present; it had been in his family for generations. Haley had no idea how valuable it was; she knew only that it was beautiful and unique, and the fact that someone had taken it—just that necklace, and nothing else, as far as she could tell—was an absolute tragedy.

"Obviously the robber knew what he was looking for," Haley said breathlessly. "Mom was wearing it at the party, and he must have seen it on her. It's a really gorgeous piece, a gold chain studded with jade beads and with a heavy jade pendant carved in the shape of a hummingbird. Mom loved that necklace, always wore it for special occasions, and she always kept it in the exact same place—in the bottom compartment of her jewelry box."

"You need to call Detective Clemmons to report the theft. He can put an alert out to pawnshops. But I wouldn't hold out too much hope that you'll get it back," Merritt said.

"Oh, I'm not expecting that. I'm sure whoever stole it has got it tucked away and is keeping a low profile. I just wanted to let you know right away. This changes your investigation a lot, I imagine. Doesn't it?"

"It adds a dimension, I'd say. But keep in mind that the theft didn't necessarily occur the night your mother died. Her house has been unoccupied for ten days at this point, and it is notoriously easy to enter. Anyone who knew about her death would realize they had a golden opportunity."

"But why would someone steal only that necklace? It has to be because they saw it on her at the party and figured it must be very valuable—which it well may be, for all anyone knows. So they broke into the house in the middle of the night, thinking she'd be asleep. Only she woke up and confronted them, maybe tried to call the cops—who knows?—and she was killed. That has to be what happened, don't you agree? It just makes too much sense."

"It's a plausible hypothesis, Ms. Summersworth. Thank you for letting me know. By the way, I'm still waiting for the guest list and party photos."

"I've got them," Haley said. "I can't leave the café right this minute, but I'll drop them off at the resort as soon as I get out of here."

When the call ended, I blurted, "Haley's right. This does change everything. If the robbery happened the night Victoria died, it makes it much more likely that she was murdered—most likely by someone who knew about that necklace and wanted it very badly. A party guest, probably."

"Or a staff member," Merritt added. "Staff are responsible for the vast majority of thefts at resorts and hotels. Haley mentioned this herself. When we see Detective Clemmons next, remind me to mention Pia Valente. She was alone in the house for several hours the morning the body was discovered, long enough to poke through the jewelry box."

"Pia?" I said with some surprise. "She struck me as exactly the kind of person who *wouldn't* steal from her employer."

"You've got to stop trying to protect people just because you like them, Blunt."

Was that what I was doing? I didn't think so. "Well, whatever way you cut it, the number of potential suspects just ballooned."

"I'm not so sure. This is only the second day of the investigation, and we've already made excellent progress, more than I think you realize. I expect the net to start tightening soon. Tomorrow, possibly. At the funeral. I strongly suspect that the murderer will be there."

"So you've determined that Victoria *was* murdered?"

"I'm almost certain of it."

I was mystified by this assertion, which I saw no basis for. As far as I was concerned, we hadn't come close to resolving that question. "I must have missed something. Care to share your reasoning?"

"Wouldn't you rather figure it out for yourself, Detective Blunt?" There was an unpleasant teasing in her voice; she was mocking me for my ambition.

"Sure. I'd like that very much," I said gamely. "But right now I have no idea who could have murdered Victoria Summersworth, and I really don't see how you would know either. Monty? Scott? Pia? Robin? How about Pat Tucci?" I threw out the name offhandedly. "She's the only person so far who had a grudge against Queen Victoria, as she called her. But if Pat killed her, she probably wouldn't have admitted to hating her so much."

"You left out Neil Summersworth and Lauren Perry." Merritt seemed pleased by my omissions.

I groaned, and in a surly voice that did me no credit I said, "Are you sure you're not just indulging your own ambition? You *want* there to be a murder so you can have the pleasure of solving it!"

Merritt responded with a faint smile that could have meant anything.

CHAPTER 21

Beach Party

I dropped Merritt off at the Lodge, left Horace in the parking lot, and strolled back to the staff dormitory. It was a beautiful, balmy evening, smelling of lake water and newly mown grass, but alas, it was not mine to enjoy. I had work to do. When I got to my room, I grabbed a Diet Coke out of the mini fridge, split open a bag of salt-and-vinegar potato chips, opened my laptop, and began slogging through the various tasks I'd been assigned.

1. The Wild Goose Resort's financial issues. Neil had given us a general description this afternoon, when he'd laid the charge of overspending against his brother. Merritt had requested a more detailed picture, but I had no idea how to get it. That kind of information wasn't exactly hanging like ripe fruit to be plucked from the branches of the internet. I wondered now whether I hadn't oversold my fact-checking skills during my interview.

2. Stephen Hobbs, CPA, whose business card I'd found in Victoria's satin clutch. He was a partner at a forensic accounting firm in Burlington. I checked his professional bio and social media and got the usual background, which was nothing special. He was fifty-ish and round, with a half-bald egg-shaped head. He'd lived in the Burlington area all his life, enjoyed fishing and folk music, was married to a woman named Evie, and had three children, whose names all began with *M*. I called his office to set up an interview, but it was after six and the place was closed. I made a note to call again in the morning.

3. Victoria's laptop. I'd already started wading through it last night, using her dead dachshund's name as a password. I gave it another hour. It was slow going and mostly uninteresting.

4. Her medical files. I got her Keychain password off a document cleverly marked *pswds* (why do people do this?), so I was able to get into her MyHealth account on her health network. I found no mental or physical illness beyond the high blood pressure and high cholesterol we already knew about. No record of an appointment at the local hospital on the afternoon of her party, so maybe she'd been visiting someone.

5. CCTV footage from the Meadow Gate apartments. Luckily, Detective Clemmons was still on duty when I called the police station. He agreed to get the film ASAP. Merritt's promise of shared credit must have done its work, because he seemed eager to help.

Now there was nothing left to do but head over to the Bungalow and raid the deceased woman's office. I dreaded it—not only because it meant spending another couple of hours wading through paperwork without a clear idea of what I was looking for, and because I didn't want to be in a dead (almost certainly murdered, according to Merritt) woman's house by myself, but also because it was still bright and beautiful outside. The sunlight was truly, actually golden, and the bracing scent of pine was drifting through my open patio door.

If Trevor were here, we would go for an evening swim or take a nice walk through the forest. He hadn't returned my call last night, which was vaguely worrying. He'd called this morning while Merritt and I had been interviewing Scott Summersworth, and I'd forgotten to call him back. We hadn't spoken to each other in almost thirty-six hours, which was unusual for us. I missed him, wanted to share with him everything that was happening in the investigation and hear how his rehearsals were going. I tried calling again, but his phone was off.

I thought about the lovely secluded beach I'd stumbled upon yesterday morning, how the cliff had given way to a serene blue inlet where willow trees went right down to the shore and dipped their leafy branches into the water. I had a sudden hankering to be there, soaking up nature's beauty, instead of in this stuffy old room with rickety furniture and a pilled bedspread. *All work and no play makes Jack a dull boy.* I could certainly relate to that feeling. Olivia would be a dull girl if all she did was root around in dead people's files digging up dry facts.

I retraced the wrong turns I'd made yesterday. As I got closer to the beach I heard a low, rhythmic thumping—bass turned up too loud, so that the melody of whatever was playing was all but lost. A party, obviously. I almost turned around, but I was curious.

The beach was quite busy. There were about twenty people there, all my age or younger, and many were wearing the staff uniform of navy pants and white polo shirt. There was a bonfire, with hamburgers and hot dogs being roasted over the open fire, and there were a couple of big coolers of drinks.

There was no reason why I should recognize anyone, but out of habit I scanned the crowd for a familiar face. Not seeing anyone I knew, I turned and headed back the way I'd come, but then a voice accosted me. "Wait. Don't go."

There was soft thudding behind me, bare feet on sand, and then I was face-to-face with the good-looking guy who'd driven me in a golf cart to the dormitory yesterday.

"You're not leaving, are you?" He was panting from his dash to intercept me.

"Yeah, I am. I just came here to chill for a bit. I didn't know there'd be a party."

"We do this from six to nine every Wednesday. Just our way of letting off steam."

It seemed that everything at the Wild Goose Resort had a date and time attached. Flower arranging, Monday, one to three. Beginner's tennis, Tuesday, three to five.

"Management doesn't love it," he said, "but they turn their heads as long as we clean up afterward. And the guests don't know about this place. Except you, of course. How did you find your way here?"

I explained getting lost the day before.

He nodded solemnly, as if my answer impressed him somehow, though I didn't know why it should. "Now that you're here, why not stay awhile? Can I get you a beer?"

I didn't have a good reason to refuse. The atmosphere was nice. Everyone seemed happy, full of energy and high spirits. Even though there appeared to be some college-age kids there, I didn't see anyone throwing up, and the idea of hanging out with people close to my own age did appeal to me. "Sure," I said.

He told me his name was Greg and introduced me to more people than I'd ever be able to remember: kitchen workers; grounds workers; a couple of guys who repaired things like broken doors, bicycles, and golf carts; lifeguards; swimming and sailing instructors, etc. Because there weren't enough local workers to fill the seasonal jobs, the resort imported young people who were happy to get a not-bad paycheck, a room at the resort, cheap meals, and a chance to spend the summer months by Lake Champlain, carousing and having as much sex as possible in their spare time. I envied them their temporarily carefree lives. How different talking to them was from the dismal conversation I'd had with my boss that afternoon!

Still, my investigatory instinct was not asleep. After a sufficient period of friendliness had passed, I said, "Too bad about the owner of this place. I hear she committed suicide."

"Suicide? Nah. They just want us to think that. Actually, she was murdered," a shirtless guy with a lot of red chest hair said. He laughed very loudly afterward, which was jarring.

When his laughter subsided, I asked the hyena what his evidence was.

"There's no evidence," Greg said to me. "It's a conspiracy theory. Derrick here follows QAnon. Next he'll be saying she had a child sex ring in her basement."

"Hey, don't knock conspiracy theories if you haven't tried them. We were right about alien spaceships. The military finally admitted it," Derrick said.

"So there's no real evidence that she was murdered?" I was scraping the bottom of the barrel with this, but there was always a chance I'd find a drop of truth there.

"Actually, there is," Derrick said.

This prompted a chorus of skeptical hoots.

"Seriously, all kidding aside, I did hear something about the Russian Mafia. You know those creepy-looking fat Russian guys who come here every summer? The ones who always have sexy models on their arms? They've had their hooks in this place for years. Apparently the Summersworth family wasn't laundering their money properly, and boom—next thing you know, the owner's dead. Thrown off a balcony like an oligarch. That's how you know a Russian did it."

"Jesus, Derrick. You never stop, do you?" Greg said.

"That's just what I heard," Derrick said with a shrug. "I'm not saying it's true."

"Who did you hear it from?" I asked.

"I'm not going to say. I don't want to get anyone in trouble."

Greg leaned toward me and said sotto voce, "Derrick's a golf caddy," as if that explained everything. Which it sort of did.

Just then, another guy muscled into the conversation. He seemed overly pleased to see me. Perhaps all the employees of the Wild Goose Resort were trained in perpetual delight. "Ms. Blunt!"

I looked more closely. It was Jason, reservation specialist.

"You know who this is, don't you?" Jason asked the group. "This is Olivia Blunt, assistant to the famous private investigator Aubrey Merritt. They're here from New York City, looking into the mysterious death of Mrs. Summersworth. They think it was murder."

Greg turned to me with new respect. "No shit."

I shrugged. "We don't know it was murder. We're just checking it out."

"But that's what they think it is," Jason said, "or else they wouldn't be here. They're getting the total VIP treatment, by the way. Everything free."

People started clamoring to know what I knew, whether there were suspects, and if so, who they were. The whiff of murder had gotten everyone excited. I felt like a minor celebrity.

I didn't tell them anything, of course. Not that there was much to tell. I did, however, ask them to get in touch with me if they heard anything interesting, and they eagerly agreed.

By this time the sun was setting. I'd had a hot dog and two beers. When I stood up to leave, Greg put on his tennis shoes, then followed me to the path. "Where are you going?"

"I have work to do," I told him. I wanted to sound mysterious, but it might have come off as prim.

"Like what?"

"I have to go to Mrs. Summersworth's house to do some investigating." There was no doubt about it now: I sounded totally pompous. But the rapt attention of so many people my age had gone to my head, and I couldn't resist extending my allure a bit.

"Really? That's cool," Greg said. "But you're going the wrong way."

"Am I?" I looked at the path snaking through the forest. It was the same one I'd come in on, wasn't it?

"You know how to get there?" Greg asked.

"Yeah, I think so. First I go to the Lodge, then cross the street, go a ways up a road, hang a left, and take that road to the end."

"Okay. But if you want to get there faster, you can take the Cliff Walk." He pointed in the opposite direction. "You pick it up over there."

I saw a path heading south into the woods. There was even a small sign that read CLIFF WALK.

"It will take you straight to the Bungalow. Save you fifteen minutes at least." Noticing my hesitation, he added, "It gets a little rocky the higher you go, but it's still light out. You'll be fine."

I looked at the trees and sky. Everything was a beautiful burnished gold, as if the earth were being briefly gilded before surrendering to dusk.

"I'll go with you if you want," he said helpfully.

He seemed like a nice person, and he was, of course, very good-looking. I was tempted to let him come with me, but I also felt that I shouldn't, precisely *because* he was so attractive and seemed so nice.

"No, thanks. I'll be fine," I said.

"Hey, if you're not doing anything later, maybe we could grab a beer or something?"

"Oh, thanks. But I'm busy tonight. Like I said, I have work to do."

"Tomorrow?"

"I'm busy tomorrow too."

"Yeah. I guess you must be working pretty hard on this case, right?" He shuffled his feet. "Any free time this weekend?"

"No. Sorry. I'm busy every day." It didn't seem fair to leave it at that, so I blurted, "I'm more than busy, actually. I'm engaged." He looked confused, so I added, "To be married. Engaged to be married."

He blushed slightly, but quickly rallied. "Oh wow. That's really great. Congratulations on that. So, um, I guess I'll just say: enjoy your stay at the resort!"

"I will, and . . . thanks for asking." I said good-bye and hurried off toward the Cliff Walk.

The trail rose through a forest of pine trees, getting rockier as it went. Eventually the cliff face on my right blocked the rays of the setting sun, plunging the path into shadow. I picked my way along in the gloom, pebbles and loose gravel skidding under my smooth-soled sneakers. I would have to return on the road, I thought, as the Cliff Walk would be unsafe in the dark.

Pausing on a granite ledge, I looked out over the lake through a break in the trees. It was deep blue and seemed to go on forever. A large bird was coasting over its surface, barely flapping its wings, riding an updraft with ease. Was it an eagle? I ought to know that much, at least, the bald eagle being the official bird of the United States. Whatever it was, it had a majesty and grace I knew I wouldn't soon forget.

As the trail climbed higher, the forest fell away, revealing a sheer drop to the jagged boulders below. There were no waves to speak of, no crashing surf, as there would have been at the ocean. The lake was a much quieter body of water. You could almost forget it was there, which was ominous in its own way. The trail continued to rise, making a hairpin turn to traverse the rock face, finally dumping me onto a flat grassy area at the top of the cliff, where the last of the sunset warmed my face like a soft farewell kiss.

I walked along, and soon I came upon Pat and Robin Tucci's weathered bench. A cigarette butt was ground into the packed dirt at its base. I imagined Pat Tucci sneaking a smoke out here all by herself, taking in the gorgeous view as she boldly waited for death to find her.

A chill came over me, and I had a sudden, intense yearning, almost a physical need, to talk to Trevor. I checked my cell phone. Coverage was strong up here where the Tucci and Summersworth homes were located. I sat down on the bench and pressed his number.

He picked up right away, and said in a rush, "Hey there. Where the hell have you been?"

"I called you last night. You didn't return my call."

"You should try checking your voicemail once in a while, Olly."

"Oh, sorry. Anyway. Here we are now."

"It's nice to hear your voice."

"It's nice to hear yours too." I wanted to say more than that, something deeper, but I couldn't find my way to it.

"So, how's the crime fighting going?" he asked.

"I'm not optimistic," I said. "Turns out there was a robbery, which may or may not complicate things, depending on when it happened. And there's no way to know, so what difference does it make? The funeral is tomorrow. Merritt is convinced the deceased woman was murdered and that the murderer will be there. I don't see why they would be. If you murdered someone, would you go to their funeral? I certainly wouldn't."

"You sound upset. What's going on?"

"I'm not upset. What makes you think I'm upset?"

"I don't know. You just sound kind of negative, like something's bothering you."

I fell quiet. On the path the whole way up, I'd been thinking about the conversation with Greg and about the big step of marriage, specifically the vow of fidelity. Trevor and I had always been exclusive, which had seemed like the easiest, most natural thing in the world. From the minute we got engaged, though, every aspect of our relationship had begun to feel a little different—weightier, riskier, more consequential. Unsettling thoughts—doubts, you could call them—had occasionally crept over me. *Marriage jitters*, a friend had rather blithely explained, but it hadn't helped me to know that premarriage anxiety was common. And now my brief interaction with Greg had dragged the issue of exclusivity into fresh, harsh focus. I knew that not too many months from now, Trevor and I would stand before 117 witnesses (that was the latest guest count) and solemnly vow to be faithful to each other *for the rest of our lives*—which meant that I would be promising to say no to every guy who asked me out ever again, even the attractive ones like Greg, who in another life I might have enjoyed getting to know.

Was I capable of doing that? Did I want to? Suddenly I wasn't so sure.

My long silence caused Trevor to say, "Out with it, Olivia. What's on your mind?"

"Have you ever thought about . . ." I wasn't sure how to finish the question, so I started over from a different place. "You work with a lot of attractive women, right?"

"Yeah, I'd say so."

"Do you ever feel attracted to them?"

"Well, sure."

"A lot?"

"Um, I wouldn't say *a lot*."

"Have you ever wanted to go out with one of them?"

"Olivia, what's going on?"

"I was just thinking . . . when we're married, are you okay with being faithful? Forever?"

"We talked about this before, didn't we?"

"That's not an answer."

"But we did discuss it, Olly. We really did."

"Okay, but I need to talk about it again."

He sighed.

"Trevor?"

"All right, I think I know what's going on. You met some guy. He probably has big muscles and a great tan, unlike me. You kind of want to sleep with him, and you're wondering if you should."

"I didn't say that."

"No, but you're wondering."

"I guess so. But not sleep with him. Just, like, have a beer."

"Which might lead to . . ."

"Possibly."

There was silence on the other end of the phone line. Then: "Are you going to do it?"

"Of course not!" The question startled me, even though it was reasonable, given what had gone before. "I was just thinking about marriage, Trevor, about being faithful forever. It's a lot to promise, a lot to give up, don't you think?"

"You want an open marriage?"

"Are you kidding? No way!"

"So what's the problem?"

"I just think we ought to be really clear about what we're agreeing to—the vows and everything. Really think about them, and be sure of them. At least, as sure as we can be."

Several seconds passed. Then: "I'm sure. Are you?"

As I searched for what was truest in my heart, my jitters dissolved. "Yeah. I'm sure too."

"Then good for us," he said, his voice warmer and more relaxed.

"Yes, good for us," I said happily. "Isn't this amazing, Trevor? We're doing something really big, you know. Really big."

"I can't think of anyone I'd rather do it with."

"Well, that's sort of the point, isn't it? Because if there *were* someone else—"

"Olly. You're going in circles now."

I smiled. That was Trevor—always clear and sensible, always with both feet on the ground. I felt lucky to be marrying him. Blessed. "You know, I was thinking, if we're still here on Saturday, I could probably get Merritt to give me the afternoon off so I could drive back to New York and go to your opening. It's only a six-hour drive. If I left at noon—"

"Olivia, listen. I said it was okay, and it really is. This is your first investigation, and you need to learn a lot and make a good impression. You'll have plenty of opportunities to see the play."

"Okay, if you're sure . . ."

"I am. There is one thing, though. Did you call my mother?"

"Oh god. I'm sorry. I forgot."

"Do it as soon as you can. It's no big deal, just something about flowers. It would mean a lot to her."

"I'll call her tomorrow," I said firmly, fully intending to keep my promise.

CHAPTER 22

Good Grief

I saw the steeply pitched roof of the Bungalow rising above the treetops and proceeded along a narrow path of packed dirt, brushing overhanging vines and branches out of my face as I went, until I suddenly came out to a sheer, dizzying drop. I stopped short, teetered on the edge of the cliff. The lake lay far below, huge boulders visible under the clear water. The breeze felt stiff and cold in my face. My heart pounded as I retraced my steps along the trail. I needed to be more careful. Either I'd missed the turnoff to the Bungalow or there wasn't one. I kept a close watch and soon spied a definite thinning in the underbrush. I picked my way through it, keeping an eye out for potential hazards.

Sure enough, a skinny path led to the residence. Four or five rough wooden steps on the side of the house brought me up to the deck where Victoria Summersworth had spent the last moments of her life. Everything on the deck looked just as it had when I'd been here with Merritt yesterday. There were the large propane grill, the chairs around the outdoor table, the spa chaises in a row. My eye rose to the floodlight over the sliding door. I thought I saw it flicker in the gray dusk, and my heart started pounding crazily once again.

I clearly remembered using the inside switch to shut the fixture off. Had someone turned it on? I squeezed my eyes, opened them slowly, and looked again. The light was off and remained that way. I stared a few seconds longer, just to be sure.

I was not a suspicious person. I didn't believe in ghosts. Nevertheless, I found myself wondering if Victoria's spirit had been trying to communicate with me. Was she hovering nearby at this moment, gently urging me on? Or was she drifting about restlessly, in a foul mood, waiting for her killer to be found and brought to justice so she could be released from this earth for good? Under my breath I whispered, *Sit tight, Mrs. Summersworth. We're working on it.*

Feeling like a burglar myself, I slid the heavy glass door open and slipped into the house. The place was dark except for a low light burning in the front hallway. The stale air bristled with the odors of floral decay and untimely death.

I switched on a table lamp and the room sprang to ordinary life, the cranberry couches and all the floral pillows lending it that sweet, soporific old-lady aspect. *Don't be afraid,* I told myself. *Even if Victoria's ghost really is gliding invisibly nearby, if she bothers you at all it will most likely be to help.*

I made my way down the hall. My courage lapsed as I passed the basement door, which for some reason was not completely closed. What if some rando crazy guy had entered the unoccupied home and was lurking down there? Or the killer himself?

I turned into the office/den at the front of the house. It was dark green and book lined and thickly carpeted in earth tones. It looked like so many other interiors at the resort—nice and unobjectionable, as if the designer had consulted a mainstream magazine for a nanosecond and simply copied the ideas in it.

I had settled myself at the desk and started pulling out drawers when, dimly, I heard what sounded like a moan. I froze, sucked in my breath. It came again. I listened hard. Now it sounded like an animal in pain. A trapped raccoon? A second later I was able to identify it conclusively. It was a human being, crying. A woman. I nearly passed out. It was Victoria's ghost!

Stop it, I scolded myself. *That can't possibly be true. And in case you decide to do your job and investigate, it's coming from the second floor.* The functioning adult in me left the den, marched resolutely to the foot of the stairs, and called up in a loud, assertive voice, "Who's there?"

The sound stopped abruptly.

"Are you all right?" A dumb question, as she clearly wasn't.

Silence. Whoever it was didn't want to talk. But I couldn't very well leave her alone when I knew she was in distress.

"I'm coming up," I called out. Fair warning seemed in order.

"Don't bother. I'm fine!" came the testy retort.

"Obviously not," I replied. The crier's curt response gave me added incentive to mount the stairs and stride down the hall to the doorway of Victoria's bedroom, where a light was shining.

Robin Tucci was sitting cross-legged in the middle of the king-sized bed. She was surrounded by silk scarves, dozens of them, a medley of brilliant colors and patterns. One of the scarves was draped between her hands, which she held like bookends in front of her face. I saw that a drawer had been pulled out of the dresser and lay overturned on the end of the bed.

The look on her face was strange and complicated, a cross between agonized and angry. "What are you doing here?" she barked.

"I might ask you the same thing."

She dropped the scarf and scooched toward me until she was perched on the edge of the bed, bare feet flat on the floor. Her Roman gladiator sandals lay nearby. "I'm grieving."

"You were crying."

"So? That's what people do when they grieve."

"Okay, I'll leave you alone, if that's all it is."

She raised her eyebrows.

"Sorry. I didn't mean it that way. I know it's a lot. Grieving, that is."

Robin gave me a fierce look and rose to her feet. For a split second I could see her mother in her—protective, aggressive, loyal, willing to go to the mat if she had to for the things she cared about. It crossed my mind that if she were a dog, she'd be a guard dog. A Rottweiler.

"I asked what you're doing here," she said in a menacing voice.

I thought it best to answer honestly, if vaguely. "I'm searching for clues that might shed some light on the manner of Mrs. Summersworth's death."

Robin looked disoriented for a second, as though I were speaking a foreign language that she had to mentally translate. Then she shook her head. "You're kidding, right?"

"No."

"Oh my god, wow. Now I've heard everything. You people. Who the hell do you think you are? Sherlock fucking Holmes? Why don't you go back where you came from and leave us all alone?"

"You seem upset." Lame remark number two.

"Of course I'm upset! My boss, and my best friend, is dead. Dead—do you understand? Dead!"

For a flash I thought she was referring to two people. Then I realized she was talking about Vicki. Vicki was her boss *and* her best friend—two roles in one.

"I'm sorry for your loss." I was on a roll with the lame remarks.

"All I wanted to do was come here and cry without anyone telling me to be quiet or trying to make me feel better. I wanted to *feel* it, you know? The grief. The pain. For once in my life I wanted to scream my head off because someone I cared about—someone I loved—is dead. But can I do that? Can I have that time to myself? No. Because *you* have to come along and ruin it. You, whoever you are. Good god. Your boss isn't even a real detective. She's a PI, for Christ's sake. I bet she spends most of her time spying on cheating spouses."

"That's not true. Merritt Investigation Agency doesn't handle marital-conflict issues. We have much more interesting cases to solve."

"Oh please. You're impostors, both of you, swaggering in here like big shots. You know full well that you can't find a killer where none exists. But you don't mind taking their money, do you? *Searching for clues.* Oh my god. You should be ashamed."

At this point I was pretty sure that any defense I made would only inflame her further. As it turned out, I didn't have to say anything, because she sank back onto the bed and started to cry again. It seemed that, once begun, her grief must and would pour out of her, whether she wanted it to or not.

Again, I was flummoxed. I could leave her alone, sobbing out her heartbreak; or I could stand there like a mannequin until she stopped crying long enough to yell at me some more; or I could react the way I wanted to, like a human being witnessing another human being's distress. I chose the latter, or rather, it chose me. Propelled by reactive empathy, I perched next to her on the bed. I stopped short of making lame remarks or opening my mouth at all. I just put my arm around her heaving shoulders. To my surprise she leaned into me, tucking her graying head against my chest, and proceeded to wail like a defenseless child to whom a terrible injustice had been done.

She eventually straightened up and patted her eyes. I grabbed a box of tissues off the nightstand and offered it to her. She plucked out a few tissues and used them to dry her eyes and blow her nose, still heaving and gulping as her emotion tapered off.

"I didn't want her to die," she murmured.

"Of course you didn't," I said tenderly.

"You don't understand. You don't get it at all."

She was right about that, but I didn't want to agree too readily. I waited quietly as the last of the sadness drained out of her, leaving her as limp as a rag doll, with splotchy skin and reddened eyes, the lashes still wet.

"Sorry," she whispered hoarsely, more in embarrassment than in remorse.

"Don't worry about it," I said.

"It's just . . . it's just . . ." She swept out her arm in a grand gesture that took in more than just the bedroom. "This was my life. Right here, in these rooms, in this house. And now it's over."

"So true," I said, and winced because, on second thought, that wasn't the right thing to say.

"But what's done is done." Her stiff, resolute tone indicated that she was going to man up and face reality.

I nodded in support of this.

Neither of us had said anything about the overturned drawer and all the bright, flimsy scarves scattered across the bed. They'd been bothering and/or intriguing me from the moment I first laid eyes on them, as scarves are often objects of sexual fetishes. At least that was an idea I'd picked up somewhere.

"Do you know anything about a missing necklace?" I asked.

"A missing necklace? This is the first I've heard of it."

"It's the one she was wearing the night she died."

"You mean the jade hummingbird?"

"Yeah, that's the one."

Robin crossed over to the dresser, opened an ornate jewelry box, and rummaged inside it, frowning. "It's not here. Pia must have taken it."

"Why Pia?"

"She knows the house, where things are kept. It's almost always staff," Robin informed me matter-of-factly. "They'll steal anything if they think they can get away with it."

Wanting to take the spotlight off the housekeeper, I shifted the conversation to another topic. "Do you feel like a cup of tea?"

Robin laughed, which I didn't expect. But the laugh had a ring of relief and pleasure in it. "Sure. Why not?"

We went downstairs to the kitchen and I filled the kettle with water.

She opened the refrigerator and took out two bottles of beer. "Wouldn't you rather have a beer?"

"Yeah, but are you sure it's okay?"

"It's not like there's anyone here to stop us. Besides, someone has to clear out the refrigerator before all the food goes to waste, and that person will probably end up being me—it's not like anyone else is going to do it—so you're just helping me out." She took a bottle opener out of a drawer, flipped off the tops of the two bottles expertly, and handed one bottle to me.

"To Vicki. May she rest in peace," Robin said, lifting her bottle.

"To Vicki," I seconded. *I probably shouldn't be drinking on the job*, I thought. Then I remembered that I'd had two beers at the beach party, so that train had already left the station.

Robin perched on a stool at the counter, and I leaned against the marble island. We talked about hiking and about the kind of wildlife you find in the woods. I satisfied my curiosity about bears. (Vermont has black bears, which aren't especially dangerous to humans. It's the brown ones you have to watch out for.) She asked me about my job and I explained a few general things—the kinds of issues PIs usually handle, etc.—without saying anything specific about the case Merritt and I were currently working on.

"You know you're wasting your time here, right?" she said after we'd talked for a while. "I mean, have you even figured out if it *was* a murder?"

I naturally chose not to pass on Merritt's strong suspicion that it was. I didn't understand it myself. Instead I explained that I was not at liberty to discuss the case.

She shook her head and said, "Pathetic." But she didn't sound as derisive as she'd been before.

After she left, I returned to the den and searched the deceased woman's papers for hours, dutifully jotting down dozens of miscellaneous facts. Not one was worth following up on, and I trekked back to the dormitory at midnight with dry eyes and a headache.

CHAPTER 23

RIP Victoria Summersworth

The day of Victoria Summersworth's funeral was warm and sunny, the air full of the drone of bees and that late-summer heaviness that speaks of ripening harvests and, appropriately, endings. I parked on a treelined street in north Burlington, and Merritt and I walked the short distance to the wrought iron gates of the Angel of Mercy Church. It was an old stone church with a bell tower that looked like it belonged in an out-of-the-way English village. The walkway consisted of slabs of slate similar to the grave markers that tilted at precarious angles in the tiny churchyard. I thought that there couldn't possibly be a more charming place to say a final farewell to a loved one, though it was also immediately clear that if Victoria Summersworth's position in society was what I'd been led to believe, the church wouldn't be big enough to accommodate her mourners.

We were twenty minutes early; Merritt had insisted on it. We walked up a few stone steps and stood in a shaded corner off to one side of the open arched doorway, where we could observe the mourners at close range as they entered the church.

It hadn't occurred to me back in New York City that I would be attending a funeral, and I'd packed nothing suitable. The dressiest outfit I'd been able to come up with was a white button-down shirt tucked into a pair of wide-leg beige linen pants. Needless to say, I felt self-conscious, especially as Merritt was wearing a gorgeous dress of charcoal gray silk, her arms bare, her wrists adorned with tinkling silver bracelets, her hair brushed back smoothly from her forehead. Draped loosely across her shoulders was a diaphanous dove gray shawl threaded with metallic strands of silver that picked up the sheen of her hair, and she wore dangling pearl drop earrings and pale pink lipstick.

Mourners began to trickle through the gates. Some clustered in small groups on the lawn, waiting until it was time to go into the church. I was surprised to discover that I could identify quite a few people: Pia Valente, looking not at all like a jewelry thief; the rather fearsome mother-daughter duo of Pat and Robin Tucci; ruddy-faced Monty Draper in a too-shiny suit; a procession of delightfully varied purple hats with ladies underneath them—among them Carla, the apparent leader, and Sandra, the gently scorned.

I recognized Stephen Hobbs from the photo on his company's website. Also an older white-haired gentleman whose picture I had seen on the Kingfisher website. This was Arthur Doyle, the moneyman of Kingfisher. Although just past eighty, and suffering from medical issues, according to Neil, he projected a vitality that younger men might envy. Indeed, the spark in his eye suggested that age-related cognitive decline was minimal. He must have felt my gaze on him, because at one point he glanced toward me sharply, and our eyes briefly met.

Neil Summersworth came through the gate a pace or two ahead of a woman I took to be his wife, a thick-waisted blonde with a boy on either side of her—Colby and Caleb, I surmised, both dressed in stiff navy suits, both looking awestruck and a little frightened.

Neil approached Arthur Doyle and clapped him on the shoulder. He moved in close for a word in the older man's ear, and the latter nodded vigorously.

Detective Clemmons lumbered up the steps in a roomy, well-worn black suit, his long face sagging, broad shoulders slumping in the heat.

"I assume Haley told you about the missing necklace," he murmured to Merritt, wiping his sweaty brow with a handkerchief.

Merritt nodded.

"It doesn't change anything as far as I'm concerned. If a thief murdered her in a robbery gone wrong, we would have seen signs of struggle in the house and defensive wounds on her body. My guess is that the thief entered the domicile unlawfully after she was deceased. I put my money on a staff member."

Of course, I thought. *It's practically been decided.*

"What about the CCTV footage from Monty Draper's apartment?" Merritt said.

"I checked it myself. Draper passed through the lobby at one fifty-two a.m., eight minutes before the estimated time of death. Looks like he's not your man, Mrs. Merritt." The detective stuffed his hands into his pockets.

Merritt and I exchanged skeptical glances. You didn't have to be a genius to know that Draper could have exited the building through a rear door after he crossed the lobby, then driven right back to the Bungalow, arriving in plenty of time to kill Victoria Summersworth— all while relying on the CCTV footage to support his innocence if questions were ever asked.

The footage posed another problem for the bridge champion as well. Draper had insisted that he left the Lodge at about eleven, and Scott Summersworth had confirmed that time. So where had he been during the more than two hours between the time he left the

Lodge and the time he arrived at the Meadow Gate apartment complex? Might he have paid a late-night visit to his beloved? If so, the black sedan Pat Tucci sighted at approximately one a.m. could indeed have been his—in which case he'd lied to us.

Merritt thanked Clemmons and adjusted her shawl. The gesture managed to eloquently convey dismissal, and the detective trudged past us into the church.

I'd been keeping an eye on the widening stream of mourners flowing through the doors. Now I nudged Merritt.

Lauren Perry walked past us. She gave no indication that she'd seen us, though it would have been hard for her not to. She was wearing a well-tailored black suit with black hose and heels, her blond hair coiled into a neat chignon at the nape of her neck. She was accompanied by a broad-shouldered man with a thick, scruffy beard—no doubt the farmer husband Pat Tucci had told us about—and the three little girls (Constance, Viveca, and Paulette), dressed in similar pink dresses, their hair in chignons like their mother's, although Paulette's had already partly fallen out. No stuffed pony this time.

Merritt and I were among the last to enter the church. The air was cooler inside, and the light was softer, more forgiving, as if the balm of heavenly solace was gently washing over us. We slipped into the last pew—I was relieved to find myself on the aisle, given my occasional episodes of claustrophobia—and for a few minutes we waited shoulder to shoulder with others of the packed assembly. Then a hush descended, the organ began a ponderous, plodding hymn, and the casket was carried in on the shoulders of six pallbearers, who set it gently on a trestle in front of the altar before disappearing through side exits.

Out of the corner of my eye I picked up a sudden motion. It was Scott Summersworth rushing past me down the center aisle. He wore a navy blazer over khakis (clean and pressed, at least) and a loosely knotted tie that telegraphed the message *I really don't want to be wearing this tie.* He scooched into the front row, causing a small commotion as his siblings and their families all shuffled down to make room for him. I noted the withering glare he received from Neil, and the anxious glance that came from Haley, who quickly replaced it with a relieved smile. Lauren stared straight ahead, unwilling to be affected. She seemed to exist in a self-enclosed bubble, and her three look-alike daughters, also staring straight ahead, seemed to be in bubbles too.

As the last reverberating chord of the hymn faded, the minister stepped up to the podium. He was a forty-something man with a clean-shaven face and a kindhearted voice that instantly soothed. He welcomed the congregation and acknowledged the sadness of Victoria Summersworth's passing, but also the joy of a life well lived. His wise words were so well-balanced and smoothly delivered that my attention slipped right off them. Within minutes my thoughts had turned to murder.

I scanned the parts of the church I could see from where I was positioned. People were crammed together tightly in the pews. The back area had filled up with latecomers. Warming up from the press of so many bodies, the air felt ever more close and cloying. My nose picked up drifting clouds of perfume and body odor. If Merritt was correct, the murderer was nearby.

Who was it? One of the four children? One of their spouses? The sullen assistant or her crotchety mother? The gold-digging boyfriend? A Purple Hat Lady? I wasn't ready to put my money on any one of them, and if Merritt had a favorite, she wasn't saying.

The thundering opening chords of another hymn jolted me out of my reverie. The congregation reached for hymnals and rustled pages until, by some weird telepathy, they all managed to arrive at the right page. They then proceeded to chirp, rasp, and warble through the verses with out-of-practice voices that were almost drowned out by the organ. Only one voice in the vicinity rose to meet the challenge. It was Merritt's. A strong, clear soprano, she bravely and beautifully sang Victoria Summersworth to her rest. Her time in St. Anne's children's choir had clearly not been wasted.

The service wrapped up later than it should have, with a folksy guitarist delicately quavering Don McLean's "Starry, Starry Night," about the death of Vincent van Gogh. *"I could have told you, Vincent, this world was never meant for one as beautiful as you."* I wondered about the song choice until I recalled that van Gogh had killed himself. This was the only part of the program that nodded to the fact that the deceased had allegedly committed suicide.

The Summersworths filed out of the church first, followed by the rest of the mourners, from successive pews from the front of the church to the back, until at long last Merritt and I, going with the sluggish flow, found ourselves spewed onto the lawn.

The family members were lined up near the gate, receiving condolences from those who cared to give them. Soon they would be whisked off to the cemetery, where the second part of the ceremony, the burial, would take place. I noticed Scott in particular. Jumpy and disheveled, he stood out from his more composed siblings. His eyes were so red that I thought he must have been crying, and my heart went out to him. Then he pulled a handkerchief out of his pocket and wiped his nose hastily, and I remembered what Neil had said: *If he's truly clean now, good for him, but I'm not holding my breath. . . . It won't last.*

The Purple Hat Ladies were congregated near Merritt and me, close enough that I could hear them discussing which cars would be taken to the cemetery and who would ride with whom. One of them piped up, "I don't know about you gals, but when this is over I'm going to need a frozen peach daiquiri."

"Vicki's favorite drink! What a wonderful idea," someone said.

"Absolutely. We'll get drunk as skunks in her honor," gravel-voiced Carla said.

And then came a softer voice—tentative, almost a whisper. "There he is, girls, the one I told you about. He's over there, under that tree. Do you see him? Wait. Don't all look at once!"

But they all did look at once.

"Where did you say he was? What tree?"

"Where? I don't see him!"

"Is that him? The stalker? You mean that kid over there?"

"For pity's sake, Sandra, he's just a teenager!"

I saw him too—the alleged stalker. He was tall and thin, with a mass of curly brown hair that blocked half his face. He was wearing a blazer with an embroidered patch in the shape of a coat of arms on the breast pocket. I vaguely recalled seeing a similar patch some-place, and I racked my brain trying to remember where it was. The answer flashed into my mind. It was in the photo album on Victoria Summersworth's coffee table, left there on the night she died. The teenager in that photo was wearing a graduation gown with a seal just like that one. Not the same teenager, obviously, but they did look alike—the same body type, which could be described only as . . . lanky.

The young man seemed to sense that he was being singled out. Shuffling nervously, he glanced over at the Purple Hat Ladies. A rather wild look came into his eye when he realized they were all staring back at him. Moving quickly to the gate, he pushed and shoved his way through a knot of people who were blocking it.

"Look! He's running away! See? Now do you believe me?" Sandra whispered loudly to her friends.

His hasty exit didn't necessarily suggest consciousness of guilt, in my opinion. The avid attention of a gang of postmenopausal women in purple hats would spook anyone.

Nevertheless, I turned to Merritt and said, "Have Haley take you to the cemetery. There's something I need to do." Before she could object, I was off after the teenager.

Whoever he was, he needed to explain himself.

CHAPTER 24

A Mother's Love

By the time I reached the sidewalk the alleged stalker was a block away, striding quickly in the direction of downtown. I jogged after him and called out, "Excuse me! Could I talk to you?"

He didn't stop or slow down; he didn't turn around to see who was calling. He broke into a run.

Now, that's *consciousness of guilt*, I thought.

I ran after him. We covered a few blocks at full tilt. Then he slowed down, glanced over his shoulder, realized that I was still following, and streaked ahead again.

"Hey! I just want to talk to you!" I called. That only made him run faster.

When he turned down a side street, I figured I'd lost him, but I arrived at the corner in time to see him making another turn. He appeared to be zigzagging through side streets, trying to shake me, which he would succeed in doing pretty soon. Rather than continuing to chase him, I decided on a different strategy. As he seemed to be headed downtown, I realized that if I just kept going straight along the main road, I might be able to close the gap between us. If

I couldn't cut him off, I could at least get to the pedestrian shopping area not long after he did.

My lungs were burning by the time I got there. I bent over, panting, hands on knees, cursing the dressy sandals I'd worn. When I caught my breath, I stood straight and scanned the crowd. The shopping area was full of couples, kids, singles, and a mad number of dogs. People were strolling, walking into and out of stores, drinking coffee, and eating ice-cream cones. A golden retriever was also eating an ice-cream cone someone had plopped onto a paper plate for him. But for all that commotion, there wasn't a single lanky teenager in a navy blazer anywhere.

There was, however, an aromatherapy shop called Green Mountain Magic. It was right next to me, in the northeast corner of the mall. Two stories, with a rainbow banner that said OPEN hanging over the door. Curtained windows on the second floor suggested a private residence; there was also a modern addition in the rear and a driveway on one side.

Aromatherapy. Someone had been talking about that recently, but I couldn't remember who it was or where I'd heard it. Yet I sensed that it was significant, that in some murky way it was connected with Victoria Summersworth. Having lost the mystery teen, and with my boss successfully pawned off on our client, I decided to go in.

A bell tinkled as I stepped across the threshold. The dense, musky smell of patchouli hit me right away. The store was smaller than I expected. It was actually just the front room of the residence. There was shelving on either side and, straight ahead, a glass counter with an empty stool behind it. Beyond that, a beaded doorway led to a darkened hallway and, presumably, the rest of the house.

I was the only customer, which made me uncomfortable, as I really had no intention of buying anything but was just following some inchoate investigatory whim. For form's sake, I glanced at some of the products on the shelves: essential-oil gift packs, a variety of diffusers, lots of soaps and lotions, lots of candles. I was just about to leave when I heard, "May I help you with something?"

The voice belonged to a fifty-something woman with a broad, fleshy face and wide hazel eyes. She was comfortably stout, dressed in a breezy multicolored caftan, and she had long, curly hair that was graying unevenly: the gray parts were rough and wiry, while the still-blond parts were smoother. It looked as if the battle of aging was happening on her head, and the good guys were losing.

"I've just come from a funeral," I said, "and I'm looking for something . . . ah, um . . ."

"A celebration of life," she supplied.

"That's it exactly," I said.

She pulled a heavy wooden tray out from under the counter and set it on the glass. "I like to create personalized blends for my customers, depending on their spiritual needs. Can I interest you in a custom oil?"

"Um, sure." I really wanted to ask how much custom oils cost, but I hesitated. My need to watch my spending always embarrassed me a little. As she removed five or six little glass vials from her case and set them on a suede mat, I decided that it would probably be okay to use the agency's credit card, as the purchase could conceivably be classed as a business expense.

Noises were coming from the living area on the other side of the doorway—a heavy bump, a metallic scrape. The beaded curtain shivered.

The woman looked up at me sadly, blinking her expressive eyes. "I can see that you're in terrible pain from your loss."

"Actually, I wasn't really personal friends with—"

She wagged her index finger at me. "That's not the loss I'm referring to. It's *your* loss I'm sensing. The funeral service brought that old pain back to you, stirred it up, and that pain led you here to find solace and healing."

"Oh. Okay." I took a moment to scan my psyche to see if she might be right, if there really was some ancient grief afoot, in need of an elixir, but all I could find was my usual psychic suffering, forced into temporary remission by intensive detective work.

"I know, I know. . . ." The woman clucked sympathetically. Behind her, a screen door squeaked open and slapped closed. "The world seems very dark right now. You feel alone and abandoned. But there is peace beyond the veil. Your loved one is resting in that sweet tranquility even as we speak."

As she was talking she'd been uncorking the glass vials. Now she brought out an empty one and removed its rubber stopper.

"I work intuitively," she explained, "so I never create the same therapeutic balm twice. In your case I have a clear urge to begin with energizing lemon verbena."

I found that a tiny bit insulting. Did I appear to be phlegmatic? Is that how the world saw me?

There was a motion outside the side window, a whoosh of movement on the driveway next to the house. I turned my head in time to see a young man on a bike, pedaling hard out of the driveway. Those thick dark curls were a giveaway. It was my mystery teen. He'd swapped the blazer for a sleeveless hoodie.

I turned to stare at the woman behind the counter. For a long moment I was silent. Then something clicked. Aromatherapy. A beaded curtain from the sixties. Robin Tucci's voice: *She just looked the other way for years, and eventually it ended.*

I said, "The funeral I just came from . . . it was for Victoria Summersworth. Everyone around here seems to have known her. Did you?"

She'd been putting a drop of oil into the vial with a pipette. Her hand paused in midair. "Excuse me?"

I repeated the question.

Slowly she laid the pipette on the counter. To her credit, she didn't equivocate. "Yes. I knew her."

"You didn't go to her funeral," I observed.

"It wasn't my place." She averted her eyes.

That was a strange answer. I wasn't sure how to follow up, so I said, "The kid who just left here, the one on the bike . . . I assume he's your son."

She nodded tentatively, unsure where I was headed.

"He was at the funeral."

"Was he?" She was pretending it was insignificant, but I saw anxiety on her face.

"He was wearing a navy blazer with some kind of emblem on it. Does he go to private school?"

"Yes, Morton Academy."

I looked around at the dingy walls and scuffed floor, at the faded colors of her caftan.

"He has a scholarship," she added, as if she'd guessed my question.

"Morton Academy . . ." A couple of puzzle pieces floated together and clicked into place. It would make sense if the young man in the photo album was Warren Summersworth. I did the math. Warren died ten years ago. The young man in the school blazer looked to be in his late teens. He would have been eight or nine when Warren died.

I took a wild chance. "Is his father around?"

She sighed deeply, put the stopper back in the vial. She looked frankly into my eyes, sizing me up. Finally she said, "Who are you? And why are you here?"

I told her the truth: the famous private investigator I worked for; the investigation we were conducting into Mrs. Summersworth's death; the mysterious sightings of a young man, presumably her son, at the resort; and the chase that had brought me to her shop.

"Your son was noticed hanging around Victoria Summersworth.

First at a pool where she was swimming with her friends, and apparently at some other places too. Finally at her birthday party the night she died. Then today he showed up at her funeral and ran like lightning when I called to him. I'll have to inform my boss, of course. She'll undoubtedly have some questions for him. Depending on how he answers them, the police could be brought in."

The woman looked down at the glass counter, at all her little vials, and slowly shook her head, but it wasn't a gesture of refusal. It was the surrender of a weary mother with a teenager, a mother who was feeling her powerlessness. "I had no idea. He promised me he wouldn't go near the family."

"What did he want?" I asked.

She shook her head again in disappointed acceptance, like someone who has run a good race, only to hit a wall. "You never told me your name," she said.

"Olivia Blunt."

"Nice to meet you, Olivia. I'm Heather Morrissey. You said the police could be notified."

I nodded.

"Would you care to join me for a cup of tea?"

She led me through the beaded doorway into a hallway crowded with a skateboard, coats and bags on hooks, and a messy array of shoes on the floor. From there we moved into a small kitchen with yellow curtains, a chipped porcelain sink, and old appliances. Magnets of all sizes and shapes were stuck to the refrigerator door: Niagara Falls, Disney World, Acadia National Park . . . I sat at a white-painted table while Heather made the tea.

"I suppose it doesn't matter now. It will all come out eventually," she said as she set the kettle on a gas burner.

"You were Warren's mistress," I said, to focus her.

She sighed. "I was a silly romantic girl. I thought he loved me; I actually believed he'd leave his wife for me. He wasn't happy, you see. At least that's what he told me many, many times." She shrugged. "We hear what we want to hear, right? Took me far too long to learn that, but I doubt I'm the only one. So when he didn't leave, didn't leave, didn't leave—one year after another going by—I decided that a baby would be the thing to convince him. I wanted a baby anyway, and I was getting older, so why not? Except that when I announced that I was pregnant, he did exactly the opposite of what I wanted him to do. He rejected the baby, and he rejected me when I wouldn't agree to an abortion. He made me choose: him or the baby. I chose the baby. And that was it—the affair ended. I was left to face the fact that Warren wasn't the man I thought he was. Not the love of my life at all, not even close. Of course, anyone could have told me that, and some people had definitely tried. But I'd been wearing rose-colored glasses that didn't get a single scratch on them for years, until they shattered into a thousand pieces all at once.

"Tristan saved me. In the end I realized that all I'd really wanted was to love someone and be loved in return. I had that with Tristan. Once I got over my broken heart I was actually very happy. He was a beautiful baby who grew into a beautiful boy, and now he's a wonderful young man." She poured the boiling water into the teapot and brought it to the table. "Milk or sugar?" she asked.

"Both," I said.

"But"—she sat down heavily at the table—"there were a couple of years in his early teens that were touch and go. He was skipping school, falling behind academically, getting into trouble. The kids he was hanging around with were the worst in the school. Alcohol, drugs, including methamphetamine. Heroin too—it was cheap and mixed with fentanyl. I was terrified. He had a friend who actually died." She poured milk into her tea and stared into the cup as she stirred it with a spoon, overtaken by the scenes inside her head. Eventually she picked up the thread of her story. "If Warren had been alive, I would have swallowed my pride and gone to him. But he wasn't, so I went to Vicki. I knew all about her charitable work and community initiatives. And, strange to say, we already knew each other, because once she'd come into the shop and made some purchases. We'd talked about essential oils—which oil for which purpose, et cetera—but it was crystal clear that each of us knew who the other was. I guess you could say we were sizing each other up. It was remarkably civil. I thought she seemed very nice, actually, not at all the ogre Warren had described her as. Of course, that didn't make me doubt him. Nothing could have done that.

"So, I went to Vicki and described the situation. I asked her for tuition money, so I could send Tristan to a boarding school with better supervision and counseling services. I really just wanted to get him out of Burlington, away from his so-called friends. She couldn't have been nicer. Not only did she agree, but she did something better. She created the Warren G. Summersworth Memorial Scholarship Fund at Morton Academy, his alma mater. Her only stipulation was that the first recipient would be Tristan Morrissey— no questions asked. No transcripts, no recs. The school complied, and Tristan ended up transferring in the middle of his sophomore year."

She closed her eyes halfway and gave a wistful smile. "I'd always told Tristan that his father was a guy I'd met in a club in Montreal and had a one-night stand with, that I didn't even know his name. I never had any intention of telling him who his real father was. I figured he'd been rejected once and he didn't need to be rejected again. What I didn't count on was that he would look exactly like Warren and that he would end up becoming a standout athlete and the captain of the soccer team at Morton Academy, just like Warren was. All you have to do is look at the team pictures—father and son are practically interchangeable.

"Naturally, Tristan had wondered how he'd managed to get a

fancy scholarship that he hadn't even applied for. I'd made up a crazy story about entering his name in a lottery, and that had worked for a while. Then, just this year, he got it into his head that he ought to know more about the guy whose scholarship had paid for his education. He read all about Warren Summersworth, saw all the team pictures and other photos, and discovered that, for some reason no one in the administration would explain to him, he'd been specifically named as the first recipient. So he figured it out. One day he came to me and told me he knew who his father was.

"What could I do? I had to admit the truth. I told him my story—our story—and begged him to stay away from the Summersworth family. I was sure he'd be hurt, a bastard son showing up out of the blue. Obviously, he didn't listen." All this time the spoon had been making a slow circuit in the porcelain cup. Now she placed it gently on the saucer. "What was I thinking? I forgot to put the cookies out."

"Tea's enough for me right now." I was thrumming with excitement and a terrible dread. Was Tristan Morrissey connected in some way to Victoria's death? Was it possible I'd found her killer? For the sake of the investigation, I hoped so. For Heather's sake, I most definitely hoped not.

"I need to speak with Tristan," I said.

"You and me both."

"Do you have any idea where he is?"

She hesitated. "Look, I told you all this because you said he might be questioned by the police, and I want you to know that he's a good kid. I can't say for sure why he went out to the resort and attended the funeral, but I am certain he did nothing wrong. So if you think for even one moment that he could be . . . implicated in something"—she shook her head at me sternly—"you simply couldn't be any further from the truth."

"I appreciate that, Heather. All the more reason why I should speak to him as soon as possible. If I can just clear up a few things, then maybe I can keep other people from getting involved."

She sighed. "He's past the age when he tells me where he's going. But he's a busboy at the Harp and Plough Tavern for the summer, and he's got the dinner shift tonight. Starts at four thirty, gets out around nine."

CHAPTER 25

A Mother's Mistake

The sign on the glass door of the Screamin' Beans Café said CLOSED FOR A PRIVATE EVENT, but Haley saw me and waved me in. About two dozen people were milling around in the cheerful café, which occupied the first floor of a Victorian house on a street adjacent to the University of Vermont's campus. The tables and chairs were charmingly mismatched and painted in thick, globby coats of pastel hues—sky blue, strawberry, and lemon yellow. There was an indie soundtrack playing, and there was a surprising amount of convivial laughter, as if everyone here, though still attired in funereal black, had agreed en masse to drop their solemn masks and return to their regular, happier selves.

Merritt was seated at a table in a corner; she was talking to the Asian woman who had been at Haley's side during the funeral, and who I took to be Sumiko, Haley's wife. With her uncanny sixth sense, the detective turned her head and raised her disapproving eyebrows at me a mere moment after I'd clocked her. *Where the hell have you been, lowly assistant?* was the message I received.

Not that she'd bothered informing me of her whereabouts. After my visit to Heather Morrissey's aromatherapy shop, I'd raced to Horace, then sped to the cemetery, only to discover that the burial was over. A few leftover mourners were clustered near a thigh-high mound of brown dirt at the side of Mrs. Summersworth's freshly dug grave, but everyone else, including Merritt, was gone. I called her phone, but she didn't answer. I figured she'd forgotten to turn it back on after silencing it during the ceremony, though it wouldn't have surprised me to learn that she'd kept it off after that on purpose, as a way of punishing me for abandoning her at the church. Luckily, I'd been able to locate her through the friend-finding app on my phone.

I'd once taken the time to explain what this app was and how it worked, but she'd sighed and wriggled like a precocious child with a boring teacher, and I'd had no idea if she was even listening. Her attitude toward technology was consistently skeptical and dismissive, even when she utterly relied on it the way everyone else did. She seemed to have no impulse to learn, wanted only to mock. On one occasion she'd informed me, with inexplicable indignation, that when she was in college, students used typewriters. She seemed to think this was a badge of honor instead of one of the many pathetic hardships of the pretechnology era, akin to washing clothes in a creek.

I scanned the crowd and noticed Scott Summersworth and Pia Valente standing in a small group, their arms looped comfortably around each other. I was glad to see them together out in public. Maybe now, with Victoria gone, they'd decided they could finally "face the wolves," to use Scott's phrase. In any case, he didn't look great. His eyes were still red and watery, and his skin had a sickly pallor. Looking closer, I wondered whether he wasn't leaning slightly, whether tiny Pia wasn't in fact bearing some of his weight.

There were some notable absences. In particular, Neil and Lauren and their families. Was it my imagination, or was a family schism revealing itself—Victoria's biological children in one camp, her stepchildren in another? Also missing were Arthur Doyle, Robin and Pat Tucci, and the Purple Hat Ladies, who I imagined were planted on barstools somewhere, throwing back peach daiquiris in maudlin debauchery.

I went over to a buffet table and made myself a sandwich of turkey, lettuce, and sliced tomato, with some pickle spears and chips on the side. I also grabbed a can of Diet Coke. Since I couldn't carry any more than that without appearing inelegant, I decided to come back later for the coffee and pie.

"Olivia! I'm so glad you're here! I was wondering where you were." Haley smiled her kind, charming smile. "Come. I want you to meet my wife, Sumiko." She took me by the elbow and led me on a zigzag path between the tables. "Please don't think less of us for putting on such a casual luncheon. We could have reserved the dining room at the resort and had the chef do a fancy meal for us, but Wild Goose is the last place I want to be right now. Too many memories of Mom, and we were all just there for her birthday party. I told Sumiko: no big meal. Cold cuts are fine. Who wants to eat after a funeral anyway? People just want to go someplace to relax and be together."

We reached the table where Merritt and Sumiko were sitting. My boss shot me a second hostile look. She was definitely hopping mad. I figured she'd forgive me when she found out about the progress I'd made in the investigation.

Haley introduced me to Sumiko Yamada. She was slender and athletic, with an aura of unhurried grace. She was wearing a well-tailored sleeveless black dress. Her jewelry consisted of a polished white rock on a silver chain around her neck, and numerous beaded friendship bracelets stacked on her wrist. Her long, glossy hair fell loose from a center part, framing her face.

Her greeting was brief and cool, and I immediately got a sense of how their relationship probably worked. Haley was the sail, Sumiko the anchor; Haley the spender, Sumiko the saver; Haley the gregarious dreamer, Sumiko the practical one.

The three women picked up the conversation they'd been having before I arrived.

"She was the same as always. Happier, maybe. It was a party, after all." Sumiko's voice was soft, but clear. She gave each syllable its due.

"Not troubled in any way?" Merritt asked.

Sumiko shrugged. "Not that I would know."

Merritt paused, tilting her head as if detecting a subtle odor. "Did you like your mother-in-law, Ms. Yamada?"

Sumiko glanced at Haley, who nodded very slightly.

"We had our issues," Sumiko confessed.

"Care to explain?"

Another glance at Haley, who said, "Go ahead. You might as well tell the truth."

"My mother-in-law didn't like *me* very much." Sumiko bit out each word with difficulty.

Haley immediately intervened. "She did, really. She just couldn't . . ." Her voice broke off.

Sumiko stared directly at Merritt, competing for her attention. "She didn't like me because one, I'm Asian; and two, I'm the lesbian who corrupted her daughter."

Haley started to object.

"Haley, stop. Don't interrupt. You said to tell the truth, and that's what I'm doing," Sumiko said.

Haley cast her eyes down. She looked mortified.

Sumiko told her story. "Vicki showed up here one afternoon after Haley and I had announced our engagement. She asked to speak to me privately. I said sure, thinking she wanted to discuss wedding arrangements or something nice like that. The two of us sat right over there." She pointed to a table by the window. "I brought her some iced coffee with lots of milk and two sugars, just the way she liked it, and before she'd even taken a sip she looked straight at me and said that if I married Haley, it would ruin her life. She predicted that this café—which she called Haley's business, even though it's actually *our* business—would never succeed, because people wouldn't want to buy food from two lesbians. We'd be ostracized and subjected to prejudice everywhere we went. She even suggested that we could be victims of violence. She offered me money—a lot of money—if I would promise to go back home to Denver. She had her checkbook with her. *If you really care about my daughter, do the right thing and leave her alone* was what she said. Her exact words."

Haley had her hands over her face. I could see that her cheeks were aflame.

"She apologized to me a week later," Sumiko said. "I believe it was a sincere apology. I accepted it, as much for Haley's sake as for my own, but there's no denying that what she said hurt me deeply. The homophobia wasn't the worst part. It was the offer of money— the idea that she saw me as the kind of person who could be paid to abandon someone I love. I know a lot of people thought the world of Vicki. I know Haley completely adored her. And the two of them worked it out eventually. They ended up closer than they'd ever been. But for me . . ." She shook her head. "I never felt comfortable around Vicki after that. Once someone shows you that side of herself, it's hard to forget."

The four of us were quiet for a few moments, in honor of what had been lost. I happened to have a mouthful of turkey sandwich, and I dared not chew for fear that the noise would be disrespectful.

Haley said, "I never thought of my mother as a bigot. I never even suspected that she could be that way. I mean, I grew up here, in one of the most liberal states in the country, and I went to an artsy prep school and UVM." She nodded toward the door; the heart of the campus was a few blocks away. "I guess I'd just assumed that the world had moved on from all that old prejudice. To hear that my own mother had said those things was terribly upsetting."

"What did you do?" Merritt asked.

"After I got over the shock, I was livid. My mother was the one to put on the occasional scene in our family, but I discovered that I was quite capable of my own. I drove out to the Bungalow and let her know exactly what I thought of her narrow-minded, hurtful, damaging opinions.

"I said it was cowardly of her to go behind my back, to corner Sumiko like that, and that attempting to buy Sumiko off was a shameful and disgusting act. I told her she needed to seriously reflect on what she had done, and if she could find her way to being truly sincere, she needed to apologize to the amazing woman who would soon become my life partner. And to me. I informed her that she wouldn't be coming to the wedding unless a sincere apology was offered, that if she refused to rebuild the bridge she'd burned, thus forcing me to choose between her and Sumiko, I would choose Sumiko without a moment's hesitation.

"I also informed her that she was a hypocrite. All that caring for the homeless and the sick, all the talk about tolerance and diversity— it had all been a load of rubbish. She was a total fraud."

Haley paused for breath, and in the sudden quiet her spent anger seemed to sizzle in the air. I was a bit breathless myself; I couldn't imagine what it must have been like to be on the receiving end of such a thorough indictment.

"How did she react?" Merritt asked, her voice quite mild in comparison with Haley's.

"She was crying by the time I was done. She said the last thing in the world she ever wanted to do was hurt me. She begged me to be patient with her, and I said I would be. Then I just left. I figured I ought to go right away, before the situation escalated and we ended up saying things we'd regret. I felt horrible, of course. I'd never spoken to my mother that way before. I was shaking all the way home."

Haley reached for her iced tea, and I could see that even now her hands were trembling a little. "A few days later she texted and asked if we could go for a walk, which we did. I let her say her piece." She sipped, then swallowed with difficulty, as if there was a lump in her throat. "Turns out, it wasn't so much hatred or prejudice that had made her act the way she did. It was her fear of what would happen to me. In her day, she said, people lost their jobs and were socially ostracized, and some people killed themselves or just led lonely, unfulfilled lives."

"And she didn't want that to happen to you."

"Correct. She said that years ago she'd had a friend who came out of the closet. She was a wife and mother—everyone thought she was straight—and then, lo and behold, she left her family to go live with another woman. In revenge and disgust, her husband screwed her to the wall in a terrible divorce, and managed to get sole custody of their kids by telling a lot of lies about how she went to lesbian clubs and slept around. And no one came to her defense. Not one person. Not her family or the friends she'd had for years. The woman went into a depression, and her new relationship failed, and the last thing Mom knew about her was that she'd moved out of state. Mom said that ever since then she'd been terrified that one of her kids would be gay and suffer the same fate. Then she admitted that she herself had turned her back on this woman, who used to be one of her closest friends. She said it had given her shame for twenty years."

I blurted, "Then she should have known how her rejection would affect you and Sumiko."

"That's exactly what I said," Sumiko chimed in.

"Things affect people differently," Haley said. "All I know is that

Mom felt terrible about how she'd treated Sumiko and wanted to make amends, and she did. And because Sumiko is the kind, wonderful person she is, the apology was accepted, and we all moved on. With scars, of course, but with deeper understanding too."

Haley reached out, clasped her wife's hand, and continued. "My mother wasn't a hateful person, Ms. Merritt. I know that to be true. She was just very scared of what could happen. The way she talked about that experience, I got the feeling that what happened to that woman had actually traumatized *her* in some way. She'd never been able to shake the horror of knowing that a person's life could be ruined so easily. I think, for Mom, being cast out of society was the cruelest thing she could imagine. And losing your children because of it—well, that was unthinkable."

"She supported your marriage after that?"

"Yes," Sumiko said. "I give her credit for that. But honestly, she always seemed a little afraid of me."

"She knew you had every right to hate her," Haley said.

Sumiko pressed her shoulders back to stretch her chest, and she took a swig of her partner's iced tea. "Are you sorry you asked how I got along with my mother-in-law, Ms. Merritt?"

"Not at all."

"It doesn't help you much with your investigation."

"At this stage there's no telling what might be helpful. I'm getting a clearer picture of Mrs. Summersworth all the time, and that's what I need right now," Merritt said, with a thoughtful frown.

CHAPTER 26

Sex, Lies, and Videotape

I was maneuvering a slice of cherry pie onto a plate at the buffet table when the bell over the door tinkled and I heard Scott Summersworth's voice saying a hearty hello to someone. I glanced up to see Monty Draper. He'd removed his tie but was still in his shiny suit, the top buttons of his shirt open, displaying overtanned skin. His gray-blond hair rose from his forehead in a stiff Elvis Presley peak. The two men clasped each other in a tight hug with mutual thumps on the back.

"Glad you could make it, Monty," Scott said as he released his friend.

"Wish it wasn't under these circumstances," Draper said.

Circumstances you might have authored, I muttered silently.

I glanced across the room to Merritt, who, no surprise, was well aware of who had just walked in the door. From the position of her chair and the slant of her head, I knew she was watching Draper surreptitiously.

He glanced around the café skittishly. He looked shaky and diminished somehow, like someone who'd been through something. I caught the exact moment when he noticed Merritt sitting across the room. His face blanched and he made a quarter turn, only to spot me on his other side. I acknowledged him with a nod. At the same time, Merritt stood up and started to make her way over to him. He did a double take, realized he was cornered, spun on his heel, and booked it right back out the front door of the café.

We followed him into the parking lot. I got to him first. "Mr. Draper! Can we have a word?"

He turned slowly, his former nervousness completely gone. Instead, an easy smile spread across his face. Ignoring me, he called out to Merritt, who was hurrying to catch up. "Mrs. Merritt, what can I do for you?"

She got to the point. "On the night of Mrs. Summersworth's death, you said you dropped her at her house between nine thirty and ten p.m., returned to the Lodge for a few drinks with Scott Summersworth, and drove home at about eleven thirty."

"That's right." Again that easy smile.

"And yet CCTV footage shows you crossing the lobby of your apartment building at one fifty-two a.m."

He took on a gently pensive aspect for a few moments. I was pretty sure that whatever came out of his mouth next would be a lie. Finally he offered an explanation we couldn't prove or disprove. "I went for a drive."

"Did you stop anywhere? An all-night convenience store, for example? Someplace with security footage that could corroborate your statement?"

"No."

"What would you say if I told you that a dark Buick Regal was sighted in Mrs. Summersworth's driveway at approximately one o'clock on the morning of her death?"

Merritt was lying. We didn't know the make and model of the car Pat Tucci saw. She had made that point quite clearly when I'd been too hasty in concluding whose it was.

The easy smile vanished. Draper looked over our heads and shuffled his feet. I wondered whether he was about to bolt and prepared myself for another chase, not that I knew what I would (or could) do to a man much larger than myself if I caught him.

Then, once again, he settled himself, and a great sigh came out of him. "Okay, okay. You've got me. I went to see Vicki after I left the Lodge. It didn't feel right that she'd left the party early. I just wanted to make sure she was okay."

Brava, boss, I thought. *Your little lie paid a dividend.*

"And *was* she okay?" Merritt asked.

"Yeah, yeah. She was fine. She was in a good mood, actually."

"You drank some brandy and spent some time in bed—is that right?"

He frowned. "I don't see how that's any of your business."

"What time did you leave the house?"

"I didn't happen to check the time. But you just informed me that I was in the lobby of my apartment building at one fifty-two in the morning, so, working backward, I must have left her house at about one twenty-two. Well before the estimated time of death."

"Only thirty minutes before," I butted in. "Not far off the coroner's estimate."

He glared at me, but didn't bother replying.

"Why didn't you stay overnight at the Bungalow, Mr. Draper?" Merritt asked. "Isn't that what lovers do?"

He gave a gruff, self-conscious laugh. "Not me. Who wants to wake up in the morning hungover, with a dry mouth and nothing to wear but the clothes you had on the night before? You have to act all lovey, when all you really want to do is go home and shower and get on with your day. You end up gulping a cup of coffee and making some piss-poor excuse about why you need to skedaddle, and the next thing you know, you have a very unhappy lady on your hands. Better to leave at night, with the good memories fresh in her head. Leave her wanting more, if you know what I mean."

I did, and wished I didn't.

"Why did you lie?" Merritt asked.

"It's not rocket science, is it? Vicki died that night. The cops said it was suicide, and that's what I believe, but in case you haven't noticed, there are a couple of people around here who don't like me very much, and I figured it wouldn't be long until one of them pointed a finger at me. Then the cops would be hauling me down to the station, trying to pin it on me, like they do—and you know that's what they do. 'A bird in the hand . . . ' appears to be their motto. Only some fool who trusted the police would admit he was anywhere near the scene of a suspicious death. I've got nothing to hide, but I'd rather not get tangled up in a murder investigation."

"Not quite true, Mr. Draper," I said. "You have plenty to hide."

His gaze raked over me roughly. "Oh, so you did some checking, did you? Of course you did. So you know I got arrested a few years ago in Las Vegas for kiting checks. So what? I had a streak of bad luck at the blackjack table and didn't get around to paying all my debts. It happens—not that I'm proud of it, but I'm not going to wear a hair shirt. I did sixty days at Club Fed and got on with my life. I cleaned myself up, got myself away from the poker and blackjack tables, stopped hitting the booze so hard, and got serious about playing bridge in legit tournaments. Found out I wasn't so bad at it. And here I am today. The picture of lawfulness."

Awfulness was what he should have said. And he drank more than a little; at least that's what Pia Valente, who routinely tossed his empty bottles into the recycling bin, said.

Merritt looked at me. "What did you find out about the son, Jeremy?"

"He exists. Bio as described," I informed her.

Draper sputtered, "Oh, for god's sake. You ran a background on my kid too? Well, let me tell you a few things about Jeremy. He's as straight as they come. Did his service in Afghanistan. Honorable discharge. You want to look that up, you go right ahead."

Merritt cocked her head. "What are you really doing here, Mr. Draper? Why Vermont? Why the Wild Goose Resort?"

"I came out here for a new start, like I said. The gig at the resort was perfect for me. The pay is shit but it's enough to cover rent, and the job keeps me out of trouble. Not exactly the high life I was used to, but it's been good, a good life for this old gambler. I actually love it, if you want to know. The Tufted Duck Bridge Club is something I happen to be very proud of. I've become a happy man here, and Vicki helped me do it. That woman had the heart of a saint, so help me god. *And* a sense of humor. You tell me where you can find a woman like that. She would have been my queen if she'd lived. I figure you're thinking I did her in. Give me one good reason why I would. But I do have a word of advice for you, Mrs. Merritt: if you ever find the bastard who did it, don't tell me who it is, or you'll have two murders on your hands." His color had risen, and his chest had swelled against the buttons of his shirt.

"Now, if you don't mind, I'm going home." He walked the short distance to his dark blue Buick Regal.

Merritt and I watched him get in. When he drove by us, the car passed too close for comfort. I had to step back, pulling my boss with me. "Asshole," I muttered. His eyes gleamed at me in the rear-view mirror as he drove away, and I knew the near miss had been intentional.

I felt gloomy and uneasy as we drove back to the resort in the late afternoon. Clouds had moved in, the first since we'd arrived in Vermont, and the wind had come up forcefully in one of those sudden summer gales like the one that ended Warren Summersworth's life years ago. It lashed the tops of the trees and ripped leaves from branches, sending them tumbling across the asphalt. When the rain finally started, it came down hard. Horace's windshield wipers slapped and jerked erratically back and forth, as if fending off attackers coming at us from all sides.

It was fitting weather to cap off Victoria Summersworth's funeral day. Her life had been publicly celebrated, prayers had been said, hymns sung, and her casket had been lowered into a fresh grave in front of many witnesses. Her story was officially over. Her burial was like the words you find at the end of a book: *The End.* Family and friends would move on with their lives now, into a world that no longer included her. The forgetting would begin.

And we were no closer to finding her murderer.

If that person had indeed attended the funeral service as Merritt had predicted, I certainly hadn't seen him. Or if I had seen him, I hadn't known who I was looking at. It chilled me to realize that a killer could have been standing right in front of me, that I could have been staring straight into his face, into his eyes, without knowing that he'd sent a defenseless older woman to her death. Now the event that may have brought Merritt and me into near proximity to him was over. Would we ever get that close again? He'd evaded Detective Clemmons's grasp easily enough; would he slip through Aubrey Merritt's fingers as well? In my mind's eye, I envisioned the smoky silhouette of a faceless man disappearing into a bank of swirling fog, leaving nothing but the fading echo of evil laughter behind.

Of course, there was Tristan Morrissey to consider. I hadn't met him, not officially, hadn't spoken a single word to him except for yelling at him in the street. He looked like an ordinary teenager, rather uninteresting as murder suspects go. Yet he fell smoothly and easily into that category. On several occasions he'd been noticed hanging around the victim creepily, and he'd shown up at her funeral in the same sneaky way he'd attended her birthday party— without an invitation and against his mother's stern advice. These were suspicious acts, to say the least.

But what motive could the teenager possibly have had for killing Victoria Summersworth? *She* wasn't the one who abandoned him before he was born. Instead, she'd done the opposite by coming into his life in his adolescence and helping him out of the rut he was in. And she'd done this despite the fact that he was the child of her husband's mistress, and thus a person she might have been forgiven for wanting to ignore.

This was the moment when I should have told Merritt about Tristan Morrissey, his relationship to Victoria Summersworth, and his troubling behavior. But something held me back. Teenagers are notorious for behaving irrationally, and then, as logically follows, being unable to explain their actions satisfactorily to others. (I was familiar with this tendency, as I'd been ordered by various authority figures to account for myself many times in high school, and the interactions had usually ended with me in even more trouble.) I could easily imagine young Tristan mumbling vague and contradictory answers, not because he was being evasive but because he was developmentally incapable of understanding his own motives, much less of making them clear and sensible to others. I pictured him getting confused by hostile, rapid-fire questions, becoming defensive in response, blurting one or two smart-ass remarks, and finding himself being dragged down to the police station for further interrogation. The experience could well be traumatic. And once the shadow of doubt had been cast, it might never be fully lifted off him. Society's suspicion could conceivably follow him for the rest of his life. People might always wonder if Tristan Morrissey had gotten away with murder.

What, really, had he done to deserve such hostile scrutiny? Spied on some old ladies? Crashed a party? Attended a funeral in his prep school blazer? These actions may have been unwise, but they were far from criminal.

But . . . was I being too soft? Too much the bleeding heart? Was I confusing my own adolescent immaturity with his? Tristan Morrissey might look like an ordinary teenager, but what did that really mean? Ted Bundy had been a teenager once, and then a very harmless-looking law school student who everyone thought was super nice. Who could say for sure that Tristan wasn't a serial killer too, at the start of a heinous career? After all, he'd once hung around with kids who did drugs. It was only his mother's desperation and Victoria Summersworth's generosity that had saved him from likely run-ins with the law.

If I hesitated to share with my boss what I knew about him and he went out and killed again, the guilt for that death would be on me. I would always know that if only I'd been tougher—if I'd had the cojones of a true, heartless investigator, if I'd followed the clues as I should have, like a nose-to-the-ground bloodhound, bereft of human emotion—I could have prevented it.

I turned to Merritt, who was bouncing gently on the squeaky passenger seat as Horace splashed over a series of shallow potholes that any other car would have taken in stride. Her thoughts seemed to be elsewhere, as they often were when we were driving. I cleared my throat and told her everything I'd learned about Tristan and his mother, including my misgivings about treating a person as young as Tristan as a suspect in a murder investigation.

She listened with interest, and when I was done, she said, "I used to feel the same way you do. One does always want to protect young people. Then I worked a case in which a ten-year-old set her house on fire to kill her sleeping parents. Another one, in which a thirteen-year-old plugged a toaster into an extension cord and dropped it into the bathtub where his sister was soaking. Tristan Morrissey might be a nice-looking young man in a spiffy blazer, as you described, but he is at heart a rejected child. Recently he's been spending his time surreptitiously observing his half siblings living in the lap of luxury, and he has no doubt passed some hours comparing their charmed lives to his own life. And he's been forced to cope with what happened to his mother—how she was cruelly betrayed by one of the wealthiest men in Burlington, how as a cast-off mistress she's had to live off the paltry profits of an aromatherapy shop while her rival, Victoria Summersworth, very publicly thrived. Think about it, Blunt. How could Tristan Morrissey *not* be seething with resentment?"

I sighed heavily. I'd obviously been letting my empathy take the lead again. But must I always suspect the absolute worst of a person? I honestly didn't know if I could.

"We need to talk to Tristan Morrissey ASAP," Merritt continued. "I suggest intercepting him as he gets off his shift at the Harp and Plough tonight; that way his mother won't be around to buffer him. If it makes you feel better, you can go by yourself. It will be less threatening than if we both confront him, and he might be more willing to open up to someone closer to his age. Be friendly. Go easy. But do find out what the hell he's been up to and why."

A rush of excitement coursed through me. A solo assignment! It was only the third day of the investigation, and already Merritt trusted me enough to send me out on my own.

"You can count on me," I assured her, having no idea what was in store.

CHAPTER 27

Zzzzip It

The Harp & Plough Tavern was located on the country route that stretched between the Wild Goose Resort and the city of Burlington. Over the past few days I'd passed it several times without paying it much attention. Set well back from the road, it was the kind of gracious colonial house you saw all over New England—many of such houses falling into decay, others enlarged and rehabbed to accommodate modern families or commercial purposes. This one belonged to the latter category. It was freshly painted in a pumpkin color with glossy black shutters. Green canvas awnings shaded the first-floor windows. Although it was the middle of the week, the dirt lot was packed with nice-looking cars. I parked at the end of a row and walked to the main entrance.

A wooden plaque near the door informed me that the house had been built by one Ezekiel Pruitt in 1789. That was nice, I supposed. I had a jittery feeling, almost like stage fright, as I ventured inside. This was, in a way, my opening night. I thought about Trevor, about how he must have felt before he walked onto a stage in front of hundreds of people and pretended to be someone he wasn't. I was doing the same thing, sort of. Only I didn't have a preset script and I hadn't bothered to rehearse. Yet the stage was already under my feet. I stood tall and took a deep breath. *Piece of cake,* I told myself.

The public area of the tavern consisted of a warren of denlike rooms with low ceilings crossed by hefty wooden rafters. The floors were wide pine planks, worn and warped, scuffed and dinged, from centuries of foot traffic, but they'd been stained and polished in a way that turned their flaws into assets. Lining the walls were bookcases stocked with leather-bound volumes probably purchased by the carton from dozens of estate sales, and heavy damask drapes enhanced the cozy atmosphere. Pewter and brass fixtures gleamed in the dim light. The maw of an ancient stone fireplace in the main dining room was big enough to walk into.

I sat with a Diet Coke at the bar, observing the servers and busboys at their work as I reviewed the questions I would ask the witness. They were fairly obvious. What was harder was choosing the demeanor most likely to disarm a teenager. I needed to be friendly, as Merritt had suggested. But I was more familiar with the psychology of youth than she was, as I'd inhabited that country myself not long ago, so I understood intuitively that I also needed just the right undertone of menace so that the poor kid would get the impression that he'd better not lie to me, lest I bring the full weight of the law crashing down on him.

It was eight fifty. The teenager would be getting off work in ten minutes, but I still hadn't seen him anywhere. Maybe I should have gone around to the service entrance and waited for him there. At nine o'clock I asked the bartender if he would be kind enough to summon Tristan Morrissey for me. The bartender replied that Tristan had gone home early. His mother had picked him up, citing a family emergency.

Darn! My first professional interrogation had ended before it began, with the witness slipping away well in advance of my arrival. I hated that I'd have to tell Merritt that.

I wasn't too surprised, though. After I'd left her this afternoon, Heather had probably had another think, questioned why she'd trusted me and volunteered so much information. She must have wondered what her son had been up to hanging around the resort and crashing the funeral, and she probably wanted to get his story out of him before anyone else did, so she'd booked it over to the Harp & Plough to pluck her wayward boy away from danger.

Disappointed, I scooped a few peanuts out of a shallow bowl and put a bill on the bar to pay for my Diet Coke. On my way out the front door of the tavern I happened to glance into the main dining room, and I stopped in my tracks. Lauren Perry and Arthur Doyle were at a table tucked half out of sight in a corner on the far side of the big stone fireplace.

There was, of course, no reason why they shouldn't be having a late dinner together. Neil had mentioned that Doyle was Lauren's godfather and had been a friend of the family since early days. They seemed very deep in their conversation, and I wondered what they were talking about.

I returned to the bar, picked a stool with a sight line to their table, and ordered another Diet Coke. I knew from Lauren's website that she lived outside Stowe, the alpine vacation mecca where well-heeled tourists went to ski in the heart of the Green Mountains. She and her husband owned a twelve-hundred-acre organic farm where they grew the various kinds of wildflowers that were the main ingredients in the array of skin-care products that they produced in an on-site lab and fulfilled from a new ten-thousand-square-foot warehouse, still under construction. As far as I could tell, the magic of their products resided chiefly in what they did not contain:

GMOs, toxins, fillers, artificial colors, synthetic chemicals, or additives of any kind. The company, called Lauren Perry Skincare, Inc., was only ten years old, but it had already become quite successful, selling products online and in department stores across America, and Lauren herself had achieved celebrity status in the skin-care world.

Doyle was still wearing his natty funeral attire: a navy double-breasted pin-striped suit with a lavender tie and pocket square. Lauren had changed into a soft pink off-the-shoulder peasant blouse. Her hair was braided and pinned up in a complicated style, revealing a thin neck and a sharply defined jawline. As I watched, she straightened up and her neck grew long—she reminded me of a pointer that'd caught a whiff of fox. I wondered if she'd sensed me watching her, but no, she seemed to be reacting to something Doyle had said. That's when I glimpsed a long green necklace hung around her white throat, its pendant hidden in the folds of her peasant blouse.

The green beads looked very much like jade. I bet that if I could manage to sneak a peek at the pendant, it just might turn out to be a hummingbird.

I made a half turn away from them, keeping Lauren in my peripheral vision. After a while she stood up, tucked a little green purse under her arm, and headed in the direction of the ladies' room. I slipped off my barstool and sauntered after her. I washed my hands at a sink until she emerged from a stall. As she was washing her hands at the sink next to mine, I stole a glance at the pendant.

"That's a really pretty necklace," I said.

"Oh, thank you." Smiling, she held the pendant out for me to see. "It's a hummingbird."

I leaned in for a closer look. "It's so delicate."

"It was my great-grandmother's." She let the pendant fall against her blouse; then she shut off the faucet and took a closer look at me.

"Do I know you? I feel like I've seen you someplace before." Her eyes narrowed. "Yes, I remember now. You're with that . . . that detective." The way she said *detective* made it sound like *cockroach*.

"I am, actually. We met you in your brother's office at the Wild Goose Resort yesterday morning. My name is Olivia Blunt, in case you forgot. I'm Aubrey Merritt's assistant."

Her face went rigid. "You're not following me, are you?"

"Not at all. I came here to meet someone else"—*your illegitimate half brother, if you really want to know*—"but he didn't show."

"Too bad," she said insincerely. She grabbed some paper towels from a dispenser and started drying her hands.

"Did you know that a necklace very similar to the one you're wearing was reported stolen from your stepmother's house?"

"Stolen?" She reared back, eyes wide. "You're kidding, right?"

"I'm perfectly serious."

Tossing the paper towels away, she took a tube of lipstick out of her purse and began applying it carefully while looking in the mirror. It was a deep plum color, more daring than anything I would wear. "Who reported it, may I ask?"

"Does it matter?"

She smacked her lips together, retracted the lipstick, and slid it into its tube. "I bet it was Haley, the little busybody. Or maybe sad-sack Robin. They'd both like to get their hands on it."

"So you admit you took it?"

"Took it? It's mine, for Christ's sake."

"I was under the impression that it was given to your stepmother as a wedding present."

"Yes, by my father. But it wasn't his to give. It came from my mother's side of the family. My great-grandfather picked it up in China. So you see, it's a Simmons asset, and should have come to me when my mother died. My father made a mistake when he gave it to his second wife—a mistake I've now corrected."

"You could have made that case when the estate settled."

"Made a case to whom? Settled with whom? I don't need permission to claim my own property, and I owe no one an explanation. This necklace was my great-grandmother's, my grandmother's, my mother's, and now it's mine. My only regret is that I didn't take it sooner."

A loud flush echoed in the tiled room and a woman came out of a stall, shot us a disapproving look, washed her hands quickly, and left.

"Shall we go someplace else to talk?" I said.

"Why would we? I don't have anything to say to you. You want to conduct your pointless little investigation? Fine. Go ahead. But please stay out of my business. Oh, and by the way, tell Haley to go fuck herself."

I finished drying my hands and tossed the paper towel into the bin. Now both sisters had given the exact same message to me. I had no intention of delivering it to either of them.

Lauren jostled out of the ladies' room, pushing her way between two women standing just inside the door, gaping at us. I followed her down a hallway like a persistent journalist, and I got a few more questions in.

"What kind of relationship do you have with Arthur Doyle?"

She whirled around to face me. "Oh my god! Will you please mind your own business? Who the hell do you think you are?"

"Are you aware of any financial trouble the resort is in?"

She froze. Her face twisted into ugliness and her voice descended to a near hiss. "You are so far out of your depth, it isn't funny. The finances of our family business are *not* your concern."

"Well, they could be, if—"

Pinching two fingers together, she made a slashing motion across her glossy plum-colored lips, accompanied by the sound *zzzzzzip*. "Shut up now. Just shut up. Your time is up. I won't be speaking to you again, ever. Don't. Even. Try."

She stormed back to the dining room, and I returned to the bar feeling a little shaky, as if I'd just stumbled off a Tilt-A-Whirl. As I put another bill on the bar, to pay for my second Diet Coke, the full weight of what had just occurred settled on my shoulders. I'd blown my first solo foray! Not because I'd failed to question Tristan Morrissey—which, while disappointing, wasn't technically my fault— but because I'd royally pissed off Lauren Perry, an important as-yet-uninterviewed witness who would now be less inclined to speak freely to Merritt and me, if she was willing to meet at all.

Sure, the fact that I'd solved the mystery of the missing necklace was a nice bonus that could conceivably impress my boss, but its real value to the investigation was negligible, since the stolen necklace had turned out to be completely unrelated to the murder. What was likely to stick in Merritt's mind was the unnecessary rift, the unforced error, with the most elusive of the Summersworth children.

As I walked glumly to my car, I saw Lauren Perry and Arthur Doyle peeling out of the parking lot in a black Mercedes, driving way too fast. Lauren flipped me the bird as they sped past.

CHAPTER 28

A Long Night

Merritt answered the door in the resort's complimentary white terry cloth bathrobe and bare feet. Her ultracasual attire unsettled me. I fully expected to be criticized for my mistake with Lauren Perry; hearing about my errors from an unshod senior in bedtime clothes would only make it worse. I would have preferred my boss to be dressed up when she dressed me down.

"How'd it go with the teenager?" she asked, stepping aside to let me enter the Blue Heron Suite.

I sank into a roomy armchair. The door to the balcony was open, admitting a cool night breeze. Despite my nervousness, it was a pleasure to be here, ensconced in luxury. Relieved that we were starting our discussion with the easier of the two topics I had to report on, I explained that Tristan Morrissey had left the Harp & Plough before I arrived, having been picked up by a no doubt worried mother.

Merritt didn't seem too concerned. Retreating to the area of the room where the mini fridge and electric kettle were located, she asked over her shoulder, "Seltzer? Coffee? Tea?"

"Seltzer, please."

Her laptop was open on the coffee table, her thick black reading glasses next to it. My curiosity was roused. I had no idea what she got up to when our day was over, especially since she seemed to be pushing all the drudge work over to me. I knew she wouldn't have been scrolling through social media, which I'd heard her call "the rot at the core of modern society," and as far as I could tell she didn't read for pleasure. So what had she been doing on her laptop before I arrived?

I peeked at the screen. On it was a page from a newspaper—the *Los Angeles Times. Oh, she's just reading the news,* I thought. *Completely normal.* But why would a New Yorker read the *LA Times?* Wasn't LA where her ex-husband, Theodore Ferro, moved after their divorce? I stole another glance at the screen. The article appeared to be a film review. Before I could see what the movie was, I felt Merritt's eyes on me from across the room and I looked up with what I hoped was an innocent expression.

"Lemon in your seltzer?" There was a thread of frost in her voice.

"Sounds good!" I said too enthusiastically.

After she put my glass and her mug on the coffee table, she reached over and gently pressed the lid of her laptop down.

I reported the rest of the evening's events—Lauren having dinner with Arthur Doyle, the missing jade necklace, and Lauren's rationale for taking it.

Merritt seemed pleased, and I mentally patted myself on the back.

"By the way," she said, "I talked to Neil this evening. He promised to call Lauren in the morning and persuade her to meet with us. With any luck, we'll see her tomorrow afternoon."

This was when I definitely ought to have mentioned my testy exchange with the witness and her fiery declaration that she never wanted to see me again.

I paused, searching for the right way to introduce the issue. I couldn't find a good one, though, and I stayed quiet longer than I should have.

Merritt, sipping her tea, regarded me curiously over the rim of her mug. "Is that all, Blunt?"

I looked for my courage and didn't find it. To my shame and for temporary relief, I lied. "Uh-huh, that's all."

"All right. If that's really all you have to say . . ." Leaving the rest of the sentence unfinished, she added, "Make sure you call Haley and Detective Clemmons to let them know the necklace was found. And don't worry too much about Tristan Morrissey. We'll swing by his house tomorrow and see if we can catch him at home."

She knows I'm holding something back, I thought.

I left shortly after that and trudged back to the staff dormitory in the dark. I dreaded to think what might happen tomorrow when Merritt and I appeared at Lauren Perry's door and my lie was inevitably exposed.

I stayed up late, scribbling in my brown suede journal. Day three of the investigation had flown by. I'd neglected to write down my questions for day two, and so much had happened over the course of the last forty-eight hours that I wasn't sure I could remember every potentially significant detail. But I couldn't afford to lose track of anything, not if I wanted to prove my worth to Merritt. Meanwhile, on a personal note, my hope of getting back to New York City for Trevor's opening on Saturday night had all but vanished. It was already late Thursday night, and Merritt and I were nowhere near a solution, as far as I could see.

The new unanswered questions, added to the twelve from day one, poured out of my pen.

Summersworth Investigation Day 2

13. Scott and Pia together. Significant?
14. Trail of dirt on VS's beige Berber rug. Must be accounted for.
15. Vicki unusually late to party (45 min). Why?
16. Source of historic rivalry between Scott and Neil? Scott denies knowledge of same. Relevant?
17. Wild Goose Resort's alleged financial issues. Connected to VS's death?
18. Missing twenty minutes when Vicki left club. Possibility that she lied about whereabouts. Where did she go? Why? If lied, why?
19. Scott: no alibi
20. Monty: no alibi
21. Neil, Haley, Robin, Lauren: no alibi. NO ONE IN THIS CASE HAS AN ALIBI!!
22. Scott. Addict. Current or former? History of anger/ stealing from VS. Significant?
23. Why do supposedly intelligent women like Victoria Summersworth fall for disgusting misogynists like Monty Draper? IGNORE THIS QUESTION. IT IS BEYOND THE SCOPE OF THIS INVESTIGATION.
24. Victoria's will. Any recent changes? HOW DO WE NOT KNOW THIS YET?
25. VS's connection with forensic accountant Stephen Hobbs. Explore.
26. Did VS intend to fire Scott? Was Scott aware? If so, possible motive.
27. Rumored involvement of Russian Mafia. Totally ridiculous? Okay to ignore?

28. Does Robin Tucci have a scarf fetish? NOT A SERIOUS QUESTION. JUST CURIOUS. :)

Summersworth Investigation Day 3

29. Tristan Morrissey, illegitimate son of Warren Summersworth, likely seething with resentment. Engaged in stalking behavior. Get to the bottom of.
30. Sumiko Yamada. Troubled relationship with VS. Significant?
31. Monty's blatant LIE about early-morning whereabouts. Extremely suspicious.
32. Lauren's hatred of VS. Possible motive. Explore.

Writing these questions down was like sticking them on a corkboard with a tack. I could take a few steps back and look at them there, pinned and wiggling like mini hostages, definitely not slipping through my fingers, but that didn't mean I was any smarter when I finished the list than I'd been when I started. Indeed, the more witnesses we interviewed, the less hopeful I was becoming. Over the last three days the questions had only multiplied, and now it felt like there were far too many, more than we'd ever be able to answer, even if we stayed at the resort for weeks. To make matters worse, I had the uneasy feeling that significant clues were blowing past me all the time without my having . . . well, a clue.

With a dejected sigh, I began another list.

Things to do:

1. Inform Haley and Detective Clemmons that jade necklace was found.

2. *Remember to get guest list & party photos from Haley.*
   (She said she would drop them off yesterday after work,
   but so far, no sign.)
3. *Take full responsibility for mistake re: Lauren Perry.*

I went to bed and lay awake for a long time, watching shafts of moonlight roam across the ceiling and listening to the soft hoots of owls and the rustlings of other woodland creatures outside my door. My mind teemed with shadows and whisperings of its own. Details forgotten or misplaced. Jagged edges. Loose ends. Teasing threads. Mysterious energies were twisting and swirling on the fringes of my consciousness as I fell into a restless sleep.

CHAPTER 29

Financial Crimes

Stephen Hobbs, CPA, was the kind of person you might stand behind in a grocery line without noticing. He offered Merritt and me seats on a low couch in his bland office on the seventh floor of an equally bland steel-and-glass office building in downtown Burlington. The back of the couch was angled away so that Merritt and I had to cant our torsos forward to avoid conducting the interview in undignified semireclining postures. The chair Hobbs occupied was higher and wider, thronelike in comparison—but it didn't make him look like a king, a prince, or even a minor duke. He was too fidgety. A wrist executed one undulating tie flip after another, and his tasseled loafers squirmed on the institutional gray carpet as if looking for a place to hide.

The square brown glasses didn't help either. They were too big and heavy for his face. He had to keep pushing up the center of the frames with his index finger to rest them on the bridge of his nose. Then, like an eyeglasses version of Sisyphus's rock, they immediately slid down again.

It had taken a bit of wrangling to get the appointment. When I spoke to him first thing this morning, the accountant had flatly refused to see us, insisting that he needed permission from Neil Summersworth to discuss his mother's case. So I'd had to get Neil on the phone, which was easier said than done. Luckily, Neil was amenable and had agreed to call Hobbs.

Hobbs was clearly shaken by Victoria Summersworth's death. "Such a terrible thing. I'd spoken with her earlier that week, and she'd seemed fine. Then my wife and I were at her birthday party, and anyone could see that she was in her element—smiling and dancing the night away, with a friendly word for everyone. I was shocked when I heard that she'd taken her own life later that night. Totally shocked. I still find it hard to believe."

"You met with her to discuss the resort's financial records—is that right?" Merritt said.

Hobbs nodded.

"And you also shared your findings with Neil?"

"That's right. He showed up here unannounced at around five o'clock on Wednesday, just as I was leaving for the day. He was clearly in an agitated state. Apparently he'd just had a meeting with you, Ms. Merritt, in which you'd mentioned that my business card was in his mother's purse the night she died. He wanted to know if his mother had hired me, and if so, why. Usually I don't disclose that information, but this case was different. I knew Victoria would want him to be informed of what was happening at the resort. If he hadn't gotten in touch with me fairly soon, I would have called him myself. As it was, we were able to spend a couple of hours together going over the books that night."

"Your conclusion?" Merritt asked.

"In a nutshell: someone has been systematically embezzling from the Wild Goose Resort for at least the last four years. An average of four hundred thousand dollars a year was paid out to nonexistent vendors with offshore bank accounts. Payments for liquor that was never delivered, renovations that never happened, golf course improvements, landscaping machinery, interior decorating, fleets of boats, and so on. It's the simplest scam there is. Forensic Accounting 101." Hobbs smiled briefly, as if this type of fraud were an old favorite he particularly enjoyed.

Merritt asked how it worked.

"The criminal creates a fake invoice from a fake company and buries it in a stack of legitimate invoices, and it gets paid along with all the others. In most cases, the invoice specifies a bank account number for payment, and the money is electronically wired."

"Doesn't someone at the resort notice that there are no new sailboats or lawn mowers?" I said.

"Not necessarily. You see, it's not uncommon for a parent company to provide administrative services to a smaller subsidiary. It's generally considered a cost-cutting measure; why pay for two accounting departments when you can get by with one? In this case, Kingfisher Development handles the Wild Goose Resort's basic accounting matters, such as accounts receivable and accounts payable. The people in Kingfisher's business office have no way of knowing whether the vendor invoices they receive from Wild Goose are legitimate or not. They just pay what comes across their desk. Likewise, the people at Wild Goose have no way of knowing that fake invoices are appearing at the Kingfisher office along with the real ones they send."

"So I could send Kingfisher a bill for, say, floral centerpieces and have them wire a payment into my personal account, and no one would check to see if the floral centerpieces actually arrived," I said.

"You got it. We see this kind of thing a lot in family-owned businesses. Procedures are lax because there's too much trust and an unwillingness to update procedures. It's the old 'but we've always done it this way' excuse. Bigger companies put all sorts of safeguards in place to prevent this kind of fraud."

"Who could have done this?" Merritt asked.

"Anyone who was aware of the split function. Possibly the resort manager, who would have known that invoices weren't checked against goods and services, or someone at corporate who knew the same thing. Even a savvy vendor could be behind it."

I remembered Scott Summersworth's words: *I learned to source practically every item this club uses. . . . You name it, I know where to get the best quality at the cheapest price.*

Hobbs continued. "They usually start with something small and hard to trace—in this case, most likely a food order—and see what happens. They get bolder over time, as they see how well the scheme is working."

"Four hundred thousand a year is pretty bold," I said.

"That's the average. It rose year by year. My team went back through four years of records. The fraud could have started before that."

"The scheme wasn't working too well lately," I pointed out. "Neil Summersworth had been complaining about mismanagement at the resort—too much spending, not enough earning. He blamed it on Vicki and Scott's extravagance."

Hobbs nodded. "That's usually what happens. Greed gets them in the end."

"Where did the money go?" Merritt said.

"Finding it is the next step in our process. It's a bit trickier, takes a bit more time, but it can be done. I intend to start working on that now, as Neil gave me the okay to proceed when we spoke."

"Why didn't other audits pick this up?" she asked.

"I'm not aware that there were other audits. Even if there were, a typical accounting firm might not have noticed. We're forensic accountants; our specialty is in uncovering exactly these kinds of irregularities."

"And you told all this to Mrs. Summersworth?"

"I gave her the preliminary findings over the phone the Tuesday before she died—July twenty-fifth. We made an appointment for her to come in the following Monday, July thirty-first, for a thorough discussion. When she realized that my wife serves on the hospital board with her, she was kind enough to invite us to her party."

"Where you gave her your business card."

"Yes, so she'd have my office address for our meeting."

"Did you tell anyone else about the embezzlement?"

"Just Neil, and now you. Of course, Victoria may have confided in someone."

Merritt and I exchanged glances. I could tell we were remembering the same thing: Scott's anguished cry—*Stop accusing me!*—on the Thursday of that week, two days after Victoria learned of the embezzlement, and two days before her death.

"How did Neil react to the news?" Merritt asked.

"He was livid. He believed his brother, Scott, was responsible and said some choice words I won't repeat. I tried to calm him down, but he was very angry when he left here. I got a text from him later that night, instructing me to hang on to the records, as I would be called to testify in a criminal case."

"Against his brother," I supplied.

"That's what I assumed."

Merritt and I were both a bit somber, a bit startled, I think, by the news that someone had been ripping off the resort to the tune of four hundred thousand dollars a year. And the crime was ongoing, the theft growing larger and bolder by the year.

"It has to be Scott," I said glumly. I couldn't say I liked Scott Summersworth, but I didn't dislike him either, and it disappointed me to think of him as a thief.

"Possibly," Merritt said. "In any case, at this point we have nothing linking the missing money to the murder."

"Honestly, how could they *not* be related?" I said with some sass in my voice. "Or are you suggesting it's just a coincidence that Victoria learned of the embezzlement four days before she was murdered?"

We were strolling down a paved pedestrian path along the shore of Lake Champlain, a few blocks down from Hobbs's office building. It was just before noon—humid, windless. Sunlight sparkled almost too brightly on the glassy surface of the lake. The pavement radiated heat.

"Let's sit down." She motioned to a bench. We sat, and she angled her body to face me, removed her big sunglasses, and fixed her vivid blue eyes on me. "Okay, Blunt. Put it all together for me."

I experienced the sudden flush of tension I was used to getting when Merritt put me on the spot. I took a deep breath and exhaled slowly, giving myself a few moments to analyze the facts and come up with a plausible scenario. Then I said, "Vicki found out about the embezzlement on Tuesday, July twenty-fifth, and confronted Scott that Thursday. She probably wanted to give him a chance to exonerate himself, to prove to her it wasn't true. He denied any wrongdoing and stormed out of the house yelling, *Stop accusing me!* Then there was the party on Saturday night, and Vicki was dead the next morning. Ergo: Scott killed her before she could report the embezzlement to Neil."

"How did he know she hadn't already informed Neil?"

"Maybe she told him that when they argued."

"For that matter, why *didn't* she inform Neil right away?"

"Because she had a meeting to go over the numbers in detail with Hobbs the following week. She probably wanted to get clear on the facts before she brought Neil into it. Also, her birthday party was only a few days away—a big public shindig. She knew Neil would go after Scott in an unholy fury as soon as he learned about the embezzlement. She might have decided it would be better for everyone involved to enjoy the party and the last bit of peace in the family before the shit hit the fan."

Merritt was listening so hard that it made me self-conscious. I really wanted to get this right. "Neil had no idea who Stephen Hobbs was until we spoke to him on Wednesday. The minute we left his office he drove over to see Hobbs and found out about the independent audit his mother had commissioned. Now he's planning a lawsuit against his brother and keeping quiet about it until he gets his ducks in a row. At the funeral yesterday I saw him enter the churchyard and make a beeline to talk to his money guy, Arthur Doyle. He had an urgent look on his face."

"You were doing fine until you got to that last part," she said. "Please do not infer motivations from facial expressions you see from afar."

"Point taken."

"So, what did Scott do with four hundred thousand dollars a year—roughly one point six million total?"

I shrugged. "Anything. Nothing. What does it matter? We know he stole from his mother, so why wouldn't he steal from the resort? He's an addict, remember?"

"Vicki's friend Carla said he's in recovery."

"Every time we've seen him he hasn't looked right to me. Even at the funeral—his own mother's funeral!—he was late, he was dressed like he'd just rolled out of bed, and he was very clearly sniffling and red eyed."

Merritt gazed across the lake to where a small sailboat was floundering in the still air. "It's possible that Victoria suspected someone else of embezzling the funds. She confronted that person—

someone we're either overlooking or haven't met yet—and they killed her."

I frowned. "Who besides Scott would know how to rip off the resort?"

"You heard what Hobbs said. Employees, vendors." She sounded pleased to have added a barrel of new suspects to the list.

I folded my arms across my chest and said nothing. It was frustrating that every time I thought we were getting somewhere, stitching some pieces of the puzzle together, Merritt turned right around and unstitched them. Sometimes it felt like she didn't *want* to solve the case.

A familiar-looking figure was coming down the street toward us. Short gray hair, a rather mechanical gait, a red T-shirt tucked into cargo shorts. It was Robin Tucci, carrying several shopping bags. One bore the logo of a well-known sporting goods store.

I waved and called hello. After the friendly beer we'd shared in Victoria's kitchen I felt kind of close to her—closer than I should have, probably, given that she was a suspect.

She looked over, and when she saw it was me, she scowled and abruptly turned down a side street. It couldn't have been more obvious that she wanted to avoid running into Merritt and me.

Merritt gave a snort of amusement. "There's your pal. Spending freely, it appears." I had naturally reported my encounter with Robin at the Bungalow.

"More likely retail therapy than embezzlement," I said, coming to Robin's defense for no reason other than kind forbearance for a person who'd been crying on my shoulder very recently.

Merritt put on her Guccis and said, rather lazily, from behind the two big black circles that hid her eyes, "No comment, my dear Blunt."

I didn't bother trying to defend myself.

As we were walking back to the car, she asked, musingly, "Do you have allergies?"

It was an odd, out-of-the-blue question. By then I was used to the way her mind jumped around erratically, so I simply said, "No. Do you?"

"I do. Did, I should say. I seem to have outgrown them. That happens, you know. The allergy just goes away. No one knows why."

She wasn't just making small talk—she never did that—so when she didn't say more, I probed. "How is that relevant to anything we've been discussing?"

"It's ragweed season. Years ago I would have been red eyed and runny nosed standing in that churchyard."

I was totally in the dark. I knew she wasn't digging for sympathy for her formerly allergic self. There was a reason for this confession, and I was supposed to figure it out. *Red eyed and runny nosed. Standing in that churchyard.* The answer came to me.

"Okay, I get it. You're saying that what I took to be Scott's addiction could have been an allergy."

"Just so. If Scott is currently in recovery, he wouldn't have been stealing from the resort to support a drug habit, at least not recently, so the embezzler would most likely be a different person, with a completely different motive."

I frowned. Perhaps I was glowering.

"Don't look so disgruntled, Blunt. I'm only reminding you to keep an open mind."

CHAPTER 30

Kingdom Come Farm

We turned off Route 100 at a rustic sign that read KINGDOM COME FARM, and we started up a dirt road flanked by a storybook pine forest. The heat was searing; the air buzzed with the drone of cicadas. About a half mile in, the road curved, and we came out to a complex of buildings: a large Vermont barn, rehabbed and freshly painted in traditional red; a towering old grain silo with a silver cap; a scrappy trailer home with one end sinking into the ground; and a big, immaculate white farmhouse from the early nineteenth century, boasting several brick chimneys and a green tin roof. Farther along was a small lot where several cars were parked.

An old tabby cat moseyed across the road, forcing us to stop, at which point four barking dogs bounded out from somewhere—a border collie, a German shepherd, and a couple of mutts. I drove slowly through the noisy chorus and parked outside the barn, where a hand-carved sign painted in soft clear colors swung over the main door. LAUREN PERRY SKINCARE, it read, in a gentle script wreathed with garlands.

I stepped out of the car, giving the dogs time to stare, sniff, and wander off. The air was suffused with fragrance, and when I looked around I saw why: rolling hills covered in blooming wildflowers undulated in three directions, eventually blending into a forest on the hazy horizon. Except for the purple lavender, I couldn't identify any of the plants, but I recalled some of the flowers mentioned on the company website: dahlia, lisianthus, and larkspur.

Merritt and I entered the barn. It had been refurbished into a modern office with a waiting area and reception desk, a glass-enclosed conference room, and five or six office doors studding a long hallway. The only sounds were from an air conditioner pumping cool air out of overhead vents and a telephone ringing far away. The place smelled minty—not sweet, like candy, but fresh and bracing, like the plant.

A twentysomething employee in faded jeans appeared and said, with a relaxed smile, "Ms. Perry will be with you in a moment." She led us into the conference room, which was dominated by a long table of reclaimed wood, sliced down the middle by a row of different-sized cacti in clay pots. The arrangement was meant to look casual and artless, but it was carefully calibrated interior design: the kind of coffee-table art in which one clay pot a half inch off center would ruin the effect—in some people's estimation, at least.

Lauren swept into the room before we could sit down. Irritability sizzled off her like oil off a hot frying pan. "I have nothing to say to either of you," she commenced. "This whole thing is a waste of time." She cast an especially harsh glare at me, but didn't mention what she'd said to me last night. I tried to look small and meek. I pressed my lips into a tight line to indicate how totally zipped they were.

Then I noticed that she was wearing the jade necklace, and my eyes widened in surprise. It was indeed an eye-catching piece, especially here, set off dramatically against her black T-shirt. Cheeky of her, I thought, given that she'd known we were coming.

Never one to waste time, Merritt pointed to it. "Tell me about that. Not the necklace, but why you think you had a right to take it from your stepmother's house."

Lauren's eyes got cold and beady. "Let me tell you something, Ms. Merritt. Nothing that Victoria Summersworth owned was, in my opinion, legitimately hers."

"I'm curious why you think that, Ms. Perry," Merritt said mildly.

"I'll be happy to tell you. My feelings about my stepmother are clear to everyone: I didn't like her. I've never hidden that. But I didn't kill her."

"I didn't ask if you did."

"But that's why you're here, isn't it? To rule me in or out as a suspect. It's insane that I have to be subjected to this ridiculous travesty. But Big Brother Neil told me I must cooperate. He thinks that's the fastest way to get rid of you. So I'll be a good girl and do what he asked." She gestured to the table. "Please sit down, and do forgive me if I don't offer you any refreshment. You won't be staying long enough to enjoy it."

Merritt and I sat on opposite sides of the long table while Lauren took her place at the head, straight and confident, presiding over us as she must have presided over all the staff meetings that had helped build her company. She reminded me of Neil—the palpable sense of power, the confidence bordering on arrogance.

"First, a history lesson," she said. "My mother's family, the Simmonses, had a successful logging business; they bought up all sorts of land and started developing it. They worked hard and basically built out Burlington. As their reward, they bought a beautiful summerhouse set on seven hundred gorgeous acres on the southeastern shore of Lake Champlain. My grandmother and mother spent wonderful summers there with their family. My mother grew up and went off to Bennington College, where she met my father, Warren Summersworth. They married, and he took over running the family's development business, because that's what they did back then: the men ran things and the women stayed home. He eventually convinced her to convert the summerhouse into a hotel and the seven hundred acres into a resort. Okay, fair enough. She didn't like it, but she went along with it to please him. Then she died of breast cancer, and a year later he came home with Little Miss Shit-for-Brains from Vergennes, and she became our mother.

"My father made the biggest mistake of his life when he married Miss Vicki, whose only demonstrated skill in her then thirty years of living was writing crappy press releases. He gave her way too much power over the resort. The first thing she persuaded him to do was to add those two eyesores, those wings, to our summer-house. Then all the rest, all those cheap, chintzy little places: the pools, the craft barn, the bike barn, the red barn, the fuck barn, the piss barn, and that god-awful golf course. It just went on and on—seven hundred gorgeous acres turned into a Disneyland of bad taste, with hordes of strangers tearing around in golf carts like they owned the place.

"Finally, after years of unhappy marriage, he died in a tragic event witnessed only by her and my drug-addled half brother. Convenient, huh? Now she was running the resort by herself, and before long she brought the idiot half brother on board, and together they continued destroying a formerly beautiful corner of the earth that neither of them had any right to own in the first place." Lauren's face twisted into a haughty sneer. "Ask yourself how you would feel if you were me."

"Really bad, when you put it like that," I blurted.

Lauren slid a dismissive glance in my direction. *Enough noise from the minion.* She turned back to Merritt. "Now you understand. If anyone wanted to kill Victoria, it was me. But I didn't do it. I just took my mother's necklace back. So sue me."

Merritt frowned. "Hold on. I'm confused. Your father's death was described in the newspaper as an accident, but you seem to be implying that your stepmother and half brother were involved somehow. Did I hear that correctly? Is that what you're suggesting? Do you have any evidence for that?"

"I'm not a detective; I don't need *evidence*. I'm just a daughter who loved her father, and I will tell you that my father knew boats, the weather, and the lake as well as anyone in this state. He would never have died the way he did."

"Come now, Ms. Perry. Even the best sailors in the world are occasionally knocked overboard by swinging booms. Surely you're aware of that."

"My father's death was no accident, Ms. Merritt. If you want evidence, I give you this: Scott hated my father. So did Victoria. I think I'll leave it at that."

Merritt appeared perplexed for a moment, and then she said, "Well, well. You're giving me a lot to think about. If you really do believe that your stepmother conspired with your brother to murder your father, in addition to all the other things she allegedly did to you—ruining your family's land, taking ownership of family heirlooms, et cetera—it strikes me that you would have had a very strong motive for murder."

Lauren threw her head back and laughed. "Wouldn't you just love it if I had killed her? What a good story it would make! Cinderella slays the wicked stepmother!"

"I doubt anyone would see you as Cinderella," Merritt said dryly.

"Well, we'll sadly never get to see the movie, because the police don't have a shred of evidence against me and neither do you."

Merritt leaned forward, interested now. "What makes you so sure?"

Lauren smiled sweetly. "Because there isn't any. Because I didn't do it."

There was a sound behind her, and she looked over her shoulder at a great hulk of a man who'd appeared in the doorway. "Ah, my love, there you are. Would you see our guests to the door?"

Lauren's husband, Eric, was in charge of cultivating and harvesting the many acres of wildflowers that eventually, after an elaborate process of drying and extraction, became the concentrated organic serums that comprised the company's high-end skin-care products. He didn't look like a farmer, though, or what I imagined a farmer to be. With his brawn and gruff clumsiness and thick chestnut beard, not to mention the big boots he was wearing, I would have pegged him for a lumberjack. Somehow you just knew that his handshake would be meaty, tight, and warm with dried sweat, and that if he told you he was going to do something he probably would.

Honoring his wife's request, he strode over to the conference table, and his advancing bulk was like lava flowing down a mountain slope toward us. I reflexively stood up and braced myself against his force. Merritt followed suit.

"I'll walk you out." His voice was surprisingly soft. I supposed he didn't need to be loud to make his point; his body did his talking for him.

We didn't bother saying good-bye to Lauren, as she was scrolling through her phone.

Eric accompanied us to the car. When the dogs ran around our legs, barking and carrying on, he didn't call them off.

"So. What's your opinion of Lauren now? Do you still find her intriguing?" I asked Merritt when we were safely on I-89, headed back to the resort.

"She's certainly very angry. And not afraid to show it," she said mildly.

"What she said about her father's death . . . do you think there was anything in that?"

"Hard to say. She's bitter enough to suggest something like that out of spite. She may even believe it." Merritt sighed in vexation. "Do you see what I mean about these tragedies, Blunt? They have a long half-life in a family. There's always unresolved blame, guilt, recrimination—it muddies the water."

"What if she's right, and Victoria and Scott really did conspire to murder Warren?"

"Unless she provides evidence or Scott confesses, there's not much we can do."

Merritt lapsed into silence. I figured that facts, connections, and impressions were swirling around in her brain, so I didn't interrupt her thoughts. It wasn't until we were approaching the Burlington exit that she spoke again.

"The skin-care industry is a very tight, very competitive market. I can't imagine it was easy to start and grow a business like hers. She obviously has brains, talent, discipline, and guts. You have to give her that."

I grunted. I didn't feel like giving Lauren Perry anything.

Merritt's cell phone jangled as we took the exit. Jim Clemmons's voice rumbled over the speakerphone. "Hello, Mrs. Merritt?" He didn't wait for an answer. "You need to get over here right away. There's something you need to see."

CHAPTER 31

Twisted Metal

A narrow road curved gently with the lakeshore. There was no shoulder or breakdown lane, just thick underbrush encroaching from the sides. The yellow center line had faded, and seasonal freezing and thawing had caused deep cracks in the asphalt. It was the kind of half-wild country road only locals would know about.

I pulled over as far as the road would let me. An ambulance was parked ahead, and two police cruisers contributed a silent drama of swirling blue lights.

Detective Clemmons was speaking with a white-suited member of the forensic team. A second forensic investigator was kneeling farther along, an open silver case by his side. Officer Grout stood guard nearby, one hand wrapped around the handle of her baton, the other rested on her holstered gun. She saw me and pretended she didn't. When the forensic person went away, Clemmons waved us over. His face was grim.

"Hit-and-run. He was dragged. I want to warn you: it's not a pretty sight." He brought us closer to the scene. The bike was a mangled mess of twisted steel, forlorn without its rider, whose body in brilliant spandex lay about fifteen feet ahead.

I looked away, looked back, looked away again, in a cycle of horror and fascination that was literally making my head spin. I knew immediately that I would never forget what I was seeing, that it would be added to my personal store of horrors exactly as it appeared to me in that moment. First Victoria, now Neil. Mother and son, broken to death. That's the phrase that came to me: *broken to death.* Like a smashed porcelain vase. Or a shattered glass window. Or a painting slashed into a million tatters. Broken to death. That was Neil Summersworth, whose soul no longer resided in the ruined temple of his once-perfect body.

A sensation of numbness spread up from my core and started to crawl across my brain. The air felt thick and suffocating, and the trees began to whirl. By the time I realized I was going to faint it was too late to save myself. My legs gave way. The ground started racing toward me. Merritt caught me on one side, Clemmons on the other. They dragged legless me over to a cruiser and propped me against it. Someone handed me a Dasani bottle. It was none other than Officer Grout. I screwed off the plastic top with a trembling hand and gulped the water, eyes averted from Grout's smirk and Merritt's probing stare.

"You with us, Blunt?"

I jerked my head in what I hoped was a nod.

"You sure?"

I swallowed more water and gathered some words from a far region of my brain. "I didn't pass out." This was a mark in my favor, or so I imagined.

"No, but you were just about to. It's nothing to be ashamed of. Are you okay now? Can I leave you here?" She was obviously eager to get back to examining the scene.

"I'll come with you."

"You don't have to. I don't need you for anything."

She couldn't have said anything more motivating than that. Her not needing me was exactly what I didn't want. I stood up straight, gulped more water, and looked her in the eye.

"Let's go," I said.

She shrugged. "As you wish."

When her back was turned I poured the last of the water over my head. The cold, wet fingers running through my hair brought me back to alertness.

The police were stringing yellow tape around the scene. We stood behind it.

Clemmons pointed down the road. "You can see there wasn't enough room on the shoulder for Summersworth to move over when he heard the car behind him. You'd expect to see skid marks anywhere from there"—he swung his arm along the pavement—"to there."

"There aren't any," I observed.

"Correct."

"Maybe the driver didn't see him," I offered.

Clemmons shook his head. "This is a straightaway." He swept his ever-sweeping arm to the road behind us. Indeed, this section was straight as a pin. He walked several paces. "Summersworth was probably hit right around here. See? There would have been plenty of time for the driver to notice the bicycle, slow down, and pass. But, as you can see, the driver didn't do that. And after the collision, he didn't stop the car; Summersworth was dragged a good twenty feet."

I shuddered.

"Then he backed up and ran over him again," Merritt pointed out.

Clemmons nodded grimly. "Yup."

Run over *twice*? I had to look. I took a few steps toward the heap of bright spandex lying in the road and realized Merritt was right.

Neil Summersworth's legs were crushed, indicating where he'd been run over, but that wasn't the only injured area. There were literally tire marks across his chest as well. My stomach filled with bile and crumpled in on itself.

"Doin' okay there, Blunt?" Merritt said.

"Totally fine," I assured her as my gut roiled and sweat broke out all over my body. I took a moment to steady myself, then carefully retraced my steps, sending up a silent prayer of gratitude that the tires hadn't squashed his head. If I'd seen brains leaking out of a broken skull I probably would have had a heart attack and ended up in the ambulance myself.

Merritt turned to Clemmons. "Got a time yet?"

"Forensics says it was recent. Late morning, early afternoon."

"Who found him?"

"Passing motorist. The guy over there."

Up the road a bit a disheveled man was leaning against the driver's-side door of a Honda CR-V with Vermont plates. He was chewing a fingernail, staring at the ground. He looked like he was in shock. Or at the very least, like he wished he could be anywhere else. Just then his gaze rose, encountered the dead body (still there!), and fell to the ground again.

"Go tell him he can leave," Clemmons instructed the stony-faced Grout. "Make sure you've got his information first." Grout left her boss's side obediently and swaggered over, her wide hips giving a jaunty sway to her holstered gun.

"Neil Summersworth did fifteen miles on his bike every lunchtime," I supplied, "along the same route. The shore road, his receptionist said."

"That's the name of it: Shore Road. A good place for bicyclists, as it's not well traveled. Just two narrow lanes."

"He'd been having trouble with his bike," I added. "Had a flat tire a couple of days ago."

"A bike malfunction wouldn't explain this," Clemmons said. "He's wearing a smartwatch, so we'll be able to trace his route, find out what time he left the office, and what time the watch stopped recording his movement."

Two EMTs filed by, rolling a gurney between them. With a *one, two, three*, they hoisted the corpse onto the gurney, then covered it with a sheet, and Neil Summersworth's remains were whisked away. Just like that. Here and gone. Alive one moment, dead the next. It felt unreal, almost like a magic trick. Now you see him; now you don't. Meanwhile, the birds were chirping in the trees and the sun was shining brightly. It was another lovely day in Vermont. Pretty soon everyone here would break for lunch. As Merritt and I walked back to the car with Clemmons, I wondered if I'd dreamed the whole thing.

No doubt Merritt's mind was working at lightning speed, these new facts making all the facts that had gone before them shift and rearrange themselves. I was still too stunned to try to make sense of anything. It wasn't just because this was my second corpse in three days, and that this one was right in front of me, not in a photo, and a lot more gruesome. It was because of the suddenness of the death. I'd talked to Neil that very morning, when I asked him to give Stephen Hobbs permission to speak with Merritt and me. When we'd visited Neil at his office two days ago, he'd been the picture of health and vitality, a man in the prime of his life, a family man with two growing sons—strong, successful, enviable in every way. Only a few hours ago we'd learned about the missing money, his anger, his intention to file a lawsuit against his brother, and now . . . this. He was dead. Someone had waited for him to leave his office, then followed him and killed him.

The death could have conceivably been classed as an accident, just like Victoria Summersworth's had been, if the driver hadn't backed up and run over Neil again, proving murderous intent. This killer hadn't had either the time or the inclination to bother with subterfuge. Could it have been the same person who'd murdered Victoria, or were there now two killers to track and bring to justice?

When we reached the car, the three of us stood in a small huddle. Clemmons said to Merritt, "We promised we'd share information. Well, I've done my part. Now it's your turn. You've been talking to the family. What can you tell me about this?"

Merritt obliged. She told him about the independent audit commissioned by Victoria Summersworth and the accountant's discovery that someone had been stealing hundreds of thousands of dollars a year from the Wild Goose Resort. She explained that Neil Summersworth had recently been informed of these facts, had immediately suspected his brother, Scott, and had advised the accountant to prepare to testify in a criminal case. She went on to say that Scott had been a cocaine addict for years, that he'd apparently had temporary periods of sobriety in the past, and it was unclear whether he was using at this time.

The obvious next questions revolved around what, if anything, Neil had told Scott. Had he shared the results of the accountant's audit? Accused Scott of embezzlement? Threatened him with a lawsuit? In other words, had Neil given his brother an excellent reason to want him dead?

Clemmons's face had reddened; his facial muscles were twitching. "What you're telling me is that Scott Summersworth had motive, as well as means and opportunity."

"Possibly. If he thought Neil was onto him." Merritt measured the words carefully, as if to model caution.

Clemmons's jaw jutted out aggressively. He stood up straight, giving himself an extra inch or two of height, and puffed out his chest. "I'll bring him in for questioning this afternoon."

We got into the car and Clemmons walked away. As I started the engine, Merritt said in a low voice, "Get us back to the resort fast. I need to talk to Scott before Clemmons does."

"You think he did it?"

"He doesn't strike me as a killer, but it's possible he felt cornered and saw no other way out. We'll be able to tell fairly quickly, I think, as long as we get to him before the cops scare the wits out of him and the lawyers counsel him to play dumb."

"And if it wasn't him . . . ?"

"Then we've got a brutal murderer on our hands who may already have killed twice and will think nothing of killing again."

CHAPTER 32

In the Crosshairs

Maybe Adam Driver would be able to pull off a convincing short-notice show of grief for a person he'd murdered himself, but I doubted Scott Summersworth had that kind of talent. That was why his reaction to the news of his brother's death strongly suggested to me that he was innocent. It was an authentic jumble of disbelief, denial, shock, and what I perceived as genuine fraternal sadness shot through with a lifetime of stubborn resentment. In other words, when Merritt informed him that his brother was dead, the victim of a hit-and-run driver over on Shore Road, Scott Summersworth turned into a very convincing burbling, blustering mess.

We were in his office, where Merritt and I had cornered him. The three of us were seated around a small coffee table littered with old issues of *Yankee* magazine. He was wearing his usual polo shirt, his abdomen straining against the leather belt holding up his wrinkled khakis. It was just before five; the sun had moved to the west and the room was in shadow. A general air of tiredness hung in the room, despite the two new photos on his desk: his mother in a straw sun hat, and a close-up of Pia Valente's face, both women wearing smiles.

When he'd collected himself somewhat, Merritt delivered more bad news. "The hit-and-run was not an accident. There's convincing evidence that your brother was deliberately and viciously killed."

Scott appeared utterly bewildered. "What? Who would do something like that?"

"That's what I'd like to know. Detective Clemmons is asking that question as well. Right now he's probably notifying your sister-in-law and will start the investigation soon after that. He intends to bring you in for questioning."

"Me? Why me?" Again he was dumbfounded.

"You see, Scott, we know all about the independent audit and the missing money."

His face drained of color. "That has nothing to do with me."

Bad move, Scott. You should have denied it, I thought.

"So you knew about it," Merritt said with ill-concealed satisfaction.

"Yeah, I knew," he said stonily, looking away. Maybe he realized his mistake. "Mom told me about it a few days before she died. She asked point-blank if I was behind it. I told her the truth. I had nothing to do with it. Nada. Didn't know a thing about it until that moment. But, I told her, now I knew why she and Neil kept accusing me of mismanagement. They thought I was overspending, that I was irresponsible. See, when you're the black sheep of the family, everyone is quick to judge. They made up their minds about you long ago. You're in a hole you can't get out of, no matter what you do."

"You sound bitter," Merritt observed.

He shrugged. "I guess I am. Anyone would be."

"Bitter enough to slip in a fake invoice every now and again? Such an easy thing to do. It must have been tempting."

He glared at her. "You're just like them. You don't get where I'm coming from at all. I want this place to succeed. I want that more than anything. Why would I drive it into debt?"

He started pacing back and forth across the room, emitting ragged sighs. He was clearly an emotional guy, the kind who wore his heart on his sleeve, and he was trying hard to pull himself together. He seemed to understand that things were moving fast, that he needed to get ahold of the situation before it swallowed him whole.

It occurred to me that he was fooling himself. Even if he was innocent of the fraud, he *was* responsible for it in a way. He'd failed to review the invoices that the bookkeepers at Kingfisher were paying out, failed to institute accounting procedures that would have prevented fraud in the first place. Whoever stole the money—if it wasn't him—had relied on the relatively obvious fact that Scott Summersworth didn't pay attention to details, that he lacked basic financial skills. I remembered his sheepish admission: *I'm more of a people person, less of a numbers guy.*

The real thief may also have known or guessed that if the club went downhill, suspicion would naturally fall on Scott—the resort's general manager, a known addict, and the family scapegoat.

"This is totally crazy," he was muttering. "Neil is dead, someone's been ripping off the resort, and . . ." He stopped pacing and turned a startled face to Merritt. It had finally occurred to him where all this was headed. "Clemmons thinks I did it, doesn't he? He thinks I killed my brother!"

Merritt's silence said everything.

"Oh my god!" Scott raised two hands to his head, as if to keep it from flying off. "You can't be serious! That is totally outrageous!"

"I'd like to help you, Mr. Summersworth," Merritt said soothingly. "Why don't you start by walking me through where you were between the hours of ten and two today?"

"Where was I? Where was I?" He repeated the question in stupefied mockery, as if it were an affront to reason and dignity. "I was here, for crying out loud. At the resort. Doing my job! Where do you think I was?"

"Doing your job. Can you be more specific?"

"I was . . . I was . . ."

Was he struggling to remember, or trying to come up with an alibi?

His face suddenly fell and he sank onto the couch. "Wait. I wasn't here. I left the club for a couple of hours to run some errands in Vergennes. Yes, I remember now. I went to the bank and the pharmacy. They'll have CCTV!" he said with rising hope. "Then I got a sandwich at a café I go to all the time. The waitress there, Stacy— she'll remember me!" He was elated. But his face turned a deathly white as he thought of something else. "Then I took my car through the car wash."

Merritt leaned forward, keen with interest. "The car wash, Mr. Summersworth—why the car wash?"

It took me a moment to grasp the implications.

Scott squirmed visibly as he felt the walls closing in. "Oh my god. This is a fucking nightmare. I need to call my lawyer, don't I?"

"It does look that way," Merritt said gently.

Back in the Blue Heron Suite later, after a good-enough room-service dinner, Merritt and I relaxed with carrot cake and cups of coffee. The night felt surprisingly cozy, as if we were finally getting comfortable with each other. I attributed this to the fact that day four of the investigation had been remarkably productive. The revelations concerning the financial crimes at the resort were taking the investigation in a promising new direction. Unless, of course, they were dragging us down a rabbit hole.

Merritt's phone vibrated, and I saw her face stiffen as she read the number on her screen. She immediately withdrew into the bedroom and closed the door. The murmur of one side of a conversation was audible. Her voice was low and urgent. By leaning toward the sound I was able to pick up a few words: "... of course I don't know.... That was years ago.... What do you want me to do? ... It's not my problem anymore." The call ended abruptly, having lasted no more than one or two minutes. Before she emerged from the bedroom, I had just enough time to pull out my phone and pretend to be checking my messages. The lines on her face were more deeply etched, and a murky gloom hung about her as she assumed her place on the couch and picked up her lukewarm coffee.

"Who was that?" I asked innocently, knowing it wasn't my business.

"No one. It's nothing." Her clouded eyes said something different.

"I hope everything's okay. If there's anything I can do to help ..." I was shamelessly digging.

"Please, Blunt. I don't pry into your personal life, and I expect you not to pry into mine. We're colleagues, not friends. Let's keep that distinction very clear."

As the relaxed mood was clearly broken, I returned us to the grubby business at hand.

"Do you really think Scott killed his brother?" I asked.

"Possibly. It's easy to see how Neil's death benefits him. Neil had been planning to fire him even before he learned about the embezzlement. Scott would have known that, or guessed it, or been warned about it by his mother. He knew the die was cast for him: he was about to be ousted from the one place on earth he loved more than anything. If, on top of that, he was going to be criminally charged in an embezzlement scheme, a career for him at the resort would be forever out of his reach. His family relationships, such as they were, and his public reputation would be seriously harmed. Basically, his life would be ruined."

She took a sip of coffee, curled her fingers around the mug. "All that is reversed now that Neil's out of the picture. Scott will most likely assume control of the family business, as neither sister has any interest in it beyond collecting their shareholder dividends. He'll be in a position to quash the results of the independent audit. The missing money, to the extent that it comes to light at all, will turn into mere 'discrepancies' that will be 'handled' by the new management. With both his mother and brother gone, Scott will be home free."

"But—"

"But what?" Merritt said impatiently, almost as if she expected me to say something stupid.

I couldn't help obliging her. "He denied everything very convincingly, in my opinion."

Merritt just closed her eyes. "Oh, Blunt. What am I going to do with you?"

It was certainly possible that I'd been wrong about Scott Summersworth, that he was indeed a talented actor who'd put on an excellent performance tonight, one I'd completely fallen for.

"If he murdered Neil, he probably murdered Victoria too," I said.

"I should think so. He needed them both out of the way. He killed Vicki to prevent her from telling Neil what she knew, and he killed Neil to clear his path to the top."

I shook my head, chagrined. If Scott had murdered both his brother and his mother, I'd gotten him all wrong. Judged too fast. Fallen for the sheep costume when I should have sensed the wolf underneath. I promised myself that from now on I'd keep my personal feelings at bay and simply do what my boss kept telling me to do: just gather the evidence and follow wherever it led. Without fear or favor, as the lawyers said. Rational. Thorough. Cold.

And right now the evidence was leading in a very straight line to Scott Summersworth's door.

CHAPTER 33

Tristan Morrissey

There was a knock on the heavy oak door of the Blue Heron Suite. The front-desk receptionist had called a minute earlier to inform Merritt that she had visitors, so we already knew who was standing in the hallway. Merritt nodded at me. I crossed the room and swung open the door.

Tristan Morrissey towered over his mother. He was probably about six feet four inches, and he was thin in the way of boys who have shot up dramatically and haven't yet bulked out into the men they will become. He slouched a bit, as if to convey that he'd never actually intended to get taller than everyone else.

His curly brown hair hung over his face on one side and was tucked behind his ear on the other, revealing a strong cheekbone and fine jawline. His eyes were hazel like his mother's, but the rest of him was the spitting image of the young man I'd seen in the photo album on Victoria's coffee table.

I greeted them, and they came into the suite—Tristan with a self-conscious shuffle, Heather with the righteous stride of a mother doing her appointed work. She was wearing a flowery blouse and shapeless white knit pants, her mass of gray-blond hair pulled back into a semblance of order. She'd applied a melon-colored lipstick that contrasted unhelpfully with her flushed pink cheeks. She went straight to Merritt.

"Are you Aubrey Merritt, the private investigator?" she asked.

Merritt admitted that she was and asked them to sit down. She offered them seltzer; Heather refused for them both. She gave the impression that they were here on urgent business. Or at least Heather did. Tristan looked more like a puppy dragged in on a leash.

Turning directly to the teenager, Merritt said, "You were curious, weren't you?"

Tristan looked at his shoes. "Uh-huh." He had understood her perfectly.

"Tell me about that, Tristan."

"I know it sounds kind of bad, like I was stalking people. But I never meant it to be creepy or anything. I just never had any family besides my mom. I always wondered what it would be like to have a dad and siblings—a real family—and then I found out my dad was dead, but I actually had two brothers and two sisters. I promised my mom I wouldn't bother them, but . . . well . . . I could at least see what they looked like, right? And see where they grew up. And sort of imagine what it would be like if I was part of their family too."

Heather brushed something out of her eye. "I couldn't give him that," she whispered unnecessarily.

Tristan put his arm around her shoulders. "Mom, you did fine. You were the best mother in the world."

"Still am," she corrected with a weak smile.

"Still are," he concurred, giving her shoulders a squeeze.

She directed her next comment rather sheepishly to me. "I told you he was a wonderful young man."

"You were right," I said kindly.

Bored with the schmaltz, Merritt broke in. "So, Tristan, you wanted to see your siblings in person but your mother had forbidden you to have anything to do with them. You felt you had to sneak."

"Uh-huh."

"How many times would you say you came to the resort?"

He squinted one eye and screwed up one corner of his mouth, as if he needed to peer through an old, foggy telescope to catch a glimpse of the right number. "Um. Ten? Maybe?"

His mother gasped. Perhaps she hadn't realized the full extent of her son's sleuthing.

"Tell me about the time you saw Victoria Summersworth at the pool," Merritt said.

He hadn't been looking for her at all, he said. He'd actually been spying on his half brother Scott, who'd retreated into his private apartment at the Lodge, so, hoping to steal a swim on a hot day, Tristan had snuck over to the one pool at the resort hardly anyone went to. Disappointingly, there were already a bunch of kids there, splashing and running around. Then a bunch of old ladies arrived, and he realized with a start that one of them was a person he'd seen in pictures—Victoria Summersworth, the woman his father had been married to when he was seeing Tristan's mother.

That's just how he would see Vicki, I thought, *not as Warren's rightful partner but as an impediment to his parents' union.*

"I thought for sure I'd hate her," Tristan continued. "But I didn't. I liked her right away. She laughed and was happy and it made me happy too. I couldn't really swim anymore, not with all the kids there, and the old ladies doing exercises in the shallow end, with the trainer yelling and blowing his whistle like it was army boot camp. I figured I'd just stay where I was, but one of the old ladies kept staring at me with a really mean scowl on her face, so after a while I left."

"And the birthday party, Tristan—why did you go? Did you want to see Mrs. Summersworth again?"

He shook his head vigorously. "No way. She wasn't the person I wanted to see. Because . . . well, you know . . ."

"Because you're her husband's mistress's child."

"Yeah."

"But you went to her party."

"Only to see my half sister Lauren. I'd sort of seen or spied on the other three already, but I hadn't laid eyes on Lauren at all. I figured she'd be at the party, so I went. It was easy to get in. You didn't need a ticket or anything."

"Someone did ask you to leave, though."

"Yeah, that was Neil."

"You didn't think to tell him who you were?"

His cheeks reddened and he shook his head mutely, as if he'd lost the ability to speak, which must have been exactly how he felt when he came face-to-face with the powerful figure of Neil.

"So, you held back from introducing yourself to Neil, but you must have identified yourself to Mrs. Summersworth at some point that evening. . . ."

"I didn't." Tristan shot a nervous glance at his mother. "*She* introduced herself to *me*."

"Tell me about that."

"So, I was in the lobby, just, like, minding my own business, when Neil came over and asked what I was doing there. He wasn't mad or anything, but he could tell I hadn't been invited and he said I probably ought to go. So I did, but then this lady followed me outside and called to me to wait. It was Mrs. Summersworth. She said she'd seen me talking to Neil and she asked if my parents were around. I think she just meant, were they at the party or staying at the resort? But I guess I got confused. I thought she was asking me if they were, like, alive, so I said no, my dad died a long time ago, in an accident on the lake, and she gave me this weird look, and then she smiled this very nice smile and said, *Hello, Tristan. I've been waiting to meet you. I'm so glad you could come."*

"What time was that, would you say?"

"I don't know. Sorry." He looked a bit worried, as if he'd gotten a test question wrong.

"No problem. What happened then?"

"We talked. She said she wanted to know all about me and how I was doing at school and stuff. I thanked her for the scholarship, and she asked if I wanted to see some pictures of my father, and I said yeah, sure, so she said she'd meet me at her house and told me how to get there and I could just go in, because the door was open."

"How did you get there? Did you drive or walk?"

"I rode my bike."

"And when you arrived . . ."

"I waited for her inside for a few minutes, and when she got there we looked at pictures of my father in an old photo album. I'd already seen some of them at school, but there were more from when he was younger and older. We talked about him for a while. She said I could look at the pictures whenever I wanted to and ask her whatever questions I had."

"Is that all?"

"She kept calling him *Warren.* It felt weird to me, but I didn't say anything. She started telling me about his other children—their names and what they did for a living, et cetera. I already knew all that, but I didn't admit it, because I liked hearing her talk about them. Then she asked if I wanted to come for lunch the next day and meet them. I said sure and she told me to come at one p.m. and my mom was invited too."

"You never told me that," Heather said to him, reproachfully.

He shrugged, a bit defensively. "I didn't know if you'd want to go. And maybe you wouldn't let me go."

Heather seemed to be about to reply, but the comment died on her lips.

"A couple more questions," Merritt said. "Did you eat or drink anything while you were at Mrs. Summersworth's house? And what time did you leave?"

"We had Coke and crackers and cheese. I think I left at . . . mm, must have been ten thirty or eleven."

"I assume you're aware that Mrs. Summersworth died that night."

He nodded solemnly.

"Some people think she killed herself. What do you think?"

"No way. She was happy when I talked to her. She seemed like the kind of person who's happy all the time."

"Did you notice anything suspicious? Anything odd in the house? Maybe someone hanging around outside? Or did she say anything you thought was strange?"

"No. Everything seemed normal to me," Tristan said. "Except, I guess, how nice she was."

CHAPTER 34

A Desperate Appeal

Late that night I was talking to Trevor in my room. I was telling him about the mangled body I'd seen that afternoon—the second tragic death in one family in so short a time—and about the embezzlement, the fifth sibling, and so on. The investigation was getting really crazy, I said. I'd pretty much given up trying to keep track of everything in my journal. Trevor was sympathetic at first, but he got quieter as I went on.

"Are you okay?" I asked after an especially long silence.

"You didn't call my mother, did you?"

My heart missed a beat. "Gosh, no. I forgot. So much happened today. We were running around from morning till night. It didn't even . . . I'm sorry, Trevor. Really, I am."

"Would you call her now?"

"Now? It's after ten. Will she be up?"

"Probably. Just call. If she doesn't pick up, leave a message so at least she'll know you tried."

"I'll do that now, promise. And, Trevor?"

"Yeah?"

"I miss you."

"Miss you too, Olly. Call me back, okay? After you talk to her."

"Sure. Talk soon."

I ended the call and plopped down on the bed, feeling ashamed of having forgotten to call my future mother-in-law. *Making one little phone call really isn't such a hard thing to do,* I scolded myself. Yet for some reason it *was* hard. My conversations with Zuzanna always felt so stilted, as if we were both determined to connect but were reading from different scripts. And now we had a specific task: to discuss flowers for the wedding. What was there to say about flowers? I tried to remember which ones I liked. Irises? Tulips? Peonies? They were all good in my book. I figured I'd just agree with whatever Zuzanna suggested. I was sure she'd suggest something, because, as we all secretly knew, she already had a very specific plan in mind.

I picked up my phone and found Trevor's mom in my contacts. To get myself in the proper mood, I was trying to remember pleasant times we'd had together, when there was a soft knock on my door. *Who could that be?* Not Merritt; she didn't know where I was staying. (She'd never asked!) Besides, she would have texted beforehand, and knocked assertively when she arrived.

"Who is it?" I said.

A whispering voice replied, "It's me, Pia Valente."

I tossed my phone on the bed and opened the door, keeping the chain on and peering through the narrow opening first. The housekeeper was huddled there in the hallway, looking compact and wary, like a kind of woodland creature that's used to being prey.

"Pia? What are you doing here?"

"I need to talk to you." There was a furtive, pleading quality to her voice.

I let her in. Affected by her clandestine manner, I checked up and down the empty hallway before closing the door and reaffixing the chain.

She was dressed in tight blue jeans and a white tank top that showed off slender brown arms. There were large gold hoops in her ears, and on the outer edge of her left shoulder there was a small tattoo of a butterfly. Her hair was in a high ponytail that swung like a pendulum when she moved.

"Have a seat," I said. "Can I get you something? I have Diet Coke and ginger kombucha."

She glanced around at the seating options—the wooden chair at the table where both my laptop and journal were open, and the old wicker chair with the flounced floral cushion—and remained standing.

"It's about Scott," she said, fear in her eyes. "The cops came to the Lodge and questioned him. They asked a lot of questions about his mother and brother, about their deaths—where he was at the time, things like that." Here her voice broke and she swallowed a sob. "They said someone has been stealing a lot of money from the resort. They obviously think it was him! And why did they ask so many questions about his mother and brother? It's like they think he killed them! It's crazy! He would never do anything like that. He couldn't. He's not that kind of person. I'm really scared."

"Where is he now?"

"He was really upset. I tried to talk to him, calm him down. I said no one who knew him would ever believe he could do such things. But it made no difference. He just got angrier and angrier. And . . . he went off in a rage." She clasped a hand over her mouth, as if to prevent the next words from escaping, but they got out anyway. "He took his gun with him!"

"His gun?" I repeated stupidly.

"His gun. The hunting rifle in his office."

I felt sick. "Where did he go?"

"I don't know!"

"Think, Pia. Where would he be going? Think hard. Did he say anything?"

"He said, *I'll give them something to blame me for!*"

"They. Who's *they*? Did he mention anyone in particular?"

"No!" Pia wailed. "That's why I came to you. You have to find out where he's going and stop him!"

I paced. The obvious objects of Scott's anger were Victoria and Neil, but they were both dead already. Who else could he be after? "I need more to go on. Are you sure he didn't say anything else?"

She shook her head miserably.

"Think back. Was there anyone he was angry with? Not just tonight, but anytime. Someone he had a grudge against."

Again the answer was no.

Pia began crying softly. "What the police said about him . . . it's not true. None of it is true."

"Are you sure, Pia? Very sure?" I asked as gently as I could.

She looked up at me with a tearstained face. "I know for a fact that he's innocent. I was with him the night his mother died."

I measured my words carefully. "Pia, I hate to tell you this, but Scott already told Ms. Merritt and me that he was alone the night his mother died. Ms. Merritt pressed him on it and he was adamant."

"He only said that to protect my family. My father is undocumented. He works here at the resort. He takes care of the grounds. Scott didn't want any attention to come to us."

"I see. So, now you're saying that you two were together the night of the party, which gives him an alibi for the time of his mother's death."

She looked me in the eye, her demeanor strong and resolute, daring me to doubt her.

"What about the hit-and-run that killed his brother?" I asked.

"I was with him then too." Her voice trembled, and her eyes skittered away from me.

"*When* were you with him, Pia? What time exactly? What exactly were you doing?"

"We were . . . in Vergennes. At that café Scott always goes to. I forget the name."

"Where else did you go?"

A gleam of sweat appeared on her upper lip. She turned and walked over to the patio door, keeping her back to me.

"Pia, please be careful," I said. "There are so many ways of checking a person's story, and you can get yourself into a whole lot of trouble by lying to the police."

"It's true. I was with him all day," she said woodenly.

"And the missing money? Do you know anything about that?"

"I'm sure he couldn't have done it. He loves this club more than anyone. He would never steal from it."

"I assume you're aware that addicts sometimes steal to pay for their drugs."

"Scott has been clean for almost a year. I know that for a fact."

"That's what he told you, Pia, but you're not with him every minute of the day."

"He wouldn't lie about that. Not to me."

I sat down on the bed, feeling sad and tired. Pia was standing by her man the way a loyal partner should, but there was a good chance she would end up brokenhearted. "You care for him a lot, don't you?" I said.

She nodded mutely, still keeping her back to me. Somehow I could tell she was crying again.

"Come on now. Have a seat."

She came slowly back and lowered herself into the wicker chair.

I opened the can of Diet Coke I had in the mini fridge and I poured the soda into two paper cups. I handed one to her.

She sipped it gingerly, with a trembling hand. At least she was accepting the comfort it symbolized.

"I'm sure Scott has a good lawyer," I said. "The lawyer will see that his rights are protected. The cops can question him all they want, but they can't charge him without evidence."

Her voice barely above a whisper, as if she didn't want to hear herself ask the question, she said, "*Is* there evidence?"

I stayed silent for a moment, and it occurred to me that this was the third and most sensitive reason she'd decided to pay me a visit. First, she wanted me to find Scott before he hurt someone. Second, she wanted to provide him with alibis, as many as he needed, however thin. Third, she wanted to *know*. Could any of the allegations against him be true? Could he have stolen from the resort? Could he, god forbid, have killed?

Merritt would probably be mad at me for spilling what I knew, but I didn't care. Pia needed the truth, and I was going to give it to her. "Ms. Merritt and I have talked to a bunch of people. There are all kinds of speculations and theories, and a lot of weird unexplained facts. But at this time there's no real evidence connecting Scott to any of these crimes."

Pia quickly made the sign of the cross.

"Why did you come to me instead of Ms. Merritt?" I asked.

"I don't like her."

"I get that. She can be a lot."

"She doesn't like me either."

I didn't argue. Merritt had been pretty tough on Pia in Scott's office Wednesday morning. Then, like Haley Summersworth, Robin Tucci, Detective Clemmons, and the entire rest of the world, it seemed, she'd leapt to the conclusion that a missing necklace had *housekeeping staff* written all over it. She'd even announced her intention to give Pia's name to the police. Pia had no idea how close she'd come to being a suspect in the apparent robbery, but she had obviously picked up on Merritt's snobbish attitude.

Pia gave me a peculiar look then—her dark eyes solemn, her lips pressed tightly together. "Scott told me something else."

"What's that?" I thought it would be nothing, some little worry, because what could be worse than what we'd already discussed? But it was worse.

"He said he didn't kill his father. I didn't know what he was talking about."

I did, unfortunately. "Scott probably shared with you that his father died in a boating accident when he was seventeen. Scott and his mom were on the boat with him. Afterward, some people whispered that they should have done more to try to save him, and maybe Scott has carried the guilt with him all these years." I didn't mention Lauren's not-so-veiled accusation that Scott and his mother had murdered Warren because they hated him.

"He didn't do anything wrong," Pia attested with flashing eyes.

I smiled at her weakly. If she could have, she probably would have given Scott an alibi for that death too.

It made me wonder. What if Lauren was right? What if Scott *did* kill his father on the boat that day, either by himself or with Vicki's help? That would explain Vicki's quick thinking in protecting him from the media and public scrutiny. It would also explain his subsequent addiction, and Vicki's constant compulsion to cover for him and prop him up.

My next thought was as inevitable as it was outrageous. Could Scott possibly have murdered *three* family members, father, mother, and brother? Wasn't there an old saying, death comes in threes?

I chuckled nervously. How Merritt would laugh if she knew that such a silly superstition had crossed my mind!

CHAPTER 35

Olivia Steps Up

As soon as Pia was out the door I speed-dialed Merritt's number. It rang and rang. When voicemail kicked in, I hung up and dialed again. Same thing. I did it again. No answer. I checked the time. Eleven twelve p.m.

The fourth time I called, I waited impatiently through the endless ringing, then left a breathless voicemail message: *"Call me back. Urgent."* Then I texted a longer message: Pia says Scott angry at being framed. Left with gun. No idea where. Please advise.

I figured she was asleep, and I debated heading over to the Lodge to shake her out of bed. But I didn't have a key to her room, and the bedroom was on the far side of the suite, so I couldn't be sure that knocking would rouse her any more than her phone had.

I called the front desk and asked the manager to ring her on the room phone. He called me back a minute later to report that she hadn't picked up. He added that he hadn't seen her since about six that evening, when the two of us went up in the elevator together.

She couldn't have left the resort without someone giving her a ride. The restaurant was closed, and I doubted she would be mixing with the boozy riffraff at the bar. My best guess was that she'd silenced her cell phone and slept through the room phone.

I stepped out onto my little patio and took some deep breaths of the warm night air until my pounding heart quieted. *What would Merritt do?* I wondered.

The answer came effortlessly. Untangling this drama involving Scott and his hunting rifle was not in her job description. She was hired to solve murders, not prevent them. I doubted she would take any responsibility for this situation at all; she would simply notify Detective Clemmons, which was exactly what I ought to do. I retrieved my phone and pointed my finger at the 9 on the keypad, to be quickly followed by 1 and 1. Then I wavered.

Why hadn't Pia called the cops herself? Answer: because she desperately wanted to keep Scott out of their sights, lest they find more crimes to accuse him of. She hadn't appealed to Merritt either. Why not? Because, for good reason, she didn't trust the famous detective to really listen to her and respect her needs. Faced with two untenable options, she'd turned to me. I was the only person she knew who might actually help her. And although I was a rash beginner who'd botched the only solo assignment she'd received so far, Pia was probably right.

She'd come to me with her heart in her hand. *You have to find out where he's going and stop him!*

I decided I owed it to Pia to accept her challenge. If I could locate Scott, I could conceivably prevent serious, possibly fatal harm to a person as yet unidentified, in addition to saving Scott from performing a criminal act. And if I couldn't locate him, no one needed to know that I'd tried.

I set to work then . . . thinking. Logically, without emotion, just as I imagined Merritt would. Ticking through the possibilities, racking up the pros and cons. What if . . . what if . . . what if . . . I paced, and raked my fingers through my hair. I had to consider all options carefully, but I also had to hurry before catastrophe struck.

I put myself in Scott's place. What would I do if I were him? I supposed it would depend on whether I was guilty or innocent. Needing to consider the two scenarios separately, I got out my pen and brown suede journal and wrote down the following:

Option #1: I, Scott Summersworth, am guilty of either my mother's murder, my brother's murder, embezzlement, or all of the above.

a. In the case of my mother's murder, I consider myself practically in the clear. The cops have already searched for evidence of foul play and found nothing. The celebrity PI isn't doing much better, as far as I can see.

b. In the case of my brother's murder, the cops can suspect me all they want, but finding enough evidence to pin the hit-and-run on me is going to be very difficult for them. All I need to do right now is deny it up the wazoo and watch them flail about.

c. In the case of the embezzlement, my first priority is to destroy the evidence, pronto. Unfortunately this will be impossible, as the independent audit is surely in digital form, and even if I could destroy the accountant's hard drive, the report will likely be backed up somewhere else.

d. Since I can't destroy the accountant's report, I will have to destroy whoever knows about it. That will be Hobbs, who actually doesn't need to be silenced, as I can thank him, pay him, and bury his report once I'm in charge at Kingfisher—which leaves Vicki and Neil, who are both dead already.

Who else might know about the embezzlement? Answer: any number of people. Which means I have a vulnerability there that I need to fix but can't without more knowledge.

Option #2: I, Scott Summersworth, am innocent of everything.

There is only one thing to do in this case: figure out who is framing me. Most likely it's the same person who committed the murders—i.e., someone who not only is aware of the financial fraud at the resort but also knows that both Vicki and Neil were informed about it.

Stephen Hobbs fits that description, but he has no earthly reason for framing me or committing a double murder. So who else could it be?

Neil learned about the missing money Wednesday night; on Thursday he was at the funeral; on Friday he was dead. Whom did he speak to in that time? It has to be someone Vicki also confided in between her meeting with Hobbs on the previous Tuesday (July 25) and her death early Sunday morning (July 30).

I threw down my pen, baffled and frustrated. How could I possibly identify a person whom both Neil and Vicki might have spoken to about the embezzlement before they were murdered? I prided myself on being able to ferret out all kinds of facts, but I didn't have a clue how to get my hands on information like that. Then a little miracle happened. A memory started nudging me, like a mouse nibbling at the corner of my brain.

I opened my laptop and pulled up the photo file labeled "The Bungalow." I scrolled to Victoria's datebook, then to July twenty-ninth, the day of her party.

And there it was. The missing link.

CHAPTER 36

A Black Mercedes

It was midnight when I left my room in the staff dormitory. We were now almost two weeks past the dark night when Victoria Summersworth met her end. The moon was full and bright—a big yellow orb that hung over the earth like a spotlight, giving every little leaf and pebble an eerie glow. I commandeered a golf cart parked outside the dormitory and puttered off at the highest speed possible, until I arrived at the parking lot where poor Horace slept fitfully (I imagined) among his sleek, shiny neighbors. Along the way I passed a couple who turned away from my trying-to-speed vehicle, and a pack of teenagers who glanced up with guilty faces, assuming I was staff. At one point a sharp peal of laughter came through the woods. Other than that, the resort was quiet.

Horace seemed to make a louder-than-usual drone in the soft air as I drove out of the resort. I'd googled the address I was headed to, and the clear, inhuman voice of my travel app directed me as guilelessly as if I were tootling off to the grocery store.

Twenty minutes later, I pulled over to the side of the road in a posh secluded neighborhood of Burlington; I was about fifty yards away from a big white colonial replica, circa 1980, that spoke of generous exact proportions and patrician elegance. It was three stories tall, with long windows on the first floor and smaller, mullioned windows on the second, with a third floor of peaked dormers set into a steeply pitched roof. Carefully sculpted shrubs softened the foundation, and the big yard was surrounded by an old stone wall—concentric circles of protection. A lamp glowed dimly from somewhere on the first floor. There was a light over the front door, another over the garage. I doused Horace's headlights.

Scott's BMW was not in the driveway. I was disappointed. I'd been so sure that this was where he'd be. Perhaps he simply hadn't arrived yet. I waited in the silent darkness, giving him time to show up.

Twenty minutes later, Scott still wasn't there, but I'd seen lights going on and off in the house, and now the garage door creaked and began to rise, seemingly without human agency. Someone must have activated it from inside. Soon the taillights of a car came to life, and a dark sedan backed slowly out of the garage and down the driveway. The last time I'd seen this car, it was leaving the Harp & Plough Tavern and Lauren Perry's slender middle finger was standing straight and brash in the passenger window.

The black Mercedes drove off, traveling fairly slowly. It didn't pass by me, but went in the opposite direction. I gently turned on Horace's engine, irrationally hoping that if I was gentle with him he would agree to be quiet, and I followed the Mercedes at a distance, keeping my headlights off on the narrow, wooded street. I rounded a curve just in time to see the Mercedes take a left-hand turn onto a bigger, busier road. Turning on my headlights, I followed the car for a couple of miles, until it turned again, this time onto the I-89 ramp. On the highway I relaxed a bit, less worried that I would lose him, as by now I'd figured out where he was headed.

———

It made perfect sense. National and international marketing. Office renovations. A state-of-the-art laboratory. A new production-and-fulfillment center under construction down in the valley. How stupid I'd been not to see it right away. She'd had help on the inside, of course. From Arthur Doyle, her godfather. The two of them so elegant, tête-à-tête at the Harp & Plough. Conspirators.

I killed my headlights again and coasted along the dirt access road leading up to the Kingdom Come Farm, letting the headlights of the Mercedes up ahead mark the path for me. There was a cutout area about a quarter mile in. I pulled in there, intending to proceed the rest of the way on foot, when suddenly the pounding drum of "Therefore I Am" shattered the silence. Startled nearly out of my wits, I grabbed my phone and muted it. The name of the caller glowed on the screen: TREVOR.

I groaned. I was supposed to call him after I talked to his mother, and I'd done neither! He'd probably been waiting all this time, checking his phone every now and then to make sure he still had service and his battery wasn't dead. I *always* called him when I said I would. I was good that way. Now I pictured him alone in our little apartment, worried, wanting to call but holding off so as to give me time to hold up my end of things.

I really ought to pick up the phone, if only to let him know I was okay. If I didn't, his fears would grow. Perhaps in the back of his mind he'd wonder if I was with someone—for example, the good-looking guy, whom I probably shouldn't have mentioned at all, as he'd been only a whim, a fleeting inclination, a brief, forgettable glimpse of a different path, one I'd known all along I didn't want to take.

But if I talked to Trevor, I'd have to explain why I hadn't called his mother, and that discussion would inevitably lead to me explaining what I'd been up to since we last spoke, and what I was doing right now.

I'd spill everything, of course, because I always did. Where Trevor was concerned, I was an open, unmysterious book. Whatever I was feeling and thinking came straight out of my mouth like a heat-seeking missile.

I knew what he would say:

1. Stay out of this. *I'm already in it!*
2. This is not your problem. *If not mine, then whose?*
3. You are not qualified. *Excuse me. I am the assistant to the detective on this case; I have already carried out important parts of this investigation on my own.*
4. It's dangerous. *Duh. Hunting for a killer is dangerous by definition; did you think I was up here playing Parcheesi?*

I realized that talking to Trevor would be one of the worst things I could do right now. It would make me doubt myself, rob me of my courage, and break the momentum of this chase. For all I knew, at this very moment Scott Summersworth was up there at the Kingdom Come Farm, preparing to shoot his sister in the face. What business did I have overthinking relationship issues at a time like this?

The phone was gently vibrating in my hand. I steeled myself and dispatched the call to voicemail with a push of my finger. Trevor and the life I shared with him in New York City were a million miles away. Right now I needed it to stay that way.

CHAPTER 37

Lauren Speaks

Scott's BMW was parked at an odd angle in the middle of the lot, suggesting a brazen attitude. Arthur Doyle's black Mercedes was pulled up right beside it.

The farmhouse was dark except for a dim yellowish porch light. Across the lot stood the huge converted barn, where a brighter, whiter light illuminated the hanging sign: LAUREN PERRY SKINCARE.

The gravel crunched under my sneakers as I approached the door. It was ajar. I pushed it gently and looked through. In the semidarkness I could make out the reception area, the glassed-in conference room, and the long reclaimed-wood table where Merritt and I had received myriad insults.

The corridor that stretched beyond this area was dark, but an open door at the end glowed with brilliant fluorescent light. I couldn't see what was happening inside, but I could hear murmuring voices, both male and female.

I slipped inside the barn and padded quietly along the corridor. When I got to the end, I pressed my back into the wall and peeked around the doorframe. What I saw was a cavernous, high-domed room full of gleaming stainless steel counters and sinks, open vats, and cylindrical vessels that looked like butter churns. This was obviously where Lauren Perry's one-hundred-percent organic products were created and produced, but there was no stinging antiseptic odor in this laboratory. Instead, the place smelled as if whole fields of wildflowers had joyfully united to offer their combined essence to the world. There were harvested wildflowers everywhere—fresh ones in big see-through plastic tubs, and dried ones spread out on trays. I could see yellow sunflowers, minty-green grasses, and something pink. The aroma was beautiful and intoxicating, calling forth sensations of health, youth, and vibrant grace. God's gift to our sense of smell. Vermont's own balm of Gilead.

Yet in the middle of the room was a sight that was not pretty: Scott Summersworth bound to a black office chair. His arms duct-taped to the arms of the chair. His torso duct-taped to its back. His calves duct-taped together. He looked angry, thwarted, more red-faced than ever. He squirmed and strained against his bonds while Eric Perry, dressed in an old gray T-shirt and loose pajama pants, stood over him holding the roll of duct tape. A long-barreled rifle that looked like the one I'd seen in Scott's office leaned against the far wall.

Lauren Perry stood beside a stainless steel table with raised sides, the kind you might see in a factory assembly line. She was wearing jeans and leather riding boots and a tight white T-shirt with a burst of flowers across the bust. Her hair was pulled into a snug ponytail.

Brother and sister were glaring at each other.

Without taking her eyes off her captive, Lauren said, "Eric, go check on the girls. Make sure the cars and all the commotion didn't wake them up. If they're up, tell them a bedtime story or something until they go back to sleep. Then pull down their shades and close their doors. I don't want them looking out windows or sneaking over here. It's extremely important that they know absolutely nothing about what's happening right now."

Eric nodded, and exited through a door on the far side of the room.

I took the opportunity to slip inside the laboratory and duck behind a row of high steel shelves that housed cardboard shipping boxes of various sizes. I squatted, checked that my phone was still on silent, and pressed the record button. Then I set it on top of the big box I was hiding behind, hoping it would pick up the conversation despite a distance of twenty feet or more.

"So, what really happened on the lake that day, Little Brother?" Lauren said. "Your mother said she was on the boat with you and my father, an eyewitness to the so-called accident. That always sounded wrong to me, but I couldn't put my finger on why. Then, the other day, I remembered something very strange. I remembered her telling me how much she hated sailboats. She said they were tippy—*tippy!*—and the wind messed up her hair. She didn't see the point of any boat, she said. *If god wanted us to live on the water he would have given us fins.* So why was the day my father died the *one and only day* in many years she decided to go sailing?"

Lauren drew closer and leered down at her captive. "Admit it, Scott. Your mother wasn't there at all. It was just you."

He groaned. "Leave me alone. I didn't do anything wrong."

"Dad always said you were a wimp, and you couldn't stand that, could you? You hated him, wanted to get him off your case." She folded her arms across her chest. "I know you did it, Scott. I've always known. Either you hit him on the head and pushed him overboard, or he fell in by accident and you stood by and watched him drown."

"That's not true! How could you even think that?" he cried, his voice strangled by wrath and self-pity.

"Your mother came up with a plausible story. The rain, high

winds, and choppy water. The boom swung round, and Dad went overboard, and you both lost sight of him. But the weather that day was perfect, Little Brother. Everyone knew that. Everyone suspected your mother was lying, but nobody had the balls to accuse her. They felt sorry for her and you and us. *Those poor Summersworths. What a tragedy.*"

Scott looked up at her with a nearly hopeless appeal in his eyes. "You're right. My mother wasn't on the boat that day. I don't know why she lied. It didn't help me. It just made me feel more guilty than I already did."

He went on in a placating tone. "Look, I know you loved Dad a lot, Lauren—more than I did, if I'm being honest. I know you've always been angry about what happened that day. But I've been over it in my head a thousand times, and I know I did everything right, just the way you're supposed to, the way Dad taught me to. And there *was* a storm that day, just not one you knew about. See, we'd taken the new Marblehead daysailer pretty far north—well past Plattsburgh, almost to Isle La Motte. The sky darkened all of a sudden, and when we looked up we could see a line squall coming. It hit us like a fist—sheets of rain and wind gusts that tore up the surface of the water. That was why the boat jibed suddenly, why he got knocked off his feet. He was seventy-one years old; he'd been hit in the head. He disappeared in seconds. It took me a while to turn the boat around and get back to where I thought he'd gone down. But in all that wind and rain, visibility was only a few feet. I kept yelling his name, thinking he might answer, but he never did, and when the squall passed a short time later and the sun came out, the surface of the lake was as calm as if nothing had happened."

Lauren snorted. "Why didn't you dive in after him?"

"Are you kidding? In the middle of a squall? When I had no idea where he was and couldn't even see him? And let the boat get away so we would both have been stranded out there? You know how stupid that would have been."

"What I know is that anyone else, any decent human being, would have worked harder to save him. That's what I know. By the way, were you high at the time?"

"What are you talking about? Of course I wasn't high! I was seventeen. I wasn't even using then."

"Uh-huh. Just like you're not using now."

In a weary voice so low that I could barely hear it, he said, "I've been clean for almost a year. Believe me or don't, Lauren; I don't care. It's none of your business anyway."

He was slumped in the chair, staring at the floor. I saw that it wasn't only the duct tape that was pressing down on him but also what he had finally understood: his sister would never believe he was innocent of his father's death, no matter what he said or how often he said it. In her eyes, he was forever damned.

Lauren wasn't finished with him yet. "Your mother's lies didn't stop there, did they? She had to tamp down all those nasty rumors, so she continued circulating your sad little story so no one would dare ask questions, at least not out loud. *Poor Scott is so traumatized. He was so brave. I saw him do absolutely everything he could to save Warren, yet he still feels responsible, so let's all be nice to him. Let's make sure he feels loved.* She made you the victim; it was a genius move. But she had to keep going with it, had to keep dragging you out of trouble, so the world would never see you as you really are. Barely graduating high school, cheating your way through college, hyped on one drug or strung out on another. Alcohol, opioids, cocaine. If it wasn't for your mommy saving your ass time and time again, you'd be in jail or on the streets."

"That's not true. I . . . I . . ."

He faltered. He had no answer for a hypothetical. Maybe he

would be on the streets. Maybe addiction would have taken him there. Maybe he *had* been protected from harsh realities by his mother's connections and his family name. It could be true. On the other hand, maybe his mother's enabling had stymied him. If he'd had to pick himself up even once, take responsibility for his own failures and mistakes, maybe he'd have gotten on his feet and stayed there. How was anyone to know for sure? What difference did it make?

Turning away from her brother in disgust, Lauren strode toward the far end of the laboratory, out of my line of sight. I heard voices. Someone else was here in the laboratory, someone I couldn't see from my position behind the wall of boxes—a man, from the sound of it. I figured it was Arthur Doyle.

Scott had watched her go, and suddenly he narrowed his eyes. Something I didn't expect to see—an expression of shrewd curiosity—settled on his face. It got sharper, more disturbed, as a thought coalesced in his mind. He strained again against the duct tape holding him to the chair.

"Did *you* kill my mother, Lauren? Was it *you?*" His tone was tentative and surprised, as if he couldn't believe where his own logic had led him, yet he was sitting up straighter and his shoulders had broadened slightly.

I heard Lauren huff with annoyance, as if the accusation were a trifle. As she came back into my visual field, she said, "Sorry to disappoint, bro. Fact is, your mother killed herself because she was a coward like you."

"I don't believe you." Scott's voice was still hesitant, but it was a bit stronger than it had been. "I think you did it and made it look like suicide. You hated her. And you wanted to get back at me. You think I killed your father—our father—so you killed my mother in revenge. That's it, isn't it, Lauren? You stand there accusing me of being a murderer, but really it's you."

He didn't seem particularly angry, only shocked by the heinous possibility that his own sister had murdered his mother. The part of him that still harbored a shred of naivete was begging her to prove him wrong.

"It wasn't me, Little Brother. Though I can't say I never *wanted* to throw her off a balcony." Lauren regarded her brother thoughtfully for a moment, then pulled over a folding chair, opened it in front of him, and straddled it, her elbows resting comfortably on its back.

"Do you remember when I started building my company?" she asked.

"Not really."

"Oh, how silly of me. Of course you don't. You were high as a kite."

He shrugged. Her bull wasn't worth his time.

"It was totally different from what I thought it would be. See, for years, whenever I would share my dream, people would whine at me, *Oh, Lauren, it's so hard to make a business successful. You'll never manage it; you don't have the skill.* I started anyway, full of doubt, and you know what I discovered? It wasn't hard at all! It was awesome! I loved every minute of it. And I'm damn fucking good at it too."

"Congratulations. I mean that sincerely," Scott said, sounding sincere even as he jerked against his bonds.

Lauren wasn't listening. She was caught up in her story. "In a few years I wanted to expand—needed to, actually—to keep the momentum going, keep the business growing and moving up. All I wanted was an investment. That was the only fucking thing I ever asked this family for. Just enough to take the next big step. I would have paid the loan back, with interest, fair and square.

"I appealed to the board. I had solid numbers to show, all my ducks in a row. It was a strong proposition, a virtual no-brainer. Neil was on my side immediately; he could see how sound and forward-thinking my business plan was. But you, your mother, and your sister all voted against it, sinking the proposal. That was the first time any member of this family voted against Neil. Why *then*, Scott? Why was that the *one time* in your life that you opposed one of Neil's recommendations? Wasn't it just to stick it to me? Wasn't it just spite?

"As if that wasn't bad enough, your mother scolded me like I was a child, telling me—get this—that Kingfisher wasn't in the lending business. As if she knew anything at all about Kingfisher, as if she'd ever in her life read a fucking balance sheet. She told me to go to a bank if I wanted a loan. Jesus. What a bitch."

"I don't remember that," Scott said blankly, sounding exactly like someone telling the truth.

"How do you think that made me feel? Can you even imagine it? Here she was, wife number two, with no legitimate claim to anything, ruining my family's property, living off my family's business, running a part of it straight into the ground, then swanning around like a queen and favoring her own worthless children—*all while denying me*. It was fucking unbearable."

"I bet it was," Scott said. "Unbearable enough for you to come up with a scheme to get the money another way. All it took was a bunch of fake invoices and a few overseas accounts that would lead back to me if anyone looked. Smart, Lauren, very smart. And you got *him* to help." Scott jutted his chin toward the back of the room.

It must be Doyle. To confirm my guess, I stuck my head out just a bit and peered around the metal shelving on which the boxes were stacked. Sure enough, there he was: a dapper, snowy-haired old gentleman. Comfortably seated in an ergonomic office chair on rollers, he was neatly attired in a crisp tailored shirt and pressed khakis. The way his legs were crossed, one calf resting on his knee, offered a glimpse of purple and brown argyle socks. His mouth was gently closed, and a look of smug amusement played across his face. He might have been watching a decent television show; that's roughly the mix of interest and detachment he exhibited.

Lauren twisted her torso to offer a fond smile to the man behind her. I had only a split second to duck back into the shadows before she clocked me. Crouching low behind the shelves, heart hammering, I whispered to myself, *Fuck, Blunt. Be careful.*

When I dared to peek out again, Lauren had returned her attention to Scott. "Art has always been loyal to the Simmons family. Did you know he dated my aunt Libby for a while? That's how he met Dad. When he and Libby broke up, he joined Dad at Kingfisher and became part of our family. He was devastated when Mom died, and horrified when he saw who Dad chose to take her place. Then, when Dad died, it galled him to see your ditzy mother at the helm of a company he'd spent his whole career building, to see her being granted decision-making power she didn't deserve. At the same time, he grasped the potential of *my* company right away. He believed in me, like he always had. When he saw how I was being treated, he was willing to do anything to help me out. So yeah, he made my little scheme work."

She did her *Sound of Music* twirl, face tilted up and arms spread wide to soak in the fluorescent sunshine. "And look what happened, Scott! Look what I did with the money I borrowed from your cheesy little resort! Lauren Perry Skincare is the only one-hundred-percent organic high-end skin-care line there is. We're offering something new and exciting, something discerning women are clamoring for. We've completely penetrated the US market and made significant inroads in the European market; soon we'll be worldwide. And all of it is done right here. Vertically integrated. Efficiently staffed. Perfect quality control. Rapid fulfillment. And we're only getting better. Honestly, Scott, if your mom had had one ounce of faith in me just a few short years ago, you'd all be making money hand over fist right now. And I probably wouldn't hate you as much as I do."

Doyle chimed in. His voice was higher and thinner than I'd expected. "I've always cared about your sister, Scott. It was obvious right from the beginning that all the brains in the family had gone to her. And she's lived up to and exceeded my expectations. Lauren Perry Skincare is poised to eclipse Kingfisher and Wild Goose combined. It's only a matter of time—a few years at most. This, right here, is where the real money is, my boy. You all bet on the wrong horse."

Scott was silent for a few moments. Then he said, evenly, "I remember when we were kids and you used to come to the house, Art. I was scared to be alone in a room with you. You always seemed sort of tricky, like there was something up your sleeve. Even as a little kid I knew that half the things you said weren't true. I didn't trust you, and that's never changed."

Scott turned to his sister with one name on his lips. "Neil. Are you going to pretend you had nothing to do with that?"

"Neil?" Lauren replied stiffly. "You can't possibly . . . Oh, for god's sake . . . I don't appreciate the implication. Neil's death is a sad thing for me. He was the sibling I liked. Sure, he was a pompous ass who loved to hear himself go on and on about environmental impact and sustainability, but all that self-absorption made him easy to fool, easy to control. Give Neil enough flattery and you'd have him wrapped around your finger. All Neil ever really wanted was to love himself. I found his simplicity endearing.

"Did you know he was all in a froth at your mother's funeral, explaining to Art that there was systematic embezzlement at the resort? He was certain you were behind it. God, it would have been so sweet to watch him fire your ass! Then, out of the blue, some yahoo knocked him off his bicycle. How does that benefit me?"

Doyle's reedy voice came from the back of the room. "There's a silver lining to that tragedy, my dear; you just haven't seen it yet.

With Neil gone, you'll take over at Kingfisher, with me by your side—the way it always should have been."

Lauren frowned and fell mute. I had a few moments to study her expression before she spoke. I saw a bloom of confusion, then traces of fear.

She turned slowly to face him. "Art, you didn't . . . ?" Her voice trailed off.

"At least he died doing what he loved," Doyle said.

I watched the blood drain out of Lauren's face. She said his name once before lapsing into stunned silence. "Art—"

CHAPTER 38

The Jig Is Up

The door on the far side of the lab opened and Eric came in. "Constance and Viveca were asleep," he said. "Paulette was up, crying because she lost her pony."

Lauren looked horrified. "Please, no. Not the pony, not now."

"No worries. I found it under the bed. She went back to sleep."

"Oh, thank god." Lauren sighed with relief, then said regretfully, "I've got some bad news, sweetheart. Scott knows."

"Knows what?"

"About the money we've been siphoning from the resort."

"Shit." Eric stared into space for several seconds, taking the time he needed to measure the breadth and depth of the calamity. Finally he said, "What do we do now?"

"We've got to get rid of him. What else is there?"

"Now? Tonight?"

"I think so, honey."

"Definitely tonight," Arthur Doyle said.

Eric shuffled to one side so the German shepherd that had been close on his heels could squeeze into the room. My heart started pounding like crazy when I saw the dog. I'd noticed him when Merritt and I visited the farm. He'd barked up a storm, carrying out his watchdog function with laudable aggression. Now he trotted over to Lauren, who scratched behind his ears, cooing, "Hello, Ranger, my sweet big boy." When he'd had enough affection from her, Ranger started nosing around on the concrete floor, eventually making his way over to Scott. As he sniffed Scott's pant leg, the bound man jerked his legs spasmodically, trying to kick the dog away.

If Ranger caught a whiff of me, or saw movement behind the boxes, I'd be in serious trouble.

Lauren and Eric had moved to the back of the room, where Arthur Doyle was seated. I couldn't see what they were up to, but I could hear their voices. I assumed they were drawing up a plan to deal with the thorny challenge posed by Scott. Having investigated the captive, the German shepherd trotted after his owners.

I drew back into my hiding place and tried to figure out what to do. There had been two murders already, and now it looked like there was going to be a third, this one imminent, and likely to happen right before my eyes. It was up to me to prevent it. There was no time for fear or hesitation. I had to save Scott, whatever the risk. And I had to do it fast.

My first impulse was to creep out and untie him. Then we could both run away. But that wouldn't work: Lauren, Eric, or Doyle would see me long before I could free the prisoner, and even if none of them did, Ranger certainly would. No, I had to distract them somehow, get them to leave the lab for a few minutes. If I'd had Lauren's cell phone number, I could have snuck outside and called her with a fake emergency. But I didn't have it, and it was a bad idea anyway, as it wouldn't get Eric and Doyle out of the building. I racked my brain for a better solution.

Question: what gets multiple people out of a building quickly?

As soon as I phrased it that way, the answer was obvious.

The door I'd entered through was about ten feet away. It would take me back the way I'd come, along the carpeted hallway, and out to the reception area and main entrance. I would sneak out of the building and call the fire department on my cell phone to report a raging blaze at Kingdom Come Farm.

I dropped down and started to crawl on hands and knees to the exit. I figured that as long as I stayed low, the metal shelving would keep me mostly hidden. The new concrete floor had a shiny epoxy coating. When I accidentally dragged the rubber toe of my sneaker across its surface, it made a squeak. I froze, waited. The adults continued talking at the far end of the room. Thank god they hadn't heard. I exhaled my held breath and proceeded at a slightly quicker pace until, a few seconds later, I became conscious of another noise: the clicking of canine nails on the same highly polished floor.

I turned my head slowly in the direction of the sound. A pair of gleaming red eyes stared at me. Ranger was seated on his haunches, observing my progress. He looked calm but I could tell he was in a state of high alertness. I tried a smile, which he didn't respond to. So, having no other choice as far as I could see, I opted to continue my crawl. My first tentative movement prompted a barrage of deep-throated barking—a warning to me to move no more. The voices at the other end ceased immediately. I knew right then that the jig was up. This was a situation I couldn't rectify.

With nothing to lose, I sprang to my feet and ran. Out of the corner of my eye, I saw the dog lunge. I reached the open door before he got hold of me, and as I passed by I grabbed the door handle and tried to yank the door closed behind me, but it was stuck on something and barely budged. I had to keep going. Ranger bounded after me as I raced along the corridor, my legs flying like pinwheels under me. In a matter of seconds I felt the dog's frothy breath at my heels.

He won, of course. He jumped on me from behind and knocked me down. I landed on my face, my chin hitting the ground hard. Then he was on my back, his big paws clawing through my shirt as he barked triumphantly, claiming his flattened prey. Perhaps on the hunt for juicier flesh, he suddenly turned himself around and sank his many teeth into the back of my thigh. I screamed. The pain was searing. I felt like a piece of steak skewered by several knives at once. I couldn't stop screaming.

Suddenly he stopped. He dropped my thigh as if it were a chew toy he'd had enough of. From inside my blinding well of pain I heard the fading echoes of a gruff male voice and assumed that Eric had called the dog off.

I admitted to being grateful, even though I knew that I was now facing an even deadlier threat.

A heavy tread approached. I twisted onto my side, propped myself on an elbow. Indeed, it was Eric. He of the broad shoulders and the lumberjack beard. Lauren was right behind. They hovered over me, their faces full of concern. Concern for themselves, of course, not me. What a picture they made. Sweet and sour. Beauty and the beast. Sharing one evil heart between them. Dumb and dumber.

"Fuck," Eric said, peering down at me. "Who the hell is that?"

"It's the detective's assistant. Lydia somebody."

"What a fucking shit show."

"We've got to get rid of them both."

My pant leg was damp, and the dampness was spreading. I felt dizzy. Little spots of light inside my brain twinkled like faraway stars. I'd had no idea that a body could bleed so much from a dog bite. I heard my own voice mutter, "You won't get away with it. Luminol will show the blood."

Eric Perry bent down, and for a frightening moment I thought that he too was going to bite me, that he would rip my cheek off my face with his big country jaws, but he only got his arms underneath me and hoisted me up, carried me like a captured runaway bride down the corridor and back into the cavernous room I'd tried to escape.

Lauren unfolded a metal chair that had been leaning against a wall. She set it next to Scott, and Eric placed me on it. "Join the club," Scott said bitterly as I too was duct-taped to the chair.

"Some club," I replied through teeth clenched because my injured thigh was now pressed painfully against the seat.

Eric, Lauren, and Doyle talked among themselves, and then Eric left the barn through the side door. Lauren kept her back to us while she and Doyle conferred. A few minutes later Eric returned, wearing jeans now, with a handgun, a big one, tucked inside the waistband.

"I'll take them out to the east field and bury them under the milkweed," he said.

Lauren was frowning, chewing her fingernail. "Okay. That works. But what about the cars? How will we get rid of them?"

"Drive them into the quarry?" Eric suggested.

Lauren shook her head. "No. There'll be a search when these two are found to be missing. The cars will be discovered eventually, wherever we try to hide them. And what if they told other people they were coming here? We need a really good plan, one that will leave us in the clear."

Doyle stood up. "Well, it's late. I guess I'll leave you to it, then."

Lauren glared at him, and he immediately sat down again.

"Wait. I have an idea," Lauren said. She picked up Scott's hunting rifle, the one that had hung on his office wall. Letting it rest horizontally on her two palms, she extended her arms, offering the gun to her husband like a ceremonial gift.

"Get it?" She looked at him hopefully, willing him to be smarter than he was.

"Get what?" he said.

The scheme Lauren was suggesting might have been above her husband's pay grade, but I understood it right away, even numbed with terror as I was.

Lauren explained it to him. "Shoot her with Scott's rifle, wipe it, and put his fingerprints on it. Then shoot him with your gun. Your story will be: You were in the house, with your sleeping family. When you heard the gunfire, you grabbed your handgun and ran out to the barn, at which point you saw your drug-crazed brother-in-law standing over the dead detective. When he then turned his rifle on you, you killed him in self-defense and to protect your family." She nodded approvingly. "Yeah, that works perfectly. These two will be dead, and you'll be a hero. And it will be a sad shame that the baby detective lost her life when she stupidly followed my psycho brother into our barn."

Eric nodded. "Yeah, that's good."

He surrendered his handgun and took Scott's rifle. "I haven't shot one of these in a while," he said.

"You're not going to miss at close range," Lauren said dryly.

Eric moved to my side and planted his feet at just the right distance to accommodate the rifle's length. He raised the gun, snuggled it against his meaty shoulder, and squinted down the barrel.

Lauren turned her back to us and clamped her hands over her ears. "Don't look," she told Doyle. The white-haired gentleman placed his wrinkled hands over his eyes like a child playing peekaboo.

I heard a metal click as Eric cocked the hammer.

I couldn't believe what was happening. I thought about Trevor. He would be very upset. I apologized to him silently. Of course, I deeply regretted that I hadn't given him the opportunity to talk me out of coming here. I said a quick *I love you* to my dead mother and living father and thanked them sincerely for everything they'd done for me. I hoped they wouldn't think it had been a waste. I tipped my metaphoric hat to Aubrey Merritt, from whom I should have learned a great deal more.

I briefly wondered who would take care of my houseplants, and then I thought about everything I would miss about this world. Sunsets and Central Park and good food and love. In my heart I said good-bye to the children I would never have. Then I prayed that reincarnation was a real thing so I would have a chance to try life again, and maybe be a little smarter next time and get myself a little further along than my twenty-sixth year.

I squeezed my eyes shut, facing my end as bravely as I could, yet still madly hoping that something, anything, would cause the man at my side to lower his weapon and let me go. Next came a wild cacophony of sounds: thumping, banging, hoarse yells, Ranger's frantic barking, and, loud and clear above it all, Merritt's voice shouting, "Drop that gun!"

CHAPTER 39

Stupid Is the Word

"Give me one good reason not to fire you," Merritt said.

That little bullet of a woman, Officer Grout, handed me a bottle of spring water, which I accepted gratefully. I barely remembered getting twenty-six stitches in the emergency room. Apparently I'd been completely hysterical, alternately sobbing and nattering on incoherently, at times begging the nurses to let me live, even though I was by then quite safe and in absolutely no danger of expiring. To say that I felt ashamed and humiliated would be an understatement. But mostly I was ecstatic to find myself still alive.

I sipped the water, my eyes cast down. Dawn was just breaking outside the window, and I was seated on the couch in the Blue Heron Suite, where Merritt had taken me, with the help of Officer Grout, who had stormed into the barn at Kingdom Come Farm along with Merritt, Detective Clemmons, and some other cops. My blood-soaked jeans had been scissored off at the hospital, and someone had donated surgical scrubs for me to wear, as well as crutches to hobble back to the resort on. The local anesthetic was wearing off and my right thigh was starting to throb painfully, in rhythm with my pulsing heart. I'd been informed that there was a big tear in my hamstring and that it would take months to heal.

"Do you have any idea how utterly, how insanely, how *enormously*, stupid you are?" Merritt's dark blue eyes were stormy, merciless. It looked as if the wrath of Poseidon was boiling in their depths.

Officer Grout had assumed a wide-legged military stance behind Merritt, who was seated in a chair across from me. I blinked in dis-belief as the little cop clearly mouthed the word *stu-pid* at me with a satisfied gleam in her eye.

The word stung, I'll admit. I would rather my boss had said how *brave* I was for having tried to save (badly) someone's life, or how *lucky* I was that she'd managed to pluck me from the jaws of death. But *stupid* was the word she'd picked out of all the ones available, and the sad thing was, I couldn't disagree.

"I think so."

"You *think*?"

"I know. What I did was stupid. Thank you for saving my life."

"I absolutely ought to fire you." Her face was whiter than its usual stark whiteness. It was strained and gaunt, every one of her sixty-plus years showing in its dry folds. She looked almost worse than I felt, as if *she* were the one who'd been seconds from the grave.

My gaze roamed across the ceiling and down to the floor—anywhere but to the space directly in front of me, where her pale, crooked fingers were tented before her mouth in the characteristic thinking pose that usually resulted in a firm pronouncement I'd not once been able to predict. Today, though, I felt pretty sure of what was about to come out of her mouth. She was definitely going to fire me.

My dream job was ending in a nightmare of my own making.

The famous detective stood up in a flurry of disgust and started to pace back and forth across the room, from the heavy oak door to the long glass windows. She was dressed entirely in black. Her silver hair looked dull and stiff. Outside, the world was awash in the soft gray fog of dawn.

"All right," she said, making a clear effort to control herself. "I'm going to give you one chance, and one chance only, to explain yourself. So you'd better make it good."

I started to mumble.

"Speak up!"

I found my voice and a smidgen of courage and told my story, beginning with how Pia had come to my room to tell me what Scott said before storming off with his hunting rifle: *I'll give them something to blame me for.* How I'd tried to get in touch with Merritt, and when I couldn't, knowing that time was of the essence, I went off in search of Scott myself, hoping to prevent him from doing something truly terrible. How logic and a clue I'd found in Victoria Summersworth's daily planner had led me to the home of Arthur Doyle, Kingfisher CFO, and how I'd followed him from there to Kingdom Come Farm, where it turned out that Scott was being held captive, his rash plan having backfired somehow.

I described everything that happened at the farm, everything that was said. I took out my phone and played back the recording I'd made. As Merritt and I listened together, our heads bent solemnly as if we were at church, it dawned on me that my solo adventuring hadn't been a complete fiasco. In fact, some rather monumental good had come of it.

I'd caught the bad guys.

There were three guilty parties, the way I saw it. Lauren Perry, who must certainly have thrown her nemesis, Victoria Summersworth, off the balcony, despite her constant refusals that she had; Arthur Doyle, who'd basically admitted to crushing Neil Summersworth under the tires of his black Mercedes to give Lauren a clear shot at total control of Kingfisher; and Eric Perry, who'd been a hair's breadth away from executing Scott Summersworth and me. All three had been partners in the embezzlement scheme, which included the elegant twist of framing Scott. Should it have been necessary, they would have dumped the murders of Vicki and Neil on his doorstep too.

My escapade had been dangerous and ill-advised, certainly. But overall, not a bad night's work.

I couldn't resist pointing that out to Merritt.

She put her wizened hands to her face, as if trying to unsee me; called me impudent and incorrigible; and asked how I could be so utterly brazen as to attempt to claim credit for anything, especially when my conclusion happened to be so stupidly (that word again!) wrong.

"Wrong?" I repeated, stupidly amazed. "How so?"

"Lauren Perry did not kill her stepmother."

"How do you know?"

A sly, mysterious smile flickered on her face. "The reading of the will is scheduled for this morning, at ten o'clock. To avoid disrupting the resort's normal business, it will take place at the Bungalow. All the relevant parties will be there, as will Detective Jim Clemmons and a cadre of officers. I'll name Victoria's murderer then."

My jaw fell open.

Merritt shook her head in the sad disappointment that I feared was becoming her habitual attitude toward me. "When are you going to ask how I found you?"

It was true that the question hadn't occurred to me. Back at the barn, in those moments of blazing terror when the hunting rifle was pointed at my head, Merritt's sudden appearance had simply been a miraculous answer to my prayer. I hadn't thought to question it. Later, in all the commotion at the hospital, I'd been too busy blubbering and blathering to anyone who would listen, and then I was gritting my teeth as the ER doctor stitched me up.

"How did you find me?" I asked.

After briefly scrolling, Merritt held up her phone. A pulsing dot indicated my present location on the western edge of the Wild Goose Resort.

"So you *were* listening!" I said.

She rolled her eyes. "Go on—get out of here. Go to your room and think carefully about whether you're cut out for this line of work. Personally, I have serious doubts. And for god's sake, wash up. You look terrible."

Officer Grout leapt eagerly to her feet and held the door of the suite wide-open for me. She audibly snickered as I hobbled out on my crutches. I finally guessed the reason behind her consistently rude behavior: the galling little woman wished *she* could be the great detective's assistant. She wanted my job.

"Not on your life," I muttered as I passed by.

CHAPTER 40

Victoria Summersworth's
Last Will and Testament

About a dozen people were there, sprinkled across four rows of folding chairs set up for the occasion, all of them facing the long table where Victoria's lawyer, Philip Drabble, sat, stiff backed and solemn, along with his assistant, who seemed to have modeled himself exactly on his boss, right down to the finely tailored dark suit, round wire-frame spectacles, and conservative tie.

The lawyers gave off a dull intellectual air that contrasted with the sunshine warming the deck, the sparkling blue waters of the lake, and the fact that the desk at which they sat was actually Victoria's frosted glass patio table, with a hole in the middle for an umbrella. In summers past the table had no doubt been home to plates of grilled hamburgers and hot dogs, rows of condiments, and heaping bowls of fruit and salad. Today the only object adorning its surface was a closed leather folder. Drabble's right hand rested lightly on its cover—a signal to all that he was in charge of the proceedings and would not begin reading the enclosed document until he deemed it the time right.

I hobbled to the last row. My right hamstring was throbbing, and I didn't dare make any abrupt movements, for fear that the stitches would break. After lowering myself carefully into a chair, I placed my crutches on the floor and waited for the show to start, but I quickly realized I'd made a mistake. I could see nothing but the backs of people's heads—a view in no way conducive to investigative work. So I picked up my crutches and hobbled back the way I'd come, then dragged an empty chair to a new position slightly behind the big table and off to one side, near the sliding glass door through which people entered and exited the deck. This turned out to be a clumsy procedure involving a lot of bumping and dropping of one crutch after the other, then some precarious balancing on one leg. An expression of annoyance flickered across the presiding lawyer's face, but he was too important a personage to quibble over the seating plan. His assistant glared at me but chose not to intervene when his boss had not done so. For my part, when I finally sat down I was quite pleased to have given myself a much better view of the assembled guests.

In row one was Neil's wife, Allison, wearing a plain black dress and chunky beads. She looked fretful and unsteady, barely put together, her hair an untidy blond nest, her face puffed out and pink. She had a friend with her, a woman I didn't recognize, who showed a sad, empathic expression to the world as she kept one arm draped protectively around the shoulders of the grieving widow.

Haley and Sumiko had claimed front-row seats as well. Sumiko looked as elegant as the day I'd met her, while Haley appeared uncharacteristically subdued. She had put on a dress for the occasion, a shapeless knit in a watery eggplant hue. Her thick calves were bare, her brown sandals but one notch higher than Birkenstocks on the fashion scale. I knew she was upset at having been excluded from the investigation, and the fact that the robbery, which she'd happily believed to be proof of foul play, had actually been committed by her sister must have been a disappointment too. As far as she and Sumiko knew, Merritt had made no progress whatsoever in finding her mother's killer. It occurred to me that I might be the only person there who knew that a murderer was about to be unmasked.

Scott and Pia occupied seats in the middle of row two. Both stared straight ahead, not touching. Perhaps they'd argued. Scott, more slumped and slovenly than usual, looked almost as wrecked as his widowed sister-in-law, though I doubted that was because of grief at having lost his brother. Last night he'd gone off in a fool-hardy rage and had almost been killed with his own gun. No wonder Pia wasn't talking to him.

Monty Draper, at the far end of row three, was jumpy and jittery. One leg crossed over the other offered him a shoelace to pick at as he squirmed his torso this way and that as if working out a golfer's kink. He'd thrown a shapeless linen blazer over white canvas pants. He kept glancing around furtively, taking stock of who else was there. He appeared to have half a mind to bolt.

The first four chairs of that row were taken up by Robin Tucci's commodious handbag, Robin Tucci, Pat Tucci, and Pat's oxygen apparatus. Daughter and mother wore the same stubborn, critical expression, as if expectation of poor treatment had already trampled their slender hopes.

The presence of Heather and Tristan Morrissey in the middle of row four surprised me. Who had invited them? The lawyer? Heather's eyes were closed. From the slow, steady movement of her chest, I assumed she was breathing mindfully. Tristan, hunched over his phone, dark curls hiding most of his face, was trying not to be there at all.

Missing from the gathering were Neil Summersworth, Lauren Perry, Eric Perry, and Arthur Doyle—Neil because he was dead; the other three because they were in police custody. Their absence was a great relief. If I'd had to look at their snide, cunning faces, I might have become a murderer myself.

Where was Merritt? I didn't see her anywhere. Motoring past the Lodge in my golf cart a few minutes ago, I'd noticed a police car parked in the curved driveway—an unusual sight that disrupted the resort's chill vacation vibe—but there was no sign of Detective Clemmons or that irksome gofer Officer Grout, who, after that morning's lip-syncing episode, I'd given myself full permission to hate.

At ten past ten, just at the point when the seated guests began to stir restlessly, Attorney Drabble cleared his throat and began the proceedings.

"As I am executor of Victoria Summersworth's estate, one of my jobs is to oversee the distribution of her assets as specified in her last will and testament. Although the reading of a will is not legally required, I believe that, in certain circumstances, gathering family members and beneficiaries together to hear its contents shows respect for the deceased, brings clarity to the process, and may prevent hard feelings among beneficiaries later. I have here"—he tapped the leather folder with a stiff index finger—"the original document and several copies. After the reading, I will retain possession of the original to file in probate court, and my assistant will distribute copies to the family members and beneficiaries named therein. If at the conclusion of the reading you believe that you heard the provisions incorrectly, or that I may have read them incorrectly, I encourage you to refer to your own copy for verification."

The proceedings were brief and straightforward. The bulk of Victoria's personal estate was to be divided in equal portions among the four children. When it was announced that Neil's portion would go to his widow, Allison started to weep uncontrollably, and her friend handed her a tissue.

Various stipulations were made. Haley was first in line to purchase the Bungalow if she wanted it, its fair market value to be deducted from her portion of the estate. The jewelry would be split between the two daughters, with a special stipulation that Lauren should receive the jade necklace that Merritt and I knew she had already pocketed. The will made no mention of the deceased woman's remaining possessions.

The lawyer shuffled some papers. Once again the attendees shifted in their seats, crossed and recrossed their legs, glanced surreptitiously at their neighbors. Robin Tucci hoisted the strap of her purse onto her shoulder as if preparing to leave. Her movements were jerky and brittle, as if she were encased in invisible armor. It was hard to tell what she was feeling. Impatience? Resentment? Fear? Anxiety? As an employee of the deceased, she was in a special category. Except for the Morrisseys and her own ill mother, she was the only individual there who'd never socialized with the others, who'd never even been invited to. She hadn't heard her name yet, and it looked as if she was already counting herself out.

Monty Draper threw an arm over the back of the empty chair next to him. His feet were planted solidly on the ground and his legs were spread wide. He'd plastered a firm smile on his face, as if he were enjoying the spectacle, uncaring of the outcome. *Let's all have some fun* seemed to be the attitude he'd settled on.

In the back row, Heather gently lowered Tristan's phone. He looked up, wide-eyed, as if surprised by his surroundings.

The lawyer resumed his professional drone. A sum of twenty thousand dollars would go to Mr. Monty Draper.

"Thank you, my love. I miss the hell out of you," Draper said out loud, and for some reason it didn't seem weird or out of place. I imagined angel Victoria, floating invisibly in the flawless sky, smiling down on him with affection. Then Monty leaned over and put his head in his hands. His shoulders heaved under the weight of his emotion.

The lawyer continued. "A sum of fifty thousand dollars to Mr. Tristan Morrissey."

At the sound of his name a startled Tristan leapt to his feet, as if he thought he was expected to walk up to the front of the group and receive a sports trophy or academic honor. When his mother whispered something, he glanced down at her in confusion, seemed to realize that nothing in particular was required of him in this moment, and sat back down. Still, he appeared rather stricken. His mother reached out and brushed his curly locks off his forehead as she must have done a thousand times when he was a little boy.

The others twisted around in their seats to lay eyes on the mysterious young man who was now blushing furiously. They had no idea who he was or what he was doing there.

The lawyer didn't stop to explain. He cleared his throat. "Lastly . . ." he said, but a murmuring had started, and he needed to repeat the word a couple of times before he'd reclaimed the group's attention. When all eyes were focused on him he continued reading, in an especially commanding tone.

"The last bequest is to Ms. Robin Tucci, in the sum of seven hundred fifty thousand dollars."

Robin gaped at the lawyer as the color drained from her face. The brittle quality I'd noticed seemed more pronounced than before. For a moment I saw her as damaged, fragile—almost as an open wound—not what you'd expect of a woman who'd just come into a lot of money. It seemed her good fortune had yet to sink in.

Her mother, on the other hand, had no trouble grasping the news. Her rough smoker's voice pierced the stunned silence that had followed the lawyer's declaration. "Yes, ma'am! Damn right! All hail to the Queen!"

Things were a bit of a blur after that. The lawyer listed bequests of ten thousand dollars each to several charities. I'm not sure anyone was listening. People were talking noisily among themselves, their heads swiveling back now and again to stare at the unknown inter-loper, Tristan Morrissey, but mostly to glare at Robin Tucci, who had made out like a bandit, and whose bequest would surely take a huge chunk out of Victoria's estate, thus reducing the value to be divided among her legitimate heirs.

At one point, in the general atmosphere of consternation, Monty Draper scooted a few seats over and stuck his hand out to Robin.

I heard him say, "Congratulations, sweetheart. See? She didn't forget you. Gave you a shitload more than she gave me. Ten shit-loads. But who's counting?"

The look he received from Robin Tucci in return was of such fierce hatred that it gave me chills. Needless to say, she didn't shake his hand.

It's Draper, I thought. *Robin suspects him. That's why she hates him so much.* The CCTV footage was an obvious ploy. He could easily have left from a back door of his apartment building and returned to the Bungalow in plenty of time to kill Victoria. Why? Because for some reason she'd decided not to marry him, and she told him so that night. How that would have stung! The high-society matron jilting the Las Vegas grifter! After all those moonlit nights and lazy days when he'd worked so hard to win her, she'd laid down her cards and taken the pot. How dare she? He was a card sharp, a profes-sional bluffer, no stranger to rough justice. To payback.

But even as I was putting my money on Monty Draper being the killer, the day's new revelation was niggling at me. Victoria's stun-ning bequest to Robin certainly gave the assistant a strong motive. Why should Robin wait dutifully until the Queen was dead to col-lect her share? Why suffer through the old girl's potentially endless dotage? Why not just dump her over the railing and enjoy a com-fortable life before she got any older herself?

Of course, that scenario worked only if Robin knew about the bequest—if she'd been told or had learned by some other means what was in her boss's will. If she had, she deserved an Oscar for her performance this afternoon. I doubted that Meryl Streep could have looked as shocked.

Attorney Drabble closed his leather folder with care. Tucking it under his arm, he stood off to one side of the deck as he waited for his assistant to finish handing out copies of the will. People were standing up, stretching their legs.

Where was Merritt? She was supposed to be here to name the killer. As outrageous as it had seemed to me, given the lack of evidence so far, I'd fully expected her to show up and do exactly that. It hadn't occurred to me that she would break her promise—that she *could* break her promise. Even now a part of me believed that she would appear momentarily to pull the proverbial rabbit out of the hat. But there weren't many moments left. Everyone would soon be gone.

I stood up, hunkered over my crutches, and peered inside the house. The living room was empty. The only possible answer was that something bad had happened; she was in some kind of trouble. I pulled out my phone to call her.

That was when the front door swung wide and she walked in, trailed by Detective Clemmons, weaselly Officer Grout, and another uniformed officer. Through the briefly open front door I glimpsed two police cruisers in the driveway and two more officers waiting outside.

I stepped back and Merritt blew past me. If she noticed me standing there, she gave no sign. She took the place of honor in front of the patio table the lawyer had just vacated.

Detective Clemmons crossed the deck and stood by the railing, facing the audience. The sun beat down on his big, drooping shoulders. The runt and her colleague assumed positions on either side of the sliding glass doors. Each had a set of handcuffs attached to their black leather belt and a holstered service revolver jutting off their hip. They were obviously barring the exit. The only way off this deck now was the way Victoria Summersworth had gone.

The guests had stopped talking. They were staring in wary surprise at the newcomers.

I returned to my seat. Someone was about to be arrested. Delight was not an appropriate emotion in such a grave and consequential situation, but I could feel the corners of my mouth turning up nonetheless. The best part of the show was about to begin.

CHAPTER 41

Aubrey Merritt Takes the Stage

This was her moment, and she'd dressed for it, in an impeccable snow-white suit and nude heels. I was too much of a rube to be able to identify brands, but both suit and shoes looked haute couture to me. Her hair was freshly slick and trim, and practically white in the sunshine. Her large sunglasses hid the upper half of her face, while the lower half was dominated by a slash of fiery red lipstick. She looked stunning and invincible. Everyone sank quietly into their folding chairs and gazed at her expectantly.

She began simply enough. "My name is Aubrey Merritt. I'm a private investigator from New York City. As many of you know, I was hired to look into Victoria Summersworth's death. I have now completed my work and am ready to give my report.

"First I'd like to say a word about the investigation conducted by Detective Clemmons and the Burlington Police Department. Given the accepted official protocols in cases of suspicious deaths, I want to assure you that the police were thorough and responsible. They made no procedural error, or any other kind of error, in concluding that Victoria Summersworth most likely died of suicide."

She nodded at Clemmons respectfully, and he nodded back.

"However, the absence of evidence does not prove, can never prove, the absence of a crime. In light of this fact, it's easy to understand why, in a case of such personal significance to her, Ms. Haley Summersworth sought my services. She preferred not to spend the rest of her life burdened by unanswered questions, nor did she want her mother's legacy to be distorted by an untrue accusation of self-harm. I admire the choice Haley made. It takes courage to seek the truth, especially when there's a chance that what you discover will hurt you.

"I believe we all owe a debt of gratitude to Detective Jim Clemmons, the Burlington Police Department, and Haley Summersworth. I mention this in the hope of forestalling future criticism of any of these parties."

She removed her sunglasses and placed them in the center of the table. "I've solved many criminal cases in my career, but this is the first time I've encountered a situation where it wasn't clear that a crime had been committed. Usually there is a bullet wound, a bloody knife, signs of strangulation. In this case there was no indication of foul play. How was I to find a killer without any evidence that a murder had taken place?

"I quickly realized that the dichotomy between suicide and homicide was immaterial for my purposes. Victoria Summersworth had clearly been killed. My job was simply to discover whether the killer was herself or someone else.

"The answer eluded me for some time. In fact, I wasn't certain of it until the early hours of this morning. I can now say with complete confidence that Mrs. Summersworth did not die by her own hand. She was murdered in cold blood, and the murderer is here today."

A gasp went up from the assembled group. Haley jumped up and cried out, "I knew it! I knew it!" Sumiko tugged her back down, at which point Haley covered her face with her hands and started to cry.

People were twisting in their seats, casting suspicious glances at one another as they tried to guess who the killer might be. I was as flummoxed as everyone else. I knew that my first choice, Lauren Perry, was incorrect; Merritt had told me so. I would have thought that Neil, Eric Perry, and Arthur Doyle would still be on the list, but Merritt had clearly said that the killer was here on this deck, which ruled them out.

I scanned the group carefully. Other than myself, seventeen people were present. After Merritt, the three cops, and the two lawyers were subtracted, eleven remained: Allison and her friend; Haley and Sumiko; Scott and Pia; Monty Draper; Robin and Pat Tucci; Heather and Tristan Morrissey. Some were clearly unlikely. Others had been shown to have possible motives, and still others seemed to have no motive at all, or at least not ones Merritt and I had sussed out. I looked for someone who seemed especially nervous, but everyone was ill at ease—either fidgeting or sunk into themselves or staring aggressively at Merritt.

At least one person must have been holding back a tremendous urge to run. Perhaps at this moment they were measuring the distance to the door, estimating how far they could get. But any escape attempt would be fruitless. Not only would they give themselves away, but the cops on either side of the door would block them immediately. The smartest thing they could do right now was sit tight and hope that the detective was wrong, or, if she did correctly finger them, hope that she didn't have enough evidence to prove their guilt.

Out of the corner of my eye I observed Monty Draper in particular. He had a skeptical "show me" expression on his face. His body language said something quite different, however. As I watched, he brought the arm that was stretched across the back of the neighboring chair into his chest, and he crossed one leg tightly over the other. For once, he was reducing the space he took up, as if to make himself less noticeable.

Merritt's sharp heels clicked on the wooden deck as she paced back and forth in front of the table. "Now I will explain how I arrived at my conclusion. My presentation will cover all the information that's relevant and that I care to provide. I will not take questions afterward, so I suggest you listen closely now."

A prickly hush descended over the group.

"You're all probably aware that a murderer needs motive, means, and opportunity—all three—to successfully carry out his deed. A simple analysis of these three factors is how a detective will usually begin an investigation. Here again my path was not as simple as one might expect.

"Let's start with the category of opportunity. Only one person of interest in this case, Arthur Doyle, had a solid alibi. Mr. Doyle was admitted to the hospital on Friday, July twenty-eighth, for a coronary stent procedure. He was discharged from the hospital Monday morning at eleven o'clock. After confirming these details with the hospital, I removed him from my list of suspects.

"Unfortunately, no one else could be eliminated. Every person questioned insisted that they were home in bed in the small hours of Sunday morning, when Victoria Summersworth fell from the balcony. As an alibi, sleeping in one's bed is clearly insufficient, even when a spouse or partner is said to be present. Not only can someone slip out in the middle of the night without their partner knowing, but a loyal partner will occasionally provide or corroborate an alibi in order to protect their loved one.

"A case in point is Ms. Pia Valente. Shortly after her lover, Scott Summersworth, was questioned in connection with the murders of both his mother and his brother, Ms. Valente came forward to provide him with two separate alibis.

"Her attempt to protect Mr. Summersworth did not convince my assistant, Olivia Blunt, whose inexperience and naive sympathy Ms. Valente was likely depending on. Nor did it convince me. While she may indeed have been with Mr. Summersworth on the morning his mother died, she most certainly was not with him on the afternoon of his brother's death." Merritt looked directly at the housekeeper. "Ms. Valente, I'm sorry to say that your lie only brought greater suspicion to both Mr. Summersworth and yourself."

"To Pia?" Scott blustered. "Why to her?"

"Because in providing you with alibis she also, conveniently, gave them to herself."

"What? You mean you think . . . Oh my god, that's ridiculous! Completely ins—"

"Please be quiet, Mr. Summersworth. I have a lot to get through."

After a bit more sputtering, he closed his mouth.

Merritt continued. "Having been able to eliminate only one individual thus far, I moved on to the category of means. Here, sadly, I had the same result: I was able to cross only one additional person off my list."

She sighed, recalling her frustration. "The problem centered on the facts that there was no murder weapon, nothing that could be located and traced back to its owner, and that no special skill had been required to effect the victim's demise. All the killer needed was enough physical strength to subdue the victim and lift her body just high enough to allow the railing to be used as a pivot point, from which nothing more than a strong push would be needed to send the victim toppling into thin air.

"Victoria Summersworth was sixty-five years old. She stood five feet four inches tall and weighed about one hundred twenty-eight pounds. Her bones were frail and her musculature was undeveloped. Almost anyone could have subdued her and lifted her to the necessary height.

"There was one exception, however: Mrs. Pat Tucci, who sits

there now with an oxygen apparatus by her side and a balled hand-kerchief in her fist. Mrs. Tucci, I submit that you are simply not strong enough to have accomplished this murder."

"Not that I didn't want to!" Pat yelled back, apparently upset at having been ruled out. She immediately started hacking. Robin pulled a water bottle out of her purse and offered it to her mother. Pat waved it away angrily, as if the gesture had offended her.

When Pat stopped coughing, Merritt continued. "With oppor-tunity and means providing minimal help to the investigation, I was forced to rely almost exclusively on the last of the three catego-ries: motive.

"As I considered Victoria herself to be the primary suspect in her own murder, I started with her. Did she have a motive to end her life? The answer appeared to be no. As far as I could determine, she was not in the least unhappy. On the contrary, she had much to live for. She was healthy; she worked if and when she wanted to at a job she loved; she had many friends and was close to several members of her family. On top of that, she'd fallen in love and was considering the prospect of a second marriage. This is hardly the situation of most suicides.

"But despite the lack of obvious motive, there was troubling ev-idence in support of the suicide hypothesis that I could not ignore.

"By far the most challenging issue was the apparent suicide note found in Victoria's bedroom. This note was examined by a hand-writing expert, who declared that it had been written by Victoria herself. Thus, it was reasonably taken as authentic by the police. I was troubled by it, though. There was no addressee, no mention of the author's intended act, and no apology. The tone struck me as odd. It displeased me both as a suicide note and as a forgery of a suicide note, since you would expect a forgery to adhere very delib-erately to accepted norms. So what exactly was this note? I turned the question over and over in my mind, until I began, uncharacteristically, to doubt myself. Was I wrong to be suspicious of such a brief missive? Were my standards for suicide notes too high? Shouldn't a woman preparing to take her own life be forgiven for doing a poor job of penning her farewell? I will admit that I endured several sleepless nights. I couldn't shake the feeling that the solution to the mystery somehow lay buried in the enigma of this note.

"Also provocative was a loosened bulb . . . there." Merritt pointed to the floodlight above the sliding glass door. Everyone looked up. "It has since been tightened and is now in working order, but on the night of Victoria's death the light was inoperable. As there was no moon that night, this deck would have been in complete darkness when the event took place, barring any electric glow that may have filtered out from the living room.

"I wondered, had the bulb accomplished the unlikely feat of failing of its own accord, in which case it was irrelevant to my investigation? Or had someone intentionally loosened it? If so, who? Victoria herself? Her killer? And why would they have done such a thing? The most likely explanation was to prevent anyone from witnessing what was about to happen on the deck, but such a precaution struck me as peculiar, as the risk of witnesses in this location appeared to be negligible at any time, but especially in the early hours of the morning.

"The case raised other pressing questions as well. I was particularly interested in the fact that something unusual had obviously been going on that evening, something in which Victoria was closely involved.

"We know that she left the Lodge between roughly nine o'clock and nine twenty, then lied about her reasons when she returned. We know that at about nine thirty p.m. her next-door neighbor saw a single light approaching the Bungalow. Then, sometime between nine thirty and ten p.m., she asked Mr. Draper to drive her home. To add to the mystery, she did not allow Mr. Draper to accompany her into the house as she normally would have. Was it coincidental that the same night on which she'd acted so suspiciously was to be her last?

"I thought not. A significant number of clues found at the scene strongly suggested that someone, possibly two people, had been inside the house with her that night. These details included a half-full bottle of brandy, two recently washed snifters in the dish drainer, and a plate and two additional glasses in an otherwise empty dishwasher. Also an unmade bed in which it appeared that two people had slept, a photo album opened on the coffee table, and a trail of dirt across the living room rug.

"Mr. Draper, of course, was the most logical brandy drinker and bedfellow. At first he denied having returned to the Bungalow after leaving the Lodge for the second time, at about eleven thirty. He later changed his story, but even with his belated confession, several details remained unexplained.

"Just as I understood the vexing suicide note and malfunctioning lightbulb to be critical issues, I soon realized that no solution would be acceptable unless I could also account for whatever behind-the-scenes activity had been afoot that evening."

CHAPTER 42

Introducing . . .

I t's usually a mistake to think that a murder investigation will be-gin and end with only one crime," Merritt continued. "When you overturn a stone, more than one beetle is likely to crawl out. In this case, there happened to be two unrelated narratives operating under the surface, gumming up, as it were, the one story I needed to reveal.

"The first centered on what appeared to be—and was, in fact—a stalker. The story first came to my attention when my assistant, Ms. Blunt, eavesdropped on a private conversation among a group of Victoria's friends."

I got a couple of dagger looks for this, eavesdropping being not only a bush-league detection technique but also flagrantly rude. I wished Merritt hadn't used that term.

"One of these women said that she'd noticed a young man hang-ing around the pool when the ladies were enjoying a scheduled exercise session. The same friend indicated that she'd spied the young man at other venues as well, but to my knowledge, specific information about those alleged sightings was not provided. It is a reliable fact, however, that a young man fitting her description of him was observed at Victoria's birthday party, and again at her funeral service.

"Could this person have killed Victoria Summersworth? It was certainly possible. His behavior was clearly suspicious. Of course, the fact that he'd allowed himself to be noticed on three different occasions, possibly more, suggested to me that he lacked the basic guile one would expect to find in a murderer. My sense was that I needed to do nothing in particular to flush him out. I had only to wait until he wittingly or unwittingly revealed himself, as he appeared to be consciously or unconsciously seeking some form of recognition.

"As it turned out, Ms. Blunt was less patient than I am. She took it upon herself to engage in a wild chase through the streets of Burlington, which, had the young man actually been the murderer, would have sent him scurrying into the shadows, adding unnecessary difficulty and delay to the investigation. When her second attempt to locate and question the young man also failed, I feared we might have lost him altogether."

I died a little on the inside as I once again became the object of negative attention. I hoped Merritt didn't intend to go on in this vein, publicly cataloging my various mistakes.

"Luckily, however, the young man's mother brought him to the resort to be questioned, and his story turned out to be as innocent as I'd expected. I would now like to introduce everyone to the young man I'm talking about. His name is Tristan Morrissey. He's entering his senior year at Morton Academy, and he works as a summer busboy at the Harp and Plough Tavern. Seated next to him, in the last row, is his mother, Heather Morrissey, the owner of Green Mountain Magic, an aromatherapy shop on Main Street in Burlington, and the longtime mistress of Warren Summersworth."

I would have expected an audible gasp, but there wasn't one. Apparently a mistress and her illegitimate child were not as shocking as I'd thought. People merely twisted in their seats to peer curiously at the strangers, then returned their attention to Merritt, eager to hear the story she would tell.

She recited the broad outlines of the narrative: how Heather, worried about her son, had approached Victoria; how Victoria had created the scholarship in Warren's name; and how Tristan, its first recipient, had eventually done some digging and been able to identify who his father was. How, despite his mother's warning to stay away from the Summersworth family, he'd ventured onto the resort several times.

"Tristan, would you be kind enough to tell the group what happened the night of Mrs. Summersworth's birthday party?" Merritt said.

When Tristan started to mumble, she interrupted him. "If you wouldn't mind standing up, please, and projecting your voice so everyone can hear . . ."

He unfolded himself to his full impressive height. He was wearing the navy blazer again, this time over a pale pink shirt and yellow tie. "I wasn't trying to stalk her, like you were saying. I mean, I did a little, I guess."

Haley broke in. "Wait a minute. I remember you. Iced coffee with extra milk and three pumps of hazelnut. You got a BLT for lunch a couple of times too. And you liked the veggie meat loaf with sweet potato fries for dinner."

"Yeah, that was me," Tristan said bashfully.

"Wow. It's nice to meet you," Haley said.

They smiled at each other.

Heather was gazing at her son in surprise. "Is that why you haven't been eating much?" Given that the answer was most likely yes, she quickly lobbed her next question. "Where did you get the money for all that?"

"Tips," he replied.

"You're supposed to be saving your tips," she retorted.

He shrugged.

She sighed.

Life went on.

Merritt said, "You told me earlier that you came to the resort to see your siblings, Tristan. Can you explain why?"

"Well, you can't tell much from social media. I mean, you see people's pictures and everything, but most of the time they're just trying to make themselves look good. And it doesn't tell you other things, like . . . um, how they walk or what their voices sound like." He frowned nervously. "I hope that doesn't sound weird."

"Not at all. You wanted to see them in person as a way of getting to know them better. Is that right?"

"Yeah, that's right. I wasn't trying to hurt anyone or, like, get in their space or anything."

"But the night of the party didn't go as planned, did it? You ended up spending quite a bit of time with the one person you say you were *not* there to see, Victoria Summersworth. As I understand it, Victoria recognized you, and the two of you began to talk, first outside the Lodge, and then here at her house."

"That's right."

"The two of you looked at pictures of your dad in an old photo album, you ate crackers and cheese and drank Coke, and Victoria invited you back for lunch the next day to meet Neil, Lauren, Scott, and Haley."

"Uh-huh."

"Were you out on the deck at any time during your meeting with Mrs. Summersworth?"

"You mean here? On this deck? No."

"Could you see the deck?"

He appeared puzzled.

"Let me rephrase. Was the outside light on, allowing you to see, for example, the table and chairs and other things that were out here from where you were sitting in the living room?"

"Yeah, the light was on. But I never came out here."

"That's fine, Tristan. Were your shoes muddy or otherwise dirty?"

"My shoes?" The question clearly took him by surprise. "I don't know. I don't think so."

"Did you at any time walk from the front door, across the living room rug, to that sliding glass door?" She pointed to it.

"No, not that I remember. I went into the kitchen when Mrs. Summersworth was getting the drinks, and then we sat next to each other on the couch."

"How long would you say you were at the house?"

"Um, an hour? Maybe an hour and a half."

"You were gone by eleven o'clock, then?"

"Definitely by then."

"One last question. Did you drive to the resort that night?"

"I rode my bike."

"Isn't it dangerous to ride your bike at night?"

"I do it all the time, to get back and forth to work and stuff."

"How do you see your way in the dark?"

He shrugged as if the answer were obvious. "My bike has a head-light."

"Thank you, Tristan. That will be all for now."

He sat down and Merritt turned to Attorney Drabble. "Would you mind telling us when Mrs. Summersworth added Tristan Morrissey to her will?"

"I don't see any reason not to." He adjusted his wire-frame glasses. "Several years ago she came to me for help creating the Warren G. Summersworth Scholarship Fund at Morton Academy. There were some legal issues to iron out. At that time she also indicated that she wanted to add Tristan to her will, which we did. I invited him here today as a beneficiary—along with his mother, since he's underage."

"So am I right in assuming that neither Tristan nor his mother knew about the bequest until this afternoon?"

"They may have guessed when I called to invite them to the reading, but they didn't know the amount until just now."

"So there would have been no financial motive to kill Mrs. Summersworth."

"None that I'm aware of," the lawyer said with lawyerly exactitude.

Merritt seemed pleased as she addressed the group. "So, as we see, it turned out that Victoria *did* have a stalker of sorts, but his story was completely unrelated to her death. Getting to the bottom of it nevertheless helped the investigation by resolving a veritable avalanche of heretofore unexplained details: the roughly twenty minutes Victoria was missing from her party, her early departure, her apparent excitement and happiness to be going home, her unwillingness to let Mr. Draper accompany her inside, the opened photo album, the glasses and plate she must have rinsed and put in the dishwasher after Tristan left, and the text message to her children. Also, of course, the solitary beam of light—which was not from a flashlight but from the headlight of Tristan's bicycle—that Pat Tucci saw from her porch at about nine thirty p.m.

"Paradoxically, it also helped the investigation by throwing into sharp relief the several clues it *didn't* explain. Namely, the dirt on the rug, the brandy snifters in the dish drainer, the rumpled king-sized bed, the car in the driveway, and how that bulb right there managed to stop functioning after Tristan left the house at approximately eleven p.m."

She was staring at the bulb with some hostility, and we all dutifully followed suit. A long silence ensued, as if we were waiting for it to speak.

CHAPTER 43

The Inner Circle

Only when I felt I had no other choice did I turn my attention to the victim's inner circle." Merritt began to pace more quickly, as if warming to her subject. "I suppose that I, like Haley, wanted to give Victoria's family and closest associates the benefit of the doubt. But with no definite solution having presented itself, I had to proceed. I began with the most likely suspect: Mr. Monty Draper."

"Sorry, love. Didn't do it," he called out.

I wasn't so sure. Honestly, I was hoping it would be him, if only to get him back for all the *love*s, *sweetheart*s, and *honey*s he'd uttered across the decades.

Merritt was undeterred. "The police never dusted those brandy snifters for prints, Mr. Draper, but I strongly suspect that if they had, they would have found yours. Ditto for the DNA they would have collected from the bedsheets if this case had been classified as a murder from the outset. You must have known you'd left a wealth of potentially incriminating evidence behind, yet you foolishly insisted that you hadn't been inside the Bungalow at all that evening, that you'd only picked Victoria up, brought her to the party, and dropped her off again, between nine thirty and ten p.m. I naturally wondered why you'd lie."

"So? I admitted it, didn't I? Didn't I admit it?"

"You did. But only after you were confronted with CCTV footage that showed you entering the lobby of your apartment building at one fifty-two that morning, and after you were informed that a dark sedan had been spotted in Mrs. Summersworth's driveway at about one a.m."

"Wait a minute. You didn't say 'dark sedan.' You said 'Buick Regal.'"

"Did I?" Merritt smiled complacently as Draper scowled. "You were wise to come out with the truth at that point, Mr. Draper, and your explanation for why you lied was convincing—I give you that—but the fact that a person admits the truth when cornered does not exonerate him from having lied when he thought he could get away with it. In fact, you had several obvious motives for ending Mrs. Summersworth's life."

"Really? Name one!"

"It was widely rumored that you were a fortune hunter."

"So? Who doesn't like a little money? It's not a crime. And if I'd been after her money, which I actually wasn't, I sure as hell wouldn't have knocked her off then. I would have waited until after we were married!" He gave a hollow guffaw at his own joke. No one smiled.

"Perhaps she'd angered you by insisting on a prenuptial agreement that would have left you with next to nothing in the event of her death."

"Prenup? What prenup? She never said anything about a prenup!"

"Hmm. Not yet, apparently. If it wasn't the prenup that angered you, perhaps it was the delay itself. You'd proposed marriage, but she hadn't accepted. She was making you wait. For what? You didn't know. You were impatient. You feared rejection. You half expected she would give you an answer that very night, the magical night of her birthday party. Perhaps your nerves were on edge. Perhaps you pressed her and she put you off. You didn't mean to hurt her. But many a lovers' quarrel has ended badly. . . ."

"I never hurt a hair on that—"

"Or did she reject you that night, Mr. Draper? After a background check."

"What? Oh, all right. You want to talk about that again, fine. Just so everyone knows: I did some time back in Nevada for a non-violent, white-collar offense, which I already admitted to Columbo here."

"But only after my assistant confronted you with the results of her research. I suspect that you didn't reveal your criminal history to Victoria, and she was just the kind of trusting person who would have accepted as fact whatever story you did tell her. Her son Neil would not have been as naive. If she'd mentioned to him that she was considering marrying you, I've no doubt that a background check would have been a quick result. Once she'd learned the truth about you, she would of course have confronted you with your lie. She might even have informed you that she could not possibly marry a convicted felon."

"No way! She wouldn't have cared one bit, I promise you. She would have understood."

"Yes, I believe she might have, Mr. Draper. After all, she had mothered two stepchildren to the best of her ability, despite their scorn and their father's ongoing affair. She had responded to another mother's cry for help, even though that woman had played a major role in her unhappiness. She had gone out of her way to anonymously assist a young boy who was in trouble, and then she made provisions for him in her will, which respected a paternity she might have been forgiven for wanting to hide. Yes, I would say that there was a very good chance that Victoria Summersworth would have accepted you just as you are."

"See? See? I told you!"

"I only wish I could say that you are a man capable of controlling your anger. Sadly, I'm not convinced of that. Nor do I believe that men such as yourself require much provocation."

Scott leapt to his feet and stared in consternation at the man in the row behind him. He was too stupefied to do anything but stutter, "Monty, don't tell me . . . you couldn't have . . . not you . . . I can't believe it . . . did you?"

"Of course not!" Monty protested in a strangled voice. "My god, Scott, how could you even think that? She's cracked. Look at her! She's a total nutjob, and she's lying through her teeth."

He probably shouldn't have mentioned lies, as it only reminded everyone of his own.

Officer Grout, the little busybody, approached Scott, put a hand on his shoulder, and firmly suggested that he take his seat. Shrugging her off, Scott nevertheless obliged, but not before shooting a look of rage, hurt, and perplexity toward the man he'd thought, and still hoped, was his friend.

I thought for sure that would be the end of it, that Merritt was about to accuse Monty outright and Detective Clemmons would soon be snapping those silver cuffs on the bridge champion's wrists. Instead, Merritt turned to the florid-faced man who'd just sat down. "Now on to you, Mr. Summersworth."

Scott reared back, pressed a hand into his chest. "Me? Why me?"

"Because you are the one person in your mother's life with whom there is a clear history of conflict—some of it quite cruel, as I understand."

"Wait. What are you even talking about?"

"Do you deny harassing your mother? Badgering her? Demanding that she give you money to support your drug habit when you were using? And then robbing her when she did not?"

"Yeah, sure. But that was a long time ago. I'm different now!"

"Then how do you explain the fact that you were heard screaming at her two days before her death?"

"Huh? What? I didn't scream at—"

"On Thursday at around dinnertime you reportedly ran out of this very house yelling, 'Stop accusing me!'"

Pat Tucci piped up, "Don't try and deny it, Scott. I heard you say those exact words!"

He looked confused for a moment, then remembered. "Oh, that. That was about something else."

"What? What were you being accused of, Mr. Summersworth?"

"Of stealing money from the resort. It was ridiculous. I've never done anything like that, and I never will. I only raised my voice to my mother because I was sick of all the lies and slander that kept coming my way. Neil was behind most of it. He and my father, if you want to know. They were always at me, ever since I was a kid. Then, from my first day as general manager, Neil was filling Mom's head with garbage about me. First, I'm accused of mismanagement, and when I do everything I can to disprove it, do either of them believe me? No. Do they back off? No. Then Mom comes at me again, this time accusing me of stealing. You better believe I was angry. I'd had enough. I couldn't get out that front door fast enough before I really did do something I'd regret."

"Would you say you have a hard time controlling your anger, Mr. Summersworth?"

"Not when I'm clean. Which I am. For eleven months. And I don't give a shit who believes me or not. Oh, and by the way, you and I both know that I *wasn't* stealing from the resort. And we both know who was. Are you going to tell that little story to friends and family now? Or do I have to wait for the indictments to come down before I can clear my name?"

Merritt nodded, respecting his anger. She looked at the group. "I think I owe it to Mr. Summersworth to mention that the reason

Lauren Perry, Eric Perry, and Arthur Doyle aren't with us today is that they were arrested in the early hours of this morning and are presently in jail, pending arraignment on a number of serious charges, including the murder of Neil Summersworth. You'll all be hearing more about it soon, I'm sure. For now, I'd just like you to know that Scott never did steal from the Wild Goose Resort. His sister Lauren did that, with inside help from Arthur Doyle, CFO of Kingfisher, and they did it in such a way as to make Scott the fall guy should the scheme ever come to light. They believed—rightly, I expect—that his well-known history of drug addiction would turn public opinion against him, helping to tighten the noose around his neck."

People shifted in their seats, murmured among themselves.

Scott said, "Thank you. I appreciate someone standing up for me—for once in my life."

"Not so fast, Mr. Summersworth. Your innocence of embezzlement and murder charges in unrelated crimes did not remove you from my suspect list. On the night of your mother's party, you still believed she was unfairly laying the crime of embezzlement at your feet. You were still angry—enraged, actually, full of a deep, historic hatred."

"What?"

"Don't try to deny it. We all just heard it in your voice. There's more than enough anger in you to commit murder."

"But I didn't do it!" he cried out.

Beside him, Pia was weeping. "He didn't do it. He was with me all night. Really and truly. With me."

"You don't have to say that anymore," Scott told her. "I'm fine. I can fight this on my own."

Ignoring them, Merritt spoke to the group once again. "I hope that by now you can understand the challenge posed by this apparently simple case—that after several days of investigation there were relatively few suspects I could exclude. I realized that the case would have to turn—that it must turn, if I was ever to solve it—on a stroke of luck. This is a very difficult and uncomfortable position for an investigator to find herself in. In essence, I was at the mercy of the detection gods. My only hope was to uncover, or perhaps simply recognize, a particular kind of clue—the kind that would point me in a clear and specific direction, while simultaneously closing off other potential avenues of pursuit. I kept myself poised, ever vigilant, ever hopeful—until, finally, this clue emerged."

CHAPTER 44

The Last Clue

Before I disclose it, I'd like to mention what had struck me all along as one of the most interesting facets of the case. No one, it seemed, in Mrs. Summersworth's orbit had had any idea that she was experiencing the kind of serious mental and emotional difficulty that would lead a person to suicide. Virtually everyone I spoke to expressed some degree of disbelief or surprise at the apparent cause of death. Even when they accepted the results of the police investigation, they did so reluctantly.

"There was one notable exception to this rule, however. Ms. Robin Tucci."

"Oh my god," Robin blurted. "Now you're going to accuse *me* of murder? Me? You're grasping at straws, Detective. You said yourself that there were too many suspects, that you needed a miracle to help you solve this case. Why was that, I wonder? Because none of us did it! She killed herself. That's right. Perfect little Vicki, everyone's darling. She took her own life, and everyone's too chickenshit to admit it. No one can face the fact that she didn't love any of us enough to stick around."

Merritt nodded. "Yes, Ms. Tucci, like everyone else, you accepted the police's verdict, but you were quite alone in maintaining that Victoria Summersworth was likely to have committed such an act. You even supplied a rationale for suicide: Victoria's chronic unhappiness stemming from her husband's long affair with Ms. Morrissey. You went on to make the singular assertion that you'd observed signs—*shifts*, you called them—that had troubled you at the time, though you apparently didn't see fit to share your concerns with anyone."

Robin broke in. "Maybe I should have said something. I wish I had, though I doubt anyone would have believed me. But I wasn't lying when I said that Vicki wasn't as happy as she acted, and that joker over there"—she jerked her head in the direction of Monty Draper—"is the reason. He's a fortune hunter and a scam artist and everyone knows it. She wasn't happy with him. She could never be happy with him."

A mysterious smile played at the corners of Merritt's scarlet lips. I'd thought she'd come here this afternoon knowing all the answers, that she had them all lined up, ready to be shot like little silver bullets out of a dazzling little gun, but now I got the impression that she was actually working things out as she went. She might know the identity of the murderer, but some of the puzzle pieces still hadn't arranged themselves perfectly in her mind. That sly little smile meant that one had just fallen into place.

Merritt addressed the group. "I'd like to take a moment to thank my assistant, Ms. Blunt, for the important contribution she made at this juncture. Were it not for one of her more egregious mistakes, I might not have found the correct path."

Oh, Merritt. Have you no mercy? There was no reason to scan the crowd to count how many people were snarling or smirking at me. I figured they all were. About six feet off my right shoulder, the runt was standing at wide-legged military attention in her appointed spot beside the patio doors. I heard her emit a weird guttural noise for which there is no adequate descriptor in the English language. I will call it a *snurf.*

Go ahead. Snurf all you want, I retorted telepathically, *but I'm not the one wearing polyester pants.*

"After accidentally stumbling upon a back route to the Bungalow, Ms. Blunt failed to notice a highly significant clue. Had I trusted her investigatory skills, I would have accepted her report as it was, never suspecting that it was incomplete. Fortunately, her inexperience and impulsivity had led her to make several previous consequential mistakes in the investigation, so I knew I had to visit the site myself to gather whatever information it might yield."

At this point I understood that there was no saving myself. I had only to endure. And, if possible, resign before I was fired.

"The route in question, which locals call the Cliff Walk, is no more than a narrow path that stretches from a secluded beach to the Bungalow. The path rises steeply through the woods, and after attaining the crest of the cliff, it crosses a flat grassy area behind the Tuccis' house until it reaches the Summersworths'. Along the way it passes a weathered wooden bench at the edge of the Tuccis' backyard. The bench commands a lovely view of the lake and is no doubt a pleasant place to sit on a summer day. I sat there myself, as I was winded from my climb. That was when I noticed a cigarette butt ground into the dirt beside my shoe. I immediately recalled the way Pat Tucci had ground her cigarette butt under her shoe when we'd first met, and how she'd picked it up so carefully, wrapped it in a tissue, and stowed it in her pocket so as to hide the traces of her smoking from her daughter. This butt had apparently escaped her diligence. Then I remembered her saying that she often went outside to smoke in the middle of the night when she couldn't sleep—a practice I'm sure her daughter was aware of.

"I remained seated on the bench and turned my head a few degrees to the right. There, in its entirety, was the deck of the Bungalow, visible through a break in the trees, a break one would notice only from this precise location. The significance of this fact was immediately clear to me. With the porch light brightly illuminating the deck, anyone sitting on the bench could have witnessed the crime. They would have been able to see not only Victoria's body falling over the railing, but whoever had pushed her.

"Who would know that this sight line existed? Only someone intimately familiar with the area. And who would know that a sighting was, if not likely at that hour, at least reasonably possible? Only someone who knew that Pat Tucci occasionally went outside at night to smoke illicit cigarettes."

Merritt leveled her fearsome gaze at Robin Tucci. "That person would have been wise to disable the porch floodlight before she committed her violent act. And if she had happened to take the Cliff Walk from her house to the Bungalow, possibly wearing hiking shoes that trapped clods of dirt in their thick treads, then she might very well have tracked dirt from one end of the living room to the other."

"Oh, come on." Robin's mocking tone couldn't mask the shakiness in her voice. "You're just making up stories about each one of us, seeing if one of us will crack. Well, I'm not going to. I loved Vicki. I had no reason to want her dead."

Monty Draper jumped out of his seat and roared, "What about that chunk of change you just got? That's plenty of motive!"

"It would be for you," Robin snarled at him, "but I didn't care about her money. I cared about her. Besides, I didn't even know about the money until an hour ago."

"Prove it!" Monty yelled.

Merritt held up her palms to quiet him. "You make a good point, Mr. Draper. Let's ask Attorney Drabble."

The lawyer cleared his throat, flipped his classic navy-onmaroon striped tie. "Mrs. Summersworth came to me a couple of

THE WORLD'S GREATEST DETECTIVE AND HER JUST OKAY ASSISTANT

weeks before she died. She said she was planning to marry again, and she knew her son would insist on a prenuptial agreement. She had some of the usual misgivings about prenups, and we talked in general terms about how we might draw up a contract she would find satisfactory. Then she indicated that she also wanted to change her will. Specifically, she wanted to raise the bequest to Ms. Tucci from fifty thousand dollars to seven hundred fifty thousand dollars. I was naturally concerned that she was redirecting such a large portion of her assets from her family to an employee. When I pressed her she gave a rather strange, incomplete answer. She said that Ms. Tucci deserved a great deal more than that for what she had sacrificed."

"See? I told you. I didn't know a thing about the money," Robin said.

"I'm inclined to believe you," Merritt said, "which means there must have been another reason you wanted her out of the way."

"This is so stupid," Robin muttered. She leaned back and crossed her arms.

"As I considered your possible motives, I reflected on a story told by Sumiko Yamada about Victoria's uncharacteristically harsh behavior toward her. Apparently Victoria had been seriously concerned about what she believed would be the cost to her daughter of living in an openly lesbian marriage. She offered Ms. Yamada a substantial sum to leave the state—an offer Ms. Yamada naturally refused. When an angry Haley confronted her mother, Victoria told a story about an old friend who lost custody of her children when she came out. Haley felt—and I felt it too, while Haley was talking—that there had been something unhinged in Victoria's reaction, something crazed in her crass attempt to buy off her daughter's fiancée—almost as if she'd had a demon to exorcise.

"No sooner had this thought crossed my mind than other details started to cluster around Sumiko's story like iron filings around a magnet. Among them: the photo of you and Victoria in your home that revealed the closeness of your relationship; your mother's bewilderment, which I share, about why a formerly ambitious woman spent three decades in a tedious job for which she was overqualified; and the fact that you'd been discovered sitting in the middle of Victoria's unmade bed, weeping uncontrollably, surrounded by a drawerful of her expensive silk scarves, some of which you clutched to your face."

"Oh my god! What are you even saying? I never touched her scarves!"

"Ms. Blunt saw you and reported those details to me. She instinctively appreciated the sensual and/or sexual nature of your behavior. Unfortunately, it seemed to have caused her some discomfort, perhaps even titillation"—I died a little more—"which may explain why she immediately discounted her intuition, on the basis that scarves are notoriously overused erotic motifs, and that therefore what she was sensing must have come from her own imagination and could not be trusted as real—as if her wise suspicion should be discounted simply because it happened to be a cliché! But my assistant hadn't been wrong at first blush, had she, Ms. Tucci? You did indeed have a sexual relationship with Mrs. Summersworth."

Robin curled her lip, unimpressed by Merritt's deduction. "It's not a crime. At least not anymore."

"But Victoria acted as if it were. In the early years of your long relationship, while she was married to Warren, she insisted on hiding the nature of your relationship, just as he hid his affair. You went along out of respect for her wishes, in the interests of the family stability she constantly touted, and because, frankly, you were powerless to change her mind. As time went by—all those busy child-rearing years passing very quickly—your love for each other deepened. She was a lonely, neglected woman with a big, sensitive heart. You were lonely too. And you were always right there: her parenting partner, her cook and housekeeper, the tireless helper who fixed the leaking sink, found the missing sock, checked the schedule, packed away all those darling Christmas decorations. You became the person she confided in, relied on, shared her joys and sorrows with. You listened when she was hurt, buoyed her when she was moody, soothed her when she was upset. She was married to you more than she'd ever been to Warren. And yet she kept you firmly in the background. Were you ever angry, Ms. Tucci?"

"Of course I was."

"Then fortune smiled. Warren died suddenly. You were delighted. You thought for sure the days of lies and secrecy would soon be over, because now there was nothing to stop you and Vicki from publicly proclaiming your love. Still, though, she delayed."

Merritt's brow furrowed. Out of genuine curiosity, she asked Robin, "Why did she delay, do you think?"

"I don't know. She kept saying she wasn't ready. Or there was something she had to do first. Or it wasn't the right time."

"It was never the right time, was it?"

"No."

"For *years*, it wasn't the right time."

Robin shrugged weakly. Her spunk was half-gone. The memory of her decades-long disappointment was filling her eyes with pain. "We were still happy," she attempted.

Somehow that one comment sucked all the air out of the spacious Vermont sky. I could see it all before me plainly: arguments, procrastination, makeups, renunciation, repression, denial. Everything gradually flattening into unhappiness. The long erosion, in Robin's case, of passion, spirit, and self.

"Were you?" Merritt asked.

Robin didn't reply. She seemed far away, as if she'd dissociated from what was happening. I wished she would fight harder to pro-tect herself. Didn't she grasp where this was headed? The rest of us were well aware of what was likely the next item on Merritt's docket. We held our collective breath, waiting for the murder accu-sation.

"The chronic unhappiness you first attributed to Vicki . . . the invisible sadness that comes from being a neglected partner . . . the dull, lonely pain that eats at you from the inside over years and years until it completely hollows you out . . . that pain and sadness were actually yours, Ms. Tucci."

Robin shook herself back to the present moment. "Say what you like. You don't know a thing about me."

"I imagine it must have been rather, ah . . . *disappointing* when Victoria took up with Monty Draper."

"Monty? Please. Monty's a joke, a low-class hustler who went after her with a lot of phony attention and flattery because she had money. I figured she'd see through him."

"But she didn't. She intended to accept his marriage proposal. You learned of it that night."

Robin's face went stony. "So what if I did?"

"How did it make you feel?"

"It didn't make me feel anything."

"Hmm. I disagree. I think you felt quite a lot. You'd been so pa-tient. For years, you'd been patient. But on the night of that party you had no choice; she put it before you so bluntly, you had to face the facts. Your beloved was a traditionalist, a social conformist, and a coward. She had neither the courage nor the passion nor the in-tegrity to claim you as her own. She probably never had. She'd strung you along for years with paltry excuses that you stupidly believed. The whole thing—the love of your life, the love to which you'd dedicated your life—was just a house of cards that now was falling down.

"The truth was, she would rather go off with a cheap faker she'd known for only a year, because he made her laugh and promised her a life in the sunshine, a life of travel and parties and fun—none of which she felt she could have with you. Because of *you*, specifically. Because of who you'd become. Let's face it, Ms. Tucci. After so many years of skulking in the shadows, you'd turned into a bit of a shadow yourself. It had been years since you smiled, since your eyes lit up with pleasure, since you laughed. You'd become a stiff, dull servant girl.

"Can you really blame Victoria for choosing a sociable bon vivant, the kind of man unafraid to shout his love from the rooftops, who made her feel like a queen? Maybe Monty Draper is a faker and an opportunist. Maybe he'd have broken her heart. If so, she would hardly have been the first old woman to dash herself to smithereens on the shoal of a last romantic dream. Now she's gone and we'll never know how it would have ended. It doesn't matter. What matters is this, Ms. Tucci: Victoria chose Monty Draper over you, and the pain was unbearable."

A tear rolled down Robin's cheek. "So what? So what if it's all true? It doesn't mean I killed her."

"How did you find out that Victoria intended to accept Monty's proposal? The party was very busy. You were putting out fires all night long, you said. I don't suppose she would have told you something that momentous, and difficult for both of you, in the midst of the festivities. And we know that in the end she didn't tell Monty that night either. The situation with Tristan Morrissey apparently took precedence for her. But somehow *you* knew she'd made her decision. How?"

"You're the detective. You tell me."

"All right, I'll take you up on your challenge. I'll also tell you exactly how I think the night went down. You can let me know if I get something wrong, but I don't think I will."

"It's a free country. Knock yourself out."

"You went to the party early. It was a busy night, as you said. Lots of details to attend to: glitches in the band's sound system, overfrozen ice cream, missing croquet mallets, and so on. You were frantic in the background, as always, while Victoria took center stage, accepting the fawning praise of nearly seventy so-called friends, some of whom brought gifts despite being asked not to: homage to the queen.

"She was radiant, dressed to the nines, chatting with her guests, dancing with her beau, smiling from ear to ear. She was ten years older than you, but she looked ten years younger and acted like an ingenue. While you played the dour-faced sentry at the service entrance, haggling with that diva of a baker whose late-arriving birthday cake looked suspiciously like a repurposed wedding cake and was just as insanely priced.

"You were jealous. Of course you were. The woman you loved appeared to be dazzled by a Las Vegas grifter who'd waltzed into her life the summer before. You couldn't believe she would take him seriously. His goals were so transparent, his strategies so trite. Nevertheless, inch by inch, they'd become inseparable and Victoria had become less and less available to you. She didn't tell you what she was thinking anymore; she told him. And the more intimate they became, the more you were pushed away, until eventually you were no more to her than a pale assistant. When you could have been, should have been—when at one point you actually had been—so much more.

"You knew Monty would propose marriage eventually. That was his game plan, as everyone could see. You consoled yourself with the idea that she wouldn't take that last, drastic step—that when it came right down to it, she would stop short of joining her life with a man like him, a man who belched in public, made crude jokes, and kited checks. You figured that when the fling was over, she'd come back to you, her lifelong, if secret, partner, and the two of you would take up where you'd left off. You still believed that you were the person she would marry in the end, when she found her courage finally, as she'd once hinted she might, and as you had faithfully trusted she would. You trusted her, Ms. Tucci, because you truly loved her, and therefore brushed away any evidence of her flaws, even when it was staring you in the face. It's sad to think of how much of yourself you'd traded, and kept trading, to keep your love alive.

"You staggered home, alone, at midnight on the night in question, exhausted from all the work you'd done without thanks from anyone, without anyone even noticing. And you found something—didn't you? A note with your name on it slipped inside the screen or taped to the door, or left someplace else where you could find it easily. A note in a fancy cream-colored envelope that read *From the desk of Victoria Summersworth*.

"It was what is colloquially known as a Dear John letter, and when you read it, your world collapsed. Everything you had built your life around—your career, your affections, your endless daily chores, all of which had been sanctified, made noble and beautiful by your hidden love—all of this was burned to ash in the space of a few dashed-off sentences. You saw your reality clearly for the first time ever. You saw that it was ugly, that *she* was ugly, and that you'd been a fool.

"In my imagination, Ms. Tucci, you're standing on the porch when you read this letter. You look across the short distance dividing your two houses and see Monty Draper's fat Buick Regal parked flamboyantly in the driveway. He's inside with her. The two of them. Celebrating their union. Making love. While you stand there alone in the dark with a Dear John letter in your hand.

"I believe the plan would have come to you quickly after that. It was perfectly simple and clear. Had you imagined it before? It's certainly possible. In any case, you went to your room and closed the door. You changed your clothes and waited. At around one a.m., you heard your mother get up and go to the kitchen for a smoke. She returned to bed and you kept waiting. At around one twenty you heard Monty's car roar off, and you knew that Victoria was alone. You went out the back door, along the wooded path, and up the stairs to the deck, where you unscrewed the bulb so your mother wouldn't see what you were about to do, if by chance another nicotine craving drove her out to her favorite spot on the bench. The sliding glass door was open—it always was—and Victoria was up in her bedroom, fast asleep in her rumpled, postcoitus bed. You woke her, coaxed her down the stairs and out onto the deck. Perhaps you let out all your rage, or maybe not. She was already dead to you emotionally, so it didn't matter anymore what did or didn't pass between you. When you tossed her over the railing, she was just a sack of bones."

Monty Draper was on his feet, his face blood filled from fury. "Why, you . . . you . . ." He lunged at Robin Tucci, who was sitting a few seats away. She recoiled, raising a bent arm to ward him off.

"I'll kill you, god damnit. I swear I'll—" He grabbed her by the hair, and then somehow, an instant later, he had his meaty hands around her throat.

The cops were on him in seconds, dragging him off. He struggled like a stuck bull as they cranked his arms behind his back and pushed him, stumbling and swearing, through the doors and into the living room. He kept hollering, promising death to Robin Tucci, his voice growing gradually fainter. I don't know what they did with him—probably put him in the back of a squad car. He didn't appear again.

We, the onlookers, were stunned into silence, shaken by both the revelations and Draper's murderous rage. Robin was pale and trembling, one small hand gently cradling her raw, reddened neck. After a while, she composed herself enough to say to Merritt in a low, cold voice, "You can't prove any of this."

"We'll see about that, Ms. Tucci. But do let me finish the story. The best is yet to come.

"After you murdered Victoria Summersworth, you set about covering your tracks by making it look like a suicide. You dragged a chair from the outdoor table and set it beside the railing. Then you knocked it over for extra effect. You returned to the bedroom and placed a note on Victoria's dresser. You didn't write it; it was the same one she'd given you—with two small adjustments: two added *s*'s. You'd probably filled them in back in your room. Here, let me read what the note said before you tampered with it."

Merritt put out her hand. Detective Clemmons took a few steps forward and placed a small transparent bag in her palm. With a click of his heels, he retreated to his position. He seemed to be enjoying his bit part in the production; he was certainly playing it to the hilt. Merritt took her heavy black glasses out of her pocket and rested them on the bridge of her nose. Squinting, she held the evidence bag a few inches from her face, and began.

"'Thank you from my deepest heart to the beautiful, loving friends who made my days so precious. It breaks my heart to say good-bye, knowing that no apology can ever heal the hurt you'll feel. There's still so much joy and pleasure in this world for you. Don't be sad, my darlings. Vicki.'

"Now let's hear it again, with two small *s*'s removed:

"'Thank you from my deepest heart to the beautiful, loving friend who made my days so precious. It breaks my heart to say good-bye, knowing that no apology can ever heal the hurt you'll feel. There's still so much joy and pleasure in this world for you. Don't be sad, my darling. Vicki.'"

There was no greater joy for Merritt than catching a criminal's little tricks, and now, with an unabashed grin, she removed her reading glasses and explained the ruse. "Victoria's penmanship was just messy enough for the added letters to blend in, though Ms. Tucci couldn't help smudging the last line a bit."

I groaned quietly. I'd noticed the smudge myself, but I'd assumed it was made by Victoria as she bid an anguished farewell to all the people she loved.

"Very nice, Detective. But you still can't prove it," Robin Tucci said coldly.

"On the contrary, enough evidence to convict you has already been gathered. You may remember the bottled water you drank in my suite a few nights ago. You left the half-empty plastic bottle on the coffee table when you went out, and I absentmindedly set it back on the drinks table, meaning to drain it in the sink later and dispose of it in the recycling bin. But I forgot, and the maid let it stay just where it was, kindly thinking I might want to finish it later. Thus was the bottle preserved. Yesterday I asked Detective Clemmons to dust it for prints, along with the faux suicide note and the lightbulb. They matched, Ms. Tucci. All three of them."

"You couldn't possibly have dusted the bulb. It's still there!" Robin pointed at it triumphantly.

"Oh, that's a new bulb. Officer Grout dropped by this morning and screwed it in."

Grout grinned proudly, as if her measly contribution was significant.

Robin was fuming. Her lips were tightly pursed and her hands were curled into fists. I could tell she wanted to erupt in anger, but words, perhaps language itself, had deserted her.

Merritt went on. "There is also a slight inconsistency in the color of the ink you used to alter the note. A search warrant for your home will likely be issued as early as this afternoon, and I expect the police will find the pen you used and will be able to match its ink to the added letters in the note. It's unlikely that in your agitated state you would have had the foresight to throw the pen away."

Merritt paused and studied the murderess carefully and rather curiously, as if she was intrigued by the woman's very existence and fully expected her to come out with a unique and interesting defense. "Would you care to say anything, Ms. Tucci, before the police lead you away?"

"Yeah. Fuck you."

Pat Tucci started to cough. She hacked so hard that her face went from white to red to blue in a matter of seconds. She flailed out her hand and located her oxygen mask, grabbed it hard, clamped it over her nose and mouth, and sucked on it like it was life itself. Several people went to her, Haley and Pia among them. Her back was rubbed. A water bottle was produced.

Robin stared straight ahead as Detective Clemmons, Officer Grout, and the third policeman approached her.

Merritt calmly slipped the Dear John note into her pocket. She clasped herself in a gentle self-hug and closed her eyes. There was an expression of tranquility on her face as the litany began.

"Robin Tucci, I am arresting you in the murder of . . ."

As the cops led her away in handcuffs, Robin glanced back at her devastated mother and mouthed the words *Sorry, Mom.*

CHAPTER 45

The Breaking Point

We drove out of the Wild Goose Resort just after one p.m., our luggage stowed in the back of the car.

I was still trying to get my head around what had happened. At first I thought Merritt must have slipped in some details I hadn't been privy to, and that was why she'd reached the solution faster than me. (I would have gotten there eventually; I was sure of it.) But when I went over everything she'd said, I saw that all the clues had been there, if I'd only bothered to look. The cigarette butt under the bench was perhaps my biggest failure. In my own defense, I'd missed its significance only because it was not itself a clue; it was only a link to a clue. In any case, if I'd only thought to check the sight line to the deck, I maybe could have gone from there to the lightbulb, and then I possibly could have wound my way to everything else. Instead, I'd been discussing marriage vows with the man I loved. I supposed if I were listing reasons to miss a clue, that would be one of the better ones. But still . . .

No doubt there were other things I should have paid closer attention to as well, but I decided to end my postmortem right there.

Merritt had done a good enough job of making me feel inadequate; I didn't need to supplement her fine work.

Besides, there was something else bugging me, something more troubling and harder to explain. In my mind's eye I kept seeing Robin mouthing the words *Sorry, Mom,* and Pat's gaunt and stricken face. Robin would probably end up in prison, probably for a long time. Her life would become about as meaningless as a life could get. And I had helped make that happen. I couldn't decide if I was proud or not. Should a person be proud of that?

As usual, the drive had been silent, but as we were approaching Albany on I-87, I found that I could keep quiet no longer. The words burst out.

"Don't you feel kind of bad for her?"

"What? Who?"

"Robin Tucci. Don't you feel bad for her? A little?"

"No. Why should I?"

"Well, I mean, she had a hard life. Doing all that maid work, and cooking for other people, and taking care of kids who weren't her own. And then waiting so long for love . . . I mean, a real love . . . the kind you can show to the world and brag about . . . and, like, go out to dinner and stuff."

"You sound like an idiot right now, Blunt."

That was it: the breaking point. It's a funny thing about breaking points: you don't know when they'll come—or even *if* they'll come— and then, all of a sudden, they've arrived, and you must do their bidding, whatever the cost.

"No, Merritt. No! It is not correct for you to speak to me that way. I'm tired of taking grief from you. All you ever seem to do is call me stupid and point out my mistakes. I've had enough of this treatment. I don't care how brilliant or famous you are. If you want to continue working with me, you'll have to treat me like a human being of worth and dignity. But I suppose none of this matters anymore.

You're probably going to fire me because I made so many terrible, horrible mistakes—like misinterpreting a smudge."

"Oh, that's right. You did get the smudge wrong, didn't you? I forgot about that one," she said in an annoyingly light tone.

I gritted my teeth. Would she never take me seriously? "Look, this relationship obviously isn't working out. I think I'll save you the trouble of firing me. I quit. Right now, right here. I quit."

There was silence in the car. All the way to Poughkeepsie, and well beyond that, the only noises in the cabin were from the wind gusts whistling through Horace's thin doors; his whining, straining engine; and the rumble of all the cars and trucks that sped past us on the highway, of which there were many.

I tried not to cry. Or scream. Or swear. Or punch the steering wheel. I didn't want to work for Aubrey Merritt anymore, but I didn't want to *not* work for her either. When I finally got back to my apartment after this excruciating experience, I would definitely need to take a bath, put on baggy sweatpants, and eat Häagen-Dazs.

As we approached the city, Merritt cleared her throat. "Do you still want to quit?"

"What's that supposed to mean?"

"I mean, now that you've had time to think about it, do you still want to quit?"

"Look, the question isn't what I want. It's what you're willing to do. Are you going to start treating me with more respect, or aren't you? It's up to you."

She paused. "What qualifies as 'more respect,' in your opinion?"

"Well, you could start by mentioning some of the things I did right. There must have been one or two."

"You drove very well. Truly. You're a very good driver, Blunt. I'm sorry I haven't made that clear."

"Is that all?" My voice was cold.

I heard her swallow, and it pleased me to think that she felt uncomfortable, even as it displeased me to think that she couldn't come up with anything nice to say about me, not even another stupid pseudocompliment.

She said, "I assume you documented the investigation very thoroughly with all your written notes, photographs, and recordings."

"Yes, I did. Not that it made any difference, since you have a steel-trap mind. Come on, Merritt. I need better from you. I must have helped the investigation in some way, or shown some kind of aptitude. There must be one thing you can point to."

She thought for a while. "Actually, there is. I meant to tell you. After Pia Valente approached you to say that Scott Summersworth had run off somewhere, brandishing his hunting rifle, you did a remarkable bit of deduction. I believe you said that you recalled a notation Victoria had made in her daily planner indicating that she'd visited the hospital on the day of her party. You remembered that Arthur Doyle had recently been having medical issues, and you put together that she must have been at the hospital to see Doyle, to seek his advice after she'd learned the results of the independent audit. You then concluded that Doyle was the other person besides Neil who likely would have known that the fraud had come to light. That was very good reasoning, Blunt. Excellent, I'd say."

"Thank you."

"It did send you in the wrong direction, of course. Scott had rushed off to confront his sister Lauren, not Doyle."

"At least I got there in the end."

"Sheer luck," Merritt said. "And very, very—"

"Don't say it. I know it was stupid." My bandaged hamstring throbbed in agreement.

"Well, we don't need to dwell on that business now. Overall, the case was a success. For the record, I also thought you showed a lot of spunk in the way you raced headlong after poor Tristan Morrissey, leaving me stranded in the churchyard. And you asked some excellent questions during our interviews. Your argument contrasting Robin Tucci with Monty Draper was quite penetrating, I thought, and turned out to be prescient in the end. And it wasn't lost on me that a certain stratum of society—housekeepers and such—are apparently more comfortable dealing with someone closer to their low social class, like you. If you want a final grade, I give you a C plus."

"That's not a very good grade."

"Your generation has been overpraised. The *C* is for basic *competence*. The plus indicates hope." She paused. "Hope for the future."

"You mean I have a future?"

"I rather like you, Blunt. And I do think you'll improve with time."

"Really? Oh. Okay."

We were quiet for a moment. Then Merritt said, "I have a big problem with this car, though. After you drop me off at home tonight, I don't want to lay eyes on it ever again."

"There's not much I can do about that. I can't afford a new car. Once I pay for rent, food, and my student loans, I barely have anything left. And don't ask about my boyfriend. He's an actor."

"I wasn't suggesting that you buy a new car. I was thinking of my car."

"How can you have a car when you don't have a license?"

"It's my father's. He died a dozen years ago, and it's been in storage ever since. It was his pride and joy, and it just didn't feel right to get rid of it. But I don't drive, so you see what the problem is. You, on the other hand . . . I wasn't kidding when I said I think you're a very good driver. What would you say if I got his car out of storage and got it all fixed up, good as new, and you drove that one instead of this . . . this . . . this pile of absolute junk?"

"Sure. I guess that could work. What kind of car is it?"

"A 1988 Bentley Continental. A real classic. It's a dark green convertible, and quite comfortable inside. I think you'd like it very much."

My brain was screaming: *a classic Bentley convertible!* But I kept my mouth closed. I didn't want her to get the idea that she could dazzle me with expensive toys. We were forging a new, more mature relationship in which I intended to be valued for much more than my driving skills. I decided to seize the moment, to self-advocate as I never had before. "Actually, what I'd really like is a fifteen percent raise."

She heaved a sigh. She hadn't been expecting that.

"Do we have a deal, or don't we?" I pressed.

"Yes, yes. We have a deal," she said with some irritation.

"And you'll treat me like a human being?"

"I suppose I could try. But honestly, Blunt, you'll have to learn to live with me, just as I'm learning to live with you. Eventually life will teach you that people rarely change; they only make slight accommodations under pressure. I think you'll find that after all this fuss and bother, and a few days of tiptoeing on eggshells, we'll both still be exactly who we are right now."

CHAPTER 46

You Were Wonderful

I hobbled on my crutches into the theater on Thirty-Sixth Street, having dropped Merritt off at home. It felt like a small miracle that I'd arrived only a few minutes late. Yesterday afternoon the solution to the mystery had seemed out of reach. Then everything had happened so quickly that I'd barely had time to think. Now I was here, as surprised and thrilled as I trusted Trevor would be.

The guy at the box office told me that the play had just started and there were still plenty of seats available, so I hastily swung myself and my bad leg into a tiny elevator that rose very slowly to the second-floor theater. As quietly as possible, I slipped inside and lowered myself into a seat at the back. I hadn't slept in about thirty-six hours, but I felt energized just by being there, in the intimate darkness that smelled of dust and old cologne.

Act one was underway. Willy Loman and his wife, Linda, were discussing his terrible, awful day as a salesman. Trevor would appear soon. I was almost as nervous as he probably was. I knew how terrified he was of the critics. They had no souls, he'd complained more than once; they drank young actors' blood. He was afraid he'd forget a line, or fall on his face, or throw up onstage, or any of a million other things he couldn't foresee that would ruin his career and destroy his self-esteem for the rest of his life.

When he came out onstage, I had to close my eyes. *Please, god, let this go well for him.* But I needn't have worried. From the moment he opened his mouth—"Biff, where are you? You're supposed to study with me today!"—I was completely convinced that he wasn't Trevor at all, but that he was Bernard, son of Charley, friend of Biff. He was earnest, honest, and pathetically endearing, appropriately exhibiting no situational awareness whatsoever. Yet you could sense the quiet dignity lurking under the raw geekiness, and in your heart of hearts you somehow understood that he, Bernard, was the horse you should bet on. Later, when Bernard intoned the wise words "But sometimes, Willy, it's better for a man just to walk away," I knew that Trevor had clinched the role as perfectly as any actor could have, and I flicked away a tear of pride (and relief).

The play went off superbly. Willy Loman died in the end. I sighed with cathartic pleasure as the curtain came down to thunderous applause.

Backstage, flocks of people were milling around. I could barely get through the door on my crutches, and then I had to squeeze and twist to get around a boisterous group who seemed to have no concern for the bottleneck they'd created. Flowers were everywhere. Champagne corks popped. Admirers shrieked and gushed. People with booming voices bumped into me without apology, and one of them stepped heavily on my toe. By the time I'd limped to Trevor's dressing room fatigue had started to creep over me. Nevertheless, I couldn't wait to give him a hug. I had to hold myself back, however, because an attractive woman about my age had already nosed into his private space, the better to pay homage.

"Oh my god. You were amazing," she gushed, drawing out the last word until it sounded like a moan.

Finally she tore herself away, and Trevor noticed me standing there. His mouth fell open. "Olivia! You made it!"

"Wouldn't have missed it for the world," I said. But that wasn't actually true. I *would* have missed it for the world, or if Merritt hadn't solved the case as quickly as she did.

"What happened to your leg?" he asked in alarm.

"Oh, it's nothing. Just a torn hamstring. I hardly need these things anymore." I waved the crutches around a bit and ended up teetering more than I'd expected.

We hugged, and I told him he was wonderful, which was entirely true. "By the way, that girl who was gushing at you just now . . . is that what I have to look forward to when you're a star? Actor groupies? Is that even a thing?"

"Olly—" he said in a fake warning voice. This meant something along the lines of *please behave.*

"I do think you're going to be a star, Trevor. You're so talented. When you do get famous, I only ask that you remember that I believed in you before anyone else did. Before you did."

"You've no idea how much that meant to me, Olly," he said, giving me another squeeze.

Someone called his name, and there was Zuzanna, his mother, pressing through the crowd of people. She was in a smart emerald green dress, and holding aloft a bouquet of lilies so they wouldn't be crushed. My heart thudded nearly to a stop. I still hadn't called her to discuss the flowers for the wedding!

After giving Trevor a big warm hug, she gave me a tentative, awkward hug that seemed to involve a lot of bony shoulders and sharp elbows. The awkwardness was probably mostly my fault, as I was still getting used to being hugged by her. It wasn't too awful. She always wore the same fragrance, a fresh gardenia scent, which I didn't dislike as much as I disliked some of the other perfumes worn by women her age, and this had given me some hope for our future compatibility.

She turned back to Trevor. "You were wonderful, darling. I'm so proud of you."

I'm so proud of you was one of her favorite things to tell her son. It always made me uncomfortable, because it sounded as if she believed that his accomplishments naturally redounded to her. I'd explained this to Trevor once, and he'd assured me that I was over-analyzing to an absurd degree.

"Have you two sorted out the flowers yet?" he said archly, as if he knew we hadn't—or perhaps couldn't.

"Let's not talk about that now. This night is all about you," I said hastily.

"Olivia is right," Zuzanna said. "We need to do something special to celebrate your stellar performance tonight. Let me take you both out to a late dinner. I've made reservations at the Lambs Club."

"Nice. I'm starving. But first I've got to get out of these clothes," Trevor said. He was still wearing his Bernard outfit: dull, brown, geeky. His hairline was damp, and there was a sheen of sweat coming through his makeup.

He retreated to a corner of the dressing room, and Zuzanna and I looked at each other blankly. Neither of us seemed to have any idea how to navigate across the gap of age and nothing-in-commonness that yawned between us. Then we both started talking at once. She asked if I'd had a chance to think about the flowers for the wedding, while I assured her that I was looking forward to discussing the flowers for the wedding. We both stopped speaking at the same time. Then we laughed.

"I like roses," I said, figuring that was a safe choice.

"Roses are lovely, of course . . . very classic and traditional, but perhaps not . . ." She sighed. "Well, I suppose I could try to make it work. Let me think about it. Are there any other flowers you really love?"

"Geraniums," I said, remembering the clay pot under which Victoria Summersworth had hidden her key. The instant the word was out, I realized it was wrong. Geraniums belonged in window boxes, not at weddings.

Zuzanna frowned at me in gentle perplexity for several seconds. She seemed to be turning a vexing problem over in her mind. Then, having come to a resolution, she said, "Tell me, Olivia—how would you feel about mixed bouquets of lilac, peony, and narcissus for the centerpieces? Then the peony again, with sweet pea and hellebores for the bridesmaids. And I just love a ranunculus with some greenery for the corsages and boutonnieres. And for you the best of all: a simple, elegant bride's bouquet of garden roses and baby's breath. There, you see? You'll get your lovely roses. They'll be especially for you."

"Perfect!" I said.

She gave me a wide, delighted smile. "Then it's done! We've decided! Now, if you'll just let me know how many bridesmaids you'll be having . . ."

"Bridesmaids?"

"Four is a nice number."

"*Four* bridesmaids?"

At that moment Trevor appeared, looking more handsome and mature than usual, as if his spectacular opening night had gilded him with a new, enduring manly confidence. "Ah, I see we're on to bridesmaids—one of Olly's favorite topics!"

"Stop. I know you're joking," Zuzanna scolded him. She turned to me. "But you *will* let me know soon, won't you? Before next weekend?"

"I definitely will."

Trevor gave me a teasing side-eye. "Really? You will?"

I elbowed him surreptitiously as I looked from mother to son. "I'm awfully hungry too."

"Lovely. That makes three of us," Zuzanna said.

Trevor led the way through the press of people and out the stage door. We found ourselves in a quiet, dimly lit alley where the humid August night felt pleasantly thick and enveloping.

Zuzanna whispered to me, "Did you find the killer?"

I nodded.

"Good for you! I just love mysteries. You've no idea how thrilled I am that my future daughter-in-law is a real private investigator. You're going to tell me exactly how you solved the case, aren't you? I'm dying to know every detail."

"I'll tell you the whole story," I said with a smile.

At least this promise would be easy to keep.

Acknowledgments

I am lucky to have wonderful friends and colleagues who helped transform what was once just a glimmering idea into an actual book. Writers Holly Robinson, Leonard Rosen, and Joan Sawyer read early drafts of the manuscript and offered excellent commentary and advice. Hank Phillippi Ryan and Joanna Schaffhausen are invaluable sources of support. I couldn't have found a better editorial team than Tom Colgan and his assistant, Carly James, whose wise suggestions brought sparkle and polish to Olivia's story. Additionally, I am indebted to the whole talented team at Berkley— everyone from the copy editors to the design, production, marketing, publicity, and sales professionals. Their expertise and enthusiasm are the forces behind so much of a book's success. Deep gratitude goes to Esmond Harmsworth for his insight, integrity, and constant faith in me, and Elena Steiert's thoughtful suggestions were much appreciated. As always, I send my endless love to Robert, Ben, and Ellen Sophia, along with a heartfelt shout-out to Becca and Tyler for making our family bigger and better.